T0281952

Other Books by Rebecca D. Elswick

Mama's Shoes
No Stopping Her

The **DREAM**
is *the* **TRUTH**

Rebecca D. Elswick

Artemesia
Publishing

ISBN: 978-1-951122-97-3 (paperback)
ISBN: 978-1-963832-03-7 (ebook)
LCCN: 2024941866
Copyright © 2025 by Rebecca D Elswick
Cover Design © 2025 Geoff Habiger
Cover Photo © Rebecca D Elswick

Artemesia Publishing
9 Mockingbird Hill Rd
Tijeras, New Mexico 87059
www.apbooks.net
info@artemesiapublishing.com

For Hugh

"If there ever comes a day where we can't be together, keep me in your heart. I'll stay there forever."
— A.A. Milne, *Winnie the Pooh*

"Ships at a distance have every man's wish on board. For some they come in with the tide. For others they sail forever on the same horizon, never out of sight, never landing until the Watcher turns his eyes away in resignation, his dreams mocked to death by Time. That is the life of men. Now, women forget all those things they don't want to remember and remember everything they don't want to forget. The dream is the truth. Then they act and do things accordingly."

~ Zora Neale Hurston, *Their Eyes Were Watching God*

1912

Chapter 1

TWO DAYS SHY OF Zelda Ryan's tenth birthday, she went into the forest to gather Shepherd's Purse and came back with a dead baby. Zelda's mother was a midwife, and she needed Shepherd's Purse to make a poultice to stop bleeding. It was May fifth and Shepherd's Purse was in bloom on Rock House Mountain, and thanks to her grandmother, Zelda knew every nook and cranny of the mountain. Zelda was named for that grandmother, a healer who now in her old age was called Granny Zee. Like Granny Zee and her mother, Zelda wanted to become a healer. Zelda knew some people called them witches, but when those same people needed help with sickness or to catch a baby, they came to fetch them. Like now, her mother had been sent for to tend to Ruth Berger. Ruth was not but thirteen, but she was bleeding so heavy from her woman parts she had taken to her bed.

That morning the mist rose and fell, rose and fell, like the mountain was breathing. Zelda loved the forest like a person, and since she could remember, Granny Zee had taught her the names of the mountain plants and how to use them to make medicines. Zelda had a special connection with Granny that her sisters Isabelle and Eleanor didn't have. They only cared about boys and dresses with ribbons. But sometimes, Zelda caught Granny Zee looking at her with a sad face, and then yesterday, she overheard Mama and Granny arguing about her. Mama had said, "Do not take away the last of her childhood," and Granny had said, "Zelda already knows she is different."

It was true. Zelda knew. She knew no other girl who could converse with spirits, but it was all a lark—a game to play in the forest. Until today.

A cold snap had come to the mountain, sprinkling frost on the newly blossomed blackberry bushes. Granny Zee called it blackberry winter because the cold came every year when the blackberries bloomed. Zelda walked through a muddle of frost patches, crunching under her boots like broken glass. A patch of Shepherd's Purse was up ahead so she got the trowel out of the gathering bag. She heard the nearby cry of a blue jay and watched a robin disappear inside the branches of a poplar tree, a large worm dangling in her beak.

"Morning Miss Robin. Congratulations on that juicy worm. I hope you don't mind if I work around your tree. My mama needs these plants."

The cold seeped through her woolen dress and into her knees as Zelda dug. Mama used the whole plant, not just the tiny white blooms. Shepherd's Purse had two sets of leaves, upper ones near the blooms that were small and tooth-shaped and larger leaves crowded at the base. The blooms brushed against her face and she wrinkled her nose. Shepherd's Purse smelled bitter, but Zelda smelled something else. Blood. It's bitter, rusty scent filled her nostrils.

Zelda gagged. She rubbed her nose until her eyes watered, but the dank metallic smell got stronger. She dropped the trowel and ran.

Up the mountain she went. All around her the mountain woke, like a great cat humping its back to stretch. A titmouse landed on a twig and called *peter, peter, peter*. A dragonfly whirred in front of her face, then dipped and was gone. The path grew steep, but on she ran. The spirit's voice whispered on the wind, "The faerie place."

Granny Zee told Zelda many stories about the faeries. When the Irish and Scots crossed the ocean and settled in the Appalachian Mountains, the adventure-loving faeries had come with them, hidden away—some right in their pockets. Zelda had never seen the faeries, but Granny Zee had. She called them the wee folk and said some had wings that glittered gold and silver. Granny said she had watched them dance on Midsummer's Eve at the faerie fort.

The first time Granny Zee took Zelda to the faerie fort she was just five years old. It hadn't looked like Zelda imagined a fort would look—nothing more than a mound of earth surrounded on three sides by huge rocks. Granny said there was a door in the mound that only the faeries could see, and they lived inside this dirt fort away from human eyes.

Zelda slowed when she saw the scarlet oak that stood across from the faerie fort. She sat down on a flat rock and stilled herself, even though her thoughts darted all over the place like marbles spilled from a box. She had promised Mama she would gather the plant and bring it to the Berger house for Ruth. Mama was counting on her. But the spirit said to come here, and the stink of blood was at this place.

The ground between the rocks and the tree formed a shallow basin littered with cup-curled leaves. Their scarlet color had darkened as they lay under last winter's snows until the earth looked bloody. Over her head the new green leaves of the oak had unfurled with a red hue. She looked up and whispered, "I'm here." And that's when she heard *hoo-hoo-hooooo*.

An owl hooting in the daytime meant death.

With outstretched hands Zelda stumbled over the tree's roots that rose above the ground. She placed both hands against the trunk, the cold, knobby bark rough against her skin. She turned her head to the left and pressed her cheek against the tree. From there, she could see how the cliff jutted out from the hillside.

In an instant, Zelda was down on her knees in front of the cliff, scraping handfuls of leaves from beneath it. Wet rotting leaves piled up around her, the scent of decay filling her nose. She lay down on her stomach and stretched her arm into the space under the rock. She touched something solid and icy cold. She pulled it toward her into the light. A perfect tiny foot appeared.

"Oh! Poor thing." With both hands Zelda eased the girl-child into the day. She looked like a tiny wax figure sculpted in a perfect infant's image. Carefully, Zelda brushed away the leaves, and opening her coat, cradled the baby next to her child-ish breast.

Zelda rose and went to the flat stone. She sat down and rocked the baby back and forth, cooing to the dead little thing, while crying bitter tears. After a time, she took her out from beneath her coat and examined her. Part of the blackened umbilical cord was still attached, so she knew it was a new-born. There were no marks or bruises on her. Everything about her was perfectly formed. She had a wee bit of dark hair, and she even had tiny fingernails and toenails.

Tears came hotter and faster than before. Zelda wiped her face with the tail of her dress and tucked the baby back inside her coat. Mama would know what to do.

On the way down the mountain, she stopped and got the trowel and bag of Shepherd's Purse. She placed it across her shoulder, and the weight of the bag was heavier than the infant in her arms.

Zelda couldn't walk up to the Berger's door with a baby under her coat, so she stopped at her house, stole inside, and grabbed a basket and a piece of feed sack without her sisters seeing her. Out of sight of her house, she stopped and wrapped the baby, putting her in the basket. All the way down the path to the Berger's house she kept looking in the basket to convince herself the baby was real.

Smoke curled from the Berger's chimney; its long-crooked finger beckoned Zelda. A hound bayed from the swept front yard but when she approached, he wagged his tail. The cabin door opened and her mother stepped out. Some of her auburn hair had escaped the bun at the nape of her neck and curled around her round flushed face. She wiped her hands on her blood-streaked apron. "Zelda! Where have you been? Bring me the plants."

"Mama, I need—" But her mother disappeared inside.

Zelda mounted the steps and set the basket on the porch. She looked around for the dog, but saw he was tied to a tree. She took the gathering bag from around her neck and set it next to the basket. When she opened the cabin door, she was met by the odor of blood.

Emmaline Ryan stepped from behind a sheet hung so it divided the room. Zelda blinked, her eyes trying to adjust to the cabin's dim light. Mrs. Berger was pouring water into a huge pot on the cookstove. Zelda said, "Mama," but Emmaline interrupted her. "Where is the Shepherd's Purse?" She stepped forward and looked around Zelda like she was hiding it behind her skirts.

Zelda raised her arm and pointed over her shoulder. "Outside." Mama threw her hands in the air and said, "Well, get it! I need you to wash it and put it in the pot of boiling water on the stove."

"I can't."

"What's wrong with you?" Mama stepped around Zelda and went to the door, but Zelda was on her heels in an instant, pushing past her to get to the porch first.

"Child, what is deviling you?"

"Please, Mama, please. Close the door. I'll tell you."

Mama turned and pulled the door to. In three quick steps, she was at the basket and gathering bag. She lifted the bag and spun around.

"Mama, I have to show you something. Something I found."

Mama frowned. "What is it?"

Zelda went to the basket and gently lifted the baby, holding it out to her mother. "I found this in the woods."

Mama's hand flew to her mouth. She stifled a scream, then drew herself up, and held out her hands. "Oh, no. You poor wee bairn," she said, cradling the baby in her arms. She whispered, "The reason for Ruth's childbed fever."

Mama settled the baby back in the basket and took Zelda's elbow, guiding her down the steps to the yard. She pulled Zelda to her in a quick embrace and then stepped back. With her hands on each arm she knelt in the dirt, so she could talk to Zelda face-to-face. "I know how upset you must be, but I need to ask you an important question."

Zelda nodded.

"You have been to enough births with me to know that that baby was just born. You saw its umbilical cord was still attached. And you know about the afterbirth, a placenta—the sack that held the baby in the mother's stomach." She paused and nodded encouragement to Zelda.

"Yes."

"When you found the baby, did you see anything that might have been the placenta? It would have looked like a bloody piece of meat, roundish in shape, and the cord may have been attached to it."

Zelda shook her head and her mother squeezed her arms hard, making Zelda wince. "This is important. Think hard. Are you sure you didn't see anything like that?"

Zelda stared into her mother's icy blue eyes. The worry line on her forehead was as tight and stretched as her mouth.

"No, Mama. I'm sure. I didn't see the placenta."

Mama nodded and rose. "There's one more thing I want you to do. Go home and tell no one about this. No one. Promise me."

"I promise."

When Zelda got home, the house was so quiet a chill washed over her like she'd walked into a stranger's house. She took off her coat and boots and went straight to her room where she pulled back the patchwork quilts from the bed and crawled inside. She cried and traced the course of that day from beginning to end, as she was to do for decades to come.

Chapter 2

A WEEK AFTER SPRING vanished, it swooshed back across Rock House Mountain beckoning forth buds and blossoms. The sun warmed the ground and new growth rose in the morning mists, the air thick with its scent.

Zelda made sure Eleanor and Isabelle weren't following her. She wanted to tell Cece about finding the dead baby, and she knew Cece wouldn't come out to play if her sisters were around. She hated being the youngest. Her sisters were always deviling her. Since Zelda had let it slip that she was playing with a new friend named Cece, she had caught her sisters following her when she went to play at the old cabin. Isabelle had called Cece her make-believe friend, and Eleanor said Zelda was playing by herself. Mama told Zelda to pay them no mind. She told Isabelle and Eleanor that if they needed something to do, the quilts they were supposed to make during the winter weren't finished.

The rhododendrons and honeysuckle would soon veil the path Zelda followed to the old cabin. She liked that. She liked lifting the tangle of honeysuckle and wiggling through to emerge in a secret green place. This morning, she was watchful of snakes. The warm days would bring them out, and she had no quarrel with them as long as they didn't bother her. Granny Zee said snakes had their place on the mountain just like people. Zelda knew this was true, but she was glad Daddy had made her a walking stick to thrash and scare them off.

The air smelled sweet like Christmas cake. Zelda breathed it in so fast she got dizzy. She stopped on the path where the honeysuckle vines were already thick with growth. The blossoms were not yet the gingery-orange they would be in summer but rather were the color of fresh cream her daddy skimmed from the morning's milking. She plucked a flower from the vine and sucked the sweet nectar from it like Granny Zee taught her. She pinched off long strands of honeysuckle and wound them around her neck until she had enough so she and Cece could make necklaces and wreaths for their hair. A grasshopper zinged off a strand, extending its z-legs to take flight, and disappeared into the honeysuckle fortress, making Zelda laugh. She realized this was the first time she had laughed since what happened to Ruth Berger.

The old cabin was down the mountain a ways. There really wasn't enough of it left to call it a cabin—parts of two walls stood, but the roof had caved in and the porch was a pile of rotted wood. The stone fireplace was mostly intact, but some of the chimney had fallen in, forming a cairn of chimney stones that were moss-covered, even in the cold of winter. Ivy had taken over the ruined walls and jumped to the fireplace, making a canopy that served as a make-shift roof.

On a warmish day in February, Zelda had first seen Cece sitting under the old cabin's roof of tangled vines. The mid-winter thaw had turned the air on Rock House Mountain so thick Zelda thought she could float down through it like a marble dropped into a jar of honey. After three days of rain the mountain snow melted, except for clumps here and there on the hillside that looked like porous steppingstones. Freshets ran down the mountain like curled silver ribbons. Streams appeared overnight where there had been none. Mist rose from the icy water and floated above the surface like specters in dreams.

Zelda placed sticks and twigs in the water and followed them down the mountain until they either disappeared or got stuck. She was having so much fun, she didn't realize she was near the old cabin until its sadness wrapped around her. That day, she didn't hurry away from the misery that lay over it like a heavy winter cloak. Instead, she let it draw her closer and went to sit among the chimney stones.

Zelda knew melancholy was not limited to people. Places had sorrows like gardens had weeds. Granny Zee had told her that sometimes the only way to deal with sadness was to talk about it to somebody who listens. Zelda sat down on a moss-covered stone and while she listened, Cece took shape.

Cece was the prettiest little girl Zelda had ever seen—skin as pale as the dawn and big green eyes with long black eyelashes. And red hair—long and curly, tied with a big white bow. She wore a brown dress with puffed sleeves made from shiny material and a starched white pinafore. She held a doll she called Patty Cake.

Since that day when winter had masqueraded as spring, Zelda had gone to the old cabin to play with Cece. Everything was fine until her stupid sisters followed her and Cece went away. It was weeks before she came back.

But this morning, Mama told her to go outside, and Zelda

left without a word. She knew Mama was grieving at the heart. After staying by Ruth Berger's side for three days and nights, Mama had come home so weary she merely said, "Ruth has passed," then she hugged and kissed her daughters and went to bed.

That night when the white moon rose with its scarred face, Zelda woke to the sound of Mama crying. She opened the bedroom door enough to see Mama and Daddy sitting in the kitchen. Daddy was trying to get Mama to drink tea, but Mama was shaking her head. Mama said, "If only Ruth had told someone and not tried to have the baby by herself."

Daddy said, "Would you tell John Berger?"

Emmaline and Jack Ryan stared at each other. They were of one mind about most things in this life, especially when it came to people like John Berger who treated his livestock better than his family.

Mama sighed. "There will be no funeral. No words will be spoken over Ruth to ease her into the next world. They aren't even going to lay her to rest in the cemetery."

"Where are they burying her?"

Mama shook her head. Daddy stood and put on his jacket. "I'm going over there with my shovel. I reckon all he can do is tell me to leave."

When Zelda got to the old cabin, she found Cece sitting by the tumble-down fireplace with Patty Cake. Cece clapped her hands when she saw the honeysuckle. While they decorated themselves and the hearth, Zelda told Cece about Ruth Berger. She began with finding the baby and pieced together the rest of the story from what she'd seen at the Berger's house and what she'd overheard her parents say.

Zelda went home when the sun was high in the sky. She found Daddy sitting on the front porch in the ladder-back chair. Zelda stared at him. She wasn't sure what was wrong, but he looked different, somehow, almost like an old man. She studied him. His fox-colored hair lay in a wave across his high forehead. He had on his old brown work-shirt, and there was mud on his boots and his pants' legs. He sat unmoving, hands resting on his knees.

"Daddy?" Zelda said.

He smiled. "Hello, baby girl."

She jumped up on the porch and threw her arms around his neck. She realized what was different: Daddy never did nothing; his hands were never still. That man sitting so still on her porch had not looked like her father.

He hugged her back and pulled her onto his lap.

Zelda whispered into his neck, "Did they bury Ruth?"

"Yes."

Zelda fell silent, staring at the mud on his boots.

Daddy smoothed back the hair that had escaped her braid. "What is it, baby girl?"

"Did they bury the baby?"

He put his hand under her chin and raised her head. "Yes, Zelda. Your mama helped them prepare both Ruth and the baby for burial. She put the baby in Ruth's arms, herself."

Zelda nodded and went inside. Granny Zee was seated at the table with Mama.

Zelda ran to her grandmother. "You're back!"

Granny Zee opened her arms wide. "Yes, child. I missed you."

Zelda rested her head on Granny's right shoulder and breathed in the scent of lavender, hyssop flowers, and rue—flowers often used at funerals. Zelda murmured, "Great Aunt Clementine died."

"Yes, she did." Granny twined Zelda's long braid around her hand. "Death comes in threes. Your mama told me about Ruth. I am sorry you had to find that poor baby."

Zelda stepped back and nodded.

Granny leaned forward and took Zelda's hand. "Fetch me my bag from the door. I believe you just had a birthday."

Zelda ran off and returned with Granny's old canvas bag. Granny said, "I tried to get back afore hand. But I bought you something I believe you will like, and I hope it will help you make sense of things."

Granny Zee pulled out a rectangle wrapped in brown paper and tied with twine. Inside Zelda found a leather-bound book with the word "Journal" stamped in gold on the cover. She ran her hand over the smooth brown cover and opened it. On the inside cover Granny Zee had written "Zelda's Book of Dreams" in large letters slanted to the left. The rest of the book was empty, clean and white like her school tablet on the first day of school. Zelda closed the book and hugged it to her chest. "Thank you. It's perfect."

Granny Zee said, "I gave you this so you can record your dreams, all the things that happen to you. It will help you make sense of them. I gave your mother one when she was your age."

Mama smiled at Zelda. "She truly did, and it helped me discover I wanted to be a midwife. You could write down all the plants you find in the forest, draw their pictures, and write how they can be used to heal or help people."

Zelda nodded at her mother. Granny Zee said, "Emmaline,

don't you have some milk over there for this girl?"

While Mama went to get the milk, Zelda slipped onto Granny Zee's lap and wrapped her arms around her neck. She whispered in Granny's ear, "The forest told me where to find Ruth's baby."

Granny smoothed Zelda's hair off her forehead. She took Zelda's face in her hands and looked into her eyes. "You are one of the chosen."

Zelda looked up and saw Mama holding a cup of milk, tears slipping down her face.

Granny Zee saw it, too. She said, "Now, Emmaline, this young'un will be just fine. You knew since her birth this was coming."

Mama handed Zelda the cup and said, "Zelda, why don't you take your milk and go out on the porch?"

Zelda stood to go, but Granny Zee put one hand on Zelda's arm and the other on Emmaline's. "No, child, sit down." She let go of Zelda and took her daughter's hands. "Emmaline, we don't need to be talking behind her back. It's time she knew about *an dara sealladh*."

Granny Zee and Zelda walked side-by-side up the mountain until they came upon a patch of all-heal. The June morning was already hot, so Zelda was glad they had climbed to this shady spot. The purple all-heal blooms clung to reddish stems with lance-shaped leaves. Zelda had already drawn it in her journal and written about how Granny Zee used it to make tea. All-heal tea made a good gargle for sore throat, and Granny Zee made it into a salve for sores.

They cut stems of all-heal until their bags were full, and then Granny Zee sat down and patted the spot beside her. "Have you thought over what I told you about *an dara sealladh*?"

Zelda nodded and plucked a blade of grass at her feet. "Mama calls it 'the sight.'"

"Yes, that's right."

Zelda shaded her face with her hands and looked into Granny Zee's eyes because they always had something to say. Today, they were asking Zelda to understand. She said, "I call it the knowing."

Granny Zee nodded. She put her hand on Zelda's shoulder then tucked a strand of loose hair behind her ear. "Our gift is called different things by different people. Some would call you *taibhsear*—a seer. My Irish grandmother, Brigid O'Reilly, called it *an dara sealladh* which means 'two sights.' Your first sight is your normal sight, and your second is your special gift for knowing things. Granny Brigid was the first of our people to be born on this mountain, and she spoke the Irish Gaelic. Her mother was expecting her when they left Ireland."

"Can you teach it to me?"

Granny Zee shook her head. "I only know a bit of it. My mother and your great-gran Mary Kathryn forbid us to speak Irish, so I only remember what my Granny taught me."

Zelda frowned. "Why did she forbid it?"

"Mam wasn't like me and Granny Brigid. She didn't have the sight. She was afraid people in America would think Granny a witch. And I believe she was afraid for me because there are people who don't understand our gifts, and often, people fear what they don't understand."

Granny Zee didn't want to put too much on Zelda at one time, but it was important she learn how to handle her gifts. Granny Zee was worried because Zelda's gifts were already strong. She was much like her great-great-grandmother Brigid who had even foretold happenings back in Ireland. Brigid had predicted her brother's murder. She knew the murderer, where the body was hidden, and though it took many years, she was able to get the information to family back in Ireland. But no one in their bloodline could talk to the dead.

Zelda took her granny's hand. "Why would anybody be afraid of me? I only want to help people."

"Of course, you do! And you will help many people in the years to come, but some people don't believe that we can just know these things. Some people—a few—may say the devil told us these things. You have to be careful who you tell about the knowing, as you call it."

Zelda nodded. A breeze lifted the hair around her face as she smiled up at her granny.

Granny Zee said, "Your Mama tells me you have a new friend?"

While Zelda talked about Cece, her grandmother listened, occasionally nodding. When she said her sisters called Cece an imaginary friend because she wasn't real, Granny Zee interrupted her. "Oh, she's real. But your sisters can't see her because they don't have your gift. Do you know what I mean?"

Zelda looked into Granny's eyes and slowly nodded. "Because I have the knowing."

Granny said, "Cece is a haint—a spirit. Only you can see her. She is at the old house because she died there. Like my people, her parents came to these mountains from Ireland. Their name was Adair. As I recollect, Cece died during an out-break of typhoid."

"What's typhoid?"

"Many mountain people died of typhoid. It makes a bad headache and fever that can last for weeks. Some people break out with rose-colored spots. And it's real easy to catch. It comes from infected food or water and other infected people. Back then, people thought if water moved over rocks, then it was clean. They didn't know that typhoid was caused from unclean water, and since the ground was so rocky that it was hard to dig a well, they often built their homes near a stream. That was where they got their water, but it was also used by their animals. They washed their clothes in it, and they built their outhouses close to it."

"When did Cece die?"

"Now, that I don't know. It was before my time. I remember hearing stories about the people who had lived there, and how when their daughter died, they left here."

Zelda asked, "But why can *I* see her? Why could I find that poor little baby?"

"Some spirits cannot rest when they die. They are supposed to pass on, but they stay in this world. I believe that sometimes they do not understand that they died."

"But why me? Why do they talk to me?"

"Because that is your gift—your knowing—as you call it."

Zelda folded her hands in her lap. She thought about what Granny Zee had just told her. It filled in some blanks—like stepping out of a darkened room. The day she found the baby, something inside of her had changed. She saw people differently now. Before, they were people who breathed, whose hearts beat. Now, she sensed their fears, their disappointments, and their sadness. She wasn't sure this was the way she wanted life to be.

Granny placed a hand on her knee. "I will be here to guide you. You must come to me. Together we will figure it out."

1990

Chapter 3

*A child is coming to the mountain. She was born behind the veil,
and her gifts are ripe like a blossom ready to burst into flower.
My guidance will be the rain that nurtures the child's gifts into
surrender. This was told to me by the spirits of the forest.*
~ from Granny Zee's Book of Dreams

ADDIE BURIED THE SECRET ring deep in the heart-shaped pocket of her dress. With her other hand, she grabbed her mother's wrist and tugged her down the hall. Her Tinker Bell backpack swished back and forth on her thin shoulders as she step-skipped through the crowd of parents and children gathered in the hallways of Coal Valley Elementary School.

They neared the kindergarten area where a menagerie of brightly colored animals bloomed on the walls and the rooms vibrated with childish voices. Her mother rubbed the top of Addie's head, smoothing the short flyaway curls. Addie's hair was getting thicker, and it was darker than the chestnut brown it had been before. Her mother's fingers instinctively found the one silvery-white strand, straight as a length of ribbon and as wide as a thumbnail. She twined it around her forefinger and stroked it with her thumb. An almost imperceptible pulse came from this strand of hair, like the tremor of life under the soft fur of a baby rabbit. Her mother let go and it fell among the curls surrounding Addie's pale face.

They found the line of parents and children waiting to be greeted by Addie's designated teacher when Addie suddenly broke into a run, stopping in front of a woman and little girl, their blonde hair so perfectly matched only nature could have done it. Addie's mother reached them just as Addie pulled the ring out of the pocket of her dress and held it out to the little girl, but the woman snatched it away, practically shouting, "Hey! Where'd you get that!"

Addie's mother stepped in front of the woman. "Is something wrong?"

The woman held up a small gold ring. "Is this your daughter? Because I'm positive this ring belongs to my daughter."

"I found it," Addie said, stepping forward. She pointed at Reilly who was looking at the floor. "It fell out of her pocket."

"Her what?" With one finger the woman lifted her daughter's chin and asked, "Reilly? What's going on?"

Reilly said, "I just brought it for luck."

"Oh, Reilly." The woman exhaled a huu sound through her mouth. "I told you the ring has to be sized to fit your finger before you can wear it." She turned to Addie and her mother. "I am so sorry. I feel like an idiot. You do a good deed, and I attack you. Please, forgive me."

"It was just a misunderstanding. Come on Addie; we need to get back in line."

Addie tucked her hand inside her mother's. They returned to the back of the line. Addie looked up at her mother, her eyes filled with questions. "Did I do something bad?"

"No, honey, you did a very good deed." Addie's mother crouched before her and tugged at the collar of her dress. "That other little girl was the one who did something wrong—she brought the ring to school and didn't ask permission."

Addie nodded. Now that she was sure she had done a kindness, a smile spread across her face.

"Sweetie, where did you find that ring?"

"In the parking lot. When I got out of the car, I saw it on the ground."

"How did you know which little girl lost it?"

A giggle escaped from Addie like a puff of colored smoke. "Because I saw her drop it."

Addie's eyes shone with unmistakable brightness. Her mother had not seen Addie pick up the ring, but she had looked around the parking lot, and she was certain the mother and daughter, who claimed ownership, had not been there. She said, "Addie, when you found that ring was the girl there?"

Addie shook her head in a slow side to side motion.

"Then, how did you see her drop it?"

Addie giggled. "Oh Mommy, I saw her with my other eyes."

A voice said, "Who do we have here?" A woman who looked like a teenager dressed in her mother's clothes said, "I'm Miss Hall."

Addie's mother stood and extended her hand. "I'm Margaret Whitefield and this is my daughter, Addie."

They shook hands while Miss Hall recited the speech she had no doubt given a dozen times that morning. Addie raised her chin and listened, but her foot was poised toward the classroom. When Miss Hall finished, Addie called, "Bye, Mama," and disappeared inside. Her mother raised her hand to wave, but Addie didn't look back.

A bell pealed and students and parents scattered. Addie's classroom door banged shut, and Margaret's tears broke free. She hurried out of the kindergarten pod but had to stop in the hallway to fish a tissue out of her purse. She didn't hear the woman's footsteps until she was next to her. She said, "Are you okay?"

Margaret sniffed. "I think so."

The woman nodded, and a lock of blond hair fell forward until it touched her chin. She tucked it behind her ear, revealing two sets of gold hoop earrings, the upper hoop slightly smaller than the lower. Her eyes, large and diamond blue, floated on tears that coated her long dark lashes and slipped unchecked down her face.

Margaret stared. It was the mother of the little girl who had lost the ring.

Margaret pulled more tissues from her purse and offered one to the stranger. The hand that took it had nails bitten, the cuticles ragged and torn. The stranger blew her nose and started down the hallway. She paused after a few steps and turned back, tilting her head. She said, "Well, I guess that's it."

Margaret crumpled her soggy tissue into a ball and stuffed it in her purse. They walked to the end of the long hallway and pushed open the doors together.

Outside, the mountaintops wore frothy whitecaps, reminders of the morning's dense fog, but above their peaks a bluebird-colored sky held promises of picnics and daydreams. When they got to the parking lot, the woman said, "If the fog lifts late, the day will be clear."

"Is that the weather forecast?" Margaret shaded her eyes and scanned the sky.

"No, that's just what my granny says." The woman looked at Margaret. "My name's Hannah, Hannah Lively. I apologize again for my stupid outburst."

Margaret waved her hand like she was shooing a fly. "There's no need to apologize."

"Oh, yes, there is. I feel rotten for yelling at your daughter. Why don't you let me buy you a cup of coffee?"

When Margaret glanced at her watch, the refusal died on her lips. It was only 8:30 and she had nothing to do all day. She said, "Coffee would be nice. By the way I'm—" She looked at Hannah's expectant face and, for a reason she couldn't explain, said, "I'm Maggie Whitefield."

To the rest of the world, she was Margaret Elizabeth Anne

Whitefield. No one had called her Maggie since her father died, but today she wanted to be Maggie again.

Hannah said, "It's nice to meet you."

"It's nice to meet you, too." Maggie surveyed the visitor parking lot. "Looks like everyone else left."

"What does that say about us?" Hannah grinned.

Maggie bit her bottom lip, but her smile broadened. Then Hannah laughed, and like a flame that spreads across a branch, it leapt to Maggie. Maggie giggled and crossed her arms over her stomach. Hannah laughed so hard she had to lean against her car to stay upright. When their fits subsided, Hannah said, "Well, I guess it says we are either the most dedicated mothers in the world, or we seriously need to get a life."

❦

The Corner Coffee Shop was in a part of Coal Valley the locals called Old Town, a large rectangular area that looked like a frozen frame from a 1950's film. At the north-end of the rectangle was a grand, three-story, gray stone building—the courthouse, complete with a bell tower that chimed the hour. The rest of the Early American style buildings lined-up on either side of the courthouse. Beyond, the remainder of town fanned out toward the river like the tail of a peacock.

Brick sidewalks led the way to a row of Victorian-style houses. The grandest of them stood at the corner of Maple and Riverside. It was a three-story structure painted a quiet lavender with a slate roof the color of overripe plums. White shutters and gingerbread trim gave it a friendly look, and the bottom floor housed The Corner Coffee Shop.

Maggie was about to get out of her BMW when her phone rang. The caller ID read "Mother." Maggie glanced up and saw Hannah disappear inside the café. She looked down at the phone and stabbed the END button.

Hannah waited for Maggie at the counter, where she insisted on paying for Maggie's tea and bowl of fruit. Maggie tried not to look surprised when the clerk handed Hannah a giant chocolate chip cookie and cup of hot chocolate.

They made their way to a booth by a window that looked out over the river. Maggie had barely settled in her seat when Hannah said, "Geez, I'm glad your daughter found Reilly's ring. You don't know how much trouble I'd be in if she lost it."

"You?" Maggie frowned.

"Oh, yeah, me. I'd be blamed for not protecting it. You see, my mother-in-law gave it to Reilly for her birthday. It was hers when she was a girl. They have the same first initial—she's Rita."

Maggie made an *ah* sound and picked up her cup.

Hannah said, "I knew Reilly would lose it! She's too young to have it, but Travis and his mother wouldn't listen to me. Travis is my husband." She crammed a bite of cookie into her mouth, her brow puckering into a frown.

"Addie's always finding things." Maggie took a sip of tea and held it on her tongue.

Hannah's frown deepened. "That's the thing. How did she know it was Reilly's? I didn't see y'all when we walked in." Hannah cocked her head. "No, I'm sure I didn't see you. There were only a few cars in the lot when we got there. We came early because I had to take Reilly's shot record to the school nurse."

Maggie widened her eyes and shrugged. "I guess it's just your lucky day."

"Maybe so," Hannah mumbled.

But Maggie heard, *I don't think so,* so she turned toward the window, looking for a change of subject reflected in the waters of Coal River. "Have you ever noticed how the river wraps around the mountains like a ruffle on the hem of a skirt?"

"That river?"

Maggie nodded. "We moved here from D.C. in the spring, and the mountains were so green and lush—I fell in love."

"You *like* living here?"

"I love it."

Hannah sat back and folded her arms. "Maggie," she said, "look out that window and tell me what you see."

"A river and mountains—"

"And coal dirt," Hannah said. "That's Coal Valley. Down here in the valley is where the dirt settles."

Maggie rested her arms on the table. "Sometimes," she said, "it's what's missing that makes a place special. I lived in the city all my life, and now that I'm here, I can't imagine ever going back." She looked out at the river, and her voice lowered an octave. "My day begins with the mist clinging to the mountaintops, and it ends with fireflies dancing with the moon."

The look on Hannah's face made Maggie burst out laughing. "I'm sorry. I must sound silly to you."

"Yeah, well, just wait until winter gets here."

"Does Coal Valley get much snow?"

"It doesn't take much snow in these mountains to trap you inside for so long you're ready to burn the house down to get out."

"I take it you're from here?"

"Born and raised. Spent most of my life trying to escape."

This time it was Hannah who laughed. "I'm just kidding. You should see your face."

Maggie smiled.

"So what do you do?"

"Do?"

"Yeah, I thought," Hannah lifted her hands, palms up like she was surrendering, "you were dressed for work."

"Oh." Maggie eyed Hannah's t-shirt and denim shorts, and then glanced down at her white linen dress. "I didn't know what mothers wear on the first day of school. I'm just a housewife. You?"

"I'm a stay-at-home mom. I hate that word, 'housewife.'"

Hannah tilted her head to one side and smiled. A dimple appeared in her right cheek. But it was her eyes that were striking—watercolor blue and perfectly round with long lashes, the kind that made men stare and women jealous. Hannah's lilting mountain accent and animated hands were enchanting. Even the way she slipped off her shoes and sat with one foot tucked under her was charming.

"What does your husband do?" Maggie asked.

Hannah frowned. "My husband goes to work, comes home, and eats-drinks-sleeps football. That sums up Travis Lively." She shrugged. "Except in summer, then it's baseball or any sport that requires a ball. Travis thinks there are three seasons: football, basketball, and baseball. What about your husband?"

"J.D. is an attorney. Politics is his game. Unfortunately, it's a year-round sport."

"Tell you what," Hannah flicked her wrist so that her hand fell back, "let's not talk about husbands."

"Agreed."

The shop door opened and a draft of heat slipped in, announcing a group of students from the Appalachian Law School. Its campus was on the other side of Coal River, but a walking bridge connected it to Old Town. The slap of their flip-flops on hardwood was almost as loud as their voices. Maggie and Hannah watched them get drinks and pastries and come trooping past them. One young man carrying an enormous book bag slung across one shoulder smiled at Hannah and said, "Hey," his eyes lingering on her face just a second too long.

When they were out of earshot, Maggie said, "How does it feel to be *hit on*?"

"Oh, stop." Pink flooded Hannah's cheeks. "He's too young for me—that is, *if* I was looking."

"Too *young*! You're what, twenty-four?"

"Twenty-five."

"That's what I thought. I'm the old lady here—almost thirty."

Hannah grabbed their cups. "Be right back with refills."

Their cups were empty again before Hannah blurted out, "Why did you cry?"

Maggie didn't want to tell Hannah about Addie's fragile health. She said, "I'm just an over-protective mother. Too sentimental for my own good."

"Yeah, me too. Reilly's my only child."

"Addie's my only child."

Hannah studied the ring of chocolate in her empty cup. She picked up a napkin and wiped the table around her cup, even though the area was clean.

Maggie didn't trust herself to speak, so she turned toward the window and watched the river pulse with sunlight.

"I'm sorry," Hannah said. "I don't know what's wrong with me. I used to think of all the things I could do when Reilly went to school, but now, I don't want to do any of them."

Maggie nodded.

Another group of students came in, and Hannah said, "I guess we should go. But let's do this again."

Maggie smiled. "Sure."

Maggie was in her car when Hannah called out.

"Maggie?"

"Yes?"

"It's lightning bugs. We don't call them fireflies."

"Thanks. I'm already in trouble with the gardener for calling the creek a brook."

"Gardener? Don't you mean yard man?"

"Of course, the yard man." Maggie laughed and started the car. She drove through town with a smile on her face until her cell phone rang.

"Margaret." Her mother's voice was cold and composed. "Why didn't you call me back? Surely, you're home by now."

"Sorry, I got busy."

This excuse sounded lame even to Maggie, but she wasn't prepared for her mother's scathing response. "How do you know my granddaughter isn't sitting in a corner crying?"

"Because" Maggie snapped, "as soon as we got to her classroom, Addie waved good-bye and went off with the other children. She didn't even look back."

"But my granddaughter needs special care."

"Mother, your granddaughter has a name. It's Addison.

And she *had* cancer, Mother. Cancer. She's been cancer free now for almost a year."

"I'm well aware of her name, and I maintain Addison is a surname, not a given name."

Maggie knew her mother would not say the big c-word, but would rather pick on something like Addie's name, so she ignored the slight. Years ago, she had adopted what she called a Gandhi approach with her mother, practicing "peaceful resistance."

"Addie doesn't want anyone to know she had cancer, and I'm respecting her wishes. Besides, J.D. doesn't want me to broadcast our daughter's illness."

"Well, if J.D. doesn't want anyone to know—"

"No, he doesn't."

Judith Hudson's voice rose to an all-out whine. "If you had just stayed around D.C., instead of moving to that god-forsaken place. I mean—"

Maggie interrupted. "Mother, you have never been here." She switched tactics. "Oh, and Mother, Addie insisted on wearing the pink dress you bought her."

"I hope you took a picture." Her mother's tone softened.

"I took several. Look, Mother, I have things to do before it's time to pick up Addie."

"All right, Margaret, I'll speak with you later."

Maggie pushed the end button. She looked down at her sweaty palm and realized she was gripping the phone like the arm of the dentist's chair—only the dentist numbed you first.

She turned into her driveway and the world balanced. Her mother could call, but she couldn't "pop-in" unannounced like she had in D.C.

The hundred-year-old house came into view. Maggie had overseen the remodeling, taking every precaution to keep its Early American personality. There were times she could sense its past lives, hear her footsteps echo those who had lived here, loved here, died here. She had always wanted to live away from the city in a house with a sloping lawn, a place where she could watch the seasons change. Maggie was in love with this rugged little town. There was a peace in Coal Valley, a sense of life moving through its proper courses. It was the kind of place she wanted to live and raise her daughter, away from the politics and parties of D.C., away from her mother.

J.D.'s BMW was blocking the garage. Maggie stepped out of the car just as J.D. burst from the house. He stopped short and waved a folder in the air. "It was your responsibility to give the housekeeper specific instructions not to touch my desk."

Maggie's hand flew to her throat. J.D. stalked past her and opened his car door. He practically yelled, "If you *had* told her, then she wouldn't have cleaned my office and mixed up the files on my desk, *and* I wouldn't be here getting the correct one." He slammed the door, the engine roared, and Maggie was left standing in the driveway.

Maggie walked around the house to the sunroom. She removed her shoes, slipping the straps over her wrist. Her housekeeper, Ida, cleaned the kitchen on Mondays, and the last thing she wanted to do was to make small talk. She hurried to the living room. The heavy silk drapes were open and sunlight laid golden stripes on the polished floors, creating the sensation the floors were moving. Maggie put a hand on the white grand piano to steady herself. A cabinet banged shut in the kitchen, and she darted out of the living room. In the front foyer, she glanced down the hallway that led to J.D.'s office. She had to talk to Ida about *not* cleaning it. But not now. Not today.

Feeling like she was sneaking through her own house like a thief, Maggie hurried upstairs and down the hall to her bedroom. She went to the French doors that opened onto a balcony and stepped outside, wiping away hot tears. Nothing had changed.

A breeze drifted down the mountain, and Maggie shifted in her chair so she could see the brook edging their property. The weeping willows along the periphery tossed in the gentle wind. She leaned her head back and inhaled the heady scent of freshly mowed grass. It was a lovely blue-sky day—her daughter's first day of school—an event that not so long ago she feared would never happen. She was happy Addie was well enough to go to school, but how was she supposed to let go?

For three years, Maggie had enfolded Addie's body in her arms during chemotherapy, watching the poison drip into her body. She had not cried.

When the vomiting started, she had held a cold cloth to Addie's forehead. She had not cried.

When Addie screamed while she urinated, Maggie discovered it was because the chemo turned her urine into liquid fire. She had not cried.

When she gathered the strands of hair as they fell out, she had tied bright jeweled bows around Addie's bald head. She had not cried.

Then today, Addie had positively danced into the kindergarten class. Without her. And this time she cried. The tears she had held back all those years welled up until Maggie thought she would drown in them.

The day edged toward noon and still Maggie lingered on her balcony. The sun ripened until it dangled in the sky like a golden peach, and the cicadas woke to praise the heat. Did the world move slower in these mountains?

And then there was Hannah—a wonderful surprise on an otherwise miserable day. She was as refreshing as diving into the ocean after running across hot sand. Hannah had made Maggie feel like she counted—like she was important. Easy to talk to and quick to laugh, Hannah had said "y'all" and explained she was from a "holler," a narrow valley between the hills that ran through this part of central Appalachia like blood-rich veins.

Maggie remembered Hannah's eyes, full of questions about why Addie had known the ring she found belonged to Reilly, but she had accepted Maggie's feeble answer and let it drop. Maggie couldn't explain to Hannah her daughter's "gift" for finding lost keys, misplaced cell phones, and the lipstick holder of her husband's latest lover. She couldn't explain it to herself.

Maggie left the balcony and went to Addie's room, a mixture of soft pastels and white furniture. She paused in the doorway, admiring Peter Pan's Neverland—the way Addie imagined it—as a mural covering one wall. Peter Pan, Tinker Bell, and the three Darling children flew across the sky, the city of London spread below them. Only the little girl wasn't Wendy; it was Addie who followed Peter Pan and Tinker Bell with pixie dust swirling around them.

Maggie lay down on Addie's bed and looked up at the pink canopy suspended from the ceiling. She switched on the Tinker Bell lamp and the canopy glittered. Each night, Addie looked up at it and said, "Goodnight, Mama. I'm going to Neverland."

For three long years, Maggie had fought for her daughter's life. Addie's cancer had consumed her every waking moment and haunted her dreams. *Treatment. Chemotherapy. Radiation. Prognosis.* Fear had been her life. And where had her husband been when she needed him?

The day the chemo treatments had taken the last strand of Addie's hair, she had come to Maggie with a gold lipstick case in her tiny hand, purple with bruises from the IV. Inside the case had been an expensive lipstick so dark red it looked black—a shade Maggie never wore. Addie's words still haunted her. "Look what I found in Daddy's pocket. Can you give it to the pretty lady? She's looking for it."

The pretty lady, she discovered, was a new attorney at J.D.'s Washington office. He had sworn he had no idea how her lipstick case had gotten in his suit-coat pocket, but Maggie could come up with several scenarios, none of them innocent.

A Boyd's Bear her mother had given Addie for her first Christmas lay on the pillow. Maggie picked it up and looked into its soulful eyes. As soon as she could talk, Addie had pronounced the bear "Wiggle Worm"—only it sounded like "Iggle Um." Addie took Iggle Um everywhere, by slipping her forefinger inside its tag. She carried all stuffed animals that way, shunning those whose tag didn't make a loop for her finger. Every trip to the doctor, every stay in the hospital, every treatment she endured, Addie had taken Iggle Um. Maggie whispered, "What would you say if you could talk?"

Maggie took Wiggle Worm and sat down in the rocking chair. She murmured the familiar prayer, "Father in heaven, heal my child. Take away her pain. Let her sleep be peaceful. Take away her sickness."

The cancer was gone, but the scars were tender and fresh. Every time Addie slept later than usual or said she wasn't hungry, Maggie worried the cancer was back.

Before the cancer. After the cancer. Maggie's life was divided between the two as if a black line was drawn down the middle. Before the cancer, Addie's life was measured by a baby's natural time markers: first time she slept through the night, first time she rolled over, first tooth, and first word. What a joy it had been to record all the milestones. Then Addie took her first step, and Maggie's days were filled with chasing after her daughter and watching her discover the world.

After Addie got sick, everything stopped. No more milestones to record. Life became a horror of doctors, hospitals, and treatments. Lost were the pictures of birthday parties and holidays Maggie would have treasured. The bedtimes she would have cherished. And through it all, where was her husband? He chose that time to turn to other women.

Maggie placed Wiggle Worm in the rocking chair and went to her bedroom. She opened her closet and pulled out the movable rack of shoes, sliding her hand into the toe of one of the red high heels she never wore—a perfect place to hide the mysterious lipstick case. She smiled, remembering J.D.'s face when she had told him, "Well, if she asks, tell her this pretty lady won't give it back."

The gold case was like a smooth stone in Maggie's hand. She took it to her dressing table, sat down, and switched on the lighted mirror, examining her face. She opened the case and removed the purple tube of lipstick, pulling off its top and twisting the base until the cylinder of blood red appeared. She carefully applied a thick coat. "Well J.D.," she said and smacked her lips together. "What do you think?"

Chapter 4

Between night and day abides an elusive recess, indefinable in the cycle of time. When the sky purples into blue, the gate to this interstice opens, and spirits reveal themselves to those who, like me, seek them.
~ from Granny Zee's Book of Dreams

HANNAH LIVELY KNEW EXACTLY who the Whitefield's were from the newspaper. He was a government attorney the new Appalachian Law School had lured from D.C., but even if she hadn't seen their pictures, it wouldn't have taken her five seconds to figure out Margaret Whitefield wasn't a Coal Valley housewife, or as people in this town were apt to say, "She ain't from around here."

Hannah filled the sink with soapy water and put the breakfast dishes in to soak. She wiped the crumbs from around the sink and adjusted the cutting board, so it covered the burn marks on the counter. Her kitchen was a 1970s-harvest gold nightmare, and she'd lost count of the times Travis had promised they were going to update it.

With a glass of sweet iced tea in her hand, Hannah went outside and settled in the swing. She shouldn't have pretended she didn't know who Maggie was, but damn it—she wasn't expecting her to be so, well, nice. She had been ready to dismiss Maggie as someone outside her price range. Who wears a designer dress and high heels to her daughter's first day of school? But instead of some snooty city girl, she had met a mom, just like her, leaving her only child on the first day of school.

A breeze crossed over the deck, and Hannah inhaled late summer's perfume. Maggie was nothing like the girls Hannah had known in high school. They had never gotten past being cheerleaders or wannabe prom queens, and some of those same girls were at Coal Valley Elementary this morning, smiling and greeting her like an old friend. It had been like a high school flashback. These so-called friends were the reason Hannah frequented The Corner Coffee Shop. None of them ever went there.

The coffee shop was Hannah's safe haven. There, she imagined she was one of the law school students who frequented the place—who had classes and study groups, who had a purpose

Hannah knew she didn't really belong there. If anyone belonged amid the polished wood and coffee smells it was Maggie. Maggie was lovely in a Julia Roberts sort of way—like one of those women who is attractive but then she smiles and her whole face transforms into gorgeous.

Something nagged at Hannah about Maggie. On the outside she looked self-assured, but she reminded Hannah of a stray cat that had shown up hungry and frightened at her granny's back door. Hannah had only been six or seven, and she had wanted to rush over and scoop it up, but Granny Zee had stopped her. "If you approach a strange cat too fast it will run. Go slow and give it time to get to know you."

Hannah rubbed the cool glass across her forehead then set it on the deck. She fashioned her hair into a small bun and let it fall back to her shoulders. Maggie's long dark hair had been pulled into a thick ponytail.

"Maggie," she said, "I'd kill for your hair. Wait! And your perfectly arched eyebrows. And your flawless skin, full lips, and white straight teeth. And. And. And." Hannah laughed but it caught in her throat. Maggie was exactly who she had wanted to be when she was a little girl dreaming of a life beyond these mountains—beings she loved and hated with equal passion.

She understood why Maggie saw them as otherworldly, filled with mist and mystery. She had spent her childhood roaming the woods, learning their secrets from her mother and grandmother. What would Maggie say if she knew Hannah was from a long line of mountain witches?

❧

The minute Travis got home, Reilly scrabbled onto his lap and threw her arms around his neck. "Daddy, I love school!"

Travis transformed when he was with his daughter. No matter how busy or tired he was he always gave her his undivided attention. Right now, the lines around his blue eyes crinkled as he smiled down on Reilly. His sun-streaked blonde hair had gotten so long he'd parted it in the middle and had it looped behind his ears. A blush of new sun was on his face like he'd spent the day boating on the lake.

Travis threw back his head and laughed, and Reilly giggled, putting her hand shyly over her mouth. A flush of warmth went through Hannah like she had taken a drink of hot cocoa on a cold day. She went to them and put her hands on Travis's shoulders. This was the Travis she wanted—the Travis who paid attention, the Travis who showed his love. The Travis she had lost.

The minute Reilly went off to play, Travis picked up the remote and switched on ESPN. Hannah sat down across from him. "I met Maggie Whitefield, today. Her husband is the dean of the law school. Their daughter's in Reilly's class." She paused. "Travis, did you hear me?"

"That's good, babe."

"What's good?"

"Tell me later? I'm trying to watch this."

The phone rang, saving Hannah and Travis an argument. When Hannah finally wrestled the phone from Reilly, Granny Zee said, "I believe Reilly enjoyed her first day of school, but how did you fare?"

Hannah sighed. "It was a bit sad."

"Reilly told me an interesting story about a little girl who found her lost ring—a ring she wasn't supposed to take to school."

"I had no idea Reilly took that to school! So, when this little girl walks over and shows it to Reilly, I—well, I may have over-reacted."

"With that Irish temper?"

"But I apologized. Even bought the little girl's mother a cup of coffee—wait—tea."

Granny chuckled. "My question is, how did the child know the ring belonged to Reilly?"

"Exactly! And there's something else. That little girl had an angel's kiss."

"Did she?"

"Her dark brown hair had one silver lock above her forehead."

Granny Zee went silent.

Hannah shifted the phone to her other ear. "Granny? Are you there?"

"Yes, dear, I was just thinking. It's been many years since I saw an angel's kiss."

"I didn't even tell you their names," Hannah said. "Maggie Whitefield and her daughter, Addie. Her husband's the new dean of the law school. You probably saw the article about them in the paper."

"No, Hannah, I know who they are. I was expecting them."

A shiver worked its way up Hannah's spine. "Expecting

them? Why?"

"Maggie and Addie are going to become important in your and Reilly's life."

Hannah knew Granny was never wrong, but exactly how was this "uptown girl" going to be important to them?

October presented Indian summer to Coal Valley. Sweaters and scarves were put away and sandals and shorts were once again wardrobe staples. Daytime temperatures soared into summer digits where the heat pooled, waiting for the night to sweep it away.

Reilly Lively and Addie Whitefield spent so much time at each other's houses that Hannah and Maggie were becoming as close as their daughters. Hannah was surprised at how satisfying it was to have a friend—someone who simply *liked* her for who she was, a person who sought her out because she was good company and not because of her husband's agenda.

And then Addie caused Reilly to get into trouble at school.

When Hannah burst into the principal's office, Maggie was already there. Hannah looked from Maggie's black slacks and lavender silk blouse to her cut-offs and t-shirt that read HAND OVER THE CHOCOLATE AND NO ONE GETS HURT. Then, her eyes fell to her feet. After the school's phone call, she had run out to the car barefoot before running back inside where she grabbed the first shoes she saw—fur topped ankle-boots. She realized she must look like a deranged Eskimo.

The principal, Ms. Goodall, was seated behind an enormous desk with nothing on it but a telephone with a row of lighted buttons and a gold-embossed nameplate proclaiming PRINCIPAL. She gestured Hannah toward a chair and waited for her to sit down before saying, "First of all, and most importantly, no one got hurt, but Reilly and Addie left the school grounds together and disappeared into the woods behind the school." She paused for dramatic effect before adding, "Without permission." She lowered her pointy chin and looked down her beakish nose, giving Hannah and Maggie her most withering look, one that no doubt terrified children and teachers alike.

Hannah glanced at Maggie. She could tell that Ms. Goodall's "look" was working on her. Maggie wore an expression like someone who was used to being chastised. But, oh heck no, that look wouldn't work on Hannah! She said, "That doesn't sound like Reilly or Addie. Unless they had a really good reason."

"Reilly said she was helping Addie find Timmy, a fellow kindergartner who had decided he was going to run away from school," Ms. Goodall said.

"Well, it sounds like they did a good thing. I mean, they found the boy and brought him back, right?" Hannah looked over at Maggie for conformation, but she stared straight ahead.

Ms. Goodall sighed. "The boy was discovered missing after morning recess. The children were questioned about his whereabouts. I, myself, told the students how important it was for them to tell if they knew anything about where Timmy had gone."

Hannah said, "Well, I have no doubt your talk with the children made them want to run right up to you and tell you everything, but let's say for the sake of argument the girls were afraid to tell."

Maggie glanced at Hannah, then pressed the fingertips of her left hand to her forehead.

Ms. Goodall narrowed her eyes. "Mrs. Lively, if the girls had told us that Timmy was hiding in the woods behind the school, we could have found him without having to call the police. Instead, in the confusion, they slipped away and went into the woods—"

Hannah interrupted. "Where they found the boy and brought him back. So essentially, our girls are in trouble for finding a missing child."

A rash of bright pink flooded Ms. Goodall's face. "Mrs. Lively, the girls are in trouble for leaving the school property without permission. They had an opportunity to tell their teacher where Timmy was and they didn't." She paused for effect. "Mrs. Lively, a lie by omission is still a lie."

Hannah looked at Maggie who now had the palm of her hand spread across her forehead. She turned back to Ms. Goodall and pointed her index finger at her. "You know, here's where I have a problem. I don't see it that way. I want to talk to the girls."

Maggie suddenly sprang to life. She shook her head. "I don't think that's necessary."

Hannah crossed her arms and stared hard at Maggie before turning to the principal, who sighed and picked up her phone. No one spoke until a knock sounded on the door and Miss Hall entered with Addie and Reilly in tow. Before Ms. Goodall could speak, Hannah said, "Hey, girls!" She motioned the girls over to their chairs.

Maggie said, "Hello, sweetie," and took Addie's hand.

The girls now stood facing their mothers. Hannah said, "So

girls, I heard you found a lost boy today?"

They nodded. Then Addie said, "We had to go and get Timmy because of the bad snake."

"A snake?" Hannah turned toward Ms. Goodall. "You didn't say anything about a snake."

Ms. Goodall's face flushed. "This is the first I've heard of a snake." She glared at Miss Hall. "You didn't say anything about a snake."

Miss Hall looked from Ms. Goodall to the girls. "This is the first I've heard of a snake."

Addie said, "Timmy was sitting on a rock and there was a snake under it. It was going to bite him."

"Yeah," said Reilly, "that's why we went to save him."

Addie piped up. "It was brown, and it was a bad snake. Mama, remember you told me about bad snakes?"

Maggie nodded. She smiled to reassure Addie.

"Well, there you go," Hannah said, like the matter was settled. "Thanks girls. You can go back to class with your teacher now. We'll see you after school."

Ms. Goodall said, "You may go, Miss Hall."

When they were gone, Hannah stood and faced Ms. Goodall. About to speak, she instead looked at Maggie and raised her eyebrows. Maggie immediately sprang to her feet. Hannah said, "I assure you that Reilly and Addie will never leave school grounds again without permission."

"That's right," Maggie said. "We will give them a strong talking to."

Ms. Goodall frowned but rose slowly from her desk. Hannah walked to the door and Maggie followed. With her hand on the doorknob Hannah turned to face the principal. "I know how happy you are that little boy was found safe and sound. I hate to think what could have happened if the girls hadn't found him."

Ms. Goodall wasn't going to let them go without the last word. "Understand that if anything like this happens again, there will be strict consequences."

Maggie said, "Of course," but Hannah was already out the door.

Hannah and Maggie were in the parking lot before Maggie said, "I'm so sorry about this. I will talk to Addie. I promise she won't get Reilly in trouble again." When Hannah didn't reply, Maggie put her hand on Hannah's arm. "I hope you'll continue to let them play together?"

Hannah stopped abruptly and wheeled around to face Maggie. "I just have one question."

"What?"

"What *really* happened?"

Hannah was prepared for Maggie to sidestep the issue but instead, she burst into tears.

"Come on," Hannah said, putting her arm around Maggie and guiding her to her car. "Get in. We've got time for a cup of tea before school's out."

Without a word, Maggie climbed into the car and took the tissue Hannah offered. By the time they got to The Corner Coffee Shop, she had composed herself. They went inside and Maggie found a seat while Hannah got two tall glasses of sweet iced tea.

"Before you say anything about today," Hannah said, "I want you to know I'm not mad at you or Addie. But I will be if you lie to me."

Maggie's mouth fell open. Hannah held up her hand and said, "Hear me out before you say anything."

Maggie nodded.

"Yesterday, when Addie was at our house, she came running to me and said she saw my lost earring." Hannah's hand instinctively went to her earlobe, and she fingered one of the gold hoops. "It's been missing for a couple of weeks and, when Addie said she found it, I expected it to be in plain sight, not to be snagged in the threads of a folded towel."

Hannah paused and gave Maggie a long look. "The towel was on the top shelf in the middle of the stack."

Maggie's eyes widened.

Hannah put her hand on Maggie's wrist. "Addie led me to the shelf in my bathroom and pointed to the towels. She said, 'You don't have to be sad anymore. I know you're sad because you lost your earring. The one your mama gave you.'"

Maggie's eyes trailed down to Hannah's hand and back up to her face.

Hannah said, "Those earrings were the last gift my mother gave me before she died."

Maggie covered Hannah's hand with hers. "I'm so sorry."

Hannah never knew what to say to that except "me too," so she just nodded. She said, "Look Maggie, nobody asked the real question today—how did Addie know where to find that little boy? Obviously, the principal and Miss Hall think Timmy told them where he was going before he slipped away."

Maggie nodded and looked down at her hands. "I can't explain it, but Addie has a... gift for finding things—especially if she thinks the person connected to it is sad—but honestly, this is the first time she ever found a person."

"Finding things and people," Hannah said. She sat back and folded her arms. What she didn't tell Maggie was that after what happened yesterday, she had called Granny Zee and now, all she could think about was what Granny had said—the sight, the two sights, the touch, the sixth sense—call it what you want, Addie had the gift. She *knew* things.

Chapter 5

*I learned about ancient Celtic festivals from my grandmother.
The harvest festivals: Lughnasadh signals the beginning of the
harvest season in mid-August, between the summer solstice and
autumn equinox; and Samhain, celebrated from dusk October
31st to sundown November 1st, marks harvest's end and winter's beginning. The spring festivals: Imbolc, also called St.
Brigid's Day, signals the beginning of spring; and Beltane,
observed on May 1st, marks the beginning of summer.*
~ from Granny Zee's Book of Dreams

ZELDA DAVIS WOKE TO find the world had turned to fog.
She made a cup of ginseng tea and slipped on her red
cardigan, rolling up the over-long sleeves. She went to sit on the
patio in the morning mist and wait for the sun to sweep the fog
from the mountaintops. As she sipped tea, a legion of fog ghosts
surrounded her, draping a milky shawl across her bent
shoulders. The fog's cool touch on her skin brought back
childhood memories of freshly washed sheets hanging across
ropes stretched between two oak trees. She and her sisters
would chase each other, the wet sheets flapping against their
bare arms and legs. The sheets called to memory her mama's
sweet lavender bush. Mama added lavender to the rinse water,
knowing its fragrance repelled insects and calmed the senses,
offering a soothing night's sleep.

There was too much to do today to sit and recollect her
childhood. After all, there was hardly anyone left who called
her Zelda. For many years now, she was known as Granny Zee.
Some days, she had trouble understanding why she was still
living. She had outlived her sisters, husband, two of her children, and everyone who had grown up with her on this
mountain.

The celebration of Samhain would begin at sunset and end
tomorrow at twilight. This ancient Celtic festival marked the
end of harvest and the beginning of winter when the darkness
grew long and the days short. The children called it Halloween,
but like her Irish ancestors, Granny Zee called it Samhain, the
beginning of the darker half of the year.

In the pantry, Granny found her biggest terra cotta pot. She set it in front of the fireplace and prepared to smudge her home. Her mother and grandmother had smudged their houses on each Celtic festival to purify and cleanse the house and its objects and balance the aura and energies of everyone who lived there. Granny Zee cherished the scent of herbal smoke wafting through the rooms, and like she did as a child, she stood where the smoke would touch her so she might feel its cleansing power.

Into the bottom of the pot, Granny Zee placed a handful of cedar chips. To this she added two scoops of pine needles. On top, she placed a bundle of garden sage, lavender, mugwort, and white sage—all dried and bound together with twine. Before lighting the herbs, Granny Zee bowed her head and said the harvest prayer her grandmother had taught her: "I come to this place with pure intentions and an open heart. I give thanks for the abundance in my life and will share the harvest of the earth with those I love. I will meditate on the sacredness of life in the silence of the forest. With these herbs, I will turn the negative energy in this place into light. I invite the spirits of Mother Earth to guide me."

Granny Zee struck the match and touched it to the cedar and pine. "Cedar, connect me with the spirits of people and animals. Pine, cleanse and purify this place." When they began to burn, she lit the bundle of herbs. "Mugwort, connect me with nature and protect my dreams. Sage, give me a healing hand and a lucid mind. Sweet lavender, I call on you to restore balance. Calm and soothe my life." When everything was burning, Granny Zee gently blew out the flames, leaving the herbs smoldering so the smoke would drift through and smudge the house.

She inhaled the dusky scent and closed her eyes, savoring the memories gathering around her: Mama's smudging pot placed on the table that held her family's Bible; her grandmother's smudging pot that held in the scent of the herbs long after they were gone; her own smudging pot circled by her children dancing in the smoke. She opened her eyes and watched the smoke spiderwebbing through the room until it disappeared from sight.

Now, it was time to prepare a feast for the wee folk. Granny had her recipe for apple faerie cake and all the ingredients set out on the counter: softened butter, eggs, flour with a pinch of salt and baking powder, sugar, and cinnamon. She peeled apples from her own trees, shredding them into a bowl. She hoped the wee folk wouldn't mind that she used an electric mixer because her old hands had gotten too warped with arthritis to mix the batter by hand. Before pouring the batter into the pan, she stirred in a drop of vanilla and a handful of black walnuts that she had harvested, shelled, and chopped herself.

When the cake was baked, Granny Zee prepared the faerie basket. In years past, her daughter, Emma, and later her grand-daughter, Hannah, had helped bake the cake and take it to the forest to leave for the wee folk to find. Now, she had a great-granddaughter, and she hoped, one day, Reilly would want to know the old ways. Hannah and Reilly kept her going, even though Hannah pushed against the mountains with all her might. Granny Zee had watched her granddaughter grieve for a life she thought she wanted, when Granny knew in her heart that Hannah belonged here.

Granny Zee placed a cloth embroidered with sunflowers in the bottom of the faerie basket. In the center, she placed a slice of the fresh apple cake. Around the cake she arranged a cup of heavy cream, her shiniest apple, a block of chocolate, and sprigs of fresh mint—things she knew the wee people loved. It was important to keep them happy, or they could wreak havoc in her garden.

Granny Zee slipped on her leather brogans with gripping soles so her step would be sure. She wore her red cardigan and a matching knitted hat to ward off the morning's chill. Across her shoulder, she hung a canvas bag that held her spade and shears, the tools of her profession—a gatherer of plants and herbs to be used in her medicinal remedies. Even though Granny Zee was not going gathering, she never entered the forest without her tools. And last, she slipped the basket over her arm.

Before she set off into the forest, Granny Zee took up her walking stick from its place next to the back door. As she climbed the mountain path, she sang, "My Wild Irish Rose," humming the parts pitched too high, for she knew the spirits liked music. It didn't matter that the fog still cloaked the mountain path, her feet knew the way. Granny's very being was woven into the tapestry of Rock House Mountain.

When she reached the scarlet oak, Granny Zee placed the basket at the base of the faerie fort and said, "Wee folk of the forest, accept this autumn offering of sweet treats." She knew not to call them faeries. Her grandmother had taught her they preferred "wee folk" or "wee people." She had also taught her it was not wise to anger the wee people.

A group of stones formed a natural bench in front of a

mound of earth that rose up from the ground like the hump of a camel. This was the faerie fort where her grandmother had told her the faeries lived. She sat down on the stone bench and breathed in the moist, earthy scent of fog. Above her, fog garlands stretched between the bare branches, while below her, the star-shaped leaves had flamed scarlet and dropped, fashioning a carpet around her bench. Granny Zee sighed. For seven decades, she had sat in this very spot, watching squirrels forage for acorns. She closed her eyes and listened. Her time on earth was passing, but she knew her days were not yet done.

When Granny Zee opened her eyes, the fog was gone, and sunlight moved between the tree's branches like a child peeking around her mother's skirts. She went to the basket and discovered it was empty. The wee folk hadn't left a crumb. Granny chuckled and picked up her things. There was still much to do for the feast tonight, so she made her way back down the forest path.

Tonight, the veil between this world and the next one would lift, allowing the dead to revisit the living. The evil dead would not pass fire, so Granny Zee would place lanterns all around the outside of her house and light a bonfire near her back door. In olden times, the Scots-Irish carved out the inside of turnips and placed candles inside to ward off spirits. They also wore masks to disguise themselves from the wandering dead. When her own children were small, Granny had helped them carve jack-o'-lanterns out of pumpkins and make masks. She told them how the wearing of masks and costumes for Halloween came from the Celtic feast of Samhain, when children in Ireland and Scotland went from house to house, asking for gifts of food and coins. The people willingly gave these gifts in fear there was an evil spirit lurking behind the mask.

Back down the mountain, Granny saw the sun had climbed high in the sky, so she decided to lay the fire before she went inside. Ten smooth stones placed in a circle would hold her fire—one stone for each member of her family. In the center, Granny Zee placed bundles of twigs and broken branches she had collected in the forest. Tonight, after the fire took hold, she would add seasoned hickory and poplar logs. From that fire, she would take burning wood into her house and light her hearth. It was important to bring Samhain's fire inside to protect her home from the coming darkness of winter.

Before she prepared the evening feast, Granny put the kettle on for tea and heated a bowl of vegetable soup. She switched on the television that sat on her kitchen counter and smiled when reedy pipe organ music filled the kitchen. Why was it people wanted to be scared? These silly Halloween movies weren't scary. Now, being alone in the forest when a banshee screams—that was scary. She switched the channel to the home-shopping network and ate lunch.

Colcannon was the Irish dish Granny was going to prepare, just as her grandmother and mother had made for Samhain. She went to the pantry and filled her apron with potatoes and set to peeling them while she listened to the woman selling shoes on the television. When the potatoes were ready, she got out her biggest cook pot and placed it next to the sink, so she could toss in the washed and chopped potatoes. She covered them with water, added salt, and set the pot on the stove. While the potatoes were cooking, Granny got another cook pot and prepared the cabbage.

While she waited for the pots to boil, Granny Zee watched the sales lady talk about the newest thing in walking shoes: "All leather with a special cushioned heel to absorb the shock of walking, available in six colors." When the water boiled, she set the timer and went back to watch a model, in a spiffy jogging suit, strut around in the all-leather walking shoes. She did like that new brick red color. By the time the cabbage was drained and buttered, and the potatoes were cooked tender, Granny Zee had called in her order for the walking shoes.

Granny's mother had insisted that two things were required to make good colcannon: make sure the potatoes were dry before adding the milk and butter and hand-mash the potatoes. After a brief rest for her hands, Granny Zee chopped the cabbage into bite size pieces and mixed it into the potatoes. The dish was finished, but when she was a girl, her mama would observe the old Irish custom of adding charms to the col-cannon—a button, thimble, coin, and a ring.

According to the legend, the charms were portents for what would happen in the coming year. The legend said the one who found the button would remain unmarried. The one who found the thimble was in danger of becoming a spinster and had best change her ways! The one who found the ring in her colcannon would marry, and the one who got the coin would come into money. Her older sisters had always wished to find the ring, and somehow, Granny Zee always got the coin.

There was nothing better with a bowl of colcannon than a fresh hunk of cornbread, so Granny Zee took down her mixing bowl and got out her iron skillet. She turned on the oven and put a scoop of Crisco in the skillet. Her mama had used lard, but Granny Zee had promised Hannah she wouldn't use lard because she said it was "bad for you."

As if she had conjured her, the phone rang, and when Granny answered, Hannah sang out, "Happy Feast of Samhain!"

Granny Zee laughed. "And how are the festivities going at your house?"

"Peter Pan is running around here somewhere. We're getting ready to meet Tinker Bell at her house, and when we can't delay them another minute, Maggie and I will let them start trick-or-treating. Are you sure you don't want us to bring the girls to see you?"

"Oh, no, dear. I don't want you coming up the mountain with dark coming on. It's not safe to be on the mountain tonight."

Hannah laughed like Granny's warning was a joke, and sadness pressed down on Granny Zee's chest like a heavy hand. Hannah had grown up with the old ways, but now, she chose not to join in. Instead, she took Reilly trick-or-treating and did all the modern silliness that had nothing to do with a true celebration of Samhain. Granny Zee said, "Maybe next year you can bring Reilly up, and I'll teach her how to make colcannon. Do you remember how we hid the charms inside?"

"I remember." A silence followed.

"Be careful tonight," Granny said.

"I won't let any ghosts or goblins get us."

"It's not just the dead you need to be wary of," Granny said.

Granny Zee placed the skillet into the oven so the Crisco would melt. She mixed corn meal and flour, baking powder and salt. She added milk, one egg, and a scoop of melted Crisco into the mixture, stirring until it was just a little lumpy. Before she poured the batter into the skillet, she checked to make sure it was hot, so the bread would have a thick crunchy crust.

The afternoon was edging closer to dusk when Granny Zee smoothed her fall tablecloth over the dining table. It was dark green and embroidered leaves in amber, russet, burgundy, and ginger tumbled around the edges. She arranged pumpkin-shaped placemats, one for her, and one for each invited guest. On these she arranged her best dishes and silverware. She folded matching green napkins and tied them with orange and green plaid ribbons. She placed a crystal bowl full of her best polished apples in the center. Around the bowl, she put four big pumpkin scented candles. It was almost time.

Granny Zee laid kindling and wood on her hearth to be set alight with fire from the Samhain bonfire. The timer dinged, signaling the cornbread was ready.

With all the food covered and put on the stove to keep warm, Granny Zee went through the house lighting candles.

41

Then, she went outside and lit two lanterns at the front of the house and one on each side. It was almost time to light the bonfire, but first, Granny Zee sat down and waited for Samhain to begin.

Her thoughts turned to Hannah. Her absence left an ache in her side. Her granddaughter did not love these mountains. Granny Zee knew this to be true. Since she was a little girl, Hannah had talked about moving away—going to the city. When she was a teenager, she couldn't wait to be the first person in her family to go to college, and the day Hannah left, Granny Zee feared she would never come back. And then, Hannah's dreams had shattered, and Granny had watched her shrivel like a forgotten flower.

Darkness rose up from the ground and began to paint shadows on every measure of Rock House Mountain. Why did people call it nightfall? Darkness doesn't fall. It rises up from the ground, creeping up tree trunks, around house corners, and into windows. It wraps around every rock, spreads a velvet cloak over the grass, and then sails through the forest and up the mountain until it reaches the sky. Tonight, the dead spirits would rise with the darkness and walk the earth again. Granny Zee was ready. It was time for the fire.

Granny Zee walked slowly around the circle of stones, touching a lighter to the kindling until the flames leapt from twig to branch, snapping and popping into blue-red flames. The pyre blazed and sent plumes of smoke into the night sky. Granny Zee stood back and watched as the spirits gathered around the flames. She smiled and clasped her hands over her heart, and a gush of tears warmed her cheeks.

There was her beloved husband. From the darkness came her mother and father, her grandmother and grandfather, her sisters, and her dear, dear Emma.

She picked up the stick of kindling that had caught with the fire of Samhain and went to the back door. She opened it wide and held the fire up to the night. "Come in dear family. Come in and share in the feast of Samhain. The table is set and dinner is ready."

Chapter 6

The first of my bloodline born on Rock House Mountain was Brigid O'Reilly. She was born with a caul—a thin birth membrane covering her face. Mountain people call this rare occurrence "being born behind the veil," and like they believed, the spirits of this mountain favored her with many gifts. But to the caulbearer, these gifts can become a millstone. The caulbearer must take the clouds with the sun.
~ from Granny Zee's Book of Dreams

MAGGIE PARKED NEAR THE back of Hannah's house and walked up the steps to a wooden deck that ran its entire length. She tapped on the kitchen door and opened it. Hannah popped from behind the door so fast it reminded Maggie of the jack-in-the-box Addie had loved as a toddler. In her faded jeans, over-sized sweatshirt, and bare feet, she looked like a teenager. Her hair was pulled back with an ornate silver clip that should have looked out of place with her outfit, but on Hannah it was perfect.

She smiled and led Maggie into the dining room that had oak paneled walls and avocado green carpet. A swath of carpet, more worn than the rest, led from the doorway to a rectangular table and six chairs. The only other furniture in the room was an open front hutch, jam-packed with an array of odd dishes and knickknacks.

"Sit down," Hannah said, waving her hand toward the table where an apple pie scented candle burned next to plates of grilled cheese sandwiches and cookies. "Sorry lunch isn't fancier, but today I'm about as useless as buttons on a dishrag."

Maggie smiled. "This is perfect."

They made small talk about the girls and Halloween, skirting around the issue of Addie's strange talents until Hannah cleared away their plates and brought in mugs of fragrant hot tea.

"You said you understood about Addie and her... ability, but there's something more I want to tell you about her." Maggie's eyes searched Hannah's face. "Addie is a cancer survivor."

"Oh, honey!" Hannah grasped Maggie's hands that were clutching a napkin like a lifeline. "Why didn't you tell me?"

Maggie wanted to confess that J.D. had decided they were not to talk about it. Instead, she said, "Because Addie doesn't want anyone to know," and consoled herself that she was telling a degree of the truth.

"But you said *survivor*, right? She's okay?"

"She's cancer free."

"Thank God," Hannah said, leaning closer to Maggie.

Maggie dropped the napkin and gripped Hannah's hand. She let the words push the burden up and out of her. "It began when she was two. It was almost Christmas. The pediatrician thought it was a cold and an ear infection. He prescribed antibiotics, but the day after Christmas came and she wasn't getting better, so he changed her medicine. Three days later, Addie refused to eat or drink. She was admitted to the hospital for fluids and tests."

With one hand Maggie held onto Hannah—with the other, she blindly searched for the napkin. While she talked, she crumpled it into a ball, holding it in her fist. She said, "But those *routine* tests came back abnormal, and that led to a bone marrow test, the first of many nightmares. The diagnosis came on New Year's Eve—acute lymphoblastic leukemia, or 'ALL.' It took two years of treatment, but she's in remission—cancer free for a year now."

"That's wonderful! And I totally understand why you didn't want to talk about it. Just know I'm here for you, Maggie. I mean it."

A slight smile brightened Maggie's face. "Thank you."

Hannah picked up their cups. "This tea's cold. Let me get us a fresh cup."

They settled down with steaming mugs and were silent for a while. Then, Maggie put her cup down and smoothed her hands across her lap. "At first, I thought Addie's new *sensitivity* was somehow connected to her illness because the first time it happened, she was in the hospital undergoing chemo."

Maggie relived that night. A nurse had been taking Addie's vitals when Addie looked up at her and said, "Stop being sad. Your white kitty is at the blue house with two, two, two, on the wall." The poor woman had been shocked because she hadn't told anyone her cat had been missing for three days because a plumber had accidentally let her outside. The nurse had thanked Addie, and when she got off work, she had driven around her neighborhood and found a blue house with the address two twenty-two. Her cat was indeed there. The family had found her hiding in the bushes.

Hannah said, "Did the nurse ask how Addie knew?"

Maggie shook her head. "The next night, she brought Addie a white stuffed cat. Grateful and bewildered, she told me she had worked in pediatric oncology for ten years and had seen many things she couldn't explain."

A silence passed. Maggie turned back to Hannah. "What did you mean when you said you knew from personal experience how Addie can find things?"

"It's my grandmother," Hannah said. "She's a healer, and she has abilities like Addie—and I hope you won't be mad, but I told her about Addie."

Maggie straightened. "What did she say?"

"She'd like to meet you and talk about Addie."

A deep sigh rose from Maggie. "I would like to talk to her. When do you think she could see me?"

Hannah stood and picked up the plate of cookies. "Come with me to the family room, and I'll call her right now."

The room had the same carpet and paneling as the dining room with a modest brick fireplace at one end. An entertainment center rested against a wall across from a comfortable-looking leather sofa piled with multi-colored throw pillows. A coffee table with a stack of *Sports Illustrated* was parked in front of the couch, and a recliner that had seen better days was angled toward the TV.

Hannah tucked herself into the corner of the sofa, pulling her bare feet up under her. She dialed her grandmother, and Maggie watched her friend transform right before her eyes. Her face brightened and her voice took on a slight childish lilt. After she said good-bye and tossed the phone on the table, she said, "Granny Zee wants us to come for tea on Friday."

"Oh, wow, that's day after tomorrow."

Hannah said, "She's anxious to meet you."

"Why do you call her Granny Zee?"

Hannah laughed. "Her name is Zelda, and since I can remember, everyone has called her that. Actually, my great-great grandmother was also Zelda, and my Granny Zee says that's what people called her."

"I can tell your grandmother means a great deal to you."

Hannah smiled. "She means the world to me. She's been my rock since Mama died."

"Were you close? You and your mother, I mean."

Hannah nodded. "We had our ups and downs, but she was a good mother to me and my brother."

"I didn't know you had a brother?"

"Stevie is two years older. He lives in Pineville."

"I always wanted a brother. I don't have any siblings. Father died from a heart attack when I was fourteen. Did I ever tell you he was the only person who called me Maggie?"

Hannah smiled and shook her head.

Maggie put her mug on the coffee table and turned to Hannah. "Do you want to tell me about your mother?"

Hannah nodded. She took a sip of tea and stared into her cup like the words she wanted to say were floating there. "Her name is Emma. She was a stay-at-home mother to me and Stevie. She never held a job. She didn't even finish high school. She dropped out when she was sixteen and married my father who was twenty-five."

Maggie blinked hard. She had never known someone whose mother was a high school dropout. She hoped her surprise didn't show on her face.

"She died four years ago in an accident."

"Car accident?"

"No." Hannah fidgeted in her seat. "She was shot in the back by a man hunting in the mountains behind her house."

"Oh, my God!" Maggie reached across the couch and took Hannah's hand. "I'm so, so sorry."

"You know, I always heard of a 'freak' accident, but I thought an accident is an accident, right? Then, my mother was mistaken for a deer. Suddenly, the freak-part made sense."

Maggie nodded. She looked down at Hannah's hand in hers; she couldn't remember the last time she had held anyone's hand besides her daughter.

Hannah said, "Mama was gathering bloodroot. She often walked in the woods at dawn and gathered plants for Granny Zee's remedies. But that morning it was foggy, and she was wearing brown pants with a tan hooded sweatshirt. A hunter wandered onto the property and mistook her for a deer."

Hannah scooted closer to Maggie and said, "Did you get to say good-bye to your dad?"

Maggie nodded. "Papa lived for three days before a second heart attack took him away. He was a doctor, and I know, now, he realized he wasn't going to make it."

Hannah nodded. "Mama and I had talked on the phone the night before the accident. Her last words to me were, 'I'll see you tomorrow.'"

Tears stung Maggie's eyes. "Oh, Hannah, I'm so sorry. At least I got to say good-bye to my father."

Hannah sat up and put her feet on the floor, wiping tears from her face. "You know," she said, "the worst argument I ever had with my mother was over marrying Travis."

"Didn't she want you to marry him?"

"Just the opposite. I got pregnant, and my parents, especially Mama, wanted me to get married. It was practically a shot-gun wedding. Like in the movies—when the girl's father shows up with his shotgun and forces the boy, who got his daughter pregnant, to marry her. Only in this case, the gun was pointed at me."

Maggie said, "But a lot of women have babies without getting married. Things are different now. It's not like it was fifty years ago."

"It is around here." Hannah leaned toward Maggie. "You don't know much about small towns, do you? Or maybe I should say you don't know much about Coal Valley—here, people make it their *business* to know other people's dealings and relationships. When a woman pushes a baby in a stroller down the street in New York, nobody gives it a second thought, but when a woman walks down the street in Coal Valley with a baby, everybody knows her and who the baby's daddy is. Not to mention the parents of the mother and father."

Maggie frowned. "But the social circles I grew up in are just as judgmental. Girls are supposed to do the proper things—go to college, and then marry someone acceptable. If you don't follow 'the rules' the least that can happen to you is to be talked about. The worst is you will be shunned, but that depends on how much money your family has."

Slowly, Hannah nodded. "That's the difference between you and me—money. Money gives you options, Maggie; you can't deny that."

"No, you're right. Money changes things."

Hannah said, "Do you know what my father said when I told him I was pregnant?"

Maggie shook her head.

"'You made your bed. Now go lay in it.'"

Maggie's hand flew to her mouth. *Never* could she imagine Papa saying something like that to her. Her mother, on the other hand—

Shame. Hannah had been shamed into marrying Travis by her parents, who said an unwed mother brought disgrace on the whole family. Even Granny Zee had not defended her, and Hannah didn't have the strength to have the baby on her own. And after what happened, marrying Travis had turned out the best thing to do.

"Do you want to hear the most bizarre thing of all?" Hannah asked. "I had planned to marry Travis. We were high school sweethearts."

"Okay, now I'm really confused. I thought you didn't want to get married?"

"Travis wanted to marry me."

Maggie threw her hands up in the air. "So, you were supposed to get married because he wanted to, and your family wanted you to? What did *you* want?"

Hannah looked at Maggie, but her eyes saw something far away. "What did I want? I wanted—more." She swiped at sudden tears. "What I wanted then is the same thing I want now—a different life with a man who really loves me. And one that I really love. Travis threw his life away and mine, too." She saw the question in Maggie's eyes and said, "But that's a story for another day."

What Hannah couldn't explain to Maggie was what growing up in Coal Valley had been like. Here, there are families who've lived in the same holler for two hundred years. How did she justify that, right or wrong, good or bad, what a family member does in a small town reflects on the whole family? How did she make clear that in a mountain town like this, things change slower than other places? And people don't always forget past slights. All her life, she had heard her father talk about "those sorry Jacksons." He said the whole family was too lazy to work. He also went on about "those thieving Bedfords," who he said, "Would steal the nickels off a dead man's eyes." It didn't matter that Granny said that way of thinking went back to the clannishness of their people and their Scots-Irish heritage. What mattered was how that way of thinking had tied her to Travis and these mountains like a fly stuck to flypaper.

Hannah jumped up and started pacing. "Maggie," she said, "if it wasn't for Reilly, I'd leave Travis and end this ridiculous excuse of a marriage."

Maggie went to Hannah and put her hand on her arm. She said, "Oh, honey, believe me I understand. In fact, I have a confession. What I said about Addie not wanting anyone to know about her cancer is true. But J.D. is the real reason I didn't tell you. He decided that when we came to Coal Valley it would be better not to tell anyone."

"Better for who?" Hannah snapped.

"Him. Better for him."

"Then your husband's like mine—an asshole."

Maggie stuck out her chin. "Yes, he is. If it wasn't for Addie's illness, I'd take her and go. I haven't loved him in years."

The weight of their words dropped on them like an invisible net, drawing them closer together. Hannah was the first to react. She grabbed Maggie's hands. "Let's do it!"

"Do what?"

"Let's leave."

"Leave?"

"Leave! Go! Run away!" Hannah shook Maggie's hands up and down. "Not right now. I know it's not possible now, but we can plan. That is, if you mean it. Do you really want to leave your husband?"

"More than I've ever meant anything in my life. But I can't leave now. For all his faults, J.D. loves his daughter, and Addie needs him."

"She won't always need him."

Maggie looked at the half-smile on Hannah's lips. She asked, "What do you mean?"

"Let's sit down and talk about this."

They sat down on the edge of the couch, their right knees touching.

"The girls are going to grow up," Hannah said. "That's when we do it. It will take years to make this happen. At least it will for me. I promised myself I would go back to school and get my degree when Reilly started school, and I haven't done one thing toward that goal."

Maggie murmured, "High school." She took Hannah's hand. "We can leave our husbands when the girls graduate high school."

Hannah wanted it so much—was desperate for it. Life had to be more than this. It had to be more than just waking up in the morning and going through the motions of life until she could go to sleep, wake up, and do it all again. She looked down at her hands. She wanted to live the truth again—she deserved it. She was going to go back to school—study again. Start over.

Maggie put her head in her hands. "My life is a sad movie and I'm trapped there, watching the same parts over and over, but I never get to the end. I want to get to the end, and I want a new episode with a—" She hesitated. "With a happier ending."

Hannah stood and pulled Maggie to her feet. She said, "We can do this together. Let's make a pact. Let's promise right here—today—to help each other realize our dreams."

They joined hands and looked into each other's eyes. With clear steady voices they said, "I promise."

Two days later, Hannah and Maggie were on the road to

Granny Zee's house. Maggie looked out at the frosted morning. The mountains' colorful splendor had sifted down from the trees and become a tawny carpet on the earth's floor. Their finery had been replaced by a stark black and white beauty that made the landscape look like an old lithograph.

Hannah turned onto a bridge that crossed the Coal River. Just past it, they bounced over railroad tracks and a smaller bridge came into view. Across it, the road narrowed, and Hannah said, "This is Little Creek Holler."

The creek ran parallel to the road and was about its same width. The water was dark with white frothing like dollops of cream. It spilled over rocks in a myriad of shapes and sizes. Mist rose and danced like streamers in praise to the pale sunlight.

Houses and the occasional mobile home crowded the creek bank. Bridges connected road to land. Some were sturdy wooden or concrete structures, while others had missing boards and gaping holes. Maggie wondered how anyone dared drive a vehicle across, but vehicles were indeed parked on the house side of the bridge. It occurred to Maggie the houses were built to fit the narrow embankment, many of them two-storied. In some instances, the front porch was three big steps from the creek.

The road climbed. Maggie was looking up at a house perched on a ridge when the car veered toward the creek. An enormous coal truck was barreling toward them, and even though she realized Hannah was getting out of its way, she grabbed for the door handle like she was going to have to jump out to save herself. Maggie had driven past coal trucks on the highway, but this was too close for comfort.

Hannah stopped until the coal truck blew past, brakes groaning, smoke spewing from the exhaust pipes that stood out on either side of the truck like chrome antlers. The driver waved at Hannah, who waved back. "Who's that?" Maggie asked.

"No idea. Just being friendly. Travis used to drive a coal truck for his uncle, and he said people waved at him all the time."

"Your husband drives a coal truck?"

"Right now he works in a mine office. He knows a lot about coal and how mines work, but he still drives when his uncle needs him."

Maggie digested this information. She asked, "Why was that truck on this road?"

"Because there are coal mines up in this holler."

The road continued to climb, and another coal truck passed, heaving under its weight. When the driver waved, Maggie joined Hannah in waving back.

Hannah said, "I can't wait for you to meet Granny Zee. Are your grandparents still living?"

"Papa's parents died before I was born. I vaguely remember my mother's father."

"What about your mother's mother?"

Maggie mumbled, "She lives in Paris."

Hannah's head whipped toward Maggie. "I'm going to go out on a limb here and guess you don't mean Paris, Kentucky."

Maggie shook her head. "She lives with her sister, my great-aunt Amelia. After Grandfather died, Grandmother went to Paris for a visit and decided to stay."

"Have you been there?"

"Not since Addie's illness."

"Paris, wow."

Before Maggie could think of something to say to that, Hannah turned left and said, "This road goes all the way to the top of Rock House Mountain. Somebody in my family has lived on this mountain since before the Revolutionary War."

The road twisted and climbed, trading the creek bank for the foothills. Driveways sloped upward toward houses and mobile homes on lots carved out of the mountainside. As the houses became fewer and farther between, the shadows deepened. A forest of barren hardwood trees took over the landscape. The bare branches were so close together the dense winter sunlight made tiny silver slashes between them.

Around the next curve, a two-storied house appeared that Maggie would swear had been plucked from the English countryside. It had no front porch, but rather stood on its own without preamble. It would have been just a modest house made from wood and stone, had it not been for the lavish stone chimneys that flanked either end.

"Isn't it lovely?" Hannah turned left and drove up a graveled road that curved around to the back of the house. The grounds were beautifully landscaped, raked and groomed for winter.

"It's enchanting! I feel like I've stepped back in time."

"My Papaw built it with his own two hands. Come on. Let's go in. I'm freezing!"

Hannah tapped on the back door and pushed it open. She called out, "Granny Zee, it's Hannah. I brought Maggie."

The aroma of fresh baked gingerbread and burning hickory wood laced with fresh cut pine made Maggie light-headed.

A fire glowed in the impressive stone fireplace nested in the far wall. A comfortable-looking blue gingham sofa and chairs were grouped close to the hearth. At the other side of the long open room, a kitchen gleamed white, with Williamsburg blue table, chairs, and china cabinet. An old-fashioned copper tea kettle rested on an even older stove that shined like a new one. A small television was on the counter, its channel turned to a home shopping network Maggie recognized as QVC.

Hannah said, "There you are!"

A tiny woman with a halo of white hair entered the room. She wore an over-sized red cardigan over a black velour pantsuit. Maggie smiled and extended her hand. This little woman, in her over-sized sweater, reminded her of the bright red Cardinals that were so plentiful in these mountains.

"Welcome, dear," Granny Zee said. She took Maggie's hand in both of hers. "I've heard so much about you."

Granny Zee's strong grip surprised Maggie. Her hands looked like gnarled tree roots, and their touch told her of all the years they had toiled in the soil. Granny Zee looked as frail as a matchstick, but her blue eyes sparked with life.

Maggie said, "Thank you, Mrs. Davis. I'm happy to meet you, too."

"Now, you must call me Granny Zee. Everybody does. I told Cece it was time to steep the tea. I knew you'd be here any minute." Granny Zee shuffled over to the stove.

Maggie turned toward Hannah with a *who's Cece* look, but Hannah had her back to her. Maggie slipped off her coat and went to hang it on a coat rack carved from honey-colored oak. "This is beautiful," she said, sliding her hand across the warm wood.

Hannah turned and swept her hand in an arc across the dining room furniture. "Papaw made it—the table and chairs, and the china cabinet, too."

Granny Zee placed a plate of what looked like biscuits, but smelled like gingerbread, on the table. She said, "Hanson was a right good hand at furniture making. Now, set down. Tea's ready."

Maggie spotted an orange cat curled up in a rocking chair drawn close to the fireplace. She guessed that was Cece.

Granny Zee hurried to the kitchen. "You know what they say, 'an ounce of ginger a day keeps the doctor away.'"

Maggie whispered, "I thought it was an apple?"

Hannah whispered back. "She's almost eighty-eight years old; maybe she knows something we don't."

Granny Zee came back with a delicate looking teapot decorated with tiny shamrocks that Maggie recognized as Belleek Irish china. Granny put it in front of Hannah and said, "Sweetie, will you pour?"

Maggie looked from Granny Zee to Hannah, and two pairs of eyes the same clear arctic blue looked back. Granny Zee slid two gingerbread biscuits onto a plate and gave it, and a small pot of honey, to Maggie. "I hope you like my gingerbread."

"Thank you," Maggie said. She took a sip of tea, and peppermint filled her senses. "Delicious." She smiled at Granny, who was clearly pleased.

A peacefulness pervaded the room. A vision of her father sitting before the fire flashed before Maggie, and she knew he would have loved this place. The wood-paneled walls glowed golden in the firelight. A braided rug in muted shades of blue and brown was centered before the stone hearth. On the sofa rested a knitted throw with matching pillows. Maggie spotted an open book on a chair-side table, with what must be Granny's reading glasses lying on top. One wall was filled with shelves of books and photographs. Maggie felt like she had stepped into Addie's dollhouse.

Granny Zee turned her attention to Maggie. She patted her hand and said, "Now, I can put a face on the Maggie that Hannah talks about."

Maggie smiled. "You have a lovely home. The fireplace is incredible."

"Thank you."

There were bundles of plants hanging in the kitchen, a drying rack, and frames netted with gauze hooks. Granny Zee pointed. "I'm drying some sweet violet, beebalm, chamomile, and mugwort."

"What are they for?" Maggie asked.

"The chamomile is for my teas, but you have to be careful with it because it thins the blood. The mugwort is good for aches and pains. It makes the best foot bath for tired feet, and my mama always planted it in the chicken yard because it keeps lice away. When you got the grippe, pour boiling water in a bowl and add a fistful of beebalm. Let it steep a minute and then put a towel over your head and lean over the bowl and inhale the steam. And that sweet violet is left-over from my jelly making." She stood and disappeared through a door in the corner of the kitchen and came back with two small jars. She gave one to Hannah and one to Maggie. The label read "Sweet Violet Jelly" in Granny's spidery handwriting.

Maggie asked, "Is grippe a cold?"

Granny nodded. "Beebalm is good for upper respiratory

infections and flu."

Maggie took another sip of tea and the warm delicious liquid coursed through her. "This tea is wonderful."

"It's my own recipe," Granny Zee said, "ginseng and peppermint, with a few other things sprinkled in."

Maggie said, "I've never known anyone who made her own tea, or for that matter, anything else."

Granny Zee beamed. She patted Hannah's hand and said, "We're from a long line of healers. My Mama, Emmaline, was a midwife, and my grandmother, Zelda, was a healer. I'm her namesake. In her late years, they called her Granny Zee, too."

Granny leaned toward Maggie like she was imparting a secret. "Some people called Granny Zee a witch." She chuckled. "But many people in these mountains would've died if not for her. She learned the healing ways from her grandmother, Brigid O'Reilly, who brought them from Ireland."

"O'Reilly," Maggie said, "is that where Reilly gets her name?"

Hannah nodded.

Maggie savored another sip of tea. "Granny Zee," she asked, "isn't ginseng the plant the Chinese think so highly of?"

Granny nodded. "It grows good here on the mountain. It especially likes these poplar trees and a damp soil. I've got mine planted so I can harvest every year. It takes four years from the time you plant the seeds till the time you can harvest. A ginseng seed lays in the ground for eighteen months before it sprouts. You harvest it in the late summer or early fall, before the first frost."

"How did you learn all of this?" Maggie asked.

"My grandmother taught me the old ways of caring for the sick, just like she taught my mama. Now, my mama's gift was for catching babies. My Granny birthed babies too, but she took care of all kinds of sickness. In her day, they called women who did doctoring a 'granny woman.'"

Maggie spooned honey on her biscuit. "So, could any woman become a granny woman?"

Granny Zee shook her head. "A true granny woman has the gift. A healer knows how to make medicines with plants and how to read the signs. Just like the ginger in this bread is good for the blood. And if the blood is healthy, the heart stays healthy. Ginger tea is good for just about anything from colds and headaches to rheumatism."

Hannah smiled at Granny Zee and placed her hand on Granny's shoulder. Granny covered Hannah's hand with hers. A tangible sadness settled over Maggie. She had never had a loving granny in her life.

Granny Zee patted Hannah's hand. "Now my granddaughter here has the healing hands. I keep telling her she needs to go on and finish her schooling and help people."

Hannah smiled. "I'm planning to talk to you about doing exactly that."

"Nothing would make me happier," Granny said.

A log popped, and the sweet scent of hickory escaped from the fire. Maggie closed her eyes and inhaled. When she opened them, Granny Zee was staring at her. "You want to talk about your daughter."

Maggie looked into eyes as blue as the surface of a southern lake. "Yes."

Granny Zee nodded. "From what Hannah told me, she has what my Irish grandmother called *an dara sealladh*—the sight. When I was a girl and it happened to me, I called it the knowing."

Maggie nodded. "Did Hannah tell you Addie is a cancer survivor?"

Granny took Maggie's hand. "Yes, and I know that when a person has walked the path between this life and the next one and come back to this world, it changes them. In most cases, it makes them more in tune with the world around them, but with your daughter, I suspect it's more than that. Would you agree?"

Maggie sighed in defeat. "Yes," she said, looking over at Hannah who smiled encouragement.

"I'm curious about something," Granny said. "Was there anything unusual about Addie's birth?"

"Unusual?" Maggie frowned.

Granny leaned forward so she could look directly at Maggie. "I've been wondering if she was born with a caul over her face."

The air crackled like some unseen entity had been unleashed in the room. Maggie gasped. "How did you know?"

"I was a caul baby, myself. Mountain people call it being born behind the veil. The proper name is caulbearer, and I believe it is a gift from God. Being a caulbearer can be hard, especially when you're young and you don't understand why your world is so uncommon."

"What do you mean by uncommon?"

"The best way I can describe it is you're always waiting for something to happen—always looking for a message—or finding one. Dreams aren't just dreams. Someone with the sight is always searching, and what you find may come in bits and pieces so it's like figuring out a puzzle."

Granny Zee paused to let Maggie take it in, then asked, "Was Addie's a full-face caul?"

"Yes, it was like a mask, and the doctor said it was looped behind her ears."

Maggie knew it was very rare, and she knew there were a lot of superstitions about babies born with face cauls. After Addie was born, she had researched it and learned the caul was once believed to be a magical talisman. People would attach them to paper and dry them. Sometimes they were folded and sewed together to form a pouch or purse. Sailors would pay large sums to get a caul because it was said to protect them from drowning.

Granny Zee nodded. "With some caulbearers, it's no more than being highly sensitive, or having great compassion for people and animals. For others it's stronger, like an instinct. I know you've heard people say they have a gut feeling or a woman's intuition?"

Maggie nodded.

"Then, there are the caulbearers like Addie, able to find what's lost. Others can see into the future, and some can see what happened in the past. Some see both. Other caulbearers are healers, and some, like me, can communicate with spirits. The Scots call me *taibhsear*, or one who speaks with the dead. I like to think of us as betwixt and between." She looked into Maggie's eyes. "We stand betwixt and between both worlds."

Granny Zee paused. She held Maggie's gaze for just a beat too long before dropping her eyes and concentrating on her tea. "I was about Addie's age when I started knowing things. I lived on this mountain and played in these woods. My grandmother taught me how to listen to the spirits and how to be a messenger—a link to here and the hereafter." She set her cup down on the table. "I'm not saying it's easy. There have been many times when I wished I hadn't been told things, and times I wished the spirits *had* told me things. The spirits can be fickle."

They finished their tea in silence.

Maggie looked down at Granny's hands, the tired skin and misshapen fingers. She asked, "Can you teach me about caulbearers? Help me understand and help Addie?"

"Of course, dear. I had my mama and grandmother. They helped me understand and manage my gifts. My Granny Zee was a caulbearer. There have been a number of caulbearers among my ancestors."

"Isn't that unusual? I thought babies born with a caul are rare?"

"Well, I do know they tend to run in certain bloodlines. I also know that not all people who are caulbearers have the sight, and not all people with the sight are caulbearers." She placed her hand carefully on the table. "There is something else I'm curious about." She paused and looked at Maggie. "How does your husband feel about his daughter's gifts?"

Maggie took a deep breath and exhaled slowly. She could only imagine the hell J.D. would raise over this. He would think Maggie had lost her mind and would demand she never see Hannah or her grandmother again. She said, "My husband doesn't know. He would *never* understand."

Granny Zee took Maggie's hand. "He need not know. I will help you and your daughter the way my granny and mama helped me. And Maggie?"

"Yes?"

"When can I meet her?"

1991

Chapter 7

*Spirits love the music a mountain makes. They hoard it beneath
their green skirts—a twig snapping, rain snagging on a leaf,
wind soughing through the trees, a bird's complaint, echoes of a
haint rattling its bones in the night. This morning the spirits
shook their skirts and unfurled the sounds into the sky, their
laughter echoing around the edges, and I was there to hear it.*
~ from Granny Zee's Book of Dreams

M**AGGIE PICKED UP THE** phone and punched in
Hannah's number. The holidays were over, and the
stark burn of winter had settled in, but Maggie knew it wasn't
cold enough to keep her mother away. Her visit was next week,
and she wished Hannah wasn't so excited about meeting Judith
Winthrop Hudson.

"She's only going to be here three nights and four days. I
suppose it could be worse," Maggie said.

Hannah giggled. "That sounds like one of those vacation
packages you hear advertised. 'Spend three nights and four
days at our beautiful resort for the unheard-of sum of
$999.99!'"

Maggie laughed. "She'll be here Friday afternoon; basically,
she's stopping for a weekend visit before she goes skiing."

"So, when can I come over?"

"You and Reilly are invited to tea on Saturday."

"I'm sorry I'm so curious about her, but she's your mom."

Maggie searched for the right words. She couldn't say, *No
matter how you look, or what you say, my mother is going to be
judgmental and negative,* without sounding like her mother.
Finally, she said, "Be yourself and remember, it doesn't matter
to me what my mother thinks about you, or anybody else."

Next Friday afternoon, Maggie stared out the window.
From the concrete gray sky above the ash-colored mountains to
the dull gunmetal valley, the world had turned into the god-forsaken place her mother was so fond of calling it.

Maggie had carefully planned the weekend. She knew it was not wise to leave things to chance where Judith Hudson was concerned. She had planned a family dinner for tonight, and tomorrow they would attend a fundraising dinner at the law school because there was nothing her mother liked more than a party, and J D. was thrilled to introduce his charming mother-in-law to his colleagues.

A Lincoln Town Car turned into the driveway. When her mother emerged, Maggie realized the two things about Judith Hudson that never changed were her sleek bob and stylish pantsuits. This ensemble was heather gray, and her hair just brushed her shoulders. Its color had lightened and darkened over the years. Currently, it was a sleek mocha sporting subtle blonde highlights. A picture of Granny Zee with her cap of white curls and velour pantsuit flashed before Maggie and she grinned. Granny and her mother were as opposite as Bengal tigers and alley cats. Maggie opened the door to welcome her mother before the smile disappeared.

"Mother, come in!" Maggie swung the door wide and stepped back.

"Margaret, please show me to my room. My head is spinning from that horrible drive. I must lie down." For emphasis, she pressed the palm of her right hand to her forehead.

Maggie had tea ready to welcome her mother, but Judith Hudson waved it away and instead demanded a hot water bottle and two aspirin. Maggie retreated to the sunroom where she poured a solidarity cup and stared out at the winter afternoon. She let one tear escape.

When Addie burst into the house, her grandmother led her to the den where she had arranged a huge stack of gifts, all wrapped in *The Little Mermaid* paper—Addie's latest movie obsession. Maggie now understood why her mother had so much luggage.

"But Mother, you already sent Christmas gifts." Maggie folded her arms and watched Addie squeal and rip paper.

Judith said, "I should have sent you a new mattress for that guest room."

A rush of heat flooded Maggie's face. "What?" But her mother was helping Addie try on an adorable purple coat trimmed with what looked like real rabbit fur. Maggie had made it clear how neither she nor Addie would wear real fur, but before she could think of what to do, Ida came in with a tray of tea and refreshments.

Judith said, "Margaret, what is that unpleasant smell coming from the kitchen?"

Ida stiffened. Maggie blinked hard. "Thank you for the tea, Ida." Ida disappeared into the kitchen, and Maggie stared at her mother who was now reading a book with Addie, who was still wearing the coat. "Mother, may I speak to you a moment?"

Judith followed Maggie into the living room. Maggie said, "What was that?"

"What was what?"

Maggie sighed. "Look, I'm sorry if your bed is uncomfortable, I can move you to another bedroom. And if that coat has real fur trim, Addie is not wearing it. And do not insult Ida. She is the kindest, sweetest woman, and she's been cooking all day."

"Well, do you feel better, Margaret? Attacking me? Twisting my words?"

"I'm not attacking you or twisting—"

"If you will excuse me, my granddaughter is waiting."

On Saturday, Judith spent the morning with Addie, playing board games and watching *The Little Mermaid*. At noon, they had lunch together and resumed watching movies.

At precisely one minute before two o'clock, the doorbell rang. Addie ran to answer it and came back leading Reilly, wearing a blue corduroy jumper the color of her eyes. Hannah stood off to the side, smiling. She was dressed in a gray wool skirt that hit just above the knee and a pink cashmere sweater. Dark gray stockings and low-heeled pumps completed the look. Her blond hair was secured at the nape of her neck with the silver barrette Maggie had seen before. An exquisite strand of cultured pearls lay against her neck and single pearl earrings replaced her usual gold hoops. Her makeup was light and flawless, and she had even had a professional manicure.

Maggie went to Hannah and grabbed her hands. "You look beautiful!"

Hannah smiled. Together, they followed the girls into the living room where Judith Hudson waited. Addie said, "Grandmother, this is Reilly. She's my bestest friend."

Reilly stepped forward and shook hands with Addie's grandmother, saying, "It's nice to meet you."

Maggie said, "Mother, this is my friend and Reilly's mother, Hannah Lively. Hannah, this is Judith Hudson."

Judith briefly took Hannah's hand. "Please," she said. "Sit down."

While Maggie busied herself preparing the tea, Addie and Reilly talked to Judith with the luxury that only childhood allows. When the girls went off to play, Maggie served tea and watched her mother turn to Hannah.

Hannah was warm and open, charming the social beast in

Maggie's mother simply by being herself. She did not seem the least intimidated by her but rather talked with the ease of a clean conscience at confession. Maggie wanted to jump in the air and click her heels.

On Sunday, Maggie and J.D. took Judith to church services and then to dinner at the small country club where J.D. played golf. Back home, Judith spent the rest of the day with Addie. All day, Maggie waited for the subject of Reilly and Hannah to come up. She was prepared for her mother's criticisms of her friend, but so far, she had complained constantly about everything else—the house was too cold; her bed was uncomfortable, but she refused to change rooms; Addie wasn't dressed warm enough; the food tasted "odd"; and the house was infested with spiders, because she "saw" one in her bathtub.

When Monday morning came, and the car arrived to take Judith to the airport, Maggie was exhausted from constantly sparring with her mother. Judith gave Maggie a swift kiss on the cheek, their standard farewell, but she couldn't miss a parting shot. "I do wish you'd come home long enough to get a decent haircut. You could use the spa package I gave you for Christmas, while you were there."

"Good-bye, Mother. Safe travels."

Before getting inside the car Judith turned and said, "And, tell your charming friend, Hannah, it was lovely to meet her."

The car drove away and Maggie stood in the cold, waiting for her world to realign itself.

Judith Hudson upset the balance of Maggie's life in more ways than one. Her visit, and the snowy weather that followed, interrupted Maggie and Hannah's Monday and Thursday morning outings to the coffee shop. They hadn't been able to meet for two weeks, and then Maggie came down with a cold and canceled for the third Monday in a row.

J.D. volunteered to take Addie to school so Maggie could sleep in, but a cough kept waking her, so she put the kettle on for tea. She found the tin of Granny Zee's special tea she kept hidden because she didn't intend to explain to J.D. what it was or where she got it. She could just see the smirk on his face and hear the condescending remark about "these people and their mountain voodoo."

When the phone rang, Maggie was sipping peppermint tea. She didn't want to talk to anyone, but she thought of Addie and grabbed it.

"I hope I didn't wake you," Hannah said, "but I wanted to know how you're feeling?"

"A little better. I was just drinking Granny Zee's peppermint tea."

"Put lots of honey in it. Honey's good for a cold."

"Thanks."

"I haven't got to talk to you since your mother's visit. I hope Reilly and I made a good impression."

"Oh, don't worry. I don't care what my mother thinks. You looked amazing, by-the-way. Your sweater looked like cashmere."

"It *was* cashmere. Granny gave it to me for Christmas."

Maggie coughed and cleared her throat. "I bet she ordered it from that home shopping show."

"As a matter of fact, she did."

"I thought so."

"And your pearls looked real."

"My pearls *were* real. They're Scots pearls, a family heirloom."

Maggie pretended not to hear the hurt in Hannah's voice. She plowed on. "You really surprised me. I've never seen you in anything but jeans and a sweatshirt."

"I do have nice clothes, Maggie, even if I don't dress like *you*."

The hateful words bounced off Maggie's tongue: "You could have passed for a real society icon. You fooled my mother and she's an expert."

Maggie ignored Hannah's stunned silence. She continued, "Mother thought you were "charming" and told me to tell you so. At the law school's dinner, she asked if you and your husband would be joining us. She assumed your husband was a professor."

"Imagine that!" Hannah said. Her voice shook. "I really fooled her! And you can't stand it!"

"What does that mean?"

"Exactly what I said! Your mother liked me, and you can't stand it!"

"That's ridiculous!"

"Admit it. You were so sure your mother would hate your poor hillbilly friend, and you could give her another black mark."

"That's not true."

"It *is*. You're mad because your mother liked me, and you can't like anything or anyone your mother likes. And you know what?" Hannah didn't stop to let Maggie answer. "I liked your mother."

"You spent maybe half an hour with her! You don't know what she's really like."

"No, I don't know her, and she doesn't know me. After all, you made it painfully clear I *fooled* her."

"And you did!"

Hannah expelled a bitter laugh. "You don't even realize how you just insulted me, do you?"

"What? But—"

"Maggie, if I had said how much I disliked your mother— we'd be having a totally different conversation right now. Wouldn't we?"

"That's not true."

"Yes, it is. *Admit* it. But she liked me, and I liked her, and you can't stand it!"

"No, that's not true."

"Look. If you can't admit it, then there's no reason to talk to you."

Maggie snorted. "I refuse to admit—"

"Then, good-bye."

Maggie couldn't believe Hannah had hung up on her! She called Hannah back, but the phone rang and rang. She called a third time. Come on! Answer the damn phone!

After a fourth try, Maggie went upstairs, grabbed a quilt, and took it to her bedroom balcony. The day in front of her was as bleak and miserable as she felt. She took a gulp of cold air and willed herself not to cough, but she let the tears come. *Your mother liked me. And you can't stand it. Admit it.* Hannah's words played like a song in her head.

Chapter 8

My granny called winter "the days of the hag, Cailleach." Irish legend says the deity Cailleach was an old woman hag who ruled from Samhain, November 1, to Beltane, May 1. Cailleach is also called the queen of winter who herded deer and carried a large staff. When she touched the staff to the ground, it froze instantly. When a snowstorm happened, Granny would say, "the old hag of winter is angry."
~ from Granny Zee's Book of Dreams

B Y THURSDAY MORNING, MAGGIE had given up calling Hannah. She had spent the last three days thinking about what Hannah had said, and she didn't like what she discovered. It was like picking at a scab.

It was time to face Hannah. Maggie drove to Hannah's house but found the driveway empty. She rested her forehead on the steering wheel and let the tears come. She cried and coughed until she started choking. She beat the steering wheel with her hands then forced herself to take shallow breaths and calm down. She caught a glimpse of her contorted face in the rearview mirror and pulled tissues out of her pocket. She repaired her face and got out of the car, prepared to wait for Hannah's return.

The wooden deck was glazed with a coat of early morning frost. The swing where she and Hannah had talked and laughed glistened. She sat down and closed her eyes, remembering the summer sun on her skin, hearing the slap of Hannah's bare feet on the deck. Tears started again and she jumped up, shoving the swing back hard.

Back in the car, Maggie pushed a button on the steering wheel and music filled the car.

Maggie followed Little Creek Road until she turned toward Rock House Mountain. Immediately, she passed through a portal into another world. Frost-sugared trees and grass created a ghostly world of disjointed shapes. Maggie rolled down the car window and drank great gulps of sweet cold air flavored with frozen earth. She shivered, cold but cleansed. Granny would intercede with Hannah. She had to.

A crooked finger of smoke curled from Granny Zee's big stone chimney. Maggie pulled her car around to the back of the house, where she found Hannah's car. "Of course," Maggie said.

Before Maggie could knock, Granny Zee opened the door. "Come in! Come in, dear. Take off your coat and join Hannah for tea."

Hannah sat at the kitchen table. A crystal bowl filled with realistic looking snowballs was in the center, and an empty cup and saucer waited next to the teapot. She had been expected.

"Thank you, Granny," Maggie said. "Hi, Hannah."

"Hey." Hannah's head was bent so low her hair brushed her cheeks and Maggie couldn't see her face.

Granny took Maggie's coat and waved her hand toward Hannah. "Sit down and have a cup of tea. It'll warm up your insides."

"Thank you." Maggie sat down across from Hannah, who was looking intently into her cup.

Granny Zee poured tea and pointed to the tray that held honey, milk, and her wonderful gingerbread biscuits. "Help yourself. I've got some work to do in the doll room."

The silence was deafening. Hannah glanced at Maggie and then looked away. Maggie stared down at her hands. Hannah took a sip of tea, placing her cup gently on the table. Maggie picked her cup up, looked at it, and then put it back down. They spoke at the exact same moment.

"Look, I'm sorry," Hannah said.

"I've wanted to talk," Maggie said.

They stopped.

Again, they spoke at the same time.

"I didn't mean it," Hannah said.

"I'm so sorry," Maggie said.

They stopped, again; only this time they laughed.

Maggie said, "Go ahead."

"No, you go ahead," Hannah said.

Maggie set her cup on the table and leaned forward. "I'm sorry," she began and then paused. When she began again, her words tumbled one over the other. "I'm sorry I said those terrible things to you. Please, forgive me."

The only sound in the room was a log shifting in the fireplace. Maggie hesitated, waiting for Hannah to say something, but there was silence. Maggie said. "I admit it. I didn't want my mother to like you, and I didn't want you to like my mother."

Hannah grinned. "Well, I didn't like her *that* much." Her cup clanked down on the table. Maggie turned toward her with a smile tugging at the corner of her lips. "Then why didn't you answer my phone calls?"

"Because I wanted to talk to you like this." She pointed at herself, then at Maggie, and then back at herself. "And I admit— I wanted to punish you. You hurt me." Hannah lowered her eyes. "I know I shouldn't hold a grudge. Don't you see? You are the better person here. You lashed out because you were sick and under stress. But me—I fly mad and then nurse a grudge like a damn stubborn mule."

Maggie shook her head and frowned. "No, you were right. I really didn't want my mother to like you. I thought if she didn't like you and you didn't like her, it would keep you away from her and she wouldn't say something nasty and hurt your feelings."

"Oh, honey, that's the sweetest thing anybody's ever said to me." Hannah put her hand over Maggie's. "Look, I'm new at this friend business. You are the first close friend I've had since third grade. I grew up following around my older brother and—" she lifted her leg and pointed at her bare foot, "in case you haven't noticed, I'm still a tomboy. By high school, Travis and I were together." Hannah shrugged.

Hannah stood and pulled Maggie to her feet. "Come on *best* friend. Let's sit by the fire."

On Granny's gingham sofa, Hannah perched so she was facing Maggie, sitting cross-legged. "Let's not talk about this anymore. It's over and done with."

Maggie shook her head. "Not until I say this—not until I tell you how bad I feel. I did the one thing I swore I would never do. I talked to you exactly the way my mother talks to me."

"I got mad at you, but I was madder at myself." Hannah smoothed her hair behind her ears, and her gold hoop earrings danced. "Your mother's visit was another reminder. I'm not the person I want to be. I'm just a college dropout who hasn't done anything for six years but wallow in it."

Hannah got up and put another log on the fire. A sweet scent like summer apples wafted into the room. "We were set." She turned around and dusted her hands together. "Both of us. I had an academic scholarship, and Travis had a full ride to Virginia Tech as long as he played football."

The stunned look on Maggie's face made Hannah laugh. "Which part is the surprise? Me marrying a football star or getting a scholarship?"

Hannah's face softened with the memory. "I was the envy of every girl at Coal Valley High. All the girls, even the cheerleaders and beauty queens, would have given anything to change places with me, but the star of the football team *chose me.*" She put her hands on her hips and shook her head. "Travis and me—we thought we had the world by the tail! I was going to be a physical therapist. Granny says I have healing hands."

A fountain of red and gold fire rose, feeding on the new log Hannah had placed on the fire. She sat down next to Maggie, and for a while they watched the fire zig zag up and down the log, sparking and sputtering.

"The first year was perfect," Hannah said. "Travis got tons of playing time. His name was on everybody's lips. I had all A's, and he did okay, too. I came home for the summer and got a job at the grocery store while Travis spent most of his time back at Tech in training. It was the second year when things went all to hell. Travis got hurt and had to have surgery, putting him out for the season. Then he started drinking."

Hannah could close her eyes and conjure the page in the textbook she was studying the night of the accident—*chemical bonds: iconic, covalent, and metallic*. She remembered that at precisely ten o'clock, she had gone to the drink machines to get a Coke. There she had looked out the window at the snow bucketing down on a world already ghostly white.

Sometime after midnight, her dorm phone rang. Travis's car had skidded off the road and hit a telephone pole. His friends were okay, but Travis's leg was broken—the same leg he'd injured playing football.

Hannah picked up a pillow and hugged it to her chest. "To make a long story short—there was a car accident and Travis was driving drunk. He lost his scholarship."

Maggie said, "But you still had *yours*. Right?"

Hannah turned her wedding ring around and around on her finger. "Yes, and I was determined I wasn't going to give up on my dream just because he screwed up, so I went back to school spring semester. But Travis was so miserable that I came home every weekend, and one weekend I had too much to drink, and we had unprotected sex."

"And you got pregnant with Reilly," Maggie said. "But pregnant women go to college. Why did you quit?"

"I got so sick I couldn't finish the semester."

"Sick how?"

"I was carrying twins, and there were complications."

"Twins?" Maggie frowned. "Reilly's a twin?"

"Reilly had a brother—Ryan—he only lived a few hours. They were born early, and he was so small..." Her voice choked, and she struggled to continue. "He waited for me, you know. He didn't let go until I got to hold him. Oh, Maggie, he was so beautiful. He had red downy hair and eyes the blue-green color I've seen in pictures of the Irish Sea."

Maggie put her arm around Hannah's shoulders. "Oh, honey, I'm so sorry."

A surge of heat rushed over Hannah. The day she had the twins was connected to the humid heat of summer. She and Travis had lived in a trailer that had no air conditioning, and it was so hot it was like being trapped inside a metal trashcan. She was supposed to be on bed rest, but she thought one trip to town wouldn't matter.

"I left the house once. Just once," Hannah said. "I went to the post office to get the mail, and on the way to my car, a pain hit me in the bottom of my stomach, causing me to drop everything. Gradually it eased, so I bent over to pick up the envelopes I'd dropped. That's when the second pain hit. This time it was sharp like a knife ripping through me, and I thought my water broke, but it—it was blood."

The cold of the operating room was such a shock after the summer heat that Hannah couldn't focus on anything else. There were voices. There were bright lights. There was pain. But Hannah remembered the cold. It devoured her, creeping into every pore of her body. She begged the doctor not to let the cold take her babies.

Hannah said, "It was a placental abruption—the placenta tore away from the uterus. I had an emergency C-section, and when they couldn't stop the bleeding, they removed my uterus."

Hannah mumbled she was going to wash her face and left the room. When she came back, she found Maggie sitting on the edge of the couch, elbows resting on her knees, chin in her hands. Hannah sat down next to her and for a while they watched the fire dance.

Maggie dropped her hands and straightened her back. She said, "When Addie was almost four and the cancer was in remission, I found out I was pregnant. I was happy for the first time in two years. Maybe, just maybe, I could pick up the pieces of my life and move forward."

And for a while, everything had been perfect. Thrilled, J.D. said a baby was just what Maggie needed—like the baby was a new pair of shoes or something. Then Addie caught a cold, and as a precaution, the pediatrician put her in the hospital and Maggie missed her OB appointment.

Maggie said, "Then I started to get tiny cramps on my right side. They would come and go and I began to fear I would miscarry, but I didn't go to the doctor. I couldn't—Addie was sick! But if I had, the doctor would've discovered the egg had implanted in my fallopian tube."

Hannah said softly, "Ectopic pregnancy."

Maggie had asked "what if" hundreds of times over the past two years. "What if" she hadn't missed her appointment? "What if" she had called the doctor right away? "What if" she hadn't put it off? But by the time Addie got out of the hospital, Maggie was exhausted. Addie was tired of being cooped up and demanded constant attention. When her side started to hurt, Maggie would lie down, and the pain would always go away. She had told herself that it was just the stress of Addie being sick, and since there was no bleeding, she would be fine. She had really believed she just needed to rest.

Then she woke in the middle of the night with a fever. She had crept out of bed and into the bathroom where she wet a washcloth with cold water and held it to her forehead. When a horrible pain in her side doubled her over, she tried to call for J.D., tried to get to the door, but instead she collapsed and hit her head on the sink, passing out.

Maggie stood. She went to the fireplace and stared into the flames. "That night," she said, "my fallopian tube ruptured. By the time J.D. found me, I was hemorrhaging and unconscious. When I woke in the hospital, it was all over. I still have my other ovary and tube, but there was so much damage I can't carry a child."

Maggie sat down beside Hannah and laid her head against Hannah's shoulder. When she spoke, her voice sounded small, like a child's. "J.D. and my mother blamed me. They said if I had gone to the doctor, he could have done something. And I know that's true."

Hannah put her hand on Maggie's shoulders and gently pushed her back until she could look into her eyes. "Don't you dare, Maggie Whitefield! Don't you dare blame yourself. What happened was beyond your control."

While Hannah tried to take in what Maggie had told her, she took comfort in the routine task of making tea. Since the day they made their pact to leave their husbands when Addie and Reilly grew-up, they had gotten so close, and Hannah couldn't imagine life without her best friend. Still, she had held back—a little piece of herself—because she wasn't sure Maggie really wanted to leave her husband. She knew Maggie had far more to walk away from than she did, but now, she saw none of that mattered to Maggie. She and Maggie were caught in the same web, and they weren't going to break free without each other's help.

When she came in with tea, Hannah found Maggie study-ing a wedding portrait of Granny Zee and her husband. She wore a white sheath with lace trim in a classic 1920's style. Instead of a veil, she wore a jaunty lace headband with what looked like a rose over one ear. With one hand she held a bouquet of wildflowers, the other was tucked inside Hanson Davis's elbow. He wore a dark suit and a proud smile. Granny Zee stood with one leg forward, showing off her white heels. She had a half-smile on her face, and even in the old photograph, the resemblance between Hannah and her grandmother was striking. "Wasn't she beautiful?" Hannah asked.

"You look just like her."

"Thanks." Hannah set the tea tray on the table and handed Maggie a cup.

Hannah crossed her arms over her chest and sat back, pressing her body against the softness of the couch. The raw pain of her loss was exposed after all the years she had kept it tucked out of sight. She glanced at Maggie's puffy eyes and red-tipped nose, and guilt stabbed her for every time she had thought Maggie's life was perfect. Hannah hadn't known Maggie belonged to the private society of women who had lost a child—an alliance no woman wanted to be a part of, speak of, or acknowledge. It didn't matter that Maggie had not borne the child she lost; her pain was unquestionable. A mother's grief over a lost child was as individual as snowflakes.

Granny Zee came into the room and announced the doll room was ready for inspection. Hannah led the way and made sure she and Granny entered the room first, so they could turn around and watch Maggie's face when she entered.

When Maggie entered the room an "oh" of pure delight escaped her. She clapped her hands, turning slowly in a complete circle. Dolls reposed on shelves and the window ledge, were displayed in glass cases, and were arranged atop an antique iron bed. Beside the bed was a matching cradle, and both were covered with ruffled coverlets the color of marshmallow cream. An old rocking chair held four dolls sitting side-by-side. Sunlight peeked around the white ruffled curtains, making the butter-colored walls glow. Maggie had stepped into the doll room of Santa's toy shop.

The doll in the cradle drew Maggie to her side. Made from bisque, her smooth bald head was the color of fresh cream. Her face had a pale pink mouth fixed in a permanent kiss, and her glass eyes were the color of blue innocence. Tiny feet peeked out from under a faded pink gown with hand-stitched smocking across the front. Miniature hands balled into permanent fists rested at her sides. She was old and fragile, and Maggie had never seen anything more beautiful. She stepped closer to the cradle and whispered, "You're lovely," and reached out to take the doll into her arms.

Granny Zee laid her hand on Maggie's arm. "Now, we don't touch Patty Cake. She's real old."

"Is that her name?"

"It sure is. Patty Cake's the oldest doll in this room."

"How old?"

"I don't know exactly." Granny Zee glanced at Hannah. "She's been with me since I was a girl, but she don't really belong to me. I just take care of her."

Maggie looked at Hannah, who was standing at Granny Zee's elbow. She too was looking at the doll. "Is she a family heirloom?" Maggie asked.

"Oh, she's antique for sure," Granny Zee said. "Now, let me show you some of my dolls."

Granny Zee went over to the shelves that extended the length of the wall from ceiling to floor. They were filled with dolls of all shapes and sizes, and no two of them looked alike. There were dolls with blue eyes, brown eyes, green eyes, and buttons for eyes—some eyes closed when they were laid down, some did not. There were dolls with painted pink mouths, red yarn mouths, and mouths with tiny round openings so a toy bottle would be a snug fit.

Together, Granny Zee and Hannah showcased the dolls—porcelain dolls, plastic dolls, stuffed dolls, and dolls made out of cornhusks. There were dolls with long hair, short hair, curly hair, and no hair. There were dolls wearing hats, dolls with braids, pig tails, straight hair with headbands, and elaborate hairstyles with beautiful satin bows.

The dolls were dressed in everything from bibbed overalls to wedding gowns, and most of the clothes Granny Zee had made herself. She had even knitted the booties and bonnets that some dolls wore. Each one had a name and a story about how they came to "live" with Granny Zee.

After introducing them to Maggie, Granny Zee announced it was time for lunch, and she had just the thing for a cold winter day.

A whiff of lilac tickled Maggie's nose—that gentle floral scent with a touch of pine pervaded the room. Maggie looked around the room for a scented candle but saw none.

Back in the kitchen, Granny Zee served bowls of steaming vegetable soup. She had made it during the summer from her garden vegetables and canned it in quart glass jars. Maggie had never tasted anything that delicious.

While Hannah and Maggie ate, they talked about the dolls,

and Granny Zee smiled to see them together, their friendship restored. When Maggie said it would soon be time to pick up the girls from school, Hannah rose and started clearing the table. Maggie said, "Granny Zee, may I use your bathroom?"

"Of course, dear. It's the room next to the doll room."

The pale blue bathroom had an old-fashioned, white claw-footed bathtub and pedestal sink. Even the brass fixtures looked antique, but they gleamed like everything else in the room. Maggie took off her diamond ring and put it on a shelf. She washed her hands with lavender soap, hurrying so she could make a quick detour through the doll room before returning to the kitchen. She couldn't resist another peek at Granny's dolls.

It was cold in the room, and Maggie shivered. She rubbed her hands up and down her arms. She didn't remember the room being this cold. She glanced over her shoulder to make sure she was alone and went to the cradle that held Patty Cake. She scooped her up and lay her against her shoulder, feeling a soft body beneath the gown. With her other hand, she moved some of the dolls from the bed to the cradle, so she could sit down. The comforter was too slippery, and she couldn't get comfortable, so she went to the rocking chair. She moved the dolls in the rocker to the bed and sat down, arranging Patty Cake on her shoulder. She smoothed the downy soft gown over the doll's tiny feet and began to rock. She rubbed her back, humming under her breath. She shifted Patty Cake into the cradle of her arms and smiled down at the doll, rubbing her smooth bald head.

It was Hannah calling to her that brought Maggie back from her reverie. She jumped up and lay Patty Cake down on the bed before hurrying to the kitchen. She didn't want to get caught holding the doll when Granny had told her not to touch it. She would help Hannah with the dishes, then run back and put the dolls back in their proper places.

"Are you okay?" Hannah asked.

"I'm fine. Sorry, I took so long." Her voice dropped to a whisper. "I had to look at the dolls again."

Hannah laughed. They tidied the kitchen and when they finished, Hannah offered Maggie lotion for her hands. Maggie realized she wasn't wearing her ring. She said, "I left my ring in the bathroom. Be right back."

Maggie grabbed her ring and slipped into the doll room. She had made a mental note of where the dolls belonged, so she hurried to Patty Cake's cradle. The cold in the room slipped around her neck like icy fingers and Maggie gasped. Patty Cake lay in her cradle. Maggie turned around in a slow circle, first pausing at the bed, then the rocking chair and again, at the cradle. No one had left the kitchen, but the dolls were back in their places as if she had never moved them.

Maggie inched backward toward the door, pausing in the doorway. A blast of lilac-scented air rushed at her, hitting her in the gut like an icy fist. She stumbled into the hallway, catching herself before she fell. She straightened and stepped toward the doll room, and the door slammed in her face.

Hannah and Granny Zee came running. They found Maggie standing in front of the closed door—eyes fixed—red spots glowing on her cheeks. The rest of her face was deathly white.

Maggie turned and looked at Granny Zee, then Hannah. Her voice shook. "I would swear someone slammed that door in my face."

A look passed between Granny Zee and Hannah, and Hannah bounced into action. She took Maggie's hand and tried to hurry her down the hallway, but Maggie kept looking at the door over her shoulder. Back in the kitchen Granny Zee poured Maggie a cup of tea and added extra sugar. She and Hannah sat on either side of her and urged her to drink.

"Oh, Granny," Hannah said, "Cece scared Maggie half-to-death."

Maggie's head shot up. "Cece?"

Granny Zee said, "I know. I shouldn't have showed her Cece's doll."

Maggie shot up so fast she almost knocked her chair over. "Hold on a minute! You're telling me Granny's cat did that?"

"Wait!" Hannah said. "Walter?"

Maggie turned toward Granny. "Your cat's name is Walter? I thought your cat's name was Cece. Then who's the Cece you're always referring to?"

Granny Zee and Hannah looked at each other. Hannah said, "Sit down, Maggie. Let Granny explain."

At the end of her story, Granny leaned forward and took Maggie's hand. "In many ways, Cece's story is also my story because Cece taught me I had the gift of talking to spirits. It's in our bloodline—many of the women in our family had a special gift, and folks back then were wont to call us witches. My Aunt Mary was a water witch—a dowser—and she could find water and tell people where to dig their wells. That was her special gift like mine's making medicines. Witching was just what they called it, and it had nothing to do with the devil."

Maggie's eyes flew to Hannah. "You! What about you, Hannah? Do you have powers? Are you a—?"

Hannah's nervous laugh filled the room. "Me?" She held up her hands in surrender. "Not me. No powers here."

Maggie looked from Granny to Hannah. She said, "There's still one thing I don't understand. Why is Cece here, now?"

"When Hanson and I agreed to marry, my father owned the property the old house was on and he gave it to us. Hanson hauled away what was left of it, and Cece's presence disappeared. Then, Hanson and Daddy built this house, and I thought Cece would come back, but she didn't. It wasn't until Hanson built a cradle for our first baby that Cece came back."

Granny remembered well the morning she was prettying up the house, and the sweet scent of lilacs wafted through the window. She knew it was Cece, and that night she found Patty Cake lying in the cradle. Cece never made her presence known to Hanson or the children, but she had been with Zelda while she raised her children, said good-bye to her husband, and grew old.

"I shouldn't have picked up Patty Cake," Maggie said.

Hannah leaned toward Maggie. "You didn't!"

Maggie nodded. "It's worse. I moved some of the dolls around, and I even put some in Patty Cake's cradle."

Hannah winced, and Granny Zee nodded. "That explains it," Granny said.

"But you don't understand," Maggie said. "When I came in to tidy up, I left those dolls out of place. But just now, when I went to put them back, they were arranged exactly as they were before I moved them! And then cold air blasted me, and the door slammed in my face."

Granny Zee patted Maggie's hand. "It's okay. You didn't know. Cece doesn't want anybody to fool with the dolls but me, especially Patty Cake."

Maggie gulped the last of her tea. "So, you're saying a ghost moved those dolls?"

Granny Zee nodded. "The dead have powers. I have spent my whole life learning that." She placed her gnarled hand on top of Maggie's smooth one. "The world is not always what it appears to be, but I suspect you've already learned that. I hope this won't keep you from bringing your daughter to meet me."

Maggie placed her other hand on top of Granny's and cradled her fragile bones and soft papery skin. She looked into her eyes, so filled with wisdom and mysteries that Maggie couldn't even imagine. "Granny Zee, I will bring Addie to see you. I promise."

Chapter 9

*The dead walk the earth for many reasons. Some do not realize
they are dead and do not cross over. They remain connected
with a place, which is why people say a house is haunted. Sometimes, the spirit walks around the whole place, but more often it
chooses one room or a block of rooms like an attic or upstairs.
Often the spirit is heard in the room where they died.*
~ from Granny Zee's Book of Dreams

IT WAS TIME FOR Maggie to fulfill her promise. The snowy
winter had given Addie many days off from school, and
Maggie had been lulled into her old ability to comfort herself in
the silence. But spring had returned, and Addie had gone back
to school. Her teacher had called Maggie once again about
Addie's "over-active imagination." Maggie needed Granny Zee's
help, and she needed it now.

On a Saturday morning, Hannah and Maggie set off for
Granny Zee's house with Reilly and Addie in tow. Reilly and
Addie were spending the night with Granny Zee. It had been
Hannah's idea, and Addie was so excited she had been up and
ready to go at six o'clock that morning. Now, she bounced on
the seat with excitement as Hannah took the turn-off to Rock
House Mountain.

When Maggie heard Reilly say, "Patty Cake," she put her
hand on Hannah's arm, and inclined her head toward the back
seat.

Addie said, "How many dolls does she have?"

"A whole room full."

"A big room or a small room?"

"Medium."

Addie paused to think this over.

Reilly said, "There's one doll I'm not allowed to touch."

Maggie raised her eyebrows and looked at Hannah who
had her head tilted, listening.

"Why?" Addie asked.

"'Cause she's real old, and Granny Zee says she don't
belong to her."

"Then whose doll is she?"

"Granny's friend."

"Why doesn't she keep her doll herself?"

Hannah and Maggie didn't get to hear Reilly's reply because Granny's house came into view, and Reilly squealed, "We're here!"

By the time Maggie and Hannah got out of the car, the girls had disappeared. They found them in Granny's kitchen, which smelled like sugar cookie heaven.

"Come in! Come in, dears," Granny called out. She was sliding freshly baked cookies onto a plate, and Addie was watching her with wide eyes. Reilly was carrying a platter of sandwiches to the table that already had a plate of sliced apples surrounding a bowl of caramel dip. "Look, Mama. I'm helping Granny Zee," Reilly said.

"I see you are," Hannah said, hugging her daughter. "Did you introduce Addie to Granny Zee?"

"Uh huh." Reilly bounced back to Granny and began pelting her with questions. "May I show Addie the doll room? May we go for a walk in the woods?"

Addie clasped her hands and joined in the pleading. "Oh, please! May I see your dolls?"

Hannah put a hand on each girls' shoulder. "Let's go take a quick look, and then we can have lunch. Granny Zee, you lead the way."

Maggie hovered in the doorway of the doll room and, like before, she smelled a faint breath of lilacs. After what happened the last time, she didn't want to go in, and she was relieved to see Granny Zee tell the girls that Patty Cake was not to be taken out of her cradle. Instead, she introduced them to the dolls on the bed and showed off the ones on the shelves, announcing they could play with the dolls on the bottom shelf.

The girls took their dolls to the kitchen, where they ate with them on their laps, chattering to them in the singsong, high pitched voices people call baby-talk.

After lunch, Addie and Reilly went outside to explore. Maggie was nervous about Addie going into the woods, so Hannah had them make the "cross my heart and hope to die" promise to stay on Granny's path.

As soon as the girls left, Granny Zee shooed Maggie and Hannah into the family room. "I'll tidy up the kitchen. You girls go set down."

Maggie expected Hannah to argue, but she grabbed Maggie by the elbow and practically dragged her across the room. As soon as they sat down she leaned close to Maggie, so Granny Zee wouldn't hear, and said, "I heard about Addie finding the lost doll at school."

Maggie shifted slightly and looked down at her hands resting in her lap.

"Well," Hannah said.

"Well, what?"

"Why didn't you tell me?"

"I hoped no one would mention it."

"Sweetie, I almost slapped the whore-red lipstick off Cheryl Lee's face over this."

"What! Who?"

"I got way laid by the bitch club after school the other day. Cheryl Lee wanted to know if it was true Addie could read minds?"

"Oh, God, no." Maggie pressed her hands against her forehead. "I suppose I should tell Granny Zee."

"Yes, you should."

As if she had been conjured, Granny Zee appeared. She sat down next to Maggie and patted her hand. "Tell me what, dear?"

Maggie explained the latest call from Addie's teacher. Ethan, a first grader, had hidden a classmate's doll, and even though everyone had searched and couldn't find it, Addie had walked into a strange classroom and gone right to it. When asked how she knew the doll was behind the bookcase, Addie had insisted she *saw* Ethan put Sarah's doll there. Addie's teacher kept reminding Maggie that was impossible since Addie was in a classroom on the other end of the hall.

Maggie said, "Granny Zee, I tried to explain that Ethan must have told Addie where it was, but Addie's teacher wouldn't listen. She insisted that Addie said, 'I *saw* Ethan put Sarah's doll behind the books. I *saw* it in my head. I *see* lots of things that people lose in my head.'"

Granny Zee said, "I believe it's time to teach Addie how to be unnoticed."

"But how do I do that?"

Granny leaned forward. "By telling her she must not talk about her gift to anyone but us. We will teach her together." Granny Zee rose. "Now, I believe it's a good time to take a walk and check on the children."

Granny took her canvas gathering bag from its hook, slipping it over the shoulder of her red cardigan. She retrieved her walking stick, and the trio set off into the soft spring sunshine. They hadn't gone far into the forest when they heard the girls' voices. Hannah called to them, and the girls came running. They had streaks of dirt on their faces, muddy knees, and dirty hands. The fragrance of freshly tilled earth trailed them like a shy friend.

"Look at you two!" Hannah laughed. "How did you get so grubby?"

"We're digging," Reilly said. The girls turned and ran back up the path. Maggie called, "Where are you going?"

Addie and Reilly shouted in unison, "To play!"

Maggie laughed. She stopped and surveyed the mountainside. The palest of greens to the darkest of evergreens sprouted right before her eyes. Beneath her feet, patches of green mingled with the dead sward, and newborn leaves clung to the branches overhead. She inhaled the sweet breath of spring— new growth pushing its way through the dead of winter. She smiled at Hannah and took her hand, and they hurried to catch up with Granny Zee. As the path climbed, Maggie marveled that she was hiking in the spring woods. This time last year, she was probably walking through the National Mall in Washington, D.C.

"This way," Hannah said, leading Maggie off the path. "Watch your step."

Maggie followed Hannah down a slight incline. She could hear Addie and Reilly talking to Granny Zee who sat on a large flat stone near an enormous tree sprouting pointy star-shaped leaves. Addie was standing in front of Granny, who was looking at something in her outstretched hand.

Addie called out, "Come and see what I found."

When Maggie and Hannah reached them, Maggie crouched down so she could meet her daughter at eye level. Addie's eyes were bright. Her hair curled furiously around her flushed face, the lock of silver hair made a perfect loop over her forehead. "I had to find Granny's ring," she said.

Maggie looked up at a teary-eyed but smiling Granny. Addie tugged on her mother's sweater. "It's okay, Mama. Granny Zee's not sad. She's happy."

Granny's tears spilled over, filling the labyrinth of wrinkles around her eyes. "Oh, yes, child. I am happy. Very happy." She held out her hand, revealing a ring, the dirt still clinging to it. "Addie found my grandmother's wedding ring. It's been almost a century since this ring saw the light of day."

Addie beamed, looking from her mother to Granny and back again. Maggie hugged her daughter, and Granny stood and placed her hand on Addie's head. Her blue eyes danced. Granny said, "You have a special daughter, here. A special daughter, indeed."

Back at the house, Hannah took the girls to the spare bedroom Granny had prepared for them, so they could play with the dolls and have cookies and milk. When she came back to the kitchen, Granny was now admiring a cleaned and polished ring on the middle finger of her right hand. She held it up for Maggie and Hannah to admire. She said, "My granny had big hands."

Maggie and Granny Zee retired to the family room while Hannah went to the kitchen to brew a pot of tea. Granny Zee slipped off the ring and handed it to Maggie. It was a band about a fourth of an inch wide in a woven, unbroken cord design with a patina the color of warm sunlight. Granny Zee said, "This ring was passed down from my great-great grand-mother. It's called—"

"A Celtic knot," Maggie said. "It symbolizes eternal love with no beginning and no end. It's beautiful."

Granny Zee smiled. "I'm grateful to Addie. It was lost around the time my grandmother's house burned. Mama was always sad about it because it was supposed to be passed down to her."

Maggie nodded.

"And I'm grateful I got to see Addie's gift first-hand. If it's okay with you, we can use this incident to begin teaching Addie how to be unnoticed."

"Granny Zee, I know Addie has to learn to be careful what she says about finding things, but I'm so conflicted about what to tell her. I don't want to feel like I'm teaching her to lie."

Granny frowned. "I understand. I have struggled with this myself. And I know that with age comes wisdom, but until Addie is old enough to understand her gift, we must protect her. When people don't understand us and what we can do, it can be, well... disastrous."

Maggie burst into tears. Granny put her arm around Maggie's shoulders and said, "There now. You cry it all out." Granny Zee hummed and patted Maggie's back. When her sobs subsided, Granny sang in a halting soprano, "Too-ra-loo-ra-loo-ral, Too-ra-loo-ra-li, Too-ra-loo-ra-loo-ral, hush now, don't you cry! Too-ra-loo-ra-loo-ral, Too-ra-loo-ra-li, Too-ra-loo-ra-loo-ral, that's an Irish lullaby."

Maggie said, "Thank you, Granny. That was beautiful." Granny Zee's voice was whispers of snowflakes on her face with the scent of an ocean breeze—it was the magnificent symphony of a baby's first cry.

"How about a cup of tea?" Granny Zee stood and held out her hand, and together they went to the kitchen.

Maggie walked over to the window and looked out just as a little brown bird flew by and landed on a low branch of a tree.

"Oh, look," she said.

Granny Zee peered out. "It's a wren. A wren around the house brings good luck."

"Really?"

"Indeed. There are two birds you want to have around your house—the robin and the wren. My Mama used to say, 'Kill a robin or a wren/never prosper, boys or men/the robin and the wren/are God Almighty's cock and hen.'"

Maggie laughed.

Hannah placed Granny's Belleek teapot and a plate of cookies on the table. She poured the tea, and a full five minutes passed before Maggie said, "I don't want people thinking my daughter is some sort of psychic curiosity—like the way young children look at someone who's lost a limb. And I'm afraid if Addie doesn't learn how to—hide her gift—then that's what will happen."

Hannah said, "Maggie, you and I have talked about this before—how people talk in this town and how some of them love to blow things out of proportion. I know those mothers. They are talking about Addie and what happened at school, and a couple of them were quick to bring up this has happened before."

"What do you mean?" Maggie asked.

"Honey, have you forgotten how Addie found Timmy in the woods?"

Maggie placed her cup carefully on the table. "No."

"Neither have they," Hannah said. "And—" She paused. "There's more."

Maggie stiffened like she was expecting to be punched. "What?"

"Remember I said I wanted to slap Cheryl Lee?"

Maggie nodded.

"She said her son, Jessie, gave Addie five dollars to find his Gameboy."

"What!" Maggie jumped up, knocking over her teacup. Tea splashed across the table.

Granny Zee threw her napkin over it before it spattered on the floor. Hannah ran to the kitchen and came back with paper towels.

"Sit down, Maggie," Hannah said. "It's okay. I didn't mean to upset you."

Granny Zee poured Maggie a fresh cup of tea while Hannah wiped off the table. Maggie sat down and bowed her head, rubbing her forehead with both hands.

Hannah sat down next to Maggie. "Look," Hannah said, "it's

okay. It's just kids being kids, but this could get—sticky."

Maggie leaned back in her chair and threw her arms up in the air. "I know! I'll just buy Addie a turban and a crystal ball! Get her some hoop earrings and an armful of bracelets!"

"Oh, honey," Hannah murmured, rubbing Maggie's arm. "We can fix this."

Maggie took a deep breath and slowly exhaled. "Okay, I know you're right." She turned to Granny Zee and held out her hand. "Tell me what to do."

Granny Zee patted Maggie's hand. "We have to teach Addie that her gift must go unnoticed—hidden, if you will. And I know, that in a sense, we are telling her to lie, but I believe if you use your gift for good, it outweighs all else. The things I have done have been to help people, but some people might want Addie to use her gift in ways they could profit from or worse."

Granny remembered the time she found the body of that poor woman, Vadie. What might have happened if the killer knew of her gift? What if he'd known she could find where he'd hidden the woman's body and had come after her? She had been a young girl then, and Granny Zee had protected her, and she must help protect Addie.

"Most people don't understand what we can do," Granny Zee said, "and that can lead to fear. More than that, the wrong people knowing our gifts can cloud our abilities." Granny took Maggie's hand. "I'm not going to tell you that there haven't been times when I didn't tell the truth because there have been. I'm not going to tell you that it's been easy knowing the spirit world. Some of the things I know—secrets—have laid on my heart these many years. But know this, I believe what I did was the right thing, and I'm not sorry. Looking back, I would not have done things differently. I have kept secrets. Secrets I will carry with me to my grave."

1918

Chapter 10

THE RAIN HAMMERED DOWN until Rock House Mountain became as colorless as the rain. The spate trampled the pale shoots of spring, making the ground a sodden brown mess. But babies ready to be born don't care about the weather. This Zelda had already learned. In fact, babies liked to make their entrance in the middle of the night or the wee hours of the morning. They were also liable to come during a blizzard or rainstorm, and with all this rain, Mama was anxious about Beula Dawson.

With each pregnancy Beula grew thinner. This time she was so gaunt she looked like skin stretched over a skeleton with an oval-shaped ball attached to her middle. She had given birth to five girls, ages eight and under, and her husband had made it plain that this baby had better be a boy.

Zelda and her mother went to the Dawson's cabin to see how Beula was getting on. Mama was examining her when her husband, Jimmy, came stomping into the room, smearing mud on the floor. "That 'un better be a boy," he said. "I ain't raising no more girls."

A pitiful mewling rose from Beula. Mama said, "Please, Mr. Dawson you're upsetting your wife."

"She knows."

"But, Mr. Dawson, surely you don't mean that."

Beula Dawson wailed and thrashed about. Mama put herself between husband and wife. "Please, Mr. Dawson, go. Let me take care of your wife."

Dawson put his hands on his hips and ignored Emmaline. He said, "You can cry all you want woman. But if this 'uns a girl then send it back to God."

He turned and stomped out, leaving the cabin door open so the rain blew in. The little girls huddled in the front room started to cry. Mama said, "Zelda take care of the wee lasses while I see to Beula."

"Mama, did you hear what he said?"

Mama pointed toward the little girls. "Feed them the deer stew we brought." She disappeared into the room where Beula lay, her lamentations raising the hairs on Zelda's arms.

Zelda went to the girls crowded together in the corner by the fireplace. In this dreary place, sadness floated around like dust motes. She looked around at the dirty rag rug, sagging furniture, and little else. Nothing was on the walls, not even a makeshift curtain at the window. The cabin smelled of old grease and sour milk with a trace of wet dog.

The girls attacked the stew. They leaned low over the bowls, their arms encircling their bowl in a tight hold until their faces practically lay on top of the food. While they ate, Zelda took a bowl to Beula. She had stopped crying and was sitting up in bed, her nose red and running, her eyes red-rimmed and haunted. Fear hung like a noose around her throat.

Mama said, "Beula, Zelda's brought you some stew. My husband killed a doe, and we had more than we could eat." When Beula made no move to take the bowl, Mama took it. "My Zelda is becoming quite the midwife," she continued. "Would you mind if she takes a look at you?"

Without a word, Beula lifted her dress. Zelda sat down on the edge of the bed and placed her hands firmly on Beula Dawson's bulging middle. She rubbed slowly down to the bottom of her stomach where she could feel the head on its way to the birth canal, and then she stroked each side of her belly before kneading the taunt skin, her hands moving back to the top of the hard mound. "The baby is head first," Zelda said, "and good sized." She turned slightly toward her mother and lifted her hands off Beula's stomach.

As quick as a striking snake, Beula grabbed Zelda's wrists. Instinctively, Zelda tried to pull away, but Beula dug her jagged nails deep into the soft flesh of Zelda's inner wrists. Zelda let loose a strangled cry. "Tell me," Beula said, her eyes wild. She pulled Zelda toward her. Her rank breath puffed in Zelda's face. "Tell me if it's a boy. Tell me! You know!"

Emmaline rushed over and put her hands over Beula's. "Let her go, Beula. Zelda doesn't know. I don't know, either."

Beula released Zelda and bent over her belly. She used her hands to cradle the mound that held her child. She said, "He means it. He will kill her. Oh, Emmaline, help me. Help me!" She clasped her stomach and moaned, rocking back and forth.

Zelda wanted to run out of the room, but she stepped out of Beula's reach and stayed near, watching Mama get down on her knees by the bed and comfort her. Beula grasped Emmaline's hands and begged, "I need Granny Zee. She can tell me. I need Granny Zee."

Emmaline said, "Granny Zee's gone over the mountain to

Cousin Tilly's. She is also having a baby. She should be back tomorrow. I will have her come to you as soon as she gets home. Now, you must eat this stew."

After Beula ate, Mama fixed a cup of tea and dosed it with a tincture of passionflower, lemon balm, and lavender to help Beula rest. By the time they were ready to leave, Beula was asleep.

They were not far from the Dawson's cabin when Zelda burst into tears. Mama put her arm around her child. She said, "I pray Granny Zee gets here soon. Beula don't have much time. Granny's the only person who can deal with Jimmy Dawson."

The next morning, Zelda found Mama and Granny Zee in the kitchen with a plate of half-eaten biscuits and a jar of honey. She hesitated in the doorway, but Granny Zee called her over. "Sit down, child. We are talking about poor Beula and Cousin Tilly."

"How is Tilly?" Zelda asked.

Granny Zee shook her head. "I don't know if Tilly will make it. She's lost all her babies, and I don't believe this one will live. And more than likely, this is the end of her birthing time."

"Do you think Tilly's going to die?" Zelda asked.

Mama put her hand on Zelda's arm.

"Tilly says if this baby dies, she wants to die," Granny Zee said. She stood, balancing herself with one hand pressed against the table. Her high forehead was a maze of lines drawn tight with worry. Years of working in the sun had left her exposed skin dotted with small dark patches. Zelda had a sudden flash of herself, standing like Granny Zee, bent at the waist, her hair gray, her face a web of wrinkles.

Granny Zee straightened. "I'm going to see Beula. And have a talk with Jimmy Dawson."

For three days it hadn't rained, but the sky held forth a map of gray clouds. The acrid odor of wet ashes hung in the damp air, and Zelda found herself taking shallow breaths as she walked because the air tasted like lumps of soot. Water clung to the dripping trees, dug runnels in the side of the mountain, and pooled in the crevices and dips in the ground. The scarlet oak came into view, and as always, Zelda remembered the baby girl hidden under the leaves. That was more than five years ago, but she could still feel the coldness of its dead skin against her own.

Zelda sat down on the bench made by rocks that lay in a crooked line in front of the faerie fort—a mound of dirt that rose up into a rounded hump. It was here that Granny Zee said the faerie's lived, and that she must never disturb them. Ever.

Zelda looked up at the new red-tinged leaves sprouting from the oak. She stretched her arms straight up, holding her hands palms up to the tree and closed her eyes. In a voice strong and clear she said, "Spirits of the forest, help me help them."

A sudden gust brought Zelda to her feet. Rain was coming. She hurried down the mountain path with that feeling of knowing so deep in her breast it hurt to breathe.

Granny Zee's horse was saddled and waiting in front of the house. Zelda hurried inside where she found her mother and grandmother packing their doctoring bags.

"Good, Zelda, you're here," Mama said. "Beula's labor has started, and your grandmother is heading to Tilly's. You come with me. Eleanor and Isabelle are already gone to Beula's to get the girls and bring them back here until this is done. Those little girls have already seen too much."

"Rain's going to turn to ice," Granny Zee said. She pulled on her Mackintosh and belted it snugly around her slender waist. "I must get back to Tilly. I have a bad feeling." She handed Zelda her bag. "Help me get saddled up?"

They went out on the porch and closed the door. Zelda took a step off the porch, but Granny Zee grabbed her arm. "Come to me, child. I need to tell you something important." Her blue eyes shone with concern. "I shouldn't call you child, anymore," she said, brushing a strand of hair off Zelda's forehead. "You're almost grown."

Zelda took Granny's hand. "What is it?"

"As soon as Beula has that baby, you must take it straight to your daddy. He has a horse ready and will bring the baby to me at Tilly's."

Zelda's hand flew to her throat. "But what about Beula?"

"Your mama and I have laudanum."

"But she will think her baby died."

Granny Zee clasped Zelda's face. The strength in her gnarled hands made Zelda flinch.

"We did not ask for this gift, but we have it. And with it comes much responsibility. Sometimes, that responsibility is deciding life and death. If we give Beula's girl-child to Tilly, we will be saving two lives. Or more."

Jimmy Dawson left around midnight, saying he'd be back

when his boy was born. Beula labored and cried all night, begging God to give her a son. At one point, she tried to run away, and Zelda had to help Mama hold her in the bed. Beula said she would have her baby in the woods and hide it there. Mama had to give her laudanum to keep her in the bed, but she was careful not to give her too much, or the baby would have trouble breathing when she was born.

Zelda stepped out on the porch just as the first gray threads of dawn appeared. There were no stars to wish upon like she had done when she was little, only the moon dodging the clouds that had poured endless rain upon them. She knew Granny Zee was right, but right now this gift they shared was a curse. She wished she could turn back time to the days when her only worries were getting her chores done, so she could play with Cece at the old house. Too many things were changing. Isabelle was getting married, and Eleanor talked about going away to the new teacher's college at Radford. And she *was* almost grown, and that meant learning to stand on her own two feet.

A crackling sound like buckshot hitting tin made Zelda jump. Ice was drumming the house. She pulled her coat close, taking a deep breath of cold air before stepping back inside where her mother was just coming out of the bedroom with Beula's baby wrapped in a blanket.

"A healthy girl," she said. "Now, hurry. You know what must be done."

While Zelda bundled up, Mama carefully swaddled the baby in layers. "Your father is waiting. He has a basket to carry her in."

"But Mama, it's sleeting and getting colder by the minute."

"Then you must hurry. Daylight is coming soon. It's a two-hour ride to Tilly's and two hours back. I have to hold off Jimmy and keep Beula asleep until you get back with Tilly's baby."

"But what if Tilly hasn't had her baby?"

"Granny Zee will have everything taken care of. You'll see. Now, go!"

Zelda shifted the baby, pulling the blanket over her head. She looked back at her mama.

"It's the right thing to do," Mama said. "You must believe that."

Zelda never knew why she went with her father that night. It could have been fear that Jimmy Dawson was going to come after the baby and demand it be given back, only later to have it meet with a sudden accident or mysterious death. It could have been she wanted to see Tilly with her own eyes. To see for herself that Tilly could love this poor child whose only fault was being female. Or, it could have been holding that tiny baby next to her breast on that long ride up the mountain was enough to convince her that Granny Zee and her mama were doing the right thing. Whatever the reason, Zelda handed the baby to her daddy and grasped his hand. She said, "Pull me up."

Zelda settled on the saddle and hunkered over the basket, shielding it from the cold with her body. The moon was full and ponderous, pushing aside the clouds until the sky cleared and blackened, heavy like a stone. Zelda wrestled with her heart on that long ride. Her head was clear. If she was to live her life with this knowing—hearing the dead—then she was going to have to do what she thought was right, just like Granny Zee said. It was living with those decisions she had to make right with her heart.

Dawn woke on a world turned to ice. Temperatures had dropped so quickly the rime was thick and crisp on every tree and shrub, even the rocks and ground. The horse made its way slowly, occasionally slipping, to Philo and Tilly's house where Philo met them outside and took their horse to the barn. Zelda slipped into the darkened house with the basket to find Tilly in heavy labor. Granny Zee came out of the room long enough to tell her to take the baby and sit by the fire until it was over.

Zelda sat by the fire and prayed that Tilly's baby would be born alive and healthy. She looked down at the baby slumbering in the basket and wondered what would happen to this wee girl if Tilly's baby was born alive. The baby stirred in her sleep and Zelda lifted her out of the basket. She was a miniature version of her sisters—reminding her of their pitifully thin bodies, their dirty hands shoveling deer stew into their empty stomachs. Zelda looked around at the room with its large stone fireplace—big enough to put a witches' cauldron in, comfortable furniture with knitted blankets across each piece, maplewood candle holders on the fireplace mantel, and woven rugs on spotless floors. A worn family bible rested on a side table, with an empty page for the names of Philo and Tilly's children. This was a home, and the only thing missing were the children.

Zelda closed her eyes and instantly slipped into the dreamworld. Her breath grew shallow. The buzzing of bees filled her ears. A tree appeared before her—blinding white. Its branches blossomed into long thin feathers that curled on the end like fingers. A soft wind rose and the branches swayed, spreading the scent of vanilla. A blue bird flew toward the tree and lit on a branch.

Peacefulness covered Zelda like a blanket warmed by the fire. She smiled as the soft feathers encircled the baby bird, rocking it gently as the fledgling sang the sweetest song. On the last note, the feathered branch swayed down and back up, releasing the bird. It soared upward toward the sun. Zelda opened her eyes and knew—a spirit had just left this world.

Granny Zee appeared with a tiny still bundle wrapped in a blanket. She shook her head with tears in her eyes. She went to the basket and peered in at Beula's sleeping daughter. "God forgive me for what I'm about to do," she said.

By the time Zelda and her daddy started for home, the sky had blued on a cloudless day. The sun rose golden but veiled by its lack of warmth. Tendrils of sunlight played amongst the ice-world. Ice clung to every tree and shrub, every rock and plant, forming teardrops and whorls, icicles and pickets. Light bounced off bobs of ice in dashes, shooting out into the day. It hurt Zelda to have such beauty around her when she knew what lay in the basket tied to the saddle.

"I can feel your heart hurting," Daddy said.

Zelda leaned back on his chest. He had removed his Mackintosh and his old wool jacket comforted her. She turned her head sideways, so she could press her face against him, inhaling his scent—pine boughs, wood smoke, and the faint scent of the sweat of hard work. Daddy squeezed her shoulder, and tears rushed down her cheeks. She leaned away from him and hung her head.

"Now, don't you cry, baby girl," Daddy said. "Your mam and gran did what needed to be done. That baby is better off with Philo and Tilly. James Dawson can't feed the young'uns he's got, let alone another one he don't want. Dawson is the devil hisself. He would have killed that wee girl and got away with it. Let him think his son died. If you ask me, it's justice."

Daddy's words made her heart hurt a bit less.

The only sounds in the forest came from the horse—the crack of ice under her hooves, her warm breath colliding with the cold, followed by the occasional snort. The woodland creatures had taken cover from the ice-world, but Zelda could feel them—their familiar presence a comfort.

"You're growing up, Zee," Daddy said. "This world is a hard place. Bad things happen to good people. If we can make it a little better for them, then it's our duty to do it." He grew silent and Zelda thought he was done speaking when he said, "This won't be the only time you're going to wonder if you did the right thing. If you live your life—truly live it—not sit and watch it pass by, then your whole life you're going to wonder if you're doing it right." He put his hand on her shoulder and squeezed.

The sun was edging mid-sky by the time Zelda and her father made it to the Dawson cabin. Still, the ice held fast to its woodland hosts, sun ghosts dodging from tree to tree. The only sign of life was smoke coming from the chimney. "There's no need for you to go in," Daddy said, tucking the basket under his arm. "Go home. I'll stay with your mama until Dawson gets here. Likely, he's laying drunk somewhere from drinking all night."

When Zelda got home she was so exhausted that, at first, she thought she was seeing things. Beula's girls were sitting at the table eating bowls of stew, and each girl had one of *her* dolls —the youngest had Patty Cake propped up on the table. Stew was smeared all over her porcelain face and dribbled down the front of her little white gown.

Isabelle smirked at the horror on Zelda's face. "Well, well, look who decided to come home." she said.

Zelda gasped. "What have you done?" She thought she'd had Patty Cake hidden where Isabelle and Eleanor couldn't find her. She had brought her home when she found the doll left at the old cabin. Zelda believed that was Cece's way of telling her good-bye.

Isabelle said, "While you were sitting around *helping* Mama, me and Eleanor were here taking care of these young'uns. So, we found them some dolls to play with."

"Those are my dolls!" Zelda crossed the room and grabbed Patty Cake off the table. Instantly, the youngest Dawson started to cry.

"Now, see what you've done!" Isabelle came toward Zelda like she was going to take the doll back, but the look on Zelda's face stopped her. Instead, Isabelle pretended to look contrite. "We were only trying to settle them."

"Then give them your dolls!" Zelda went to the kitchen, got a rag, and dipped it in the water bucket. She took it and Patty Cake into the room she shared with her sisters.

Eleanor came in behind her and got a ball of yarn out of a basket. Eleanor, the middle sister, was the "pretty one," with hair that fell in auburn curls down her back. Eleanor had Mama's pretty face—velvety fair skin, small nose, and big eyes with perfectly arched auburn eyebrows. Zelda's hair was lighter and just as curly, more blonde than red, and Isabelle's was darker, brown with red highlights. The sisters shared their father's bright blue eyes, but Isabelle was the only one who was tall like Daddy. Eleanor and Zelda were petite like Mama, but Zelda didn't have Eleanor's graceful ways and flawless skin. When she was little, Daddy often said, "Zee is as tough as a pine-knot."

Eleanor held up the ball of yarn. "I'll give her this to shut her up. You don't have to be so selfish with your old dolls. I have never seen you play with that one, anyway." She pointed to Patty Cake.

Isabelle came in and planted herself in front of Zelda, hands on her hips. She had their mother's figure, full-breasts and slim waist, but unlike their mother, she had a tart tongue. Since her engagement to Emerson Smith, she had become a tyrant who acted like she had to get as many hurtful jabs in as possible before she married. Zelda was cleaning Patty Cake and refused to look up at her sisters.

"Why do you have to be like them?" Isabelle said. "Why can't you be—"

"Be what?" Zelda lay Patty Cake on the bed and raised her eyes to Isabelle's face. She eased off the bed and clenched her fists at her sides, drawing herself up until she stood rigid like a plank of wood.

Eleanor looked from Zelda to Isabelle. Her face paled, and she took a step back, but Isabelle wasn't so quick to back down. She said, "Why do you have to go and do things like you're already an old woman? Why can't you have any fun?"

"Fun?" Zelda started to laugh. She looked from one sister to the other and laughed until tears poured down her face. She dropped down on the bed and wiped her eyes, her laughter fading away.

From the front room erupted cries of, "Mine! Give to me! No!" and little girl high-pitched screams. Isabelle grabbed the ball of yarn out of Eleanor's hand and hurried out of the room, saying, "Stop that right now!" but Eleanor sat down next to Zelda. She reached out like she was going to touch her sister but dropped her hand in her lap. She said, "I'm sorry about your doll. But Isabelle said..."

Zelda turned toward Eleanor and held her hands out like she was trying to catch something falling from the sky. "Do you see my hands?"

Eleanor nodded.

"I held a dead baby in these hands," Zelda said. "While you and Isabelle were here with those poor little girls, I held a dead baby next to my heart."

Eleanor's hand flew to her mouth.

Zelda dropped her hands. She went to the window,

rimmed on the inside with a line of frost, and turned her back on her sister. "Get out. I need to sleep."

Zelda heard the bed creak when Eleanor stood. She placed her forehead against the cold window pane. "You and Isabelle didn't even ask about the baby." She stayed there until she heard Eleanor close the bedroom door.

Chapter 11

ALL ISABELLE DID WAS cry. She and Emerson Smith married in June, and he was drafted in July. The war was raging in Europe and, in August, Emerson was sent to France. Before he left, he tried to move Isabelle in with his folks who lived near their new cabin in Poplar Holler, but Isabelle would not have it. Mama wouldn't let her out of her sight, anyway. Isabelle was pregnant and suffering such terrible sickness, she couldn't keep anything down. Zelda stayed busy grinding ginger root for Isabelle's tea.

October on Rock House Mountain smelled of burning leaves and pumpkin, and something akin to fear. Winter was coming, and the whole family was busy with the harvest and preparing for the cold and snow. Winter was a hard time for every mountain creature, and Granny Zee said the signs promised this would be a bad one. She had taken supper with them after she and Daddy had come back from town with supplies—flour, salt, sugar, and coffee—things they could not make themselves. Granny had also bought medical supplies. She and Daddy talked about the war and the influenza that was all around them. Granny said it was coming to the mountains, and Zelda heard fearful whispers in her dreams.

The good news was Daddy brought Isabelle two letters from Emerson. He was in Belgium and had not seen any fighting yet. Even though influenza had struck there, he was well.

Mama and Granny Zee were in a frenzy of gathering, drying, and making tinctures, salves, and ointments. If Zelda wasn't helping them, she would wait on Isabelle hand-and-foot or, like today, preserve food for the coming winter. Zelda would never again look at shucky beans without remembering the day her life changed forever.

An overflowing bushel basket of half-runner green beans perched at Zelda's knee. The sun pushed the morning toward noon, and Zelda held her cold hands, stained brown from working the beans, up to a shaft of sunlight. She flexed her fingers to get the blood flowing before she picked up another bean and stabbed it in the center with her needle. She pushed the needle through it and the bean slid down the twine to join the others. A whiff of summer came from each bean like a tiny speck of sun and rain was inside it.

Long strands of beans like these hung all over the house, drying so they could be enjoyed during the winter. It made the house smell like Daddy's summer bean patch. Daddy called the dried beans "leather britches" and loved them cooked with fatback. Zelda was thinking about how the house smelled at Christmas when Mama baked a ham and cooked a pot of shucky beans, so she didn't see the man until he had his foot on the first porch step. He said, "Is this where I can find Granny Zee Winn?"

Zelda dropped the string of beans on top of the basket and hid her stained hands in her lap. The young man standing before her had the whitest teeth and the sweetest smile she had ever seen. His longish wheat-colored hair fell across a tan forehead. He brushed the hair off his forehead, revealing straight eyebrows bleached almost white. He wore a collarless gray flannel shirt and faded brown corduroy britches. He said, "My name's Hanson Davis."

Zelda's heartbeat quickened. She said, "I'm Zelda Ryan. Granny Zee is my grandmother."

"Can I come up on your porch?"

Zelda gestured toward a ladder-back chair. "Set down while I go find her."

Zelda found Mama and Granny Zee working in the kitchen. Zelda stammered, "Gran-Gran-Granny Zee, there's a man to see you."

Granny Zee turned toward Zelda. "Well, where is he? And what's wrong with you? Your face is as red as a rosebud."

Mama practically ran to Zelda and put her hand, palm down, on Zelda's forehead. "Are you feverish?"

Zelda batted her mother's hand away. "No, I'm fine!"

Granny crossed the room, her eyes fixed on Zelda until she disappeared out the door.

"Who's out there?" Mama asked.

"His name is Hanson Davis. I've never seen him before."

Emmaline went to take a pot of boiling water off the stove. "That would be Susan Kennedy's nephew from Tennessee," she called over her shoulder. "I heard he and a brother came to live with them. Their parents died in a fire."

"Oh, how terrible," Zelda said, hovering by the door. She hoped to hear what was going on outside, but her mother was banging pots around in the kitchen and she couldn't hear a thing. She went to her room, took her braid apart, and combed her hair. It hung to her waist in long blonde ripples with high-lights of amber, ginger, and copper.

The second Granny came inside, Zelda slipped out. She went to the edge of the porch and scanned the yard. Hanson sat on a rock at the edge of the woods. He raised his hand and waved, and Zelda waved back. He stood, put his hands in his pockets, and looked down at his feet. He kicked at a rock before looking up to see if she was still there.

He started back up the hill and Zelda went down the porch steps, stopping when she got to the yard. He came the distance to her. "I wanted to say hello again. Before I left."

"Hello," Zelda said.

He grinned. "Hello, I'm Hanson."

Zelda smiled. "I know."

"Oh, sorry." He rubbed a hand through his hair making a cowlick at his forehead visible. "Forgot I told you." He dropped his head, but not before Zelda saw his deep blue eyes and long golden eyelashes.

"It's nice to meet you," Zelda said.

He looked up and smiled that wide bright smile and Zelda's stomach flipped. "Maybe," he said, "I could sit with you awhile?"

Zelda nodded. "I'd like that."

Hanson pulled a chair over next to Zelda and sat down. "Got another needle and string?"

At supper, Zelda toyed with her stew. She had trouble swal-lowing around this mysterious lump in her throat. She half-listened to Daddy talk about the work he needed to do on the barn before winter.

Mama said, "Can you find someone to help you?"

"I did. Today, I met a nice young carpenter, Hanson Davis. He's coming Friday to help me fix the roof."

Zelda stiffened her back and almost fell off her chair.

"That was the poor feller who came to see me today," Granny Zee said. "I can say that in my seventy odd years, no young man has ever asked me to help him get *in* the army."

Everyone stopped eating and stared.

"What's wrong with him?" Daddy said.

Granny Zee shook her head. "It's his feet. He enlisted, but they won't take him. He wanted to know if there was anything I could do for him. He has flat feet and is missing his little toe on one foot. Accident, I believe he said, when he was a lad."

"But he walked just fine," Zelda said.

Everyone looked at her and her face flamed.

"Noticed that, did ye?" Granny said, smiling.

"The army needs foot soldiers," Daddy said. "They don't want somebody who can't march for days on end."

Before Hanson came to see Zelda again, influenza broke out on Rock House Mountain. As Granny Zee feared, it hit hard. Within days there were fresh graves in almost every family plot. A ten-year-old was the first dead, followed by his grandfather. The dead were buried quickly without wakes or funerals. People stayed away from anywhere the sickness had been. The school closed and unless people had business, you didn't see them on the road. It was as if the mountain turned in on itself and settled down to wait out the sickness.

Families all up and down the mountain sent for Mama and Granny Zee, and Mama refused Zelda's pleas to go doctoring with them.

"It's too dangerous," Mama said. "You can help by staying home and helping me here."

Zelda appealed to Granny Zee, but she said, "I want all three of you girls to stay away from this sickness. I fear it."

Friday came and went and then another week passed, and Hanson didn't show up to help with the barn. Zelda feared the worst. "Have you heard of any sickness at the Kennedys?" Zelda asked. Mama and Granny Zee had come back late from the Anderson family where they had found the mother and father dead in bed with six children, ages ten and under with no one to care for them.

Neither answered.

"Have you? Tell me!" Zelda said.

Granny Zee said, "I'm afraid Hanson's brother died. But I don't believe he's sick, yet."

"Yet?" Zelda reached out and grabbed the edge of the table.

Granny Zee went to Zelda. "Child," she said, "people get it from being around those sick with it, and it spreads like wildfire. It settles in the lungs and chokes the life out of a person. It's not just the weak and old it's after. The young and healthy are dying just as fast or faster."

The disease spread rapidly, and Granny and Emmaline were the only doctoring the mountain people had. Some lived through the fever only to die from pneumonia. Some made it through but were too weak to get out of bed, and some who came down with the disease in the morning, died that night.

Granny and Emmaline fought with every method they had, and the whole family helped. They also struggled to keep from getting it. Granny and Emmaline cleaned their hands with moonshine after treating each patient. To try and protect their family, they wore masks when around the sick and stripped off their clothes and scrubbed themselves before they touched anything in the house. They also boiled every container and instrument they used.

Isabelle stopped feeling sorry for herself and came out of the bedroom. She took care of the milking and chickens, so Daddy could spend his days going from place-to-place feeding livestock and milking cows for people who were too sick to take care of them. Eleanor spent the day cleaning and cooking bone broth that Granny Zee took to the sick, and if she wasn't working up medicines, Zelda helped her.

The day Hanson came in search of Granny Zee, the scales had tipped from fall toward winter. During the night, a cold wind had come rip-roaring down the mountain, stripping leaves from the trees and yanking boards off buildings. With it came bone-chilling cold. By morning, winter hovered above them like a reflection on water.

Zelda and Eleanor were making bone broth. Daddy had killed a deer and what bones they couldn't break, they were sawing apart, so the marrow would seep into the broth. Granny Zee said the broth was keeping many a folk alive who couldn't eat anything else.

When the knock sounded at the door, Zelda figured it was someone looking for help from Mama or Granny Zee. She grabbed up her apron and wiped the blood off her hands and went to the door to find Hanson. "Oh!" Zelda said. She looked down at her bloody apron and her face flushed.

Hanson said, "I wanted you to know—and your father—why I didn't come back. He hunched his shoulders against the wind. "I've been building coffins."

A wind gust almost tore the door out of Zelda's hands. "Come inside," she said.

Zelda introduced Hanson to Eleanor, who had come out of the kitchen and was hovering near them. "I've got everything in the pot," she told Zelda, "Why don't you go sit in the front room by the fire."

Zelda showed Hanson to a seat and hurried to take off the bloody apron and wash up. When she got back, Eleanor had brought them coffee with cream skimmed off the morning's milk, and then disappeared to the bedroom.

"I'm glad to see you looking so good—I mean not sick or anything," Hanson said.

But it was Hanson who was thin with dark circles under his eyes. Zelda said, "Our family has been lucky."

Hanson nodded. "I lost my little brother, and Aunt Sue had it, but she's getting better." He stared into the fire.

"I'm truly sorry." Zelda put her hand on his arm. He looked at her, and Zelda saw the high gray wall Hanson had built around his fragile heart. He was huddled behind it waiting for the next rock to come hurtling toward him.

Hanson said, "I lost my mam and my dad back in the summer. That's why me and Rudolph come here to live. Sue is Mam's sister."

"Where did you live?"

"Greenville, Tennessee. I got two older brothers, but they're both fighting in the war."

Zelda intended to say she was sorry Hanson had lost his little brother and that his older brothers were at war, but instead she blurted, "Rudy left something for you in the barn. It's in the north corner on top of the rafter. Tied up in a piece of old blanket. Gray blanket. He said, 'Sorry.'" Zelda's hand flew to her mouth, eyes wide.

Hanson jumped to his feet. "What? How?" The color drained from his face.

Zelda rose and stepped toward Hanson, who took a step back like he was afraid of her. "I heard about your granny, but you?" He turned and hurried out the door, letting an icy gust sweep into the room.

Zelda ran into her bedroom and startled Eleanor, who dropped the book she was reading. "What's wrong? Where's Hanson?"

"He left."

Eleanor came to Zelda, who crumpled against her. "Oh, sissy," she said, "what happened?"

"I hate myself," Zelda wailed. "I don't want to be like this!" She dropped down on the bed and bent at the waist, rocking back and forth with her hands over her ears.

Eleanor sat down and put her arms around her sister. She held Zelda until she stopped crying and wiped her face on the hem of her dress. Zelda said, "You know how there are things— things you don't want to think about—so you put them in this tiny corner of your mind, so you can think about them later?" She sighed and stood. "Do you mind if I go out for a walk?"

"Wait!" Eleanor stood and took Zelda's hand. "Tell me what you mean, please. I want to understand."

Zelda sat back down on the bed and rubbed her hand over the patchwork quilt, made from their old clothes. She could feel the night's sleep lingering there, and she wished she could return, sink back into its softness until this time of sickness and death was over. But that was for someone else, not her. Zelda would always be akin to death.

Eleanor sat down beside her. "I mean," Zelda said, "bad things you know are going to happen, like—death." She paused and looked into Eleanor's eyes. "That's something you don't like to think about, so you put it in the back of your mind. You know you'll have to think about it someday but—"

"Oh, sissy," Eleanor said. "Are you worried about dying from this influenza?"

"No, I'm not talking about *my* death—just death. Death is something people don't want to think about, but I can't help it! The dead are always there!"

Eleanor stared at her sister. When she spoke, her voice shook. "I thought you were just learning the healing ways. Do you have *an dara sealladh* like Granny?"

Zelda blinked hard and tears spilled over. She nodded, and Eleanor pulled her to her breast. "Oh, lil' sissy, how can I help?"

Zelda said, "You can't help me. Nobody can." She stood and kissed Eleanor's cheek. "I'm going out for a walk. I won't be long."

Zelda tucked Patty Cake inside her coat. She headed down the mountain to the old house, blind to every tree, rock, and plant, propelled along by the wind. She had not been to the cabin since the day Cece vanished and left Patty Cake by the decaying fireplace.

The vines that grew across the crumbling walls were gray-green and shriveled. They swayed and creaked in the wind like a baby's cradle. Zelda shivered and sat down on a pile of rocks. She kept seeing Hanson's face—his blue eyes wide with shock, his face white like death—and worst of all, he had stepped back like he was afraid of her. Or worse.

Until she had met Hanson, Zelda thought she could live with one foot in the spirit world and the other planted firmly in this world. Granny Zee had said she could—that she would learn how to manage her gift. She took Patty Cake out from under her coat and clasped her to her breast. She was shaking, but it wasn't from the cold. Hanson had showed her just who she was—what she was—and there was nothing she could do to change it.

Puffs of snow hitting her face brought Zelda back to herself. In two days was the feast of Samhain. Granny Zee said they needed the bonfire more this year than ever—for its protection and cleansing power—and for its power in calling the spirits. Granny said the family would gather at the fire and ask for help from the spirit world.

Zelda stood. Cece had not come, so she tucked Patty Cake inside her coat and turned toward home. She had to figure this out on her own. By the time the house came into view, the snow was falling in thick twisted ropes. She saw a light on in the kitchen and guilt stabbed at her. She should have been helping Eleanor with supper. Isabelle should be there, but one never knew when she would beg off being around food, and Mama and Granny Zee would soon be home cold and weary, wanting supper. If Daddy was back, he was probably sitting by the fire with more stories of death and dying.

The minute she stepped into the house, Zelda knew something was wrong. A mewling sound like a newborn kitten was coming from the back bedroom. Daddy had added on that room when Isabelle came back to live with them because she said a married woman should not be sleeping with her sisters.

While Zelda was taking off her coat and wraps, Eleanor appeared in front of her. Her cheeks were red, and her hair was a mess of coppery curls. Her dress was stained and an odd smell like curdled milk came from her.

"Thank God you're back," Eleanor said. "I didn't know what to do! Come quickly." She turned and headed for the bedroom.

An oil lamp cast a sallow glow on a woman lying on the bed. The mewling sound was coming from the baby beside her. Zelda smelled dried sweat and the unmistakable scent of sickness. Eleanor said, "They came just after you left, looking for Granny and Mama. The woman practically threw the baby into my arms and collapsed. I didn't know what to do, so I put them in here."

"Where's Isabelle?"

"I wouldn't let her in the house. She's staying in the barn until Daddy gets home and takes her to Granny's house."

Zelda nodded. "Get me a pan of warm water, soap, and some rags. Then bring me that small wash tub and fill it with lukewarm water so I can put the baby in it. I'll try to get her fever down that a-way. Bring me a bottle of willow bark tincture and a cup of cool water. I'm going to clean them up." She eyed Eleanor. "Did they vomit on you?"

Eleanor said, "The baby did. I tried to clean her up. I gave the mother some sips of water and put some cool water on a rag and tried to get the baby to suck on it, but she's too weak."

"Hurry and bring me the stuff and then go and take off

your clothes. Wash good with lye soap."

Eleanor stood there and stared at Zelda, fear clearly written on her face.

Zelda leaned toward her sister. "Go!"

By the time Granny Zee and Mama got home, Zelda had gotten the woman to drink a cup of water with willow bark tincture. Her fever had cooled a bit, and she had stopped shivering so hard she was shaking the bed. Zelda had bathed the baby in tepid water, but the wee girl's skin was still burning hot to the touch. She had gotten a little sugar water in her, but those blue eyes stared at her unseeing. Mama sent her to wash herself and change clothes. She insisted Zelda and Eleanor stay in the kitchen.

The snow had stopped by the time Daddy got home. Granny Zee came out of the bedroom and explained Nellie Stone was the sick woman.

Daddy said, "It's close to five mile from their cabin to here."

"She walked here," Eleanor said. "The poor woman crumpled to the floor the minute I opened the door. I caught the baby before she dropped it."

"Joe was in that last Army draft that took Emerson. I thought she went back to her people, or I'd a-gone and checked on her."

"The sickness has come to our door," Granny Zee said.

The last person on Rock House Mountain to die from influenza was Eleanor. Three days after Nellie Stone showed up at the Ryan family's door, Nellie and her daughter were dead, and Eleanor woke with a blinding headache. It was November first, and Samhain had begun the day before at dusk. The sisters sat at the table, peeling potatoes, and chopping cabbage to make colcannon.

Mama followed the Irish tradition of hiding a button, thimble, coin, and a ring in the dish. The sisters had laughed about the feasts of Samhain past, and what charms they had found in the colcannon. Isabelle said, "The ring worked last year! It wasn't long after I found it that Emerson proposed, so this year I want to find the coin."

Eleanor and Zelda had laughed, and Eleanor said, "Zelda always finds the coin."

"Well, this year," Isabelle said, like it was already settled, "I'm finding the coin! You two don't need money, I do."

Zelda laughed. "It don't work that way, silly."

"I always get the button," Eleanor said. "No marriage for me!"

Granny had come that evening, bearing an apple faerie cake, filled with black walnuts and smelling of cinnamon. As always, a slice was missing. She had gone up the mountain to the scarlet oak tree and left her offering for the wee folk at the faerie fort.

As she came off the mountain, she'd stopped to inspect the bonfire Daddy had laid for the coming night, making sure the ring of rocks was in place. When they lit the fire, the family would stand inside the rocks, so that any evil spirits that might appear could not touch them. Granny Zee hoped the spirits would give them a sign that the sickness would leave the mountain. Nellie Stone and her child were the first new cases and deaths in over a week, giving her a mixed feeling of hope and dread. Hope that the worst was over, but dread that the influenza had finally come to their door.

Everyone joined in the fun. Daddy laughed loudest of all when the charms were found in the colcannon. Isabelle found the thimble and, since a thimble meant the girl was in danger of becoming a spinster, she laughed and said she was going to write Emerson a letter and tell him. There were two charms in Zelda's colcannon, the coin and a ring Daddy had fashioned from a nail. Eleanor got the button, meaning she would remain unmarried, and she joked she was lucky.

It had been the first time since the influenza outbreak that the family had gathered to celebrate and for a short time, forget. That night could have been a memory they returned to, a light in the darkness of that time, but instead, it became the last night they would ever spend with Eleanor.

After dinner, the family assembled and watched Daddy light the bonfire. When the flames began to warm them, Granny Zee stretched her arms toward the stars and said, "Spirits of the dead we ask for your help. Protect us in the coming winter."

The family recited, "Spirits protect us."

Granny cried, "Tell me, oh spirits, will the sickness leave us? Tell me will death leave our mountain?"

The family recited, "Spirits protect us."

Zelda saw the spirits gathering around the fire. She raised her arms toward the sky and stepped closer to the fire. She called out, "Speak to me, spirits!" Behind her, Zelda heard Isabelle gasp, but she did not stop. "Tell me," she cried. "Will the sickness soon leave us?"

The family recited, "Spirits protect us."

The fire popped and branches cracked, sending flames

shooting into the sky. Startled, Eleanor stepped backward, leaving the ring of stones. Zelda watched the spirits gather around Eleanor, weeping and keening. She knew they were lamenting her sister's coming death.

Samhain would be the last time Zelda ever saw Eleanor's smile or heard her laugh. But more than that, it would be the last time she had a sister she could turn to for comfort or to share in her happiness. Isabelle's bond with Eleanor did not extend to Zelda.

Eleanor lingered a week before her lungs collapsed, and she drowned from her own body fluids. The bitterness of winter had already descended on the mountain and, strangely, no new cases of influenza occurred. It was like the cold had frozen it out of existence. Whatever the reason, Zelda was glad her mother no longer needed to fight a disease that had stolen her daughter. Instead, Emmaline Ryan turned all her healing skills to helping Isabelle through her pregnancy. For that, Zelda was thankful.

The day they buried Eleanor, the weather was turning on its hinges. It had been cold and dry, but an omen of snow was in the clouds. Hanson was among the men who had gathered with shovels. After the burial, he went to Zelda at the gravesite and said, "I am truly sorry about your sister."

Zelda said, "Thank you." She turned away and started for home. Hanson fell in step beside her, leaving a wide margin between them. When they got to the point where Hanson should have turned and gone in a different direction, he continued to follow Zelda. When she swung around on him, he said, "I want to make recompense with you. I'm sorry for how I acted about Rudy."

Zelda nodded.

"May I walk you home?" Hanson asked.

"Alright."

They matched their steps stride for stride, closing the gap between them. Hanson reached for Zelda's hand and she took his. She knew he could feel the tiny dry fissures on her hands carved there by work.

The noon sun was brighter than it ought to have been. It offered no warmth but threw cheery streaks of light on the dead leaves and plants at Zelda and Hanson's feet. They did not notice, but continued side-by-side, step-to-step, hand-in-hand like they would for the rest of their days together.

1995

Chapter 12

For more than a half century, I have entered the forest when
time stands between night and day because that is the time the
mantle between my world and the spirit world is liminal. I have
venerated the spirits that inhabit my mountain, and from them I
have learned many things—not all of them I wanted to know.
~ from Granny Zee's Book of Dreams

MAGGIE STARED AT THE phone in her hand. The sudden buzz startled her, and she pressed the off button. She gripped the phone harder and pressed the talk button, dialed the first three numbers of J.D.'s office—stopped—punched off—then threw the phone across the room. It hit the couch and bounced onto the floor, landing with a dull thud. Maggie wrapped her arms around herself, cupping her elbows in her hands. She bent over until her head almost touched her knees. Great sobs racked through her, and she gave way to them, rocking back and forth. At last, she stood and retrieved the phone, this time dialing all of J.D.'s number. When he answered, the annoyance dripped from his tongue. "What is it?"

"Come home. Now."

"Whatever it is, it can wait."

"No. It can't. I just got off the phone with Mr. Liang in China."

The phone went dead.

Maggie sat down and watched the clock. Eleven minutes later, she heard J.D. come into the kitchen. He walked into the den where she sat in front of the fire, saying, "Margaret, listen to me." He paused.

"Go on," Maggie said. She looked into his dark eyes, the same whiskey-color as Addie's. His dark suit fitted him seamlessly, and his white shirt and bright blue tie completed the GQ look. She said, "I can't wait to hear this."

J.D. sat down next to her and loosened his tie. For some absurd reason, this made Maggie smile. He drew back from her like he'd been slapped and said, "Adoption was the only way. I did it for you. I did it for Addie. I know how much you wanted more children."

Maggie stood and went to the window. After days of lovely spring temperatures, the surreptitious winter was back, and the weather balanced on the brink of snow. Granny said this was redbud winter, named for the delicate blooms and buds that splashed the mountains with pinks and purples.

"Did you hear me, Margaret? I did this for you," J.D. said.

Maggie wheeled around. "And not even tell me? You adopted a baby—a life-changing event—and didn't even discuss it with me? What kind of husband does that?"

"A husband who wants to protect you."

"From what?"

"From disappointment. I didn't tell you because I didn't know if the adoption would go through."

Maggie's knees were shaking, so she sat down on the end of the sofa farthest away from J.D. She took a deep breath and caught a whiff of his cologne. He only wore Pierre Cardin Por Monsieur, an expensive fragrance from Paris. The exotic scent had traces of lavender, orange, basil, and bergamot, and it took her back to happier times when she had been content to curl up next to him and inhale his scent. Now, she wondered how many other women he'd intoxicated with that smell.

Maggie realized J.D. was staring, assessing her emotional state. The quintessential lawyer, he was deciding how to proceed.

Maggie said, "The man who called, this Mr. Liang, said the... he said the child was ready to be surrendered to us. So, you must have known for some time."

J.D. leaned toward her, his voice filled with concern and imbued with honesty. "I was waiting for the right time to tell you. I planned for us to go to China together. Your mother is going to come and stay with Addie, so—"

"My mother!" The blood surged through Maggie and her nerves disappeared. She bolted off the couch. "She knows about this? You told my mother but not me?" She crossed her arms and looked him in the eye. "So, was this her idea?"

"Of course not."

"You may as well tell me the truth."

"I told you I did it for you and Addie. I did it for our family."

"Liar!"

J.D. stood, his face reddened like he'd been slapped. "I understand I may not have handled this correctly, but believe me, I did this for you. I know how much you want another child."

"No, no, that's not it." Maggie shook her head so hard she got dizzy. She put her arms out in front of her like she was going to catch herself before she fell. J.D. reached for her, but she drew herself up and took another step away from him. "You did this for your political schemes. A nice tidy family."

J.D. took his keys out of his pocket. "I'm going back to work. We'll talk about this when you calm down."

Maggie sprang toward him and slapped his hand so hard the keys went flying across the room. "You're not going anywhere until you assure me that you're going to call this off. I don't care what you and my mother had planned; I promise you it's not going to happen. And understand this, if you ever do anything like this again, I *will* leave you." She strode across the room and retrieved the keys, tossing them to J.D. who grabbed them in an awkward catch. "Now, I'll let you get back to work. I'm sure you have lots of calls to make."

At first, Hannah thought she was hearing things. The washing machine was spinning a load of heavy towels, and she was bent over with her head in the dryer, looking for a lost sock. She raised up, sock in hand, and froze. Someone was pounding on the kitchen door. She dropped the sock and sprinted up the stairs, yelling, "I'm coming!"

Hannah jerked open the door and Maggie stumbled inside. In the five years she had known her, Hannah had never seen Maggie like this. Her eyes were bloodshot and swollen. Her pale face had red blotches on both cheeks, and her hair was half in, half out of its ponytail. Hannah's first thought was Addie's cancer had returned. She asked, "Maggie, what in the world is wrong?"

Maggie was crying so hard she couldn't talk, so Hannah took her arm and guided her into the family room, where she sat her down on the couch and then knelt in front of her. "Honey, please, tell me what's wrong."

Maggie wiped her face with a tissue she had balled up in her fist. "Just give. Me. A minute."

Hannah jumped up. "Hang on, I'll be right back."

Hannah hurried to the bathroom, grabbed a box of tissues, and rushed back to Maggie. She said, "You're scaring me to death! Did something happen to Addie?"

Maggie shook her head. "It's J.D. Oh, Hannah, you won't believe what he did."

Hannah sat down next to Maggie. "Take your time."

Maggie cleared her throat. Her voice sounded like it was being raked over gravel. "There was a phone call this morning, and a man asked to speak to J.D. I told him he was gone to work, and that I was Mrs. Whitefield. First, he apologized for calling our home telephone by mistake, and then he said... he said—"

Hannah squeezed Maggie's hand. "It's okay."

Maggie breathed in, then out, steadying herself. She leaned toward Hannah. "He said, 'Mrs. Whitefield, let me be the first person to congratulate you on your adoption.'"

"Wait! What?"

"He said our adoption!" Maggie pounded her thighs with her fists. "The man said, 'I need to confirm the date you will be here to collect the child.' That's when I interrupted him and said, 'I'm sorry. There must be some mistake.' But he said there was no mistake. He said he had been working on our adoption for some time, and he needed to know when Mr. J.D. Whitefield was coming to China."

"Wait! China? He was adopting a baby from China?"

Maggie nodded. "I called J.D. and demanded he come home. Of course, he said no; he was busy. Then, I told him I knew about the adoption. I barely had time to hang up the phone before he was home."

"What did he say?"

"The bastard said he did it. For me." Maggie swept her arms out and back to her chest, placing her hands, one on top the other, over her heart. She paused and hunched her shoulders until her chin was on her chest. "He said he thought I would be happy—that Addie had always wanted a sibling. He swore the only reason he hadn't told me was because he didn't want me to get my hopes up in case the adoption didn't go through. He said he had planned for us to go to China *together* to pick up our—our daughter."

"Oh, honey." Hannah reached out to take Maggie's hand, but she jerked it away. "Lies! All lies!" She pounded her fists on the coffee table until Hannah covered Maggie's fists with her hands.

Maggie closed her eyes and lowered her voice. "He swore it was all for me—that he knew I wanted another child. That he did it for our family." She turned toward Hannah, and a bitter laugh escaped her. "Do you know what I said then?"

Hannah shook her head.

"I called him a liar to his face and told him he never did anything for anybody but himself."

"What did he say?"

"That when I calmed down, I would see that he was right. Then he took his keys out of his pocket like he was going to leave, but I slapped them out of his hand."

Hannah's eyes went wide. "What happened?"

"His face turned blood red, and for a moment, I saw J.D. the man, not the stoic lawyer, and that's when I went in for the kill—I demanded he call if off or I would leave him."

"What did he do?"

"He took the damn keys and left."

"Oh, Maggie." Hannah laid her hand on Maggie's arm.

Maggie snorted. "And do you know what stands out in my mind?" She glared at Hannah, who didn't move. "His damn clean fingernails! When he caught those keys and made a fist around them, his fingernails were perfect. In all the years I've known him, I've never seen him with dirty nails. And that makes me hate him even more."

Hannah thoughts darted back and forth over what Maggie had said. She had only seen J.D. a few times when she picked up Reilly at their house. He had always been gracious and managed to disappear quickly, but she would be the first to admit he was a commanding presence.

J.D. was the exact opposite of blond, blue-eyed Travis. He *was* handsome in a dark distinguished way, but Travis still had a football player's muscular body while J.D. was slender like a long-distance runner.

Hannah said, "There's a bit of sun out. Let's go sit in the swing." She grabbed a throw from the couch, leading the way out to the deck. They sat down in the swing, and Hannah covered them. She pushed the deck with her foot and the swing began to move. Maggie closed her eyes and let the warm-hearted spring sun wash over her. When she opened them, Hannah was studying her face. "Are you going to be okay?"

Tears slipped down Maggie's face, but she didn't make a sound.

"Oh, honey, I'm so sorry." Hannah put her arm around Maggie's shoulders. "Damn him!"

Maggie slumped forward like she was deflating. "There's a part of me that wants that baby. That aches for that baby."

Hannah whispered. "I would feel the same way."

"Would you?"

Without hesitation, Hannah answered, "Yes."

"Now that Addie is cancer free and older, J.D. knows his hold on me is slipping. So, what better way to keep me than a baby? Think of how good it makes him look—the handsome law professor, and aspiring Congressman, goes all the way to China to get a baby for his poor wife who can't have another child. Add that to the sick child he already has—wouldn't you vote for a man like that?"

Hannah nodded.

Maggie remembered the newborn newness—the buttery soft skin under her hands, the downy hair against her cheek, the scents of sweet milky breath and a baby powdered bottom. She could imagine that baby's tiny perfect hands and feet and feel her tummy against her shoulder. She remembered how Addie rooted at her breast when she was hungry, and an unbearable ache filled her heart.

Maggie said, "I almost, almost wish..." She paused, and her voice dropped to a whisper. "I almost wish..."

The swing stopped.

Hannah asked, "What do you think would've happened if you hadn't gotten that phone call? I mean—would he have just shown up with a baby?"

"Think about it. If your husband walked in with a baby and put it in your arms, would you refuse to take it?"

"Of course not."

"That's exactly what J.D. was counting on."

Silence fell, its heaviness welcomed. The friends drifted back and forth, gulping air like they were competing for it.

Hannah put her hand over Maggie's. It was easy to forget that Maggie had lived a different life than she had—and still did. Even though they were both unhappy wives with ten-year-old daughters, there was something unreachable about Maggie's world that Hannah couldn't forget. If she took Reilly and disappeared tomorrow, it would barely cause a ripple in Travis's family. She said, "I would understand if you changed your mind. You have so much more at stake than I do."

"What do you mean?"

The phone rang, startling Hannah and Maggie. Hannah said, "I better get that."

She went inside and came back with the phone. "It's Addie. She wants to speak to you."

Hannah moved to go, so Maggie could have some privacy, but Maggie grabbed her hand and pulled her down in the swing.

"Addie, slow down. I can't understand you." Maggie covered the phone with her hand and cleared her throat so she wouldn't sound so hoarse. "No, there's nothing wrong. Nothing happened. Daddy's not here. He's at work. I talked to him a little while ago. He's okay, and I'm perfectly fine." She looked at Hannah. "Sweetie, I'm not crying. I think I'm catching a cold—that's all."

A single tear trickled down Maggie's cheek. She said, "Addie, I'm fine. I promise. I'm just visiting Hannah. I'll pick you up in a few hours." Hannah handed Maggie a tissue, and she wiped her eyes. "There's nothing for you to worry about, sweetie. Now, let me speak to Mrs. Howard."

Hannah listened while Maggie thanked the guidance counselor for allowing Addie to call.

Hannah said, "Want to go inside? I'll break out the brownies." She wagged her eyebrows up and down, and Maggie gave a husky laugh.

Back in the kitchen, Hannah put a plate of brownies covered with thick chocolate frosting on the table. "Good for what ails you," she said.

Hannah was starting on her second brownie when she asked, "I know we talk about how Addie's learning how to handle her gift, but how about you? How are you handling it?"

"Sometimes I feel like Addie's looking over my shoulder, especially where her dad's concerned. Like today, she knows when we argue, and she's protective of J.D. And I worry..."

"About?"

"I worry about what she's going to do if she realizes he sleeps around."

Hannah nodded. "Growing up's hard enough without worrying about things you can't change. Just remember, Granny and I are here for you."

Maggie smiled. The puffiness was leaving her eyes, and her face was pale, but flawless. She had left her long hair loose on her shoulders, and combined with no make-up, she looked young and vulnerable. Hannah said, "If you wanted to, you could sell that gorgeous head of hair and get enough money to divorce your husband. I'm sure some stringy-headed woman like me would pay top dollar for it."

Maggie smiled. "I'll take that as a compliment, but I don't need J.D.'s money."

"Everybody needs money! If I left Travis, and he had to give me half of everything, it wouldn't matter—half of nothing is still nothing. Of course, with your mother—"

Color surged into Maggie's pale cheeks. "I don't need my mother's money, and J.D. doesn't have any."

"Wait!"

"I'm the one with the money. The house, the cars—I paid for all of it."

A puff of air rushed from Hannah. "No wonder he planned the adoption! If he loses you..."

"He loses my money. At one time, his family was extremely wealthy. They're not poor now, by any means, but a pedigree from his blue-blooded family is the extent of his inheritance."

Hannah's voice dropped to a whisper. "Sometimes I feel like I live at the end of the world. Maggie, why do you stay? If you can go, then why not—go?"

"If Addie hadn't gotten sick, I would have, but I came so close to losing her, and she went through so much hell, that she deserves to be part of a family. The best thing about J.D. is the love he has for his child and that has made me forgive so much else."

Hannah looked down at the table. "Maggie, can I ask you something that's really none of my business?"

"Sure."

"How much money do you have? I mean, are we talking Oprah Winfrey?"

Maggie laughed. "No, not Oprah, but my father left me enough money to be independent and comfortable."

Hannah echoed, "'Independent and comfortable.' That's exactly why I want to be a physical therapist. I will never depend on a man—any man—for my livelihood."

"Are you saying you don't ever want another relationship?"

Hannah leaned forward. "I'm not saying that at all. I just don't want to ever have to stay in a relationship because I can't take care of myself. I want to be free to choose."

"Hannah, I may have money, but all my life someone has made decisions for me. First my mother and father, and then J.D., and I admit part of that is my fault. I thought I would always have my father to guide me, and when he died, I drifted—first through adolescence, then through college without pursuing a course of study that I could do anything with... I mean, a Bachelor of Arts in philosophy isn't a marketable skill."

Hannah sat perched on the edge of her seat, her eyes locked on Maggie's face. "But, don't you see?" Hannah continued. "What happened this morning was the first step in changing that. You didn't let your husband make a decision that would change your life. You took control. You're on your way, Maggie."

Chapter 13

Spring is the season when love is born, and many young maidens come to the granny woman seeking a potion to cast a love spell on their chosen man. Legends abound, but a true mountain witch knows the power of a love potion is its scent. A portion of: jasmine—its distinct, sweet, odor induces euphoria; rose—its sensual scent can lower anxiety; vanilla—its warm scent (and taste) is welcoming, subtly sensual, and relaxing; and cinnamon—its spicy scent ensures a burst of passion and energy. The potion should be rubbed behind the ears and in the bend of the elbow when the girl is near her chosen love. The scent will go straight to his heart.
~ from Granny Zee's Book of Dreams

A**T NOON ON SATURDAY**, Maggie and Addie pulled into Hannah's driveway. They had been summoned by Hannah with the promise of a BIG surprise. Addie hopped out and disappeared around the house.

The sound of a lawn mower made Maggie pause before getting out of the car. She loved the smell of freshly mowed grass, so she lowered her window and inhaled the heady scent. The noise got louder, and she realized it was coming from Hannah's front yard. She turned toward the sound just as the mower and Travis Lively appeared.

He was shirtless and his broad shoulders were golden brown. He drove across the yard and turned the mower, so it was coming back in Maggie's direction. He leaned to the right and looked down at the mower blade. His blond hair fell forward, catching the sunlight. "Wow," Maggie said. She filled her lungs with scented air and stared at this male blond vision. She muttered, "Why in the hell do you have to be so gorgeous?"

He waved and smiled at her, his sapphire blue eyes twinkling. She got out of the car on shaky legs and was at Hannah's back door before she realized how she got there. On some level it had to be horribly wrong to drool over her best friend's husband, but she couldn't help it, and Hannah had always brushed it off with "a handsome fool is irresistible."

Hannah came into the room and laughed at Maggie, who

had picked up a dishtowel and was fanning herself. Maggie said, "Did you know Brad Pitt is mowing your grass?"

"Really?" Hannah went to the window and raised the shade. "Oh, you mean that guy?" She turned to Maggie. "Too bad he's an asshole."

Maggie snorted. "It's always something."

Reilly and Addie burst into the room. "Did you show her the letter?" Reilly asked.

"What letter?"

"Mama, for heaven's sake!" Reilly grabbed a folded document and handed it to Maggie. Maggie looked at Hannah, who clasped her hands in front of her chest, hunched up her shoulders, and grinned so big her eyes looked like they could pop out.

Maggie laughed and opened the letter. The girls shouted, "Read it out loud!"

"Dear Hannah Lively. We are proud to inform you that you are the recipient of the Augusta Alexander Scholars Scholarship." Maggie squealed and grabbed Hannah who was jumping up and down. Addie and Reilly started dancing in a circle around their mothers.

"You did it!" Maggie laughed.

"You did it!" Reilly and Addie echoed.

"I did it!" Hannah squealed.

The celebrating died suddenly, and Maggie wheeled around to see Travis standing in the doorway. He grabbed a towel off the counter and proceeded to wipe sweat from his face. "Don't let me break up the party," he said. His lopsided smile was directed at Hannah.

His shoulders were so broad they blocked the sunlight flooding through the glass door. Maggie had seen Travis many times, and she loved to tease Hannah about how her husband was a dead-ringer for Brad Pitt, but this half-naked creature standing before them wasn't just handsome. To call this man, with sweat running down his face and bare chest, handsome was like calling a monsoon a little rain. She managed a weak, "Hello," while she clenched her fists at her side to keep herself from running to him and wiping the sweat off his body. Her gaze trolled from his broad shoulders and muscular chest, down to the cutoff jeans, hanging low on his hips.

Reilly said, "Daddy, we were just celebrating Mama's scholarship."

Travis dropped the towel on the counter and walked over to the refrigerator, pulling out a bottle of water. He took a long drink, giving Maggie a side view. Her eyes dropped to the ugly scar on one leg.

Travis grunted what sounded like, *yeah,* and kicked off his grass covered sneakers in the direction of the door. He padded in sock feet out of the room, and Maggie heard the TV come on.

Reilly said, "Mama can we go get pizza for lunch?"

Addie chimed in. "Can we?"

"Sure, give us half an hour." Hannah went to the refrigerator and got out two bottles of iced tea. She handed one to Maggie. "Let's sit on the deck."

They settled into the swing, and Hannah pushed the deck with her bare foot. For a while, they drank tea and swayed back and forth. The sun ruled the day. Only one cloud, a mere scrap of lace, drifted in the sky.

Hannah said, "I told you so."

Maggie raised her eyebrows.

"I told you Travis is an asshole."

Maggie sighed. "You did. But why do our husbands have to be so damn good-looking?" She turned toward Hannah. "Is there some hidden law on the books that says handsome men always put themselves first in a relationship?"

"Yeah," Hannah said. "It comes right after the law that says wives shouldn't expect husbands to help them achieve their lifelong dream."

Travis still lived in the world where Hannah worshiped him. In high school, being Travis Lively's girl was more important than a perfect score on her SAT. She'd been so proud of herself. She'd gotten the hottest guy in school. The fact that he was a football star was just a bonus, like opening a box of cereal to get the prize inside and finding two of them. But she hadn't fallen in love with Travis. She had been in love with being Travis's girlfriend.

Hannah let the swing come to a stop. "Maggie, I know women say they fall out of love with their husbands, but the truth is I was never in love with Travis—I was in love with the idea of love—the way other girls envied me. I was in love with the way people turned and looked when we entered a room. I was the girl from up a holler that had never been anywhere or done anything. Travis was my way out of here—a chance to be somebody. I told myself that it didn't matter—that Travis could have the spotlight. I convinced myself that being Travis's girlfriend and then Travis's wife would be enough. Then fate played a dirty trick on me and that's exactly what I got."

Hannah went to the flower bed and started fussing with the impatiens. Pinks and purples rioted the garden. A lazy yellow butterfly landed on a fuchsia bloom, its wings coming to a standstill like it was too intoxicated to move. When Hannah turned, Maggie was standing behind her, watching. She said, "I'm sorry, Maggie. I shouldn't take it out on you. But when I showed Travis the scholarship letter, he said, 'That's good, babe.' Nothing more." Tears slipped down her cheeks. "I'm sorry, Maggie, but it hurt! It really hurt."

"Don't ever be ashamed of your feelings!" Maggie took Hannah's hand. "I spent my youth apologizing to my mother for showing my feelings. Would you believe, I have never seen my mother cry? Even when my father died, I never saw her shed a tear."

Hannah turned her back to the flowers and jumped up, landing in a sitting position on the wall. She patted the spot next to her and Maggie joined her. For a while, they sat in silence, swinging their legs, the sun warming their backs.

When Hannah started to hop down, Maggie said, "When I was about seven years old, I was playing outside on a day just like this when a bird suddenly flew into one of our windows, breaking its neck. I didn't hesitate. I picked up the poor thing and cradled it in my hands." Maggie cupped her hands together and stared at their emptiness. She continued, "I ran to find my mother. I wanted to bury it." She dropped her hands. "I asked her for a shoebox, and do you know what she did? She marched me to the trash can and made me throw the bird away. I begged her to let me bury it, but she stood there and pointed at the trash can until I dropped it. Then she marched me to the sink and watched while I cried and scrubbed my hands until she was satisfied they were clean. And the whole time she stood as silent as a stone."

Hannah touched Maggie's arm, saying, "Sweetie, I'm so sorry."

"But, she wasn't finished with me." Maggie hopped down and leaned against the wall. "I had to be punished. I had to sit in the serenity chair."

Hannah frowned.

Maggie crossed her arms over her chest. "It was a chair in the corner of our living room. My mother would make me sit there until I could 'compose' myself. She called it the serenity chair, and whenever I got too emotional—happy or sad—she made me sit there. I had to stay in that chair, in that room, all alone until she decided I had composed myself—sometimes for hours. If I begged to be released, she made me stay longer."

Hannah thought of the big oak rocking chair in her mother's front room, how the wood complained when they rocked, her sitting on Mama's lap. How many times had Mama

117

rocked her and dried her tears? How many times had Mama helped her and her brother bury one of their pets or a dead wild thing?

The back door burst open.

"Mom! Where are you?" Reilly called.

"I'm starving," Addie whined.

"What are you guys doing that's so important?" Reilly said. "We're hungry!"

Maggie and Hannah looked at each other. Hannah said, "Let's go get pizza!"

⁂

"Are we really going to have a whole week to ourselves?" Hannah asked. She was sitting at the marble bar in Maggie's kitchen, watching her friend pace back and forth. In less than five days, Reilly and Addie were traveling to Washington with J.D., who would deliver them into the hands of Judith Hudson.

"You do realize what you've agreed to do?" Maggie asked.

"Absolutely. I agreed to a week all to myself." Hannah raised her arms, put both hands on her heart, and looked up at the sky with an exaggerated smile. "Travis is going fishing, which is a cover for a week of drinking with his buddies, and my daughter is going with your daughter to spend a week with horses—her dream come true, by the way. So, what's the big deal?" She dropped her arms and shrugged.

"The big deal is they will be staying with my mother."

"So, what's she going to do? Make them sleep in the barn? Feed them hay?"

"No, she doesn't have a barn."

"Then where does she keep the horses?"

"She boards them at Blue Ridge Stables. That means the girls will be supervised there—that's where I learned to ride."

"Of course, you ride." Hannah smiled. "Let's see, you ride horses and ski and—wait! Ice skate?"

Maggie laughed. "A little."

"I knew it! What else have you hidden from me? How about—oh, I know, ballroom dancing?"

"Okay, okay." Maggie laughed. "I won't say any more about the girls going to my mother's."

"Look, Maggie. I have finally realized my dream of going back to school and my first semester of classes starts soon. The girls and husbands will be gone for a whole week. That sounds like a slice of heaven to me."

"Have I told you how proud of you I am?"

"Only a million times."

"I do have one question, though. How did you talk J.D. into taking the girls?"

Maggie made a *hump* sound through her nose. "Actually, he suggested it. He's still paying penance for the adoption fiasco."

Hannah said, "It's a beautiful day. We should be outside enjoying it." She grabbed Maggie's hand and pulled her out the door.

"Do you want to go swimming? I can—"

"Who wants a pool when you've got a creek?" Hannah giggled and took off running across the lawn.

"Wait for me!" Maggie ran after her. Her feet glided over the freshly mowed grass. When she got to the brook, Hannah was already there—bent at the waist with her hands on her knees—laughing in between gasps for breath. She said, "I am so out of shape!"

"You!" Maggie panted. "I barely made it alive!" She held her stomach with both hands.

"Come on, kick off your shoes. We're going in."

"No, you go. I'm fine."

"Oh, no. We're both wading in the creek!" Hannah grabbed Maggie's hand and pulled her to the water.

"Wait! My shoes!"

"Better kick 'em off! You're going in."

Maggie pulled off her sneakers. The friends clasped hands, looked at each other, and stepped into the water. They opened their mouths wide, but no sound escaped, and then a collective shriek rose followed by, "C—c—COLD!" Maggie turned to scramble out of the water, but Hannah was too fast for her. "Oh, no you don't." She held Maggie's hand and pulled her into deeper water.

"Oh, stop! This is freezing."

"I know. Isn't it awesome?" Hannah took another step and the water went half-way up her calves. "Come on Maggie. It's deeper over here and there's a nice big flat rock to stand on."

"No thanks, I'll stay right here."

Hannah dipped her fingers in the water and flicked it at Maggie. "Chicken."

"Who are you calling chicken?"

"You." Hannah put both of her hands in the water and cupped them like she was going to throw water on Maggie.

Maggie put her hands on her hips. "Hannah Lively. Don't. You. Dare."

Hannah laughed. "Are you sure you don't want to come over here where the water is deeper?"

"I'm sure."

Hannah raised her cupped hands until all of the water poured out. "Okay, if you're sure..."

Before Maggie could reply, Hannah started splashing her as fast as her arms could move. Maggie shrieked and stepped away from Hannah. "Stop it!"

"Make me."

Hannah splashed Maggie, mercilessly. The water rose in the air where it hung suspended in the sunlight before raining down on her. Each time the cold water hit her skin, Maggie shrieked and writhed. She dipped her hands in the water. "Two can play at this game, sister." She flung water toward Hannah, but most of it missed her.

"Is that the best you got?" Hannah put her hands on her hips. "If you stopped trying to shield yourself with one hand and splash with the other, you might actually hit me. You need to use both hands—watch." Hannah splashed Maggie right in the chest.

Maggie scooped up water and threw it at Hannah, hitting her in the chest. She picked up speed and water pelted Hannah. "Take that!"

Water arched in the air and splattered down upon them. Amid shrieks and peals of laughter, Hannah and Maggie hurled handfuls of water. Neither saw who was striding across the lawn toward them.

Maggie knew something was wrong when Hannah froze. She wheeled around and almost lost her footing, so she put her arms straight out to balance herself. For a moment, she looked like a giant wet bird, flapping its wings.

J.D. looked Maggie up and down, taking in her wild hair and wet clothes, not to mention the water running down her arms and legs. He stood with hands on his hips—his crisp dress shirt blinding in the sun. He was cool and polished. The monogramed cuffs of his long-sleeved shirt weren't even turned back. His dark blue tie was knotted perfectly at his throat. He said, "Margaret, you have a telephone call," and then turned without acknowledging Hannah and strode toward the house.

Hannah came up beside Maggie. For a moment, they stared at J.D.'s retreating back. Then Maggie stepped out of the water and picked up her shoes. "I'll be back," she said.

Maggie took the call in the kitchen. While she talked, she pulled a handful of paper towels off the rack and dried herself. She knew J.D. was standing behind her, so when she hung up she said, "It was the Children's Cancer Center calling to confirm Addie's yearly check-up."

"That's all. That's all you've got to say?" J.D. walked around the bar so he could face her.

"That's all they said."

"You know I'm not talking about the damn phone call! Care to explain your ridiculous behavior?"

"No."

J.D. crossed his arms over his chest. "I find you playing in the brook like a damn hillbilly with your hillbilly friend, and you have nothing to say? Thank God we don't have any neighbors." He snorted. "For God's sake, Margaret, we have a pool. Why didn't you just go swimming?" When Maggie refused to comment, J.D. placed his hands on the bar and leaned toward his wife with an exaggerated stare.

As quick and precise as a striking snake, Maggie grabbed J.D.'s tie and yanked so hard his arms flew out from his body and his chest hit the bar. An *oof* sound burst from him. His face went from quick anger to surprise to something that Maggie couldn't identify. Then she realized it was fear. The kind of fear a man feels when he's facing a worthy foe.

Maggie did not loosen her grip. In an exaggerated mountain accent she said, "Well, you know us hillbillies. We like to hunt crawdads in the creek. Then we'll catch us some frogs and fry up their legs—so good with moonshine."

She let go of J.D.'s tie, and he stepped back and smoothed his tie. "What has gotten into you?" he said. "Is it this woman? I know her daughter is Addie's friend, but you don't have to spend all of your time with her. Why don't you go to D.C. with me and see some of your old friends?"

"Friends?"

"Yes, Margaret, your friends in D.C. are always asking about you."

Maggie shook her head. "Hannah is the first true friend I've ever had. I can be myself with her. She's smart and talented and she makes me laugh. But most of all, she likes me for *me*." She jabbed her chest with her pointer finger. "Not because I have the right last name, or how much money I have, or what I might be able to do for her."

"Please, Margaret," J.D. said in his most conciliatory voice. "With the election in November, I want to make sure we put forth the best impression."

Maggie sighed. "Of course, the election." She turned to go, but J.D. grabbed her arm. She looked at his hand and back at his face. "I just told you something about me—about how I feel—and all you can think about is the election. Have no fear, I won't do anything to cause you to lose the election. Now let go of me."

J.D. dropped his hand. "I don't understand you anymore. I thought you were happy that I was running for Congress. I could actually do something for these people. Hell, I could be like that West Virginia Congresswoman Lana Ryan. Those people worship that woman."

Maggie went to the door but stopped before opening it. She said, "Thank goodness these hillbillies have *you*. And thank goodness you can do something for *these* people because I consider them *my* people." She saw his eyes shift to her bare feet. "And yes, I am *not* wearing shoes."

Back outside, Maggie took a deep breath and tried to calm down. She shaded her eyes and looked toward the brook. Hannah sat on the ground with her feet in the water. Maggie looked down at her feet and wiggled her bare toes in the grass. The sun made it feel like warm velvet. She started for the brook.

Hannah looked up when Maggie's shadow fell over her. "Hey, you don't have on any shoes."

"Nope, I thought I might want to wade in the creek, again."

Hannah smiled. "So, is everything okay?"

"Yes, the phone call was to confirm Addie's yearly doctor's appointment." Maggie plopped down next to Hannah.

"I wasn't worried about who called."

Maggie pulled her knees up to her chest and wrapped her arms around them. She laid her head on top of her knees. "No worries. J.D. just thinks I've lost my mind, and he's afraid a crazy wife will cost him the election."

"Oh, yeah?"

"Yeah."

"Well, if that's all."

They sat amid the hum of bees and the call of birds. A bluebird landed on the grass and sized them up before flying away, making them laugh.

"Hannah?"

"Hmm?"

"J.D. says I've changed."

"You have."

Maggie grinned. "Well, thank God." She lay back next to Hannah and eased her feet into the cold water. "Ahh, heavenly."

Maggie let all the tension from her confrontation with J.D. leave her. When she raised herself on one elbow, she saw her friend's eyes were closed. "Hannah?"

"Hum?"

"What *are* we going to do with a week without the girls? Want to plan a shopping trip or maybe a few days at a spa?"

"I've got a better idea."

While Addie and Reilly were experiencing the city, Maggie and Hannah snapped half-runner beans, canned tomatoes, made jams and jellies, and learned how to use herbs to smudge a house. They didn't even bother to go home, but spent the week at Granny's, sharing the bedroom that Reilly and Addie used when they spent the night. It had the palest of blue walls and gleaming wood floors. The antique twin beds had white iron headboards in elaborate scrolled designs, and Granny had put feather-mattresses on top of the regular ones, so at night, Maggie sank into comfort so complete she slept surrounded by delicious softness and the scent of drying sage and lavender. The beds were covered with log cabin quilts, made by Granny, in shades of brown, blue, and yellow. When the sun came through the windows, the yellow curtains ignited with a saffron glow. Maggie had never slept better in her life.

As the week went on, Granny Zee's anticipation for her upcoming family reunion grew, and Maggie found herself caught-up in the excitement. Maggie assumed the reunion would be in a venue where weddings and such celebrations took place until Hannah pointed out that it was going to be in their family cemetery in West Virginia.

On the day before the reunion, Maggie and Hannah were peeling and slicing a basket of June apples when Granny Zee joined them. Hannah said, "Granny, why don't you tell Maggie about the family reunion?"

Granny Zee picked up an apple and a paring knife and began her story.

"I remember going when I was a girl. I don't know exactly when it started, but I do recall it was after the Great War and before WWII. We didn't call it a reunion then, we just all met together at the family graveyard to dress the graves when the circuit-preacher came. After the preaching, we'd have dinner on the ground—some of the best eating—I can still taste Mama's blackberry dumplings."

Granny looked off into the distance. Her hand reached for another apple like a blind person, feeling around the bowl until she grasped one. She continued.

"Now, in those days, a lot of places in these mountains didn't have a preacher or even a church building, so beginning in the spring, a circuit-preacher went from place to place on horseback, holding services in places that had none. They also held a service for those who had died since they had last come through. Folks called that funeralizing. Today's funerals are nothing like the ones when I was a girl. Back then, the body was prepared for burial by the women while the men hand-dug the grave. The coffin was made by a family member or neighbor who was handy with tools, and the women lined it with cloth or a funeral quilt—a quilt made especially for burying.

"If the person didn't die at home, the body was brought back there. If a family owned a clock, it was stopped at the time of death, and any mirrors were covered. Often pennies or nickels were placed over the closed eyes of the dead. Most houses were built with one window or door big enough to slide a coffin into the front room of the house.

"A wake was held before burial. People came from all around and the women brought food. Since there was no minister available, there was no actual service. Somebody might read the 23rd Psalm or say a prayer, but most people were there to pay their respects and make sure the devil didn't take the soul of the one who died. People believed the soul didn't leave the body until twenty-four hours after death. The family set watch over the dead to help ease them into the next world.

"Women were supposed to cry over the dead while the men stayed in the background. The men were usually outside passing around moonshine, but it was most times some of the men who stayed all night and set with the body. The body was usually buried right-quick, especially in the summertime.

"What we're going to do is meet at the Ryan Family Cemetery in Creekside, West Virginia, and all the descendants of Brigid O'Reilly Ryan and James Thomas Ryan are invited. This is my mother's side of the family. We'll fellowship, eat, and then the women will dress the graves. My great-grandmother was Mary Kathryn Ryan, who married Adam Murray. She was my Granny Zee's mother, and when Granny Zee married John Winn, they came over on this side of the mountain to live and the others stayed in West Virginia. It's been more than ten years since I've been over there. Thank you both for taking me."

The morning of the reunion, the sky was streaked with the grayish pink of mouse feet. Granny Zee wore her best dress, a navy-blue shift dress that was completely plain except for a row of tiny pink flowers around the neckline. Her only jewelry was a strand of Irish freshwater pearls that she said came to her at her mother's death. She wore her walking shoes and told Maggie and Hannah they should do the same. Maggie was surprised to see her climb into the SUV with her gathering bag, but then, they were after all, headed for the mountains.

Hannah and Maggie loaded the food: fried chicken, chicken and dumplings, a pot of fresh green beans, two apple cobblers, and a giant box of homemade breads—loaves, rolls, and gingerbread biscuits. The heavenly scents filled the car.

Maggie thought she was accustomed to curvy roads until they crossed into McDowell County, West Virginia. Hannah was driving Maggie's all-wheel-drive vehicle because Granny Zee had warned the road to the cemetery was steep and unpaved, but Maggie couldn't imagine it being any worse than the curvy roadway. After a few hairpin curves, she discovered she was wrong.

The trip took two hours with the last measure being a narrow road that climbed higher and higher until it reached the top of the mountain. Maggie thought the mountains surrounding Coal Valley were beautiful, but this vista was the most incredible thing she had ever seen. She got out of the car in a trance, inhaling the earth scented air, and a burden she didn't know she was carrying left her.

A troop of people greeted Granny and Hannah, and Maggie slipped away into the cemetery. A large plot of flat land sloped upward until it became part of the mountainside. The flatter section was fenced with chain link, and a wooden sign with hand-lettering announced Ryan Family Cemetery. A *woo* of wind came down the mountain and the grass around the tombstones rippled like the ocean does miles from the shore. Maggie was drawn to the gigantic oak tree at the cemetery's center. It must have been a hundred years older than any grave there, with a massive trunk and gnarled giant limbs like deformed arms that twisted and turned, some touching the ground. Maggie placed her hand on the trunk and looked up at leaves with thumb-shaped lobes, waving in the wind. She was deliciously dizzy.

"There you are," Hannah said. "Come meet the family."

The day passed in a blur of "now, who are you?" and "I'm the granddaughter, cousin, sister, aunt, uncle, and brother of." When the food was spread out and the meal begun, Maggie piled her plate with fried chicken, fried green tomatoes, potato salad, and green beans and corn straight from the garden. She ate amid the crowd, savoring the sing-song accents of mountain speech, the rise and fall of laughter, and the sounds of children at play. She swore she wasn't going to eat dessert until Hannah brought her a fried apple pie—a southern delicacy she would never forget.

After the meal was put away, flower arrangements, cleaning supplies, and hand clippers were produced. Like a colony of busy ants, the women went to work on the graves. Maggie and Hannah walked around watching and reading the headstones, some so weathered it was hard to read them.

"Who's that tall woman with Granny?" Maggie asked. "I've seen her shaking hands with everyone like she's running for office."

Hannah laughed. "That's because she's probably running for reelection. She's a Congresswoman. Come, I'll introduce you."

An attractive middle-aged woman with a broad smiling face and a shoulder-length sensible bob of auburn hair threaded with gray was talking to Granny Zee, who was saying, "I haven't seen you since my Emma died."

The woman turned warm brown eyes on Hannah and Maggie. She had a small round nose, but her lips were full and surrounded by smile-wrinkles like double parenthesis. Her minimal make-up accented her high cheekbones. She said, "Hello, Hannah," extending her hand. "Granny Zee and I were just talking about old times."

Granny introduced Maggie to Lana Ryan. Maggie said, "It's nice to meet you Congresswoman Ryan. My husband speaks highly of you."

The Congresswoman's smile didn't waver, but her eyes narrowed slightly. "I have met your husband. I believe he's running for Congress." Maggie nodded.

Granny Zee stepped forward. "Now, let's not talk politics." She chuckled and pointed to the pink granite tombstone that bore the names Philo Ryan, 1871 – 1952, beloved husband and father, and Tilly Mae Ryan, 1878 – 1960, beloved wife and mother. Granny said, "Let's talk about your folks. They were fine people. Did I ever tell you I was there the night you were born? I remember it like it happened yesterday. You were an answer to their prayers."

1924

Chapter 14

THE WOMAN STOOD IN the shadows beside the barrels of meal, flour, and brown sugar. She looked like a shadow herself, as if there was nothing under the faded brown dress but air. Emmaline Ryan approached her and said, "Hello, Vadie. It's nice to see you."

Eyes dark as coal focused on Emmaline and then turned to Zelda.

Zelda tried not to stare at this waif-like creature, but she couldn't help it. At first glance she looked young, even Zelda's own age, but then she spoke, and it was evident most of her teeth were missing. When she smiled and lines appeared at the corners of her eyes and tracked across her face, it became clear she was anything but young.

The woman brushed past Zelda on her way out of the store, and a chill tickled her neck—like the trick her sister, Eleanor, had liked to play on her of trailing a feather along the back of her neck.

While her mother made purchases, Zelda slipped out the door. The store's outside was freshly painted a dark green. A red sign nailed next to the door announced in bold white letters: Tiller Mercantile. The store front window had red checked curtains tied back on either side, so passersby could see Mrs. Tiller's presentation of goods, which today were sewing notions and gingham fabric.

It was a lazy-cloud day with wide blue skies, and Zelda had to shade her eyes from the sun to see Vadie. Zelda stepped out into the dusty road and watched Vadie come to the end of town and disappear in the direction of the King Coal company houses that spilled from the mouth of Wild Boar Holler like a handful of corn flung on the ground for the chickens.

Granny Zee and Mama had been known to go doctoring in the coal camp, and Zelda had once gone with Mama to deliver a baby. Last year, the mines had got themselves a new doctor and put up a building they called a hospital, so Daddy said there was no reason for them to go there anymore. Daddy didn't like the coal camp. He said it was because some of the people were not like mountain folk—who knew how to treat their families and animals. He said some of them didn't speak much English, had odd ways, and didn't even eat the same food as them. They even had strange religions. Mama reminded him her people were not far from being among those "strangers" from another land.

Fear. That was what made people dislike others, and Mama said it was a sin to think somebody was bad just because they were not the same as you. She said it was wrong to judge people because they looked and spoke different. She said there were many, down-right mean mountain people, and Daddy knew it. She told Zelda that she believed the real reason Daddy didn't like the coal camp was because it was by the grace of God he had kept them out of there. They had learned how to live off the land, and even though it was a hard life, they were not beholden to anyone.

Too many families had left the mountain and moved to the camp, so the men could work in the mines. Daddy said the lucky ones stayed on the mountain, even if the men walked anywhere from five to ten miles back and forth every day. That way, they could still farm and keep chickens and some livestock for when the mines quit working. Mama said it wasn't the men so much as their women who didn't want to leave the mountain.

The mines were known to close down for weeks, and sometimes months, and the people lived by charging food at the company store. That way, the miners stayed in debt to the company. When King Coal bought up the mines, it started paying its workers in scrip, tokens that were stamped like coins. The largest value they issued was a dollar. The scrip could only be used at the Company Store, so the people couldn't trade in town at stores like Tiller's Mercantile.

The coal camp houses were box-like and plain with a small front porch. They all looked the same—square whitewashed buildings with a door in the center flanked on both sides by a small cloudy window. They were built close together, either along the creek bank, like a train had derailed and left the empty cars behind, or crowded on the hillside like puffs of dust-colored clouds.

A motor car beeped, and Zelda jumped out of the road. She had been so intent on watching Vadie that she hadn't heard it. Zelda still couldn't get used to automobiles. Most belonged to the King Coal executives who lived in the big houses just out of town in the fertile bottomland. King Coal had come to the valley during the Great War and bought up the little independent mines and people's mineral rights. They had dubbed the emerging town Coal Valley. Now, there were shiny motor cars and big houses, a new church building, and the town would soon have new brick sidewalks.

Thanks to the mines, Hanson had worked steadily, building those houses, and her daddy was one of the carpenters on his crew. Hanson had made enough money to buy the materials, and it had taken almost two years, but with the help of her daddy, he had managed to build them a house. It was finally finished, so they were getting married June twenty-first—the Summer Solstice.

It was Granny Zee's idea for them to marry on what she said the Irish called Meitheamh, the "Light of Summer." She said they would be blessed if they married on one of Ireland's sacred Celtic holidays. Granny Zee had taught Zelda that the longest day of the year was important to the old Irish who knew it marked the turning of the year—the days would from here on shorten. After Meitheamh came the sacred holiday, Samhain, that began on the eve of October thirty-first. The third sacred day was Bealtaine, May first, or what the Irish called the start of the summer season. Granny Zee said there were other feast days the Irish celebrated, but Meitheamh, Samhain, and Bealtaine, were spirit days. Only on these three days was the veil between this world and the spirit world lifted, allowing spirits and the faeries to cross over from the Otherworld. Granny said if they married on Meitheamh, they would have the blessings of the spirits and the wee folk.

Zelda realized the motorcar had stopped in the middle of the road. The unfamiliar bittersweet smell of gasoline made her lightheaded, so she hurried away. She had almost reached the sidewalk when she heard her name. She turned to see someone inside the car was waving, and then the door opened, and Isabelle stepped out. She was wearing a sunshine yellow dress in the new style—sleeveless with a drop waist and straight skirt that hit just above the ankle. It had touches of embroidery in browns and greens around the scooped neckline and on the wide embroidered sash that tied at the hips. On Isabelle's tall thin frame, the dress was perfect.

"Sis!" Isabelle called, hurrying toward Zelda. Isabelle had a small brown velvet purse with gold beaded fringe over one wrist. As she walked, the fringe on it swung back and forth in a sunbeam, hypnotizing Zelda.

Zelda hugged her sister, inhaling the berry-spice of her perfume. She said, "You look beautiful!"

"Do you like my dress? It's new." Isabelle twirled, and her long curls bounced on her shoulders. "What are you doing standing in the middle of the road? Is Mama in town?"

Zelda laughed. "She's in Tiller's getting the lace we ordered for my wedding dress."

"My little sister is getting married!" Isabelle put her arm around Zelda's waist as they walked to Tiller's.

"Are you and Bill coming to the wedding?"

"Of course, I'm coming." Isabelle paused and looked down at her feet. Her voice faltered on the word "but," then she regrouped. "Bill will probably be out of town on business."

The sisters found Emmaline Ryan coming out of Tiller's, her basket filled with packets wrapped in brown paper and tied with twine. Her smile faltered when she saw Isabelle, but she quickly called it back. She kissed Isabelle on both cheeks and said, "Sweetie, how lovely you look."

"Thank you, Mama," Isabelle said. "I didn't know you and Zelda were coming to town."

An awkward pause followed, broken when the automobile appeared that Isabelle had gotten out of earlier. Isabelle said, "Well, I'm happy to see you, but I must go. Bill and I are going to dinner with his father. Something to do with business."

She turned away, but her mother's voice stopped her cold. "Your son lost his first tooth."

Isabelle whirled around, making the fringe on her purse flash in the sunlight. "Oh, my," she said. "Of course, how is Emerson Junior?"

"He misses his mama."

A quick frown followed by a smile too big and bright revealed how Mama's comment had struck home. Isabelle squared her shoulders. "Give him a kiss for me," she said, "I'll see him in a few days."

"When exactly?" Mama asked.

Isabelle stood her ground. "In a few days. It will depend on Bill's schedule."

Zelda saw one last flash of fringe as her sister hurried to the car. Her husband gave them a slight wave and pulled away. The automobile's exhaust rose like a black cloud then splintered into gray puffs.

On the way up the mountain, neither Zelda nor Emmaline spoke. They were thinking about Isabelle and the person she had become since marrying William Alexander Stockton III, son and heir to the King Coal fortune.

When the Spanish Influenza finally disappeared at the end of 1918, the Ryan family had thought they could put the horror of that year behind them. Like the other families on Rock House Mountain, they had lost a loved one, but other families had lost many more. There were families like the Murphy's that had been completely wiped out—first the six children, one-by-one, then the mother and grandfather on the same day, a week later the father died, followed a few days later by the grandmother.

Isabelle had taken the loss of Eleanor especially hard, and when she found out, in February 1919, that her husband had been killed in France, she had gone into early labor. A tiny boy was born the next day, and at first, it looked like he wasn't going to make it. Granny Zee had fashioned a box lined with lamb's wool for him and placed it in the cook stove's bread warmer—an iron box at the back of the stove. Here, baby Emerson, named for his father, had stayed warm. Too weak to suckle, Isabelle had expressed milk, and Granny Zee and Mama took turns feeding him with a dropper.

Zelda remembered Granny Zee and Mama worrying that Isabelle would die with the baby, but spring came early to the mountains that year and they rallied. But Isabelle had shied away from her son, like she feared getting attached in case something happened to him. She refused to nurse him and would go off, leaving him with whomever was available. And then, in September, she had discovered the coal company office was looking for a new secretary. She was hired on the spot.

No amount of pleading and tears could change Isabelle's mind. She insisted she needed the money for Emerson Junior, but her desperation had nothing to do with love. In truth, she had a fierce need to get away from him. After Christmas, she took a room with the Lundy sisters, two old maids who lived in a two-story house on the edge of town. The family didn't see Isabelle again until she came home for Emerson Junior's first birthday, and by then she had caught the eye of the boss's son.

Zelda and Emmaline passed a patch of bee balm, soft lavender puff balls arranged in nature's bouquets. A quivering dragonfly darted from bunch to bunch. Queen Anne's lace spread upwards toward the sun, and Zelda thought it more beautiful than any wedding gown she could wear or even imagine. She sighed.

Mama asked, "What are you thinking about?"

Zelda surprised herself when she said, "Who was the woman you spoke to in Tiller's store? The one you called Vadie?"

"I doctored Vadie's mother before she died," Mama said. "It was a sad family. They lived up Maple Leaf Holler, and as soon as the boys were old enough they left home. The father well-nigh sold the girls—there were three of them—to old men for liquor. Vadie got the worst of them all, Snow Williams, a man as mean as a striped snake."

"Snow?" Zelda asked.

"He's been white-haired as long as anybody could remember, so he was called Snow. I suspect most people, like me, long-forgot his given name."

Mama turned so she could glance at Zelda. "What makes you ask about Vadie?"

Zelda shook her head. "I don't know. When she went by me in the store I got a bad feeling."

They passed the new turn-in Hanson had cleared, so they could get a wagon or even a motorcar up to their new house, and Zelda swelled with pride. She could see the stone chimneys, tall and tan in the afternoon sun, and she imagined wisps of smoke rising up to the realm of birds. Beyond was the mountain's blue-green backbone. To her, there was not a more beautiful place, nor a finer house in town or on Rock House Mountain.

The house was built on Cece's homeplace. This pleased Zelda, even though Cece's spirit had disappeared from her life five years since. She would never forget the day she found Cece's doll, Patty Cake, left by the crumbling fireplace. She knew Cece was gone because the scent of lilacs that always followed Cece's spirit had disappeared.

It was Granny Zee who knew the meaning of the lilac bushes, five in all, planted in a row about two hundred yards from the old house. Granny Zee believed they were planted by Cece's mother because in those days, when a woman had a miscarriage, it was tradition to bury the body and plant a lilac bush over it. If Cece was the only surviving child of those poor people, no wonder they left the mountain after Cece died. It was also possible, Granny Zee had said, that one of those lilacs might have been planted over Cece's grave. When Hanson was building the house, he was careful not to disturb any of the ground around the bushes. Zelda had taken to tending to those bushes like they were on sacred ground.

Then two weeks before the wedding, Hanson almost called it off.

It started with a feeling of dread that came over Zelda as the night wrapped the mountain in dark sheets. Sleep brought no relief. Zelda woke again and again, falling end over end in her dreams. She woke pressed under its weight like a heavy fist in the middle of her back. At breakfast, she begged off her silence to a headache, so Mama went off to make her visits to pregnant women and new mothers without a fuss.

Hanson and Daddy had left at daylight to brick the town's new sidewalks, but her apprehension wasn't about either of them, of that Zelda was sure. Whatever it was, it was getting close. She closed her eyes and tried to feel it, taste it, smell it, but all she could do was remember that sensation of falling. She went to the glass jars ready for the day's jelly-making, all lined up on a table under the window. The polished glass caught the sun streaming in, making the jars glow. Zelda stared, certain if she put her hand on the glass, it would burn her. She was still staring when Granny Zee came in carrying a basket of fruit.

They were washing wild strawberries and grapes when outside someone shouted, "Granny! Granny Zee!"

Zelda and Granny hurried out on the porch, but Zelda didn't recognize the red-headed boy coming up the hill, riding bareback on a mule, holding reigns made from rope.

Granny said, "That's Joeson McCall from over Backbone Ridge. I knew something bad was coming. I spilled the salt this morning and my chair fell over when I got up from the table." She turned to Zelda. "Have you had any dreams?"

Zelda nodded. "For the past two nights I dreamed I was falling."

"I fear this," Granny said.

Tears had mixed with dirt on Joeson's face leaving streaks like war paint, but even that couldn't hide the freckles. It was hard to tell the age of this skinny boy with wide bony shoulders. What wasn't covered by shirtless filthy overalls was covered by patches of freckles. Wide-set mud-colored eyes blinked back tears under brows and lashes so light they were barely visible. Joeson slid off the mule and stumbled toward Granny Zee who had come down the porch steps to meet him.

He wailed, "You got to help Jon Jon! They're saying he killed Missy Campbell. They took and locked him up! Jon Jon never hurt nobody in his whole life!" He grabbed Granny's arm. "Please, you got to come."

Granny wrapped her arms around the sobbing boy. She looked over his head at Zelda and said, "Saddle the horses."

When Zelda came back with the horses, Granny Zee was writing a note, explaining they were called over to Backbone Ridge to Joseph McCall's. Zelda added a note to Hanson saying simply, "Granny needs me. I love you."

Bit by bit, piece by piece, the whole story tumbled out of Joeson. The Campbells had a cabin not far from the McCall's. Missy Campbell, age seven, was the youngest of a passel of boys, and Jon McCall followed her around like a puppy. The two had been playmates since Missy could walk, and her name was one of the few words Jon had ever learned to say because, even though he was fifteen, Jon looked and acted like a small child. When they went off to play yesterday, like they did most days, Jon came back alone with blood on his shirt and hands.

Granny Zee explained to Zelda that Jon had Mongolism. He was short with stubby hands and feet, had a smallish head and short neck, his face was flat, and his eyes slanted up. His tongue and lips were over large, so that his tongue protruded from his mouth, and he had the mind of a child and always would.

"I remember well the night Jon was born," Granny Zee said. "He was born under a harvest moon that hung so large and golden in the sky it looked like you could pluck it like a peach off a tree. I didn't need a lantern that night because the mountains glowed with pearly light." She paused and looked up at the sky. "You know," she said, "the faeries favor those born under a harvest moon."

Granny had watched Jon grow into a sweet child without a mean bone in his body. She didn't believe he would hurt Missy, but she knew not everybody understood about Jon, and people were want to fear what they didn't understand.

"It's those damn-know-everything Scots. The Campbells—damn them." Granny Zee spat on the ground.

"Glad they're nothing like the Irish," Zelda muttered.

Chapter 15

ZELDA TILTED BACK HER head so she could see the sky over the brim of her hat. A cobalt cap stretched from mountain peak to mountain peak without a hint of cloud. Sweat trickled down her back, plastering her dress to her skin. She looked over at Joeson whose skinny ankles hung below the mule's belly. He had a young'un's smell—rust and the earth itself, mixed with sweat.

Backbone Ridge was splashed with midday sun when they arrived. People eyed them as they passed, grudgingly acknowledging Granny Zee who rode beside Joeson. It was obvious the news of Missy's disappearance had traveled fast, and people were taking sides.

They were met in the yard by Joeson's sobbing mother, Belle McCall. Tears streamed from deep-set brown eyes. Strands of yellowed-gray hair trailed from the bun at the nape of her neck. Her skin was sun-baked and wrinkled, giving her small body the look of a dried apple. The minute they got off their horses she grabbed Granny Zee. "They took him! Granny Zee they took my young'un. He never done a thing!"

"Where is he?" Granny Zee asked.

"Them Campbell boys locked him in their shed, saying if he don't tell them where she is they'll hang him!" She clutched at Granny Zee. "He don't talk but a few words! They know that, but they keep smacking him and telling him to talk!" The poor woman fell to her knees, sorrow so heavy her legs couldn't hold it up.

Granny asked, "Where's Joseph?" She knew that Belle McCall's older children were girls who had married and left Backbone Ridge, so it was just her husband, Joeson, and Jon Jon.

"He's gone to Welch to find the sheriff. They say he's over there about some coal miners fighting to unionize."

Granny Zee wasted no time. She and Zelda went straight to the Campbell's house and knocked on the door. A big gray cat, the color of smoke, sat at the edge of the Campbell's porch, watching them with solemn eyes the same color as its fur. Zelda shivered under its gaze and Granny noticed, but before she could comment, the door swung open and Elijah Campbell pointed a rifle at them.

Granny Zee slapped the rifle to the side and pushed past Elijah Campbell saying, "Don't you dare point that gun at me, Lije Campbell! What in the name of the good God is going on? Take me to that poor child right now! And he better not be hurt or there'll be hell to pay."

At the back of the room, a woman stood in the shadows. "Marie Campbell," Granny Zee called to her, "have you all lost your senses?"

The woman took a few steps toward them, then stopped. Granny Zee strode to her and took Marie Campbell's face in her hands, turning it to the side. "Well Lije, I see you still use your fists on your woman," she said.

"Aye," the man said, "she shoudna let my lass play with that idjit."

Granny wheeled around and put her hands on her hips. "Why are you and everybody else not out looking for your daughter?"

"You mean my daughter's body! That idjit came out of the woods covered in blood!"

Marie came to her husband and tried to take his arm, but he shrugged her off. She said, "They took to the woods right where Jon came out with that cat. They was out all night. Lije just come back. Her brothers is still out there."

Lije said, "There wasn't no trace of her. That half-whit is gonna pay."

Granny Zee said, "Marie. Lije. You don't know that—"

"I do," Zelda interrupted.

They all turned to look at Zelda. She held Missy's doll to her chest. She said, "Missy is *not* dead."

Lije took a step back and his face blanched. Marie whimpered, "Yes, please Jesus."

Lije looked from Zelda to Granny Zee. He said, "I heard-tell she was *taibhsear*."

"It's true," Granny Zee said. "She is a seer."

"Don't talk about me like I'm not standing right here," Zelda said. She threw back her shoulders and drew herself up to her full height. "Call me what you want, but I'm telling you that your daughter is still alive. But we have to hurry."

Silence split the room in half—Granny Zee and Zelda on one side—the Campbells on the other. Then Granny stepped forward. "Take me to Jon."

Granny Zee sent Zelda for Belle McCall while she went with Lije to the shed. He unlocked the shed and walked away without looking back.

Jon Jon was in a corner, sitting in his own excrement. Bruises and scratches covered his face and arms. His bottom lip had been split and dried blood covered his chin. When his mother ran into the shed, he held out his arms and whimpered, "Ma-ma."

Tears burned Zelda's eyes. She stood in the doorway while Granny and Belle tried to get Jon on his feet and out of the shed before Lije changed his mind. A sudden breeze came down the mountains. The kind you see trifling the leaves at the top before you feel it down below. Dizziness swept over Zelda with the same sensation of falling she had felt the last two nights in her dreams. She grabbed at the shed door, and the rough wood pricked her skin. She looked down at her hands and saw the gray cat sitting at her feet, gazing up at her with unblinking eyes.

"Holy Jesus," she gasped. The creature didn't even look to her like a cat but rather like some sort of imitation. "Shoo, go," she said and held up her foot like she was going to kick it. But the cat sat unmoving, its unblinking gaze fixed on her.

Granny Zee and Belle managed to get Jon to the door. He smelled like rotted death, and Zelda had to step back and cover her nose with her hand. Between sobs, Jon said, "Missy boo boo."

The cat imitation, as Zelda thought of it, followed Jon. Granny Zee and his mother pulled and pushed him toward home. When Jon stopped, the cat imitation stopped and waited patiently for him to continue. When Jon disappeared into the cabin, the cat imitation sat down on the porch where it could watch the door.

A short time passed before Granny Zee came out of the McCall's cabin and went to her horse, where she retrieved her walking stick and a rope. As always, she took up her gathering bag. She stopped when she saw the cat and crouched to stroke its fur. It looked up at her with its unblinking stare. When she stood, it stood, and together they came to Zelda.

"Belle says Jon says 'boo boo' when something hurts him, so he's trying to tell us Missy's hurt," Granny Zee said. "When Jon didn't come home for supper last night, his mother went a-ways into the woods to call for him and that's when she saw that cat coming with Jon following it."

Zelda said, "Is that so strange? I mean they probably played with that cat all the time."

"No, that's just it. Belle says she's never seen it before. Besides, Belle said that Missy was the one who led the way into and out of the woods. Jon couldn't find his way."

Zelda looked down, but the cat imitation was gone. "Granny, where did it go?"

Granny Zee turned. "Look!" She pointed. "It's over there."

Cat imitation stood atop a large rock at the opening of a copse of trees, it's tail twitching back and forth with impatience. Clearly, it waited for them. Together, they followed cat imitation into the forest. It matched its pace to theirs, so they could keep up, but clearly, it was in the lead.

It was cooler in the forest, the air as fresh as a newborn's breath. The light sifted through the dense trees in darts and dashes. After about a half hour, they heard faint voices calling Missy's name, but they were off to the west. The cat had turned east toward the rocks that gave Backbone Ridge its name.

Granny Zee whispered, "Lord, please let us find her."

Zelda said, "She's alive."

Granny Zee stopped and took her granddaughter's hand. "She's alive," Zelda said with absolute conviction. "I know because I can't hear her. If she was dead, I would hear her spirit."

They followed the cat down a gully filled with rocks to a pile of shiny quartz pieces arranged in a neat circle. Inside the circle was a chipped dish filled with wilted wild strawberries and what looked like dried cream. The stones glittered in the sunlight. "Look," Granny Zee said, "the children made that."

The cat paused and looked back at them. At the bottom of the gully it turned again, leading them closer to a ledge that jutted out over a drop of about three feet to another stone ledge. A beautiful piece of quartz threaded with green and blue stripes stuck up out of the ground, but you had to go through a patch of brambles to get to it.

Granny Zee said, "They were trying to pull up that piece of pretty quartz. The brambles explain the scratches on Jon."

"And the blood," Zelda said. She managed to get through the brambles to the piece of quartz. "See," she pointed, "the brambles are broken. And you can see the dirt around the rock has been scraped back."

"She's close," Granny said.

Zelda called, "Missy! Missy!"

Cat imitation leapt past her and landed on the ledge below. It turned to her and stared.

Granny Zee said, "He's telling us she's down there."

Granny and Zelda called out, "Missy! Missy!"

A faint moan came from below, and the cat leapt again, disappearing beneath the ledge. Zelda lay down and scooted to the brink of the ledge so that her feet and legs dangled down. She kept inching backward until she got to the edge, and then she let go. She landed on the rock below her. She called, "Granny, I'm okay."

She stood up and spotted cat imitation amid a pile of rocks about a hundred yards below. Missy lay on her back about a foot from the rocks. "Missy! Missy!" Zelda yelled. The child lifted her head and tried to raise her arm.

"Granny, I see her! She's alive! I'm going to climb down to her."

"Be careful, child," Granny Zee called. "I'll get help."

Zelda pulled her skirt up between her legs and stuffed it in her waistband, fashioning make-shift trousers. Then, she half-crawled, half-scooted to Missy. She heard gun shots overhead and recognized the report of Granny Zee's pistol, signaling to the other searchers.

The child was barely conscious. Zelda took a flask of water out of her pocket and managed to get Missy to drink, all the while telling her that everything was going to be alright. She wet the hem of her skirt and wiped Missy's face. Missy whispered, "Jon Jon."

Zelda smiled at her. "Jon Jon is fine, my dear. He's home waiting for you." She stroked Missy's brow with one hand while gently feeling for injuries. Missy was scraped and scratched all over, especially her hands, and judging from its unnatural angle, her left arm was broken.

By the time Missy's brothers found them, Granny Zee had fashioned a sled out of branches and sticks. The men climbed down to Missy, and using the sled and Granny's rope, they pulled her up and out of the ravine. They carried her down the mountain toward home and soon met her parents. The first thing Missy said to them was, "Jon Jon tried to save me."

At the end of the forest, they met the coming darkness of a summer's night. Serenaded by the crickets and katydids' night-calling, they made their way to the Campbell's cabin. Inside, it smelled like fresh cornbread and fried cabbage, and Zelda's stomach rumbled. She realized she hadn't eaten but a biscuit, early that morning, but it would be awhile before she and Granny sat down at the Campbell's table.

First, they gave Missy a good going over, set and wrapped her broken arm, cleaned and put all-heal salve on her cuts and scratches, and bandaged her hands. All-heal was in bloom right now, and Granny and Zelda had already made two batches of the cooling salve.

Missy sipped chicken broth and some color came back to

her cheeks. She begged to see Jon Jon, and her father promised she could see him in the morning. When Missy went to sleep, Granny and Zelda were ushered into the kitchen where they were given heaping plates of cooked pork, fried cabbage, and cornbread with fresh-made butter. A plate piled high with sliced tomatoes and green onions was placed before them. Lije Campbell set a bottle of his best whisky on the table and poured both of them a glass.

They ate for a while in silence. Granny Zee knew it was hard for a man like Lije to own a mistake, so she said nothing when Lije started going on about how they hadn't looked for Missy on that side of the ridge because she was forbidden to play there. "I dinna think she would disobey me. She never has before," Lije said.

Granny Zee smiled. "Aye, Lije, not that you know of, anyway. In my experience, the best way to get a young'un to go to a place is to forbid them. Besides, them shiny pieces of quartz were too tempting."

"She's been bringing home some glossy rocks," Marie said. "She calls them faerie rocks. Says there's faeries in them woods, and she sings for them."

Zelda said, "Did you see the big gray cat that was hanging around here?"

Lije and Marie looked at them and both frowned. "What cat?" Lije said. "I don't keep no cats," Marie said.

Granny Zee and Zelda stayed the night and headed for home the next morning, but not before Granny Zee made sure Jon Jon and Missy were reunited. Missy said that when she tried to dig up the big pretty rock, she had stepped back too far and started to fall. She had clutched at the brambles and tried to hang on but they broke and she slid over the cliff. Jon Jon had tried to pull her up, but her bleeding hands were too slick for him to hold, so he had taken off his shirt and she had gripped it, but she couldn't hold on. She slid and tumbled down the mountain and then remembered nothing for a while. When she woke, it was night and the faeries were watching over her.

The next morning, cat imitation was nowhere to be seen. Granny Zee and Zelda rode out for home, and Granny Zee said they would not likely see it again. "Remember," she said, "Jon Jon was born under a harvest moon and the faeries favor those born such, but more than that, Jon Jon is pure goodness—pure love. One like him is born without the ability to hate or do wrong and the faeries know of his goodness."

"Granny," Zelda said, "did the faeries send the cat to guide Jon Jon?"

"I do believe the cat was a Sidhe. The Sidhe are faeries that love beauty and good. I believe Missy made that ring of quartz to please them and had left food offerings there. That, and Jon Jon's childlike goodness is why they sent the cat. The Sidhe are fallen angels who live in the woods. They are also often found near water. At Midsummer Eve, or any night there is a full moon, you can see them if you have a river rock with a hole worn in its center. You can't make the hole yourself. The hole has to be made natural, by the water, and even then the Sidhe are hard to see because they are very small and favor green tunics. It was your great-great gran, Brigid O'Reilly, who taught me about the Sidhe. She said they especially love music and adore to sing and dance."

Zelda thought this over. She said, "Missy did say she sang for them."

"Indeed," said Granny Zee. "But make no mistake, the Sidhe can do plenty devilment if they choose. They can wreck a garden overnight, so it's best not to anger them."

"How do you anger them?"

"By trespassing. Never disturb a faerie ring or faerie fort. And don't forget to offer them treats, especially on the harvest festivals."

They stopped once on their way down the mountain for Granny Zee to gather spider webs. A great patch of bushes was covered in twisted slips like white lace. Granny Zee took a twig and gently twirled the webs around and around her slender branch until she had a network of white that she would use to heal wounds. The whole time she spoke to the spiders, thanking them and assuring them their homes would be fixed again by nightfall.

When they got home, they found Emmaline finishing the last of the jelly making. Zelda washed up and helped her mother fill the last of the jars and set them in boiling water to seal. While they worked, Granny Zee recounted what had happened over on Backbone Ridge.

"I must say," Emmaline said, "Hanson was upset that you had gone."

Zelda's face flushed. "Upset. Why?"

Emmaline and Granny Zee exchanged looks. Emmaline said, "Your father said there was talk in town."

"What kind of talk?" Zelda asked.

"He came home at midday. He said two of Missy's brothers were in town talking about you."

"What did they say?"

Granny Zee came to Zelda and put her hands on her shoulders like she was trying to keep her from taking flight.

"They said, you used magic to find Missy," Emmaline said.

"Magic!" Zelda snorted. "What else did they say?"

Emmaline took Zelda's hand. "They called you a witch. And Hanson heard it. There was a fight."

"Holy God!" Zelda's hand flew to her throat. "Was Hanson hurt?"

"Not bad. Your father said it was the Campbell brothers against Hanson, and he whipped them both."

Zelda headed for the door. She threw over her shoulder, "I'm going to find Hanson."

He was at their new house, the house he had built for them. The house where they were going to begin their lives together. Zelda knew he would be there, just as she had known Missy Campbell wasn't dead.

Since the day she found Ruth Berger's baby hidden in the leaves, Zelda's life had changed, and the knowing had taken her over. But on this day of perfect June warmth, when the sky was a blue canopy over her head, the only thing she knew for sure was that one day she would be an old woman, stooped with life's burdens, living in this house alone. That was the hell of it—what she knew was just a part of the whole—it wasn't like a book in her head where she could turn the pages and see it all from beginning to end. This gift, or rather this bruise on her soul, was an entity apart from her control.

Hanson was sitting in the open doorway, legs splayed out before him. A sleeve had ripped away from his right shoulder and drops of blood had smeared his neck. The blood had come from his nose. It didn't appear broken but had taken a good smashing as had his left eye that bloomed blue and purple. Zelda dropped to her knees beside him. "Oh, Hanson. Are you bad hurt?"

He shook his head and looked down at the ground, his pale eyelashes fluttered in the afternoon sunlight. His blonde hair was streaked with sweat and dirt and plastered to his head save for a shock that stood straight up at the cowlick on his forehead. Zelda sat back and scooted so she was sitting next to him. She could see his hands, already rough from work, now with broken skin over bruised knuckles.

Neither saw the dragonfly flit from bush to bush nor smelled the heavy sweetness of honeysuckle basking in the sun. Both searched their hearts for the right words, but there was nothing that could be said without changing the future, so neither spoke. It was like the moment before a revelation that will change your fate. Until it is revealed, life goes on as it has every day with no hint that, tomorrow, you will be changed forever.

At last, Hanson sighed and laid his hand on top of Zelda's. "I thought I had reconciled myself to your," he hesitated, "gift, but when I heard him call you a witch, I couldn't abide it. I never thought you'd go off and climb all over a mountain to find a child and then be called a witch for it. I thought when we married you would stay home and make your healing remedies, and just be my wife."

"Oh, sweetheart," Zelda said, "I never hid from you who I am, or what I can do. You know I don't understand how or why I know these things, and why, for that matter, I don't know others. But what kind of person would I be if I never used my gift to help people?"

"I know you want to help people, but they were calling you a witch!" Hanson struggled up and looked down on Zelda. "They said you was like your Granny—that all the women in your family danced with the devil."

A surge of anger pushed Zelda up and she faced Hanson. "I don't give a good damn what people say! I helped Granny Zee save a little girl and keep those Campbells from stringing up a half-wit. And I will do it again tomorrow. If you can't live with that, then tell me now, before we wed."

On the third day after the fight between Hanson and the Campbells, Granny Zee found Zelda weeding the garden like a mad woman. She had just come from delivering Mary Jane Smith's eighth baby—a girl—the only child Mary Jane had born alive. Mary Jane lived in the coal camp, but she had come to Rock House Mountain to her homeplace where her old-maid sister, Hattie Mae, still lived. Hattie Mae was a superstitious Bible-thumper who called Granny Zee a witch. She'd rather Mary Jane's baby had died like all the others at the hands of the coal camp doctor, than let her birth it. Granny Zee knew what to do when a baby was born blue, and sometimes it worked and sometimes it didn't. But she didn't just give it back to God without trying to save it.

Granny Zee's good mood vanished when she saw Zelda. Hanson had been gone three days and from the looks of things, he hadn't come back. She went to Zelda and started deadheading the marigold plants, dropping the dried blooms into her pocket. They planted marigolds throughout the garden to keep the bugs from eating the vegetables. The bitter pungent smell of marigolds filled the summer air. When other flowers falter at midsummer, the ever steadfast marigold blooms on. Even at harvest, they are still in the forefront, making it through the first frosts.

"He's gone," Zelda mumbled.

Granny looked up, her hands stilled over a bunch of golden marigolds like she was praying over them.

"I saw him get on a train. In my dream," Zelda said. She sat back on her heels and wiped sweat from her face.

Granny went to Zelda. She sat down and pulled her onto her lap like she had done hundreds of times when Zelda was a little girl. Zelda melted into her and sobbed.

Granny Zee held her and let her cry. When she quieted, Zelda sat back, her face streaked with dirt, her eyes bloodshot and puffy. She sighed. "I should go talk to Mama." She stood, and Granny Zee raised her arm over her head. Granny said, "Help your poor old Granny get up."

Zelda took Granny's hand but before she gave it a pull, she gave a gargled scream, dropped it, and ran. Granny Zee struggled upright in time to see Zelda run into the house. She turned and saw Hanson approaching on horseback.

Emmaline came out on the porch just as Granny Zee made it to the first step. "Mother, what in the world is the matter with Zelda?" Granny Zee pointed at the road where Hanson was now coming up the hill. Emmaline said, "It's about damn time."

Mother and daughter greeted Hanson who asked if Zelda was home before dismounting. The swelling had gone down in his nose and the bruise under his eye had faded a bit, but the fight with the Campbell boys still marked his face.

Granny Zee said, "I'll see if I can find her," and left Emmaline with Hanson. It didn't escape Granny's notice that Hanson was all dolled up—new white shirt, crisp dungarees, and polished boots. His hair, usually so unruly that it fell every which way, was slicked back and shining like ripe wheat in the sun. Granny smiled. She didn't need the faeries to tell her that here was a man who had come to beg his love's forgiveness.

Zelda found Hanson standing beside his horse like he feared he would have to mount and ride away in a hurry. She had tidied her hair, washed her face, and was now wearing a blue calico dress the color of her eyes. She saw Hanson before he saw her, and the eyes that fell on her face were filled with love and a healthy dose of relief.

Hanson asked, "Will you go with me to our house?"

Zelda nodded and let Hanson pull her up on the saddle in front of him. She sank against his strong chest, when less than an hour ago she had lay against her grandmother's breast and cried with a broken heart.

Neither spoke on the short ride to the new house, but

Zelda could feel Hanson rehearsing in his mind what he was going to say.

Hanson helped her off the horse and tied it to a post he had put there for that purpose. He held out his hand. "Walk with me?"

Zelda nodded and took his hand. He led her to the honeysuckle arbor where they intended to say their vows in ten days' time. He said, "When I last saw you, you told me that before we married, I had to decide if I could live with your gift. Not just the things you see, but how you use it to help people."

Zelda raised her chin and looked straight into Hanson's eyes and nodded. Her heart pounded so hard and fast she thought he could surely hear its *thump-thump*. He smoothed a strand of hair behind Zelda's ear. "I love you, Zelda. I was naive to think we could live on this mountain and let the rest of the world go on about its business. What happened with the Campbell boys showed me that could never be, and that I was going to have to own up to it."

Hanson exhaled like he had been holding his breath. He put his hand in his pocket and brought out a little black velvet box. He placed it in the palm of Zelda's hand.

She raised the lid and her mouth opened but no sound came out.

"Zelda, I love you." Hanson said. "I will support you in everything you do. This ring is my promise."

He lifted the ring from its cushion of black velvet and slipped it on Zelda's finger. She moved her fingers back and forth, watching the stones catch the light. The sides of the yellow gold ring were fashioned in a delicate scrollwork design, depicting leaves reaching up and encircling a center of platinum that held a blood garnet encircled with tiny diamonds. Zelda had never seen anything so lovely in her life.

Hanson said, "This was my mother's ring. I had to go to Knoxville to find it."

"Knoxville!" Zelda cried.

Hanson nodded. "By the end of the Great War, Mama and Daddy were on hard times. I remember the day Mama took her ring to Morristown and sold it, so we wouldn't lose the farm. I weren't more than a boy, but I remember well, how hard she cried. I promised her I would buy it back one day." He took Zelda's hand and studied the ring. "I kept my promise."

"But you said you had to go to Knoxville."

Hanson nodded. "The man in Morristown remembered the woman he sold it to. Said she had lately moved to Knoxville to live with her daughter, Madeline Garvey. He knew she still had the ring because he'd tried to buy it back from her many times."

"So, you went to Knoxville to find her," Zelda said.

"I did. I found her but at first, she refused to sell it to me. I told her my story, how my Mama was dead, and how I wanted to buy that ring back from her and give it to the woman I was going to marry. It took some convincing, but she finally agreed. I was gone two days because I had to wait on the train."

"The train," Zelda said. "Oh, Hanson, I saw you in my dream get on a train. I thought you were leaving me."

Hanson put his arms around Zelda and drew her close. "I don't doubt you saw me get on a train, but Zelda my love, don't you know trains run two ways—they go, but they come back, too."

Chapter 16

TWO DAYS AFTER HANSON came home with his mother's ring, and a week before the wedding, Zelda and Granny Zee rode over to Stoney Creek to pick up Zelda's wedding dress.

The sleeveless gown was a straight white satin sheath that hit just at the ankles. Sheer organza draped the bodice and fell to the hip where it met a wide lace sash. Marthy, the finest seamstress on the mountain had even fashioned a satin flower and attached it to the sash at the hip. She'd made a smaller matching flower on a band of lace for a headpiece. Zelda planned to take it home and hang it on the back of her bedroom door where, for the first time since she had discovered her gift, she would sleep on a cloud of utter peace and contentment.

A piece of blue ribbon was sewn inside the hem of the dress for something blue, and Isabelle gave her a new pair of white shoes that had a strap around the ankle. For something old, she would tuck a lace-edged handkerchief Granny Zee had given her into her bouquet. It had belonged to her great-grand-mother and was slightly yellowed now, but her initials, B. M. O., Brigid Marie O'Reilly, were embroidered on the corner. Something borrowed would be her mother's cameo brooch.

Friday, June twenty-third was a day as close to heaven as possible. Zelda woke in time to watch the morning bloom, a great unfurling of sky and sun. At breakfast, Mama and Daddy told stories about her when she was a baby and toddler. They laughed and teased her, and Zelda reveled in their love.

When Granny Zee appeared, it was time to get busy in the kitchen. Every time Zelda tried to help, Mama and Granny Zee shooed her away, so she walked to her new house to see if everything was ready for the wedding. She wandered through the rooms, inhaling the scent of fresh cut wood, her shoes click-ing on the polished floors. She paused at the door to their bedroom. Blood flooded her cheeks when she looked at their bed. Its four posters gleamed in the light coming in the window, and the new wedding ring quilt, in shades of blue and yellow, was smoothed over the feather-tick. Streaks and slashes of sun pulsed through the muslin curtains she had sewn herself.

Zelda opened the door to the closet Hanson had built off their bedroom. Inside was a row of shelves and places to hang their clothes. Hanson said that all the big houses he built had closets, and he wanted their house to have them too. She had moved in her things before their fight, and she saw that Hanson had added his. She ran her fingers across their clothes hanging side-by-side and shivered at the intimacy of it.

Across from the bed, a lavish stone fireplace took up the entire wall. Its exact mate was on the other end of the house. Hanson had laid every stone himself, hauling most of them from the river, ten miles away. Zelda busied herself laying a bundle of sticks in both fireplaces. It was important that the first flames in the fireplaces be kindled from tonight's bonfire. Granny Zee said fire from the Summer Solstice bonfire had power to protect, and she and Hanson agreed it should be used to light their first fire.

When Zelda returned home, she found Isabelle there. "I swear," Isabelle said, "you're going to be late for your own wedding dinner! Where have you been?"

Zelda laughed. "I was just down at *my house* checking everything."

"It's time to get your bath," Isabelle said, taking Zelda's hand and leading her away from Granny and Mama who laughed.

As day cooled into evening, about fifty friends and family gathered for the pre-wedding dinner. Tables were arranged outside of Zelda and Hanson's new house and were soon filled with platters of roast pork, fried chicken, and fried green tomatoes, and bowls of potato salad, green beans, corn, and wild greens wilted with hot bacon drippings. Mounds of biscuits wrapped in towels were placed next to crocks of fresh butter.

The tables were decorated with arrangements of roses and lilies with candles in the center. These Zelda had allowed Isabelle to bring, but she had refused the bouquet of fancy flowers Isabelle had wanted to give her. She had picked her own bouquet of wild flowers—yellow buttercups, white daisies, pink lady's slipper, purple asters, and wild basil—and she had gone back down the mountain to gather some of the bee balm and Queen Anne's lace she had seen when she and Mama had gone to town. She had woven in some of the ivy she'd planted on the side of her new house—ivy that had once grown over the ruins of the old house where she and Cece had played, and for Cece, she placed a sprig of lilac in the center.

Zelda and Hanson sat at the head table where people waited on them like they were king and queen. She wore a new dress also made by Marthy for the dinner, the same blue as her eyes. When Hanson looked at her, his face filled with such pride and love that Zelda knew an answering in her own heart. She was overwhelmed with a sense of "rightness," for she knew he would love her despite her plight—despite her link to the spirit world and how it would determine her fate.

After dinner, Zelda disappeared inside to prepare for the wedding. Mama and Isabelle fussed with her hair, while Granny Zee sat close by with Mama's sister, Ellen, who Zelda thought looked just like Mama only with black hair. Aunt Ellen had come from Cumberland Gap where she lived with her husband, Silas, and six children. Uncle Silas was plump and bubbly. He had a bulbous nose tinged with red and eyebrows like hairbrush bristles. A fiddler of some renown, he was outside gathering all the musicians for later.

Ellen sat and patted her mother's hand and listened to her reminisce about her one true love—the father that Emmaline and Ellen barely remembered. When Emmaline was nine and Ellen seven, he and their baby brother, John, had died in a fire. It was the winter of 1878, and the girls had pneumonia. Johnny was three months old and Granny Zee, then a young mother, had put him in the bed with his father while she slept on the floor next to the girls. The bedrooms were on opposite sides of the house with the front room and kitchen in between them. When John woke to fire, he left the baby in the bed and ran to save the girls and their mother first. After he got them out and went back to save the baby, the roof collapsed, trapping them in a fiery death. Granny Zee said that after she lost John, she had married herself to the mountain.

While Zelda got ready, the guests prepared for the celebration after the ceremony. The food was removed, and two kegs of cider appeared. Corn-liquor would discreetly appear after dark. The mountain people were well aware of prohibition, and there were many moonshine stills hidden in the mountains. Granny Zee had made a traditional wedding cake—a fruit cake with white frosting. It was placed on a table with a white tablecloth.

Lanterns lined a path that began at the back of the house and ended where the yard sloped upward toward the mountain. There, the honeysuckle vines glowed in the fading light, their tubular orange and cream flowers sprouting gold and silver spidery threads. Honeysuckle smelled strongest in the gloaming, and the air was drenched in its sweetness. Hanson had tamed the honeysuckle arbor so that it now formed an arch between the trees, but when Zelda was a girl, it had walled-off this part of the mountain and made a secret passage to the old ruined house where their home now stood.

On this midsummer's eve, the longest day of the year, the night never won the sky. Instead, when the sun at last sank below the mountains, the sky purpled like a fresh bruise. Hanson and Preacher Slone took their place in front of the honeysuckle arch. Granny Zee, Emmaline, and Isabelle, who held her son's hand, walked up the path and stood to the right of the preacher and Hanson. Hanson's older brothers, Ellison and Tom, and his Aunt Sue and Uncle Woodrow Kennedy stood to the left. The sweetness of Uncle Silas's fiddle filled the night with "Here Comes the Bride," and the guests who lined either side of the pathway turned to watch Zelda come down the path, holding her father's arm.

But Zelda saw no one but Hanson. The cowlick he had tried so hard to tame stuck up in the evening dew, giving him an impish look. He was smiling just for her, and with that smile, all the stress of getting everything ready for the wedding slipped away. Calm like a soft breeze settled over her, and suddenly, there was nobody else in the world but the two of them. She smiled in answer, as a waxing gibbous moon rose above the horizon until it rested, the barest sliver in a lavender sky.

The glimmer from the lanterns against the white of her dress created a milky glow, so to those watching, Zelda seemed to float down the path. When her father put her hand in Hanson's, it was warm and rough like the bark of a tree, his thick fingers so strong and familiar that Zelda knew, of all the things she was not sure of in life, this—his touch—would never be one of them. His eyes searched her face like he was seeing her for the first time. Zelda knew if someone asked, she would say his eyes were blue, but that was not right—they weren't one color at all. In them she saw the colors of the mountain itself—from the dark earth to the gold of the sunset on the mountaintop—everything she loved.

The violet sky darkened to indigo as Zelda and Hanson said their vows, and Hanson slipped a gold band on Zelda's finger. At the moment Hanson kissed his bride, a haze of lightning bugs rose over the grass like tiny flashing jewels. The guests sounded a collective *ahhh* and then Mr. and Mrs. Hanson Davis turned to face them.

There was much back-slapping and hugging, blessings and congratulations, as the couple made their way to the wood stacked for a bonfire. Hanson struck a match and lit a bundle of twigs, and he and Zelda held it before them until the smoke turned to tiny flickers of orange and red. Granny Zee stepped forward and in a loud voice said, "Spirits and wee folk of the mountain, protect the union of Zelda and Hanson. They will honor the mountain as they honor each other. Give them Gra, Dilseacht, Cairdeas!"

The crowd repeated "Gra, Dilseacht, Cairdeas," Irish for love, loyalty, friendship.

Zelda and Hanson tossed the burning twigs on the waiting wood. It instantly caught, popping and crackling, sparks flying off into the new darkness. Hand-in-hand, the newlyweds moved from the bonfire to the wedding cake where they cut the first piece. Once again, they took their place at the head table as the sound of fiddles tuning-up filled the air. The music started and old-man Ranson pulled out his special playing spoons. Soon there was music and dancing as a comfortable first-dark settled over the mountain.

Hanson and Zelda danced among the fire-shadows, and Zelda knew there were more frolicking shadows than those of the dancers. Eleanor's spirit was among them. Zelda saw her smile in the swell of the blue-orange blaze—the darts of yellow-gold flames licking at the sky. But there was another spirit among the glow calling to Zelda. Large eyes burned black— what the Irish called the *taish*—the appearance—of Vadie Williams. "Please," Zelda whispered. "Not now, not on my wedding night."

At first the sheriff didn't believe Zelda.

"Now, listen, Sheriff Mullins," Granny Zee said. "If my granddaughter says Vadie Williams was murdered, then she was murdered."

"It ain't like I'm doubting your word," Sheriff Mullins said. "I know she found the Campbell's girl." He looked Zelda up and down, and it was clear to her that, in his eyes, she didn't measure up. "But this is different. I have to have evidence," he said. "And a body. Right now, it's your word against Snow's. And he says she run off."

"And I say, how could she do that with no help?" Granny Zee asked.

"Look," Sheriff Mullins said, "give me something to go on. A murder weapon. Some blood. What did he do with the body?"

Zelda stood. "He buried her in the woods."

Granny Zee and Sheriff Mullins turned to look at her. Until that moment, Zelda had not known what he had done with the body. Since she had seen Vadie's face in the bonfire the night she got married, she had dreamed of Vadie's screams, a man's laughter, and blood. But she was sure now that Snow had buried her body in the woods. Where, she didn't exactly know, but she knew where to go for help.

Zelda put her gathering bag over her shoulder and took up her walking stick. Her father had made her this stick when she was a girl, so she could part the weeds in case a snake might be resting there.

First light broke as she passed under the watershed of honeysuckle and entered the forest. At high-summer the forest was so layered with growth that the morning sun could not yet touch the ground, only scatter pinpricks of light on the plants at her feet. She stepped forward and breathed in the mixed fragrance of rotting undergrowth and rich earth, newly sprouted flower and fern. It was like she had entered eternity. The preacher talked about heaven—its pearly gates and streets of gold, but Zelda thought heaven must be like this.

Crystalline swirls of fog curled around the trees as Zelda climbed, winding her way toward the place where the scarlet oak stood guard over the faerie fort. As she walked, she focused on Vadie. Granny Zee had told her she must seek help from the spirits of the forest the same way she sought out its plants for her healing remedies. To do that, she must go to the forest, still herself, and listen.

The ground topped a rise and then sloped down, forming a basin lined with large stones of limestone and sandstone. Inside the bowl, the tree stood full with just a hint of the beautiful scarlet the bristle lobed leaves would become in the fall, but the ground was littered in the remnants of last year's crop. Crisp and curled, the leaves were still red, and Zelda shivered, remembering her dreams about Vadie—the coppery odor of her blood, the stickiness of it on her skin, her eyes open but seeing only eternity.

Zelda touched the trunk of the oak and closed her eyes. Like Granny Zee had schooled her, she used her second sight—*an dara sealladh*—emptying her thoughts and concentrating on the sounds around her. She heard the sharp cry of a blue jay high over her head, the scurry of a forest creature nearby, the zing of an insect, and the ruffle of leaves as a slight breeze passed, cooling the sweat on her face, and then silence.

How long she stood with her hands on the tree, Zelda did not know, but when she opened her eyes she saw the flash of a blade slicing the throat of Vadie Williams.

Zelda fell to her knees. She placed her hands on the ground in the leaf scruff. She took several deep breaths before she could push herself up and get to the stone bench. She sat down heavily and pressed her hand to her throat, fighting down the bile that rose from her stomach. There was more to do. She had to see where Vadie was buried.

Zelda picked up her gathering bag and took out a slice of wedding cake wrapped in paper, an offering to the faeries. She placed it in front of the faerie fort—the mound of dirt that rose behind the rocks where she sat. She said, "Wee folk, I ask for your help. A spirit has called to me. She has been buried where she cannot rest. Please, help me find her. Help me."

∂✤∂

The next day, Granny Zee and Zelda returned to town. They found Sheriff Mullins behind his desk, a mess of paper around him.

He looked up and frowned. "Got something new?"

"Yes." Zelda stepped forward. "I know where Vadie is buried."

Zelda pulled her journal out of a bag. In it were three sketches she had made yesterday after her sojourn to the forest: a ridge with trees, an old cabin with its door hanging open, and a slope covered with plants that had round leaves with ruffled edges. In the margin next to the trees, Zelda had written "sugar maple," under the cabin "homestead," and next to the plants was "bloodroot."

Sheriff Mullins studied the drawings. He closed the book and handed it back to Zelda. He opened his mouth like he was going to say something, closed it, and nodded.

Granny Zee said, "I've been to this place many times. Vadie was raised on Maple Leaf Ridge. That cabin was—"

"The Blankenship home-place," Sheriff Mullins said. He stood and picked up his hat. "Let's go."

Sheriff Mullins got a shovel and a coil of rope before saddling his horse. When they got to the old cabin, Zelda and Granny Zee waited while the sheriff went inside. He came out and said, "Somebody was here. Snow must have brought her up here when she was still alive."

Zelda said, "He told her they were leaving the coal camp and moving up here to live. She—she was happy."

Sheriff Mullins got the shovel and said, "Tell me where to dig."

Granny Zee and Sheriff Mullins followed Zelda around the cabin and into the woods. When they got to the patch of blood-root, Zelda stopped. She walked over to a tree and said, "He killed her here. Slit her throat." She walked over a few feet and stopped. "She's buried here."

Sheriff Mullins promised Granny Zee he would not tell anyone of Zelda's part in finding Vadie's body. He had known Granny Zee his whole life. He had heard people call her a witch, and if truth be told, he wasn't so sure he wouldn't agree. But witch or no, she and her daughter Emmaline had saved many people, including his wife when their first child was born dead. But this was something else. Zelda was different from her mother and grandmother. She had taken him straight to that body, and Vadie's throat was cut just like she had said.

He shivered. He had watched Zelda and he saw the pain on her face. That poor girl didn't want this. "God help her."

1997

Chapter 17

At nature's heart is the tree. They were here at the beginning.
The Bible tells us of the Tree of Life. The tree grows in silence
just as the sun and moon move in silence. A wise woman can
learn how to hear the hush of trees but only with her soul.
~ from Granny Zee's Book of Dreams

IT WAS AFTER NINE o'clock, and the day still clung to what by rights was the night sky. Maggie inhaled. Addie had gotten into the car at the theatre trailing the scent of popcorn.

Addie said, "Mom, are you *sniffing* me?"

Maggie chuckled. "I can't help it! You smell like popcorn. Did you enjoy the movie?"

"It was okay."

When they got home, Maggie and Addie lingered in the car. It had been a beautiful day with cloudless skies and a breeze that teased all the right places, and now, the stars crowded around the moon. Perhaps it was the beauty of the night that gave her the courage. Maggie said, "Addie, do you ever see anything about me?"

"Sometimes," Addie admitted.

Maggie had come this far, she may as well go all the way. "Do you ever see anything about me in the future?"

Addie's large dark eyes searched her mother's face. "I see green around you. When I see you in the future, there's always green around you."

"Do you mean green like a room that's green?"

Addie shook her head. "No, it's outside green."

"Like a forest?"

Addie shook her head again. "No, it's not a forest. I don't know where it is, but there's green all around you. And Mama, you're smiling."

Maggie's heart pounded. She smiled at Addie, who stared back like she was memorizing her face. "Well," Maggie said, "thank goodness I'm smiling."

Addie exhaled. "I'm sorry that's all I can tell you. You know, I can't control it. It's so—so frustrating. I can't turn it on and off."

Maggie nodded. "Of course. Don't be sorry. I didn't mean to make you feel uncomfortable." She paused, gathering her resolve. "Addie, do you ever see anything about your father?"

Addie bent her head so low her whiskey-brown hair poured over her shoulders, hiding her face.

Shame stabbed Maggie and she smoothed Addie's hair away from her face. "I shouldn't have asked. I'm sorry."

Addie wound her arms around her mother's neck, pushing her face into the hollow between her breasts like she had when she was small. Tears startled Maggie, and she hugged her daughter tight.

Addie was the first to pull away. "I love you, Mama."

"I love you too, baby."

Addie hopped out of the car and disappeared inside, but Maggie lingered, rolling down the window and breathing in the humid night air. The mountains were never quiet, especially at night. The *zzzz* of insects, the rustle of weeds, the hoot of an owl, the song of frogs calling for rain—together they created an inexplicable music that bewitched her. It spoke of times long forgotten when these mountains were untamed and wild with unspoiled beauty. And—green—magnificent and green. Were these mountains the green Addie saw surrounding her? She didn't think so. Addie wasn't telling her everything. There was more, hiding in her voice, and the way she practically ran from the car when asked about her father fairly shouted there was more.

The scent of honeysuckle drenched in dew wafted in the window, and Maggie wished things could stay just like this. J.D. was in D.C. and would be there most of the summer. In two weeks, she and Hannah were taking the girls to the beach. She had rented a beach house on the Outer Banks of North Carolina, and since Hannah was on summer break, she had talked her into going.

The summer was slipping by at an alarming rate, and Maggie dreaded the fall. J.D. was now a delegate to the House of Representatives. Maggie didn't need a seer to tell her his climb up the political ladder had begun. Addie was in middle school, and Hannah was going to start physical therapy school in Pineville as soon as she took the GRE, which would put an end to their already limited mornings at The Corner Coffee Shop.

This past year, Maggie had seen less and less of Hannah while she finished her chemistry degree. Going to the beach had taken some convincing because Hannah was hyper-sensitive about Maggie "paying her and Reilly's way." Maggie recalled all too well the time Hannah told her that she didn't want to be the poor relation, always looking for a handout. Since then, she had been careful not to buy anything too expensive for birthdays or Christmas, and she was careful what she spent on Reilly.

Hannah was proud to a fault. And stubborn. Maggie had learned how unforgiving her friend could be. Hannah personified the phrase, "hell hath no fury like a woman scorned." Maggie looked out on the night and whispered a prayer, "Please, don't ever let Hannah find out it was my money that financed her scholarships."

Her first morning at the beach, Maggie found Hannah sitting on a quilt spread near the ocean. At first, she wasn't sure it was her under the enormous purple sunhat, but books spread around her were a dead giveaway.

Maggie and the girls had come down two days ago, so they could open the house, buy groceries, and get things ready for their stay. Hannah had driven down yesterday, after Uncle Louis had come to stay with Granny. Granny was getting frail, and even though she insisted she had Cece to look after her, there was no way Hannah was going to leave her in the care of a ghost.

While Maggie struggled down the beach with a cooler, Addie and Reilly leapt across the sand like fawns that still had their spots. At the water's edge, they joined hands and ran into the waves. Maggie deposited the cooler next to Hannah with a loud *harrumph*. "There's fruit and muffins in the cooler."

Hannah looked up from her book. "Thanks! I'm starved."

Maggie plopped down on the quilt next to Hannah, who began consuming muffins and gulping chocolate milk at an alarming rate. She asked, "How's the studying coming?"

"Fine," Hannah said, pushing the last bite of muffin into her mouth. She chewed and swallowed, and then turned up her drink and drained it. She dusted crumbs off her swimsuit and sighed. "That's better."

Maggie giggled.

Hannah said, "Hey! I need food. I'm cramming for a test."

"When is the GRE?"

"At the end of the month."

"That's a couple of weeks away. Maybe relax and enjoy your vacation?"

Hannah turned toward Maggie and smiled. She waved her arms about and said, "I'm already enjoying it."

Maggie nodded. She lay back and was half-asleep when Hannah snapped her book shut, startling her.

"Sorry," Hannah said. "I need a study break."

Maggie sat up and stretched. "Can you believe just a month ago you graduated from college?"

Hannah snorted. "Oh, yeah. Guess what Travis said when Reilly told him I was graduating?"

"What?"

"He said, 'That's good, babe.'"

Maggie waited, but Hannah stayed silent, staring out at the waves. Maggie said, "That's all?"

Hannah pulled off her sunhat and laid it next to her. She drew her legs up and rested her head on her knees with her face turned toward Maggie. "That was all until Reilly said, 'And then, Mama's going to medical school. She's going to be a physical therapist.'"

"What did he say to that?"

"He said, 'How's Mama gonna pay for that?' To Reilly—not me—even though I was standing right next to her."

Tears surprised Maggie, and she was thankful for her sunglasses. Hannah had been going to college part-time since Reilly and Addie were in the fourth grade. Now, she was graduating with a bachelor's degree and a double major in biology and chemistry. She had maintained an A average and had already gotten accepted into a physical therapy program. All the while, she had taken care of Reilly and managed a house, *and* looked after Granny. She had done all of this for what? A smart-ass remark about money?

Maggie's blood boiled. "After all you've accomplished, that's what he said to you?"

"Oh, no, remember he's talking to and looking at Reilly, so I decided to play along. I looked at Reilly and said, 'Tell your father I have a full scholarship—tuition and books. I'm sure he remembers what a full-ride means.'"

"Ouch!" Maggie said.

Hannah turned to stare at the girls playing in the waves. "You know, that was one of the meanest things I've ever done. And I said it in front of Reilly."

"Did she know?"

"That I was talking about the football scholarship Travis threw away? Yeah, she knew."

They sat in silence for a while, lost in the sensations of sun and wind stroking their skin.

Maggie stretched out her legs and prepared to lie down when Hannah suddenly grabbed her arm. "Maggie," she said, "I didn't tell you the whole story."

"You didn't?"

Hannah shook her head. "After I said that to Travis, he looked at Reilly and said, 'Tell your mother I'm proud of her,' and then he left without ever once making eye contact with me."

Maggie opened her mouth and closed it without saying a word. Hannah stood and walked toward the ocean. She called over her shoulder, "Come on. Let's get wet."

When Hannah and Maggie returned to the blankets, Maggie draped a towel around Hannah's shoulders. "Did you know you have a strange birthmark on your right shoulder blade?" Maggie asked. She removed her sunglasses and peered closer at the inch long mark. "That looks like a Celtic marking—like a—"

"It's a Celtic double spiral. I have a Celtic triple spiral here." Hannah raised her left arm and placed her fingers in the hollow under her arm.

Maggie inhaled and exhaled slowly. "Are these natural marks?"

"Well, nobody put them there."

"Why didn't you show them to me before?"

Hannah whipped her head around and glared at Maggie. "So, I have two weird birthmarks. So what?"

"Do you even know what they symbolize?"

"Of course, I know. Granny Zee made sure of that. She says it's a symbol of female power and it gives my hands healing powers."

A sharp pain hit her leg, and Maggie realized she was still on her knees behind Hannah, posed with a towel in her hands. She sat back and slipped on her sunglasses so Hannah couldn't see her eyes. She had just discovered two random birthmarks that were Celtic symbols on her friend's body and for a reason she couldn't explain, she was shaken by it.

Hannah turned and grabbed the towel. "They're just birthmarks, Maggie. I'm not like my granny. I don't have any powers. I can't see spirits or the future."

But Maggie wasn't so sure.

The weekend passed quickly. Maggie and Hannah spent their evenings after dinner on the deck, watching the sunset. One night Maggie said, "You know how much I love the mountains, but whatever happens in the future, I want to live by the sea. Addie said she saw me in the future, and green was all around me."

"You never told me that." Hannah sat up straight.

"It was the night you told us about getting accepted at PT school."

"Did she mean green like the mountains?"

"She said it wasn't a forest, just green, and that I was smiling. I asked her if she ever saw anything about her father, and she practically bolted into the house. I shouldn't have asked. I don't want her to feel like she has to choose where her loyalty lies." Maggie looked out to sea. Night was crushing the ocean into blackness. Soon it would take the crash of the waves and the scent of brine to make the senses accept it as truly there.

Hannah sniffed back tears.

Maggie said, "Honey, what's wrong?"

"I was thinking about how we're going home in a few days. I don't want to go back."

"Oh, sweetie, you've worked so hard, and you have more hard work ahead. No wonder you don't want to go home."

"It's not that. I'm looking forward to PT school. It's Travis. Maggie, I'm so damn confused! One minute I'm fighting him tooth and nail about going to school and the next minute, he's planning how to spend the money I'll make."

Maggie stared at Hannah's face, muffled by the darkness. "What kind of plans?"

"Let's see." Hannah held up her hand. "One, he wants to buy a boat. Two, he wants to buy a camper. Three, he wants to rent a place on New River to keep the camper and boat because that's near his VA Tech buddies. Four, he wants to quit his job and 'find something out of coal mining.' And five, he wants to buy season tickets to some stupid pro-football team."

"Hum."

"Oh, yeah," Hannah continued. "When I said, 'How about using the money to send our daughter to college, or have you forgotten about her?' he said, 'Oh, yeah, that too.'"

"That too?"

Hannah stood up. "Come on, Maggie, let's take a walk on the beach."

They strolled for a while and then Hannah said, "I used to think it would be easy—I mean, when it actually came time to leave him. I have so much bitterness inside me. He ruined my life! But I wouldn't be true to myself if I didn't admit there's still a part of me that hopes he will change and make me fall in love with him. Do you ever feel that way about J.D.? Ever?"

The full moon broke through the clouds and illuminated

Hannah's face, streaked with tears. Her eyes were huge and filled with pain. Maggie shivered. "No," she said, "never."

They turned and started back. When they got back to the cottage, Maggie said, "I'm going to check on the girls." When she came back, she found Hannah outside on the deck with a bottle of wine and two glasses.

"Are the girls asleep?"

"Yes, like the proverbial baby."

Maggie sat down and sipped her wine. She watched a sailing cloud come to rest on the moon. She said, "Hannah, may I say something about Travis?"

Hannah turned toward her and nodded.

"I've been thinking about what you said—about him planning how to spend your salary—and maybe it's not that he's being selfish. Maybe it's more like he's being—immature."

"What do you mean?"

"Maybe he's being like somebody who's never had a lot of money, but still has dreams, and suddenly, that person gets a windfall and well... It's like a kid who dreams of growing up to be a fireman or astronaut or—cowboy."

"Cowboy?"

"Yeah, cowboy. You grow out of those dreams, but you never stop dreaming those *what if* dreams."

"And Travis was living those *what if* dreams of being a pro football player until the accident. So you're saying he's dreaming again."

"Yes, I guess that's what I'm saying. He's dreaming *what if* dreams."

Their last day of vacation was rainy and cool, but it didn't stop Reilly and Addie from spending most of the day at the beach. That evening, they got dressed up and went out to an upscale restaurant where Hannah and Reilly ate their first lobster. Back at the cottage, the sky had cleared and a tangle of stars now lit the sky. The ocean looked like a gigantic backdrop for the night sky.

Hannah and Maggie changed into their pajamas and kissed the girls goodnight. They took a bottle of wine and went to sit on the deck one last time. They settled down and Maggie said, "It's a beautiful night. It's looks like we placed an order for stars and got double."

"It's the most beautiful thing I've ever seen. Thank you, Maggie, for this wonderful vacation."

"You're welcome, my friend. So, what did you think about the lobster?"

A sound like *hu hu* came from deep in Hannah's throat.

Maggie said, "That's what I thought."

"Sorry, but I prefer Granny's fried catfish."

They lapsed into the kind of soft silence friends enjoy. They were of like mind—savoring the beauty of this place that wanted to be felt—not discussed or assessed like a finite object that could be weighed and measured.

The wine disappeared, and the moon rose high in the sky. Maggie startled when Hannah cried, "Look! A shooting star!"

It skyrocketed downward until it smacked the ocean, bursting into streaks of red and gold. Hannah said, "Granny would say that's a sign."

"And Granny would be right. That star means you're going to realize your dream, and be a physical therapist. As long as you have me, Granny, and Reilly behind you, you're going to catch that falling star."

Hannah began to cry. Maggie leapt to her feet and crouched in front of her. "Sweetie, what is it?"

"Why did you have to say those things about Travis?" Tears ran down her face.

"What things? What did I say?"

Hannah tried to hide her face in her hands, but Maggie grabbed them. "Tell me."

Hannah's lip trembled, "Those things you said about thinking like a little boy, dreaming of being an astronaut. Why did you say that? Why did you make me look at him that way?" She leapt to her feet. "I want him to stay the redneck asshole who doesn't give a damn about anything. I don't want him to have wants and dreams. I don't want him to be like me."

Hannah bolted across the deck, sprinted down the steps, and ran across the sand. Maggie caught up with her at the water's edge. She gasped, "Hannah, please, stop!"

Hannah bent at the waist, putting her hands on her knees. She and Maggie stood face-to-face, panting. Maggie said, "I was only... thinking out loud. Travis... may not be like... that at all!"

Hannah kicked sand on Maggie's feet. "God damn it, Maggie! Don't you know what you've done?"

Maggie shook her head.

"You gave him a heart. You gave Travis a goddamn heart!"

Hannah wheeled around and plunged into the water. The tide was coming in and a wave surged, knocking her feet out from under her. She sat down hard, and Maggie ran for her, grabbing her arm and pulling her up.

"What's wrong with you? Come on!" Maggie physically dragged Hannah until they were away from the incoming waves, and then she swung around. "What was that?" Any semblance of sympathy had vanished.

"You don't understand."

"Then explain it to me!"

Hannah sank down on the sand and drew her knees up to her chin, wrapping her arms around her legs. Maggie sat down cross-legged next to her. Minutes passed. The only sound was the ocean rocking back and forth in the darkness. At last Hannah said, "I've had to fight so hard to get my degree. So damn hard, but I did it. In spite of Travis."

"Then why do you sound so unhappy?"

"I don't know. It doesn't feel like I thought it would."

"Then maybe you did it for the wrong reason."

"What do you mean?"

"I mean—did you do it for yourself—or did you do it to spite Travis?"

Hannah suddenly became interested in the sand. "Honestly, I don't know."

"Hannah, there are times I don't understand you. You say you want to leave Travis, yet I've seen how he looks at you and how *you* look at him."

Hannah's head shot up, and she glared at Maggie.

"Don't look at me like that! It's true," Maggie said.

Hannah burrowed her hands in the sand, picking up handfuls, spilling them, scooping up more.

"I'm going to ask you something that's going to make you mad, but I'm asking anyway." Maggie paused to see if Hannah would look at her, but she kept her head down. "Do you remember every wrong anyone has ever done to you?"

Hannah kept methodically scooping and dumping sand. Maggie said, "Then here's the real question—how can you live like that?"

Hannah screeched and threw handfuls of sand toward the ocean. "I've told you I'm stubborn and hardheaded."

Maggie could feel Hannah struggling, but she knew she had said enough. She started to get up when Hannah put a hand on her arm. "Don't go."

Maggie relaxed back on the sand.

"You know I'm from a family of *unusual* women, and you know I'm good with my hands."

"You have magic hands! That time I pulled a muscle in my back, your massages worked wonders."

Hannah bent toward Maggie. "Thanks, but there's something else about me."

"You mean besides the two birthmarks you never showed me that are Celtic symbols?

A growl rose from Hannah's throat. She shouted, "Yes!" and threw her arms up in the air. "Yes, okay?"

"Then what is it?"

Hannah stared until Maggie said, "Oh for God's sake! What is it?"

"I used witchcraft to make Travis fall in love with me."

She looked so pitiful that Maggie's first impulse was to laugh, but then Hannah grabbed her arm and Maggie felt something like electricity running under her skin, she realized something new was happening.

Hannah shared how the memory of her sixteenth summer haunted her. She and Travis had flirted with each other that spring and when summer vacation started, he had promised to call and they would go out on a date. But the call never came.

Hannah had moped around until her mama sent her to Granny Zee. One day, Granny showed her a trunk she called her treasure chest. It was a beautiful old steamer trunk filled with antiques Granny Zee said had been passed down to her—a faded tartan plaid blanket from Scotland, lace edged handkerchiefs yellowed from age, a leather bag that contained her mother's midwife tools, a wooden lap desk that had an inkwell, and in the bottom of the trunk were old journals that had belonged to her great-grandmother.

One journal had stood-out from the others. Smaller and well-worn, the leather cover had a river of cracks running through it like it had been read over and over. It had beckoned Hannah to open it.

"It was my great-great grandmother's book of spells," Hannah said.

"Magic?" Maggie asked.

"All kinds—how to make amulets, talismans, candles, and charms for prosperity, luck, power, healing, and, of course, love. So, I studied it and decided I was going to use it to make Travis fall in love with me. And I did."

"What exactly did you do?"

"I made a talisman—I cut an apricot pit in half, hollowed it out, and inside of it I put seven apple seeds. I ground up some dried starwort, bachelor's button, chestnut, chamomile, and ginger, and put that in with the seeds. Last, I added a lock of Travis's hair. Then I glued it together."

"That's it?"

"Not exactly." Hannah paused and stretched out her legs. "On the longest day of the year, that we call midsummer's eve and the Irish call Bealtaine, I went into the forest at midnight and called on the spirits to do my bidding. Then I put the talisman in a little satin pouch and wore it tied to a cord so that it rested next to my heart."

Maggie grabbed Hannah's arm so hard she said, "Oww! Hey!"

"What do you mean you called spirits?" Maggie's voice rose with each word.

"I did what it said in the journal. I went into the forest at midnight on the eve of the summer solstice. According to Granny Zee and what was written in that journal, Bealtaine is one of the three Celtic spirit nights in the year when the veil between this world and the next is lifted."

Maggie said, "What do you mean lifted?"

"I mean," Hannah said, "spirits visit the earth on those nights."

The winds rose, and the waves crashed on the beach, the perfect backdrop for tales of spells and witchcraft.

"What exactly did you do?" Maggie asked. "And I swear this better not involve blood."

Hannah stood and pulled Maggie to her feet. She took a step back and said, "Watch. Here's exactly what I did." She turned to face the moon and raised her arms over her head with the palms of her hands facing the moon. She said, "O spirits of land and sky above/Hear my plea/Grant me this love/I promise to love him all of my life/O spirits of the night make me his wife." She dropped her arms and turned toward Maggie.

Maggie's heart thumped so hard she thought surely Hannah could hear it. The wind rose sharply, and with it, the air cooled. Hannah and Maggie shivered, though how much of it was the coolness of the breeze, neither could say. Maggie held out a hand to Hannah, who grasped it, and together, they turned and walked back to the house with only the wind and their silence between them.

Chapter 18

Trees have magic based on their healing abilities. The weeping willow encourages us to let go of our buried fears and desires, and grieve—only then can the human spirit find peace. My whole life I have walked among trees. I have told them my dreams and longings, my sorrows and worries, and they listened.
~ from Granny Zee's Book of Dreams

HANNAH'S FIRST DAY OF PT school dawned as clear and bright as a polished mirror. The September morning was still summer-like even though the calendar inched toward autumn. Since it was Monday, Hannah could take Reilly to school before making the hour drive to Pineville, because on Mondays and Wednesdays, her first class didn't start until 9:30. The problem was the rest of the week—classes started at eight. That had caused the first "you think you're gonna be a big shot doctor" argument with Travis.

The only solution Hannah could see was to give up PT school until Reilly was older, so she went to cry on Granny's shoulder. The minute Hannah left, Granny called Maggie, and by the time Hannah got home, Maggie waited in the swing on her back porch. She outlined her plan. Hannah was going to PT school and Maggie wasn't taking no for an answer.

Now here was Hannah, on Monday morning, taking the road out of town. She pushed a button, and Journey's "Don't Stop Believin'" burst from the radio. Hannah sang along.

Maggie's plan was a marvel. On Tuesday, Thursday, and Friday mornings, Maggie's housekeeper would be at Hannah's house at 6:00. Ida would stay with Reilly until Maggie picked her up and took her to school, and Ida would see to it that Reilly had breakfast and got ready on time. That was the second "you think you're gonna be a big shot doctor argument" she had with Travis. And it was Reilly who had ended the argument when she stomped into the room, hands on hips, and stood nose to nose with her father. She said, "I'm not a baby. Mom's going to school!"

Seeing the sign for *Mountain Empire Medical College Next*

Right, Hannah's stomach knotted and her throat tightened. She exited off the highway and passed Pineville Hospital where she would be training with physical therapists. Soon she was on campus, where she found Wagner Hall.

Hannah slipped into a parking place. She smoothed her hair behind her ears and glanced at herself in the rearview mirror, wondering why in the world she hadn't gotten a haircut. She looked down at her white cotton pullover sweater and khaki pants, relieved she had asked Maggie for advice on what to wear.

Then her eyes fell on her wedding ring. The weight of this thin gold band tugged at her heart. In one swift movement, she slipped it off and dropped it in the change tray in the car's console. Her hand went the necklace Maggie had given her for graduation. It was silver with three charms suspended from a wide circle of rose gold—a heart stamped with Tiffany's famous logo, a puffed star, and nestled between them, a round disk engraved with the medical insignia—the blue enameled letters P and T on either side. When Maggie gave it to her she said, "The heart is a reminder of the people who love you, and the star is a symbol of the falling star we saw that night at the beach. Dare to dream, Hannah, and you will realize your goal."

Hannah never took the necklace off. She shuddered to think of how expensive it was, but she promised Maggie she wouldn't fuss about it. She was, however, still embarrassed that she hadn't known the robin's egg blue box was from Tiffany's in New York. She had heard of Tiffany's, but she had no idea that every piece of Tiffany jewelry was placed in a signature blue box. Her twelve-year-old daughter had explained it to her.

Hannah grabbed her book bag from the backseat and set off. At Wagner Hall, she ran up the steps but paused at the door to take a deep breath. When she passed through these doors it would be with a weight of guilt on her shoulders for the hours of her daughter's life she would miss. From behind her came a deep male voice with an Irish accent. "Let me get the door for you."

A tall handsome man stepped around her and opened the door. When he was sure she was through the outer door, he opened the inner door and stood back to let her in.

"Thank you," Hannah said.

He took a step in the opposite direction and turned back, extending his hand. "Hello, I'm Cooper O'Shaughnessy."

They shook hands. "Hannah Lively."

"Student?"

Hannah nodded.

He pointed to his right. "Last door on the left."

"Thank you, again," Hannah said. He nodded and walked away in the opposite direction.

Once inside, Hannah paused to gather her bearings and let her eyes adjust to the dim light. The room was larger than she expected, with tiered seating. There were already about thirty people in the room, the majority of them men.

Hannah took a seat near the stage at the front of the room. Four people had appeared there, and one of them was the handsome Cooper O'Shaughnessy. He caught her eye and smiled. Hannah smiled back. Under her breath, Hannah said, "Let's do this!"

Maggie found herself seeking more of Granny Zee's company as fall fluffed her colorful skirts and settled down over the mountains. Maggie looked forward to their visits like she had once anticipated her mornings with Hannah at the coffee shop.

This late October morning, Maggie wore jeans and a sweatshirt since Granny Zee had warned her they were going out in the woods to gather persimmons. Maggie had no idea what a persimmon was or for that matter, how one harvested persimmons, but she was excited to find out.

As soon as she took the girls to school, Maggie turned her car toward Granny Zee's mountain. She crossed the bridge over Little Creek and entered an ice forest. In the sun, the frost on the trees and plants sparkled like diamonds. Maggie rolled down the window just enough to let the cold graze her cheek. She promised herself that today she wasn't going to think about J.D. and the upcoming election. He was running for a recently vacated Senate seat and if he won, Maggie feared he would try to pull her and Addie back to D.C.

Granny Zee greeted her at the door dressed in a baggy sweat suit and her favorite red cardigan. Her eyes twinkled with mischief. "Come in, dear! Come in! Now just give me a minute to put my climbing boots on and we'll go."

Maggie smiled. A vision of tiny Granny in enormous hiking boots popped into her head. Maggie doubted Granny Zee could even lift her feet in hiking boots.

Granny Zee reappeared in a red and black plaid jacket, red toboggan, and black fur lined boots that came just above her ankles. Maggie stifled a giggle. Granny Zee looked like a mischievous elf.

Granny Zee pulled gloves out of her pocket. "Oh my, I forgot to tell you to bring gloves."

Maggie said, "I have these."

Granny Zee eyed the leather gloves Maggie held up. She said, "Well, I guess they'll do."

Next to the door were two beautiful hand-woven baskets that Maggie had never seen before. Granny Zee pointed at them. "Now, if you'll get my gathering baskets, we're ready. Look inside and make sure I put the shears in the baskets."

Maggie draped the baskets on her arm and followed Granny Zee outside. Beside the back door, Granny Zee retrieved her walking stick and marched off with it held aloft like a drum major's baton. She led the way to the path that wound up the mountain like an unraveled spool of ribbon. Maggie walked beside Granny who talked about the plants all around them like she was describing old friends. When they came upon a scraggly tree, she stopped and pointed at it with her walking stick. Maggie realized in place of leaves it had odd yellow star-like blooms.

Granny Zee said, "That's witch hazel."

"It looks like it's blooming," Maggie said.

"It is. Witch hazel blooms after all its leaves fall off. My mother used a branch off a witch hazel tree as a divining rod."

"Divining rod?"

"A divining rod is a forked stick used to find underground water. My mother was called on many times to help folks find water, but she wasn't as good as Aunt Mary, her sister. Aunt Mary was a true water witch. She would walk around the property holding the forked part of the stick. When the stick bent down toward the ground then that was the place to dig your well."

"Did it work?"

Granny Zee chuckled. "It did if Mama or Aunt Mary were the ones dowsing." She plucked a twig with a blossom from the plant and handed it to Maggie. "Witch hazel is good for other things too. I gather the twigs in spring and the leaves in summer. Sometimes in the fall, I'll peel off a little of the bark. On the full of the moon, I boil the bark and leaves together to put in my liniment. It's the best stuff in the world to rub on sore muscles. I always make a batch for Mr. Hardin who lives on up the mountain." She pointed her walking stick toward the sky. "He swears by it."

They walked on until Granny Zee stopped and pointed with her walking stick. A cardinal sat on the bare branch of a tree. He looked like a little ball of flame balanced on the dark wood. "Oh, he's lovely," Maggie said. As if he heard her, the bird cocked his head to the side, so she could see his yellow beak.

"He's a show-off, alright." Granny Zee took a step toward the bird. He didn't move from his perch, but rather turned his head from side to side like he was sizing her up. She bowed and said, "Mr. Red Bird, Mr. Red Bird with your feathers so bright/ May I pass through your forest until I'm out of your sight?" The bird chirped and hopped to another twig.

"Thank you, sir," Granny Zee said.

Maggie gasped. "Granny, he answered you!"

Granny Zee chuckled. "I believe so."

The path curved right. "The tree's just up ahead," Granny Zee said.

The persimmon tree wasn't at all what Maggie expected. She imagined it would look like an apple tree, but instead it was Y-shaped with black bark and gnarly branches. The fruit looked like orange tomatoes hanging on the branches.

"This way," Granny Zee said, going off the path and passing under the tree's highest branch. On that side of the tree, the branches were low enough to the ground to easily reach the fruit. "When I was a girl," she said, "we'd shake the persimmons down. That's one of the ways you know they're ripe. Persimmons will fall right off the tree when they're dead ripe. I came out last week and picked up a whole basket full after a little shake."

Granny Zee pointed off to the right with her stick. "Set the baskets right there. We'll pick the ones that are almost dead ripe. It's the ones that are deep orange. Now, don't pull them. Watch me."

She selected a persimmon, and using her shears, cut its stem just above where it connected to the fruit. She held it out to Maggie for inspection. Maggie cupped the smooth fruit in her hand. It was soft like a ripe tomato.

"You try it," Granny Zee said.

Maggie took the shears, selected a persimmon and looked at Granny Zee for approval. Granny nodded, so Maggie cut the stem, surprised at how sturdy it was. Granny Zee smiled. "Now, put it in the basket with the stem down."

For a while, Granny Zee and Maggie snipped persimmons off the tree in silence. Then Granny Zee said, "Your husband's going to win the election."

Maggie froze with a persimmon in her hand. She said, "I was afraid of that."

Granny Zee nodded. She selected another persimmon and cut its stem. She placed it in the basket and straightened up. "Your mother's coming."

"When?"

"She plans to be here for the election."

Maggie looked down at the mashed persimmon all over her glove.

Granny Zee pulled a rag out of her pocket and handed it to Maggie. "I thought you ought to know. I don't think your mother plans to tell you."

Maggie wiped her glove. "Does J.D. know?"

"He's the one who asked her."

"Shit." Maggie put her hands on her hips.

"Honey, listen." Granny Zee put a persimmon in her basket. "This will be hard for you at first, but it's going to be a good thing. He's going to spend more time in Washington, and Addie's growing up. When children grow up, they need their parents in a different way than they do when they're little. She's an independent little thing, anyway. Reilly is too."

They snipped persimmons until Granny said, "I believe that's enough for today."

Maggie picked up the baskets, but Granny Zee didn't move. Instead, Granny stared at her with eyes like blue smoke until a chill ran up her spine. Granny Zee said, "Things are about to change for you, and it's not because of your husband. Something else is about to change."

Maggie followed Granny down the path, her thoughts tumbling end over end like clothes in a dryer. By the time they reached Granny Zee's house, Maggie was fuming. She set the baskets in the kitchen and offered to wash the fruit, but she really wanted to hurl the persimmons and pretend she was throwing them at J.D. and her mother.

"Take off your things and go sit next to the fire," Granny Zee said. "I'll make some tea."

Maggie obeyed, and in no time, Granny Zee had a pot of ginseng tea steeping. She put a plate of cookies on the table and sat down. "Help yourself."

Maggie grabbed a cookie and took a big bite. Granny Zee watched her with a smile in her eyes. Maggie chewed with her mind still on her anger, and then, the taste of the cookie got through to her. Her eyes widened. "Oh, Granny Zee, this tastes amazing!"

Granny Zee clapped her hands together. "I'm happy you like it."

"I don't think I've ever tasted anything like this before. What is it?"

"Why, that's a persimmon cookie." Granny Zee held out the plate to Maggie. "Have another while I get the tea."

Maggie took another cookie and inspected it before taking

a bite. Sweet and delicious, it tasted a little like plums and a little like dates.

"It tastes like autumn," Granny Zee said. She set the teapot on the table.

"Autumn—mmm, it does," Maggie said. "That's perfect, Granny. It's sweet but earthy like autumn."

Maggie rose and poured the tea. She handed Granny Zee a cup and sat down beside her. The steam rising off the cup warmed her cold nose. She sighed. "I wish I could hide here until after the election."

A gnarled hand covered hers. Maggie looked into Granny's eyes. The love she saw there unraveled her. "It's okay to cry," Granny Zee said. "That's why God made tears."

Maggie turned sideways and wrapped her arms around Granny Zee's waist. She buried her face in Granny's chest and cried until her tears were spent. Granny Zee held her and stroked her hair.

Maggie turned her tear-streaked face toward Granny Zee. "Would you sing that song? The one you sang to me before."

Granny Zee sang. "Too-ra-loo-ra-loo-ral, Too-ra-loo-ra-li, Too-ra-loo-ra-loo-ral, hush now, don't you cry! Too-ra-loo-ra-loo-ral, Too-ra-loo-ra-li, Too-ra-loo-ra-loo-ral, that's an Irish lullaby."

"Thank you," Maggie whispered. She kissed Granny's cheek. "Excuse me while I wash my face."

In the bathroom, Maggie splashed cold water on her face. She patted it dry and looked at her red-rimmed eyes in the mirror. She opened the bathroom door and heard Granny's Irish lullaby being sung in a sweet high-pitched child's voice, and it was coming from the doll room. Goose bumps rose on Maggie's arms. She whispered, "Cece."

When the song faded away, Maggie crept past the door without a glance. In fact, she held her breath until she reached the den. She slid into a chair and tried to pick up her teacup, but her hand was shaking so hard that, after the third try, she left it on the table.

"Are you alright?" Granny Zee asked.

Maggie nodded. For some reason she couldn't explain, Cece's singing had given her courage. "Granny, I will be okay." Granny Zee's eyes sparkled. "Of course you will."

Chapter 19

On the Celtic calendar, December 22nd is known as Nameless Day. Nameless Day is where the old saying "a year and a day" comes from—that extra day unaccounted for in a year. The Celts believed that on this "the darkest day" prayer and fasting were necessary to make the sun reappear in the new year.
~ from Granny Zee's Book of Dreams

THE PHONE RANG WHILE Maggie was wrapping Christmas gifts. It was the school nurse, who explained that Reilly had a stomachache and couldn't reach her mother or father, so could Maggie pick her up from school?

Maggie found Reilly in the nurse's office with a pale face and her arms crossed over her stomach. "Do you want me to see if I can track down your mom?"

Reilly shook her head. "Please, don't. She'll freak out and come home, and there's no reason to. I just want to lie down. And I, I... need to stop at my house and get some—some pants."

A blush suddenly bloomed on Reilly's pale cheeks, and Maggie realized what was wrong. "Oh, honey," she said, "did you start your period?"

"Yes, and it hurts. My stomach really hurts."

They got in the car and Maggie patted Reilly on the leg. "I've got just the thing to make you feel better. Tell you what— let's go to my house. You know where Addie's things are. You can find something of hers to put on. And I have female supplies."

Reilly nodded and turned to look out the window, a signal that she didn't want to talk. Maggie hadn't gone through this with Addie yet, but she knew that Reilly was right, Hannah would freak out. But Maggie decided not to call Hannah and accept the consequences.

When they got home Maggie took Reilly to her bathroom and showed her the feminine supplies. She offered to help, but Reilly assured her she didn't need it, closing the door as soon as Maggie stepped out of the bathroom. When she came back with ibuprofen and a mug of hot chocolate, Reilly was wearing Addie's pajamas and lying curled up on her side on Addie's bed.

Maggie sat down beside her and rubbed her back. "I brought you something to make you feel better," she said.

Reilly turned over and sat up. She swallowed the pills and accepted the steaming mug. They sat without talking while Reilly sipped hot chocolate. When she handed the cup back to Maggie, Maggie stood up. "Why don't you get under the covers and take a nap? You'll feel better when you wake up."

Without a word, Reilly slipped under the comforter. Maggie lingered a moment, looking down at the girl she had watched grow up, now on the brink of womanhood. "Rest now," she said, and turned to leave.

"Thanks, Maggie," Reilly said, her voice so small it was barely a whisper.

"Sweetie, there's no reason to thank me. I'm happy to help." Maggie slipped out and closed the door.

Maggie was wrong about Hannah's reaction. She didn't "freak out" as Reilly feared. It was much worse.

At 9:00 that night, Maggie found Hannah shivering on her doorstep. She was expecting Hannah to call; she was even prepared to be yelled at. She was not, however, expecting her to show up in person.

Hannah stomped past her and practically shouted in her face. "Why didn't you call me?"

Maggie froze.

"I *said*, why didn't you call me and tell me *my* child needed *me*?"

Maggie spoke softly. "I didn't call you because Reilly didn't want me to, and I thought..."

"I don't care what you thought! You should've called me."

Maggie didn't know what to say, so she waited for the next outburst. Instead of more shouting, Hannah threw herself into Maggie's arms and burst into tears.

"Oh, Hannah, Reilly was so grown-up about the whole situation. She was..."

"I'm her mother!" Hannah tore herself away from Maggie. "I should've been there." Maggie's heart wrenched at the hurt in Hannah's eyes. "I missed an important day in my daughter's life because I was in class."

Maggie grabbed Hannah's arms and forced her to look at her. "That's right," she said, "you were in class. You're going to be a physical therapist. And, your daughter is very proud of you. So, it's true, you weren't with her on the day she started her period, but ten years from now—no—five years from now, what's it going to matter?"

Hannah's shoulders slumped forward like a deflating balloon. Maggie pulled her close and hugged her. Hannah's sobs laid bare all the worries and frustrations of the past months. "Oh, Maggie," Hannah said between sobs. "I'm so tired."

"I know you are, honey, but it's almost Christmas vacation, and you get a nice long break."

Exhausted, Hannah rested her head on Maggie's shoulder. Maggie rubbed her back and sang: "Too-ra-loo-ra-loo-ral, Too-ra-loo-ra-li, Too-ra-loo-ra-loo-ral, hush now, don't you cry! Too-ra-loo-ra-loo-ral, Too-ra-loo-ra-li, Too-ra-loo-ra-loo-ral, that's an Irish lullaby."

"Granny taught you Cece's song?"

"Yes, she did," Maggie said. It was just a little lie. She couldn't explain why but she didn't want to tell Hannah how she knew it was Cece's song. Instead, she sat Hannah down and made them each a cup of Granny's calming tea.

"When's the last time you ate?" Maggie asked.

Hannah rubbed her eyes. "I don't remember."

"Did you eat dinner?"

"You mean supper?"

Maggie laughed.

"Not yet."

"Hannah, it's almost ten o'clock. How about lunch? Did you eat lunch?"

"No, I don't have time for lunch."

Maggie went to the refrigerator and started putting food on a plate. She put it in the microwave and poured them a fresh cup of tea. While Hannah ate, Maggie sipped tea. When the plate was empty, an enormous yawn escaped from Hannah.

Maggie smiled. "Granny's tea works every time."

Hannah nodded. She put her hand over Maggie's. "I'm sorry. I shouldn't have talked to you like that. I know you've got a lot on your plate, what with J.D. winning the election and your mother showing up."

Maggie smiled into her friend's sleepy blue eyes. "No apology needed. It means a trip to Richmond for his swearing in, and then his friends in D.C. are throwing a few parties, but I'm coming back without him."

"Is he putting pressure on you to stay?"

"No, just the opposite. He thinks it's important I stay in the district he's representing."

Hannah yawned again.

Maggie stood and pulled Hannah to her feet. "Go home and get some rest. And try to find time to eat. You're so thin you're starting to look like a fashion model."

The next morning, Maggie took the girls to school and then

drove to Pineville. She knew Hannah had a break from noon until 1:30, so she had time to do some Christmas shopping and then pick up something for lunch and bring it to the college. After lunch, she would have plenty of time to get back to pick up the girls from school.

At 12:05, Maggie walked into Wagner Hall with a pizza and cheese sticks. She asked a student the way to the student lounge because Hannah had said she usually grabbed something from the snack machine and studied there until her next class.

She found the room on the second floor and pushed open the door. There she found Hannah curled up in a corner chair, book open on her lap.

"Surprise!" Maggie called out.

Hannah leapt up, spilling the book on the floor. "Maggie!"

Maggie put the food on a table near a drink machine. "Lunch," she said, hugging her friend.

Maggie and Hannah were eating their second slice when the door opened and a deep voice said, "I thought I smelled pizza."

A handsome man with a head full of wavy auburn hair dropped change into the drink machine. He punched the Mountain Dew button, and then bent his tall frame so he could fish the bottle out. He turned to Hannah and Maggie and held up a Mountain Dew like he was making a toast. "You Americans know how to make a grand soft drink."

The women laughed. Hannah said, "Dr. O'Shaughnessy, I'd like you to meet my friend, Maggie Whitefield."

He stepped forward and offered Maggie his hand. She stood and took it. Hannah said, "Dr. O'Shaughnessy is one of my professors."

Maggie pointed to the Mountain Dew and said, "*Sláinte.*"

Dr. O'Shaughnessy broke into a wide grin. "*Conas atá tu?*"

"*Glemhaith!*"

"An Irish lass, are you?"

Maggie laughed. "I'm afraid that's about the extent of my Irish, but I've had a rather long love affair with your country. I even spent a semester at Trinity."

"Did you, now? And what parts of Ireland have you visited?"

Maggie paused and gestured toward the pizza. "Please," she said, "won't you join us?"

Dr. O'Shaughnessy grinned. "I'd be delighted."

Maggie looked at Hannah who was grinning like she had just pulled a wishbone and gotten the bigger half. Hannah hopped up and offered Dr. O'Shaughnessy her chair next to Maggie. The only empty chair was on the other side of the table and Hannah slipped into it. It didn't escape Maggie's notice that Hannah gave him her chair so the handsome Dr. O'Shaughnessy could sit next to her.

"Splendid," he said.

Hannah put a slice of pizza on a napkin and placed it in front of Dr. O'Shaughnessy. He said, "Maggie, you were just about to tell us the places you've visited in Ireland."

Maggie glanced at Hannah who sat back and took a bite of pizza, waving at Maggie to continue. Maggie said, "Well, Dr. O'Shaughnessy..."

"Please," he said, "Cooper."

"Cooper," Maggie said. This time, she was afraid to look at Hannah. Instead, she launched into her travels in Ireland. "My papa loved Ireland, and the first time he took me there, I was ten. He was a doctor and when he traveled to speak at universities, he often took me with him."

"May I ask what kind of doctor?" Cooper took a sip of his Mountain Dew. Maggie was struck by how the green of his eyes was like the color of the soft drink bottle.

Maggie said, "A neurosurgeon—a pioneer in laser spinal surgery. As I said, when I was ten, Papa took me to Dublin and since then, I've traveled all over, but I have a special affinity for the western country."

Cooper smiled and nodded. "I'm from Galway City, myself. My Mam and Da have roots in County Clare near Doolin."

"Gus O'Connor's pub," Maggie said, "and the Cliffs of Moher." She inhaled like she was breathing the sea air.

Cooper laughed. "'Tis the grandest place on earth," he said. He leaned toward Maggie like he was telling her a secret. "I'll let you decide if I'm referring to the pub or the Cliffs!"

Maggie laughed and her eyes sparkled. Hannah watched her shy and self-conscious friend blossom like an Irish rose. She talked to Cooper O'Shaughnessy with all the playfulness of a smitten teenager. As they shared memories of Ireland, Maggie looked like she was falling under a spell.

Cooper asked Maggie, "Are you planning a trip over in the near future?"

"Well, as a matter of fact, I was going to talk to Hannah about taking our daughters over for a visit this summer."

Hannah bolted upright. "I have an internship this summer."

Maggie said to Hannah, "We can work around your internship," but she was looking at Cooper.

"So you have children?" Cooper asked.

"Yes," Maggie said, "Hannah and I have daughters the same age—thirteen."

"Oh my, teenagers," Cooper said.

Maggie smiled. "Do you have children?"

Hannah's head shot up. She looked at Maggie with eyebrows raised and a hint of a smile on her lips. Maggie blushed.

"No," Cooper said, "no wife or children." He took a drink of Mountain Dew and Maggie passed him another slice of pizza. "Thank you," he said, "and what do you do?"

"Do?"

"Are you career orientated? You mentioned you attended Trinity College."

Maggie looked at Hannah before answering, "I studied philosophy, but I suppose you could call me a housewife—even though housewife sounds like such an archaic term."

Hannah said, "Before I entered PT school, I too was a housewife. Gee, that sounds like a disease—housewife—or worse, an addiction. Something you need to get over."

Cooper and Maggie laughed.

Hannah said, "I know, Maggie, let's call ourselves recovering housewives."

Maggie said, "I'm all for that."

Cooper laughed. "Perfect."

Maggie took a bite of pizza just as Cooper turned to her and said, "What does your husband do?"

Maggie choked. She coughed and tears sprang to her eyes. Hannah jumped up and started pounding her on the back. Maggie tried to wave her away and signal she was alright, but Hannah grabbed a bottle of water and shoved it into Maggie's hand. "Take a drink."

Maggie managed to stop coughing. She took a sip of water and wiped her eyes with a napkin.

"Are you alright?" Cooper asked.

"I'll be perfect if Hannah doesn't beat me to death."

Hannah looked sheepish. "Sorry, you scared me."

The door opened, and a group of students came in. They stopped and stared at Dr. O'Shaughnessy before making their way to the soft drink machine. He said, "Well, this has been delightful, but it appears to be time for the next class."

They stood, and Hannah gathered up her books while Maggie picked up the empty pizza box and napkins and carried them to the trash can by the door. She turned around and found Cooper looking at her. His six-foot-plus frame rested against the wall. A lock of auburn hair had slipped across his forehead. His face had that ruddy-tinge Maggie had seen often in Ireland, especially among the men who worked out in the never-ceasing wind and frequent rain. A faint reddish stubble was on his square chin, and his eyes were large and so dark Maggie wanted to drown in them. She had the maddening urge to reach up and smooth his hair.

He said, "I am very happy for my Mountain Dew addiction," his "very" sounding like *vare-a*. "Without it, I wouldn't have wandered into the midst of your pizza party."

Something inside of Maggie softened that hadn't yielded in a long time. Cooper extended his hand. "I'm very happy to have met you."

Maggie placed her hand in his, and his long slender fingers curled around it. The words to Frankie Valli's *Can't Take My Eyes Off You* came to her.

Cooper added, "Maggie," saying her name while he held her hand. The warmth of his touch couldn't equal the quiet solicitude of his voice.

"I'm happy I met you too," Maggie said.

Hannah rushed up as Cooper went through the door. She gave Maggie a quick hug before darting into the hallway, calling, "Thanks for lunch. We'll talk later," over her shoulder.

On the way to her car, Maggie realized she hadn't answered Cooper's question about her husband.

1998

Chapter 20

The ancient Irish celebrated the summer Solstice thousands of years ago. The Druids celebrated it as the feast of Alban Heriun, the time when they would praise the victory of light over dark and acknowledge that the nights will get longer, bringing the sun and moon together. Christians adopted this festival and called it St. John's Night. Many places in Ireland still celebrate St. John's Night with carnivals, music concerts, fairs, and of course, bonfires, usually lit on hilltops to simulate the sun.
~ from Granny Zee's Book of Dreams

SCHOOL HAD CLOSED FOR the summer, and Maggie was taking Reilly and Addie for a visit with her mother. Unfortunately, she would be going on to D.C. to attend obligatory social events with J.D., but right now, she was in the swing on Hannah's back porch—one of her favorite places on earth.

Two days of thunderstorms had broken the early summer heat, and the morning was deliciously cool. Maggie was dressed for traveling in navy slacks and a red and navy striped top. Hannah wore cut-offs and one of her physical therapy t-shirts. This one had a row of legs and feet on it. Under them it read, *I'm NOT Checking You Out. Just Analyzing Your Ridiculous GAIT Pattern.*

The swing made a pleasant creaking sound, punctuated by an occasional thump of Hannah's bare toe. A drunken butterfly drifted through the impatiens covering the hillside. The early morning sun heightened the bright mishmash of lavender, pink, and orange finery, and made the mountains around them seem to undulate.

Maggie said, "I gave up on Addie. She promised she will be ready if I pick up Reilly and come back for her."

Hannah laughed and thumped her toe on the deck, giving them another push.

Maggie said, "I have a surprise for you about our upcoming trip to Ireland."

Hannah glanced at her out of the corner of her eye.

Maggie said, "You'll be taking a guided tour of Trinity College, in Dublin, and its School of Medicine's Physiotherapy Department."

The swing jerked to a halt. "How in the world did you arrange that?"

Maggie laughed. "I didn't. Cooper did. In fact, he's going to meet us there."

Hannah smiled. "And just when did you and Dr. O'Shaughnessy cook this up?"

Maggie smiled. "We've talked."

"Talked, have you?" Hannah pushed the swing and it started to move.

"Yes—a bit."

Hannah laughed. She turned sideways in the swing, so she could look at her friend. "Why, Maggie Whitefield! You're blushing!"

"I am not," Maggie said, but she pressed her hand to her cheek.

"I *knew* the first day you met you were attracted to him, and it's obvious he's smitten with you. And besides, I'm thankful for all the free food I got last semester! Every time you brought me lunch, he managed to show up. I'm happy I got to watch your romance blossom."

Maggie looked down at her hands. She twisted the huge diamond wedding ring around on her finger. "Don't think badly of me."

"Oh, sweetie, I think it's absolutely wonderful. You deserve someone like Dr. O'Shaughnessy—someone who adores you." Maggie looked up, and Hannah was startled by her expression. Her face was flushed, and her eyes were dusky with emotion. Maggie said, "You know, I could fall in love with him. It would be so easy."

Hannah slipped her arm around her friend's shoulders. "Would that be so terrible?"

Maggie put her head on Hannah's shoulder. They swayed back and forth in silence. A crash, followed by the sound of a suitcase being rolled across the floor, shattered the moment. Maggie raised her head and looked at Hannah. In unison, they said, "Reilly."

The door flew open and Reilly materialized. She was pulling on the handle of an enormous suitcase that appeared to be stuck in the doorway. "Hey," she said, "I could use a little help here." Maggie and Hannah burst out laughing. Reilly rolled her eyes at them and dragged her suitcase to Maggie's car. Everyone hugged and said good-bye, and then Reilly and Maggie drove off to pick up Addie.

The house was so empty after Maggie and Reilly left, that Hannah found herself wandering from room to room. She decided to give it a good cleaning and, when she finished, she lay down to take a nap. She thought about Maggie and Cooper and wondered what it would be like to be in love like that. Hannah had never had butterflies in her stomach when a man came into the room—never lost her appetite over a man—never pined away to see a man. She had never woken up in the morning knowing she was in love. Hannah turned on her side and fell asleep.

The aroma of steaks on the barbeque teased Hannah awake. She followed it through the house and outside, where she found Travis flipping two enormous T-bones. Hannah watched her husband—the way his hair curled at the base of his neck. He wore cut-offs that were so faded they were almost white and a muscle shirt that left not one muscle to the imagination. Her eyes were drawn to the ugly scars on his leg. Even with his deep tan, the scar across his knee was obvious.

Travis closed the grill and turned around. He smiled. "Hey babe, you hungry?"

"Yes. Smells good. I'm going to take a quick shower, and then I'll make a salad."

"Already done. And I've got potatoes in the microwave." He went to the door and opened it for her. "I've got to grab a plate to put the steaks on," he said, following Hannah inside.

Placemats and silverware were on the dining room table. Hannah knew Travis preferred to eat in front of the television. "What's the occasion?" she asked.

"No occasion. I know you been working hard, so I thought you'd like a nice dinner."

Hannah smiled and went off to shower. It didn't escape her notice that Travis had remembered to get out the condiments.

She had her head under the water when Travis pulled back the shower curtain and got in the tub behind her. "Hey!" she said, turning to find him smiling.

"Thought I'd hurry you up," he said. "Steaks are ready." He stood still, waiting for her lead.

Hannah placed her hands on his chest, broad and hard, and slid them up until she reached his shoulders. Then her arms encircled his neck, and he brought his mouth down to hers. Their kisses were long and deep, and a moan escaped Hannah. Travis pulled back, his brow questioning.

She shook her head and reached for him, and this time when she moaned, he didn't pull away, but reached behind her and lifted her up to him.

While they ate, Travis talked about a guy at work who'd bought a Boxer puppy for his son's birthday and brought the puppy to work to hide it until the birthday party. He had Hannah laughing with stories of the puppy's goofy antics. She found herself telling him about the patients she would be working with and the equipment she would be using. They talked until the food was gone, and then Travis insisted she go watch TV while he cleaned up.

Hannah poured a glass of wine and retreated to the family room. She found *Gone with the Wind* on television and sat down to watch it for the hundredth time. She was surprised when Travis came in and passed up his recliner to sit down next to her on the sofa. Before long, they were laughing and doing "Scarlett" and "Rhett" voices.

When the movie was over, Travis turned off the television. In the sudden darkness, moonlight poured through the window and cast iridescent shadows on the wall. They sat for a moment in the quiet before Hannah said, "Travis, Maggie wants to take Reilly and me to Ireland."

"When?"

"Soon. When Reilly gets back from D.C."

"Well, I think you should go. It will be good for Reilly." He patted Hannah on the leg, his hand lingering on her thigh. "You too, babe. You've always wanted to go."

A wave of uneasiness washed over Hannah. She should be thrilled Travis was so obliging, but this wasn't the man she knew. Even after great sex, the Travis she knew would have come at her with a hundred reasons why she shouldn't go, with number one being money.

"The house sure is quiet without Reilly," Travis said, standing and stretching. "I believe I'll go to bed."

"Travis, wait," Hannah said. She had been trying for weeks to find a way to bring this up, but she had chickened out every time. Then tonight, Travis had been so caring and considerate—so loving—that she decided it was now or never.

Travis looked down at her. Hannah said, "Who was driving the night of the accident?"

He took a step back and put his hand up like he was expecting a blow. "Where'd that come from?"

"I've been thinking about it," Hannah said. "Things don't add up."

Travis started to interrupt her, so she rushed on. "Since I've been studying rehabilitating people with broken bones,

I've thought a lot about yours and how your leg was crushed, and it doesn't add up. I saw the car, and if you were driving, it should have been the other leg that was broken. Unless..."

Travis ran his fingers through his hair and shifted his eyes away from her face. "That was a long time ago. Just let it go."

He started to walk away, but Hannah sprang from the couch and grabbed his arm. "If you weren't driving that night, why did you say you were?"

"It doesn't matter now," Travis said, looking at the floor.

"But it mattered then! When you told the cops you were driving, you lost everything. Your scholarship, your reputation—please—just tell me."

Travis jerked his arm from her grip. "I couldn't play football again. College didn't matter after that." He stopped and lowered his voice. "Don't you see? I couldn't go back. I couldn't be *there*. I couldn't watch those guys I played with pity me." He looked down at his feet.

Hannah stepped in front of him, but he wouldn't look up. She softened her voice. "It was Roby, wasn't it?" She took his head in her hands and lifted it, so she could look into his eyes. The dark blonde stubble on his cheek and chin gave her the sudden urge to rub her face across it, but his eyes stopped her. Blue as a morning sky, they were filled with such raw pain that she shuddered. "But Travis," she said, "it *did* matter. It mattered to *me*. Why did you let me think all these years that you were the one driving?"

A deep frown furrowed his brow, and Travis closed his eyes. Gently, he pulled himself away and stepped back so Hannah had to let go of his face. "Let it go, babe," he said. "It's water under the bridge." But he didn't move. Instead, he stood still, like he was gathering his strength, and then, he reached out and let his thumb skim across her cheek. He said, "Good night."

Hannah's breath caught in her throat. She sat down on the couch and buried her head in her hands. The Travis she knew would not have taken the blame for a friend. The man she knew had always put himself first.

Hannah thought back to the days following the accident. After the operation put his leg back together, the surgeon told him he would never play football again. Hannah had been with him when he got the news, and like a black cloud covering the sun, she saw the light disappear from their lives. From that day forward, every minute of every day would be different than before the accident. The seconds, minutes, and hours would be the same, but their time had been altered. That one event had changed the course of Hannah's life as surely as if she had been in that car.

Before the accident, Hannah had been young and naive enough to think she had control over her and Travis's future, but the day the surgeon said, "I'm sorry," everything changed, forever. That day, Hannah realized that one person, one chance meeting, one wrong move, could alter everything as surely as the day turned into night and the night turned into day again.

Two weeks after the accident, Travis had gone home in an ambulance, and Hannah had stayed to take her exams. Travis could have taken his exams later and gotten credit for the semester, but he refused. She never understood why until tonight.

How could Travis have kept that locked inside of him all these years? How many times had she thrown it in his face? She had never tried to spare him her anger and disappointment. And not once had he tried to defend himself.

A hurt closed in on her heart, and Hannah lay down on the couch, curling into herself. The ache grew heavier with the gathering shadows. Travis had *not* driven drunk. All these years she had hated him for his recklessness. Blamed him for ruining her life. Hot tears overtook her.

Chapter 21

Signs are all around us, you just have to open yourself to find them. The most obvious ones are about death. My mother told me there were two signs that foretold my father's death. A week before my father died, Mama said a redbird flew in the house, and a day before he died his pocket watch, which had not worked in months, suddenly started ticking.
~ from Granny Zee's Book of Dreams

APART FROM THREE PLEASANT days, the summer was turning into one long stretch of blistering heat. Maggie couldn't wait to see Hannah and Reilly's faces when they experienced Ireland's cool weather, especially Doolin and the Cliffs of Moher. Maggie had told them the Irish people say, "If you don't like the weather, just wait a few minutes."

At the airport, check-in and baggage check went by in a blur, the four travelers made it through security, and then they sat down to wait. Hannah faced the window. She stared at three planes waiting for takeoff. She knew one of them was theirs. She told herself to breathe; it was going to be alright.

Suddenly, it was time to board the plane. It was much smaller and more crowded than Hannah had expected. Maggie explained it didn't have a first-class section, but they were near the front in business class. Maggie offered her the window seat, but Hannah refused. She watched people pour onto the plane and listened to the slamming of luggage into overhead compartments.

When everyone was seated, the flight attendants did their spiel, and the captain's voice announced they had been cleared for takeoff. When the plane started to move, Hannah looked at Maggie. "We're moving," she said.

Maggie said, "That's what we're supposed to do."

From across the aisle, Reilly said, "Mom, we're moving!"

The plane turned slowly in a wide circle. Hannah gripped Maggie's hand as the plane began to move faster. The hum of the engines turned into a roar, and then Hannah's body was pressed back into the seat. She closed her eyes, the plane lifted, and then—nothing.

Hannah opened her eyes and looked at Maggie. "What happened?"

"We're flying."

"We are?"

Maggie giggled. "I told you it's just like sitting in a chair."

Hannah said, "Piece of cake," and Maggie laughed.

In less than an hour, they landed in Atlanta. There had been no turbulence to speak of, and Hannah was over the worst of her flight anxiety, even though she gripped Maggie's hand so tight when they landed that Maggie was glad Hannah had bitten off her nails.

Reilly and Hannah were amazed by the airport—masses of people hurrying by, pulling suitcases. There were moving sidewalks, a subway train, stores, and restaurants—a city unto itself. The four made the trek to the other end of the airport where the international flights took off. When they entered the corridor, it was as if they were already in another country. Myriad nationalities milled around. Unidentifiable languages swirled in the air.

They grabbed lunch before settling down to wait for their flight. It wasn't long before the announcement came. "Flight 176 to Dublin, Ireland is now pre-boarding. People with disabilities or young children or others who need assistance may board at this time." The announcement hit Hannah in the chest like a swift punch. She even bent forward and put her hand over her chest.

Maggie grabbed her arm. "Are you okay?"

Hannah nodded her head, slowly. "Sorry, it just hit me this is real. I'm going to Ireland." A few moments later, another announcement came over the loudspeaker. "Flight 176 to Dublin, Ireland will now begin boarding first-class passengers."

"That's us," Maggie said. "Make sure you have your boarding pass and passport in your hand."

"Wait!" Hannah said.

Maggie and the girls turned around. "What's wrong?" Maggie asked.

Hannah said, "You didn't tell me we were flying first class."

"Oh, for heaven's sake, come on," Maggie said.

At the gate, Hannah watched Maggie, then Addie, then Reilly present their passports and disappear through the gate. Hannah stepped up to the attendant, fumbling to get her passport out of her bag. She finally freed it and presented it to the attendant. The whole time she was thinking how this was the first time anyone had ever asked her, "May I have your passport?"

The attendant looked at the passport, then up at Hannah. She said, "You have to sign it."

Hannah's eyes flew wide. What if they weren't going to let her get on the plane! And Maggie and Reilly and Addie will take off not knowing what happened to me. But the attendant just handed her a pen.

Hannah stood there like an idiot, searching her brand new, never-used passport for a place to sign. She could feel the people standing behind her judging her. She finally looked up at the attendant. "Where?"

The flight attendant pointed to a line that Hannah would've sworn wasn't there a minute ago. She signed her name and gave the passport and the pen back to the attendant with an, "I'm sorry."

The attendant picked up her microphone. "Ladies and gentlemen, for your information, your passport is a legal document and must be signed by the owner." She clicked off the microphone and looked at Hannah. Hannah snatched her passport from the attendant's outstretched hand and bolted through the gate. Her face was so hot with embarrassment she was surprised her hair didn't catch on fire.

When Hannah finally made it on the plane, she plopped down next to Maggie without paying attention to her surroundings. Maggie asked, "What took you so long?"

"I had to go to the bathroom," Hannah said.

From across the aisle, Reilly said, "Mom, isn't this the coolest thing ever?"

Hannah looked around. A steady line of people passed through first class on their way to the economy seats. Some of them looked at her. No doubt they wished they could trade places.

Maggie leaned toward Hannah and whispered, "Look, Hannah, I'm not going to endure a ten-hour flight in economy class. It's going to be hard enough to adjust to a five-hour time difference. Besides, I want your first trip to be perfect." She looked hard at Hannah. "Are you sure you're alright?"

"Yes, I'm just nervous." Hannah sat back and watched passengers going by. She was amazed when a woman with a tiny baby got on board, and then a woman entered with a toddler. Hannah said, "I wasn't expecting there to be kids on the plane."

"Let's just hope they sleep," Maggie said.

Finally, they were on their way. The takeoff in the big jet was more intense, and Hannah relaxed once they were in the air. Then Maggie showed Hannah how to use the television and headphones, and Hannah discovered there was a map showing the plane moving over the land. She realized it would soon be moving over the ocean, so she decided to watch a movie.

Before long, the flight attendants served dinner, and then they handed out pillows and blankets and everyone settled down and turned off their lights. Hannah couldn't believe she could go to sleep and wake up in Ireland. She looked over at the girls and saw they were already asleep. She looked at Maggie, and Maggie took her hand. "Are you okay?" she asked.

Hannah sighed. "Yes, I still can't believe this is happening. Thank you, Maggie."

"Listen, Hannah, I know how you feel about me paying for this trip, but I want you to understand, I'm doing it more for me than you."

Hannah squeezed Maggie's hand.

"I mean it," Maggie said. "This trip would mean nothing to me or Addie without you and Reilly. I want to experience Ireland with my best friend because it will make it new for me, too. Before he died, my father said something I've never forgotten: 'Happiness comes from being with the people we love, not by buying things.' Papa believed a person should accumulate knowledge and friends, not objects. He always gave me personal and meaningful gifts."

Hannah smiled. She lifted the necklace that she never took off. "Like this?"

Maggie grinned. "Yes, that's why I gave it to you. I'm so happy you like it."

"I treasure it, but there's only one problem with it."

Maggie raised her eyebrows.

"I'll have to add an Irish charm."

Maggie chuckled. "Christmas is coming."

Hannah squeezed Maggie's hand.

Maggie said, "Close your eyes and try to sleep. You're about to discover jet lag."

Hannah awakened from a dream so real she trembled with its cold. In the dream, she sat in the front seat of a car, its windshield covered with a thick shell of snow. Her arms were wrapped around her shaking body and her breath fogged in front of her. She thought she must find a way to escape when the car doors flew open and Travis and his friends fell inside, the yeasty smell of beer trailing them.

Two men squashed her between them. The vehicle started but the headlights were nothing more than a faint shadow beyond the snow-crusted car. The car lurched forward, and the snow slid off the windshield in one solid chunk. The wheels spun, and the car rocked back and forth. Suddenly breaking free, it lurched down a snow-covered road.

"Please, stop! Please," Hannah begged.

A voice from the backseat said, "Slow down, man."

Travis laughed. "There ain't nobody on the road but us."

The snow thumped against the windshield in fist-sized drops. The car picked up speed and suddenly skidded to the right. A voice from the back seat yelled, "Slow down, damn it!"

The car stopped sliding and lurched forward. Travis laughed a high-pitched, frenzied snarl. He yelled, "If we don't speed up, we won't make it up Murray Hill."

Hannah screamed when the car capped the hill, tires spinning. It hovered at the top for two seconds before taking off like a flash of prayer, gaining speed until it hurtled through the snow-white night. At the bottom of the hill it fishtailed and straightened, fishtailed again. The car lifted into the air, twisting and flipping, before landing on its top in the road with a loud thud. Their screams turned into a collective hiss, and the smell of raw fear filled the car. Upside down, the car began to move forward again, picking up speed until it careened down the road. When it hit a hump in the snow, it rose off the pavement and became airborne. A crash followed by a shower of glass and the crunch of metal rocked the car, bringing it to a halt against a tree.

Hannah screamed, "Travis!" She was pressed against the dashboard. Long white ropes of snow came through the broken windshield. The door on the passenger side hung open and in the overhead light, Hannah saw Travis face down in the snow. She crawled to him, screaming his name. By the time she reached him, he was under a white mound like a fresh burial. She clawed at the snow, trying to lift his head, but her fingers were so frozen she couldn't get a grip.

Hannah cried again, "Travis!"

He moaned.

"Oh, Travis, thank God!" Hannah lay down next to him and maneuvered under his arm. She pushed and somehow gathered the strength to roll him over. She got up on her knees and looked down into the face of Travis's friend, Roby.

Somehow, Hannah got back on her feet and turned around. She extended her arms in front of her for balance and plodded through the snow. She made it to the driver's side, but she couldn't open the door, so she trudged back to the passenger side and crawled across the seat to get to Travis who lay crumpled against the steering wheel. "Travis! Wake up!" she cried.

Hannah woke sitting upright, clutching at her throat. At first, she thought the faint yellow light was coming from the car's headlights, but then she saw Maggie curled on her side, and realized the lights illuminated the aisle of the plane.

Hannah looked around the darkened cabin. Only the tops of Reilly and Addie's heads were visible under their blankets. She burrowed under hers and tried to stop shaking. The dream was so real she could still feel the wet of snow on her skin. She whispered over and over, "Just a dream."

❧

"I thought you were going to sleep through the landing," Maggie said. She smiled at Hannah who realized the cabin was filled with light, and everyone around her was awake and eating breakfast.

"Wow, I can't believe I slept at all." She sat up. "How long before we land?"

"About an hour. Are you hungry?"

"Sure. Be right back." Hannah grabbed her bag and managed to freshen up in the tiny bathroom. When she came back, the flight attendant brought her breakfast. While she ate, she watched Reilly and Addie brush each other's hair.

Hannah watched Maggie put on lipstick. She looked as fresh and groomed as always. Hannah sighed. She knew she was rumpled from head to toe.

Maggie said, "Are you okay? We'll be on the ground soon."

"I'm fine," Hannah said. "I just..." She looked down at her hands.

Maggie put her hand over Hannah's. "What is it? Aren't you excited?"

"Oh, Maggie, of course I'm excited. This is a chance of a lifetime. I just had a bad dream and I can't shake it. That's all."

"Do you want to talk about it?"

"No, it's nothing." She looked down at her empty breakfast container and thought about Granny. "At least Granny would say it was okay to tell you since I've already had breakfast."

"What do you mean?"

"It's one of our Appalachian superstitions. Never tell a bad dream before you eat breakfast, or it will come true." Hannah knew that not all dreams were mere dreams—our minds trying to make sense out of the jumble of thoughts traversing our brains during sleep. Some were glimpses into the future. And some, like this one, was a window opened on the past. Had this dream showed Hannah what really happened that night? Had Travis been driving after all?"

The captain announced they were approaching Ireland, and Maggie grabbed her camera, pulling Hannah over to the window. A sea of white clouds parted, and the plane dropped under them into the sheer blue of the sky. Hannah didn't have time to finish her exclamation of "Look!" before the plane descended lower, revealing the aquamarine of the ocean and the green of Ireland vibrating in the sun. The most amazing green countryside Hannah had ever seen rose up from the ocean.

"Oh, my." Hannah breathed a deep sigh. "It's so beautiful and... and so *green*."

Maggie laughed. "That's why they call it the Emerald Isle." She snapped some pictures through the window and then took a picture of Hannah. Across the aisle, Reilly and Addie were pressed against the window exclaiming at the land below. Hannah took the camera and got some pictures of the girls and one of Maggie. Then the captain announced they would be landing soon and a frenzy of repacking carry-on bags started. At last, they settled down to wait for the landing.

Hannah said, "I'll tell you an old Appalachian saying that's running through my mind right now."

Maggie smiled. "What?"

"I'm as nervous as a one-legged man in a roach stomping contest."

They laughed and held hands as the plane landed.

It took them over an hour to get through Customs at Dublin Airport and retrieve their luggage, but at last they located their driver, who had more whiskers than hair. He introduced himself as John, ushered them outside, and whisked them into the mass of traffic headed for downtown Dublin. As John maneuvered through it, he explained how the roads in and out of Dublin ran one way, with River Liffey separating them. He took them down O'Connell Street, the main thoroughfare, pointing out how it was intersected by numerous shopping streets, including Henry Street and Talbot Street. They made it to the south side and, suddenly, the enormous black fence of Trinity College came into view. The Mount Clare, their hotel, was just behind Trinity.

"I hope you like the hotel," Maggie said. "It's close to Trinity College, so Papa and I always stayed here."

They entered the hotel lobby and for the first time since they'd left the airport, Addie and Reilly were speechless. The lobby glowed with rich polished woodwork and muted shades of beige and burgundy decor. The enormous check-in desk was made of highly polished mahogany and ran the length of the wall. The quintessential Irish lass stood behind it. She was tall and thin with porcelain skin and long flaming red hair. Her clear blue eyes shone when she spoke in a pure and lilting Irish brogue.

Maggie checked them in and got the keys to their rooms. "I've gone back in time," Hannah whispered, looking around the lobby. She spied Reilly staring at the hotel clerk with rapt attention. Hannah moved over to the girls. "What do you think?" she asked.

In a perfect Irish accent Reilly said, "Tis grand."

Hannah laughed and put her arms around Reilly and Addie. Maggie joined them, and the group went off to their rooms to unpack and shower before dinner. It was only 2:00 PM but their bodies were on U.S. time where it was 9:00 AM.

An hour later, they left the hotel and strolled through the streets. Hannah raised her face to the gentle breeze and a delicious shiver coursed through her. Maggie asked, "Are you cold?"

"No, it feels wonderful." Hannah laughed. "But I can't shake the feeling I've stepped back in time. You see all of these modern shops and smartly dressed people, and then you turn the corner and there's a medieval castle."

Maggie nodded. "You don't realize how new everything is in America, until you come here."

For at least the tenth time, Addie and Reilly called out, "Mom, look!" They stopped in front of a quaint bookstore, situated on the corner of a row of shops painted in jewel tones. The bookstore was royal blue with an upstairs bay window trimmed in gold. Reilly asked, "Can we go in?"

Hannah laughed. "Later! I'm starving. Let's eat now and shop tomorrow."

Maggie's step was light, and her heart was filled with anticipation. She couldn't stop smiling. Already, being in Dublin with Hannah was like being there for the first time. She was 4,000 miles away from J.D. and her mother—she was in Ireland, and Cooper O'Shaughnessy was arriving on Friday.

Maggie said, "Hannah, in four years the girls will be ready to graduate from high school."

Hannah nodded. "I think about it every day." Tears surprised her, spilling down her cheeks.

"Honey, what's wrong?"

"This," Hannah swept her arm in an arc in front of her, "is pretty overwhelming." She wiped the tears away and smiled. She didn't want to spoil the evening by talking about the dream that was haunting her.

They stopped to cross the street and Maggie kept glancing at Hannah out of the corner of her eye. She wanted this vacation to be wonderful for Hannah, but she knew when something was bothering her friend. She pointed at the building just ahead. "That's Foley's Restaurant and Pub. They have wonderful food—authentic fish and chips."

"Pub?" Hannah stopped and stared. "You mean like a bar? We're taking our girls into a bar?"

Maggie laughed. "Honey, you're in Ireland. You'll see."

Hannah didn't know what was more enchanting about Foley's, the inside or the outside. The bottom story of the building was painted white with FOLEY'S in gold letters set against a black background. Pink and purple flowers grew all along the top of the sign and spilled over the letters. Inside Foley's, the place gleamed with polished wood. They were shown upstairs to the Queen Maebh's Restaurant, a quaint place with more polished wood and old-fashioned decor. At the top of the stairs, the waitress stopped and said, "Your guest has already arrived. He's seated over there."

"Our guest?" Maggie looked around, but the room was softly lit; she thought Cooper had come early to surprise her.

Then Addie squealed. "Daddy! I knew you'd come."

Hannah watched the color drain from Maggie's face. She grabbed her elbow to steady her, but Maggie faltered only for a moment. She recovered her smile and continued across the room to where her husband sat, smiling like he flew 4,000 miles every day just to surprise her. Hannah shivered. His smile reminded her of the old-fashioned movie villains who smile when they know they've won.

J.D. stood and Addie ran into his arms. "Daddy," you're here!" She laughed and hugged him again.

"I'm surprising you and your mother. Did it work?"

Addie laughed. "I knew you were coming."

J.D. laughed at what he thought was a joke.

Maggie walked up to the table and stared at her daughter. Addie had known her father was coming. She could tell by the way Addie avoided her eyes.

J.D. waved his hand toward the table. "Ladies, please, sit down."

He pulled out the chair next to him for Maggie, kissing her cheek. "Margaret, aren't you happy to see me?" He gave an exaggerated laugh. "From the look on your face, I thought you were expecting somebody else." He laughed again.

The waitress appeared to take their drink orders, giving

Maggie a chance to compose herself. She picked up her menu and pretended to study it, her mind reeling. She would call Cooper and warn him, but first, she had to find out how long J.D. planned to stay. She knew he had come from D. C., and she doubted he would stay long.

As soon as the waitress took their orders, Addie started chattering about all the things they planned to do in the next two weeks. "Daddy," she said, "I wish you could stay with us. The whole time, I mean."

J.D. gave her a measured look. He said, "You always seem to know what I'm going to say."

Addie blushed and looked down at the table. Maggie said, "She knows how busy you are."

J.D. smiled at Addie. "I'm sorry, sweet pea, but I have some government business to take care of in London on Thursday, and then I must fly home Friday morning. So tomorrow, I'm all yours. You don't mind if I tag along, do you ladies?"

Hannah smiled at him. "Of course, not."

Thanks to Addie and Reilly, dinner was bearable. They kept up a steady banter back and forth about Ireland, engaging the waitress who told them all about her home in a little village near Cork. During the walk back to the hotel, the girls copied her expressions, exclaiming everything as "brilliant," "excellent," and "splendid," with lots of "of course" thrown in.

Back at the hotel, Maggie discovered J.D.'s bag had been sent to her room. He turned to Hannah with his most disarming smile. "You won't mind if Addie bunks in with you tonight and tomorrow night, will you?"

Hannah smiled but her eyes apologized to Maggie. "No problem. We have plenty of room."

Addie grabbed her pajamas and said goodnight to her parents. She avoided her mother's eyes, making haste to get away before Maggie had a chance to speak to her alone.

J.D. said, "Would you like to go down to the bar for a drink?"

Maggie nodded. She decided she would rather drink than be trapped in the room with him. At the bar, he ordered a Guinness and a glass of white wine for Maggie. The drinks arrived and, in typical attorney fashion, he attacked Maggie without warning. "Who's Cooper?"

Maggie took a sip of wine, composing herself before answering. "Wouldn't a phone call have been easier?" She sat back and crossed her legs, pretending to be relaxed. "Did you really come 4,000 miles to ask me that?"

"Answer the question."

Maggie leaned forward. "How dare you. I am not on trial." Her voice would have cut glass.

For a split second, J.D.'s smile wavered. Maggie knew she'd scored a point. She also knew he'd gotten hold of her phone and read her messages, the rest he'd made up on his own.

"Margaret, if you misunderstood my intention, I'm sorry. As I told Addie, I'm just stopping off on my way to London. I'm simply curious about the man who's been messaging my wife." J.D. sipped his Guinness like he was doing nothing more than sharing a drink with his wife.

Maggie caught the stress on the word "my" but ignored it. She said, "Cooper O'Shaughnessy is one of Hannah's professors. I met him at the college and discovered he was familiar with my father's research at Trinity. I asked him to set up a visit for Hannah at Trinity's Occupational Therapy College. But then, you read my messages, so you already know that."

With a smirk on his face, J.D. drained half of his Guinness. "See, that didn't hurt a bit."

Maggie knew he'd already had too much to drink with dinner. She said, "Now that I've answered your question, you answer mine. Why have you been spying on me?"

"Now, Margaret, I wouldn't do that." He sat back and put his hand on his chest like he was shocked. "It was entirely innocent, I assure you. I just happened to hear your phone get a text message and I thought I ought to look at it in case it was important."

"And what? You just happened to forget to tell me about it? Why didn't you ask me then instead of coming here to do it? Or did you want to see what else, or *who else*, you could find?"

J.D. remained silent. He stared at her, a slight smile on his face. Maggie said, "Well, at least you don't deny it."

A waitress appeared with another Guinness and glass of wine. J.D. handed his unfinished Guinness to the waitress and accepted the new one. Maggie waved away the second glass of wine. When the waitress walked away, Maggie said, "So, now, you've solved the mystery. The meeting with Cooper O'Shaughnessy, you read about on my phone, is for Hannah. Since you are so good at discovering what I'm up to, why don't you hop on over to Trinity tomorrow and check on it? I'm sure you're dying to see if they will verify my story."

"Margaret, I am a United States Senator and I don't want my wife—"

Margaret stood. "I've heard enough. Unless the next words from your mouth are, 'I apologize,' I'm going to bed."

She stared down at him, her heart pounding but she held

his gaze. He reached for her hand, but she took a step back. He said, "Okay, Margaret, I'm sorry. Sit down."

She remained standing. He said, "Please, sit down. I apologize. Please."

Margaret sat down and took a sip of wine. She grasped the wineglass tightly, so her hand wouldn't shake. If she was going to convince J.D. that she barely knew Cooper, she had to remain in control; at the same time, her mind was reeling, trying to recall the messages on her phone because she knew without a doubt, he had read every one of them.

J.D. said, "Margaret, I thought you'd be happy to see me. I've been so busy; I haven't had much time with you, or Addie."

Maggie noticed he added Addie as an afterthought. She knew it was not wise to let J.D. think he'd swept this under the rug. She had to make him understand that she knew he'd been prying into her life and that she wouldn't stand for it. She said, "You haven't been any busier than usual. That's just an excuse. I won't have you spying on me. And I won't have you showing up unannounced to try and catch me with another man."

J.D. leaned forward. His voice took on an earnest tone. "Margaret, what's happened to you? You're not the woman I married."

Maggie sat back in her chair and stared at J.D. like she wanted to fix his face in her mind, so that years from now, she could remember this moment and see his expression. "No," she said, "I'm not. I've grown and changed like a person is supposed to do, and along the way, I stopped being the person *you* want me to be and started being the person *I* want to be."

J.D.'s dark eyes flashed. His already flushed face darkened. He hissed, "When I run for governor, the last thing I need is my wife running around with some Irishman."

Maggie leaned forward until their foreheads almost touched. "In four years, Addie will graduate from high school, and I don't care if you run for dogcatcher."

She sat back and drained her wine, putting the glass in the exact center of the table. "I'm going to bed."

J.D. looked up. "I don't believe for one minute you'll turn your back on the governor's mansion."

Maggie smiled. "I guess you'll just have to wait and see, then, won't you? That is—if you get elected."

She walked away.

Chapter 22

My grandmother taught me that the number three is important to the Irish. The ancient Celts believed in three dominions: earth, sky, and sea. St. Patrick taught the Irish people about the holy trinity—the father, the son, and the holy spirit—by using a plant called a shamrock. The shamrock is an Irish plant with three green leaves that looks much like our clover, but Granny said that true shamrocks only grow in Irish soil.
~ from Granny Zee's Book of Dreams

THE NEXT MORNING, MAGGIE, Hannah, and the girls were having breakfast in the hotel dining room when J.D. joined them. Dressed in faded blue jeans and a Washington, D.C. sweatshirt, J.D. also wore sunglasses and Redskins cap. In spite of herself, Maggie smiled. J.D. was hung over and she hoped he felt like hell.

While they ate, Addie and Reilly talked over their plans for the day, but J.D. sipped black coffee. Addie explained they were going to walk about and sightsee, then have lunch, and then take a Hop-On Hop-Off Bus Tour.

"Sounds great," J.D. said.

The girls were so excited their voices grew louder. When Reilly laughed and clapped her hands, J.D. winced. Maggie had to cover her mouth and cough to stifle a giggle. Maybe today wouldn't be so bad after all.

Just after nine, they left the hotel and stepped into the bustle of Dublin. It was a balmy fifty-five degrees and the sky was a pale grey plate piled high with peach-colored clouds. Hannah confessed to Maggie she was happy she had brought jeans and sweatshirts.

They set out for O'Connell Bridge, with J.D. and the girls taking the lead. They rounded a corner and passed a group of students dressed in school uniforms. Addie and Reilly took pictures of the Irish teens, but, Maggie noticed, mostly of the boys. She poked Hannah with her elbow and motioned for her to listen to Reilly who said to Addie, "Did you see the dreamy guy with the reddish hair?"

"Which one?" Addie said. "They all had red hair."

"The tallest one. He looked right at me and smiled."

"No," Addie said. "He smiled at me!"

Maggie giggled and the girls turned around. Addie said, "Come on Reilly, let's get ahead of them so they can't listen in on our *private* conversation."

At O'Connell Bridge they paused to take pictures, and then everyone stood and gazed at the River Liffey. To Hannah, the cool morning breeze held a mysterious smell. She took a deep breath and closed her eyes, trying to decipher it. Not like home, but home shared a fecund scent with the metallic smell from the coal in the soil. This smell was fresher, saltier. She inhaled again, holding her breath for a few seconds, searching, and then it came to her. When she opened the little metal spout on the blue container of Morton's salt and poured salt into a pot of boiling water, this was the scent that rose with the steam.

O'Connell Bridge caused a flood of memories to come back to Maggie. She thought of the times she and Papa had crossed it, while he told tales of the Vikings, or Norsemen, as the Irish called them. He would point to the water and say, "They sailed up this river to plunder and take back what they could steal to Norway." He would extol the ancient history of Ireland as they strolled, explaining how the Viking raids went on for over two hundred years, and many of the Irish cities—Dublin, Cork, Limerick, and Wexford—actually began as Viking settlements.

The group continued up O'Connell Street, stopping first at the O'Connell Memorial. Maggie recited from the poem, "Easter Rising of 1916," by William Butler Yeats. "I write it out in a verse— / MacDonagh and MacBride / And Connolly and Pearse / Now and in time to be, / Wherever green is worn, / Are changed, changed utterly: / A terrible beauty is born."

Maggie continued. "The Irish rebelled against English rule by attempting an uprising on Easter Monday, April 24, 1916. It failed, resulting in the execution of the Irish republican leaders involved." She pointed out the bullet holes caused by gunfire that had never been repaired, and the angel, crushing a serpent and the faithful Irish wolfhound, on the statue.

Hannah and the girls gazed up at the statue, and Maggie realized J.D. was staring at her. She returned his stare, refusing to look away. He smirked. "Spoken like a true Irish lass."

Addie and Reilly laughed, but Maggie's face flamed. Hannah put her hand on Maggie's arm and squeezed. They walked on, and Hannah whispered, "Hang on. Tomorrow he's out of your hair."

They made their way to the Henry Street shopping district where J.D. made a big deal of spending money on the girls. At first, he followed them in the shops and encouraged them to buy something, making a big deal about paying for their purchases. Then, he handed them handfuls of Irish pound notes and let them pay themselves. Maggie and Hannah stood back and watched. Before long, Addie and Reilly were laden with shopping bags.

For lunch, Maggie took them to St. Mary's Church, a former Church of Ireland. She explained that it was now a restaurant and pub.

"I don't know if I can eat in there," Hannah said.

"Why?" Maggie asked.

"I don't know. It doesn't seem right to make a church into a restaurant."

"Wait until you see the bar," Maggie said.

"They have alcohol in there?"

"Hannah, you're in Ireland, remember?"

"I can't help it. I keep picturing a bar in the old regular Baptist church where Granny worships."

Maggie laughed and ushered them inside.

After lunch, Maggie pointed out it would be hard to deal with their packages on the Hop-On Hop-Off Bus Tour. J.D. stepped forward and offered to take the lot back to the hotel so they could go on with the tour. "I have some work to do and this will allow me to get it done before dinner," he said.

Addie protested. "Daddy, please, go with us."

"Sweet pea, I must get this done before I go to London tomorrow. You don't want me to have to work late tonight, do you?"

Addie shook her head.

"Alright, I'll see you when you come to change for dinner." He kissed the top of her head.

Hannah looked down at her clothes and back up at Maggie. This time it was Maggie who put her hand on Hannah's arm. Maggie said, "Thank you, J.D."

For the rest of the day, Maggie, Hannah, and the girls investigated Dublin. For Maggie, that afternoon was a soothing balm on the open sore left by J.D.'s surprise appearance. They began by riding atop the big red bus through the entire tour. It turned out to be a splendid day. The sun played a game of hide-n-seek with mashed potato clouds, keeping the rain at bay. The temperature stayed in the sixties and a soft ocean-touched breeze was their constant companion. For the first time in weeks, they were free of the miserable heat of Coal Valley and reveled in the outdoors.

When their bus came back to St. Patrick's Cathedral, they

got off and spent more than two hours exploring the place. They visited the final resting place of Jonathan Swift, author of *Gulliver's Travels* and Dean of the Cathedral. They marveled at the architecture, furnishings, stained-glass windows, tombs, and other treasures, such as Handel's "Messiah" on display in a glass case.

Maggie said, "At least I can say what I want about these wonderful things without J.D. here to make fun of me."

"Hey!" Hannah said, putting her hand on Maggie's arm. "He looks like a jack ass when he tries to belittle you because you know more about something than he does."

Maggie patted her friend's hand. "Thanks."

The group left St. Patrick's so in awe of the place they decided to resume their tour the next day. Maggie found J.D., without sunglasses, reading the newspaper and looking rested. In fact, he was in a famous good mood. She wondered if it was because he was leaving tomorrow, or because he hadn't found her in the arms of an Irishman.

They exchanged pleasantries, and J.D. made a big deal of taking his newspaper to the lobby, so she could rest. She did sit on the window ledge for five minutes, staring at the street below without a thought for anything or anyone. A blissful five minutes when she didn't feel anything—didn't think about J.D., or Cooper, or the future—and then Addie knocked on the door, and she and Reilly burst into the room, jerking Maggie back to the present.

At the appointed time, they met in the lobby. After J.D.'s remark about changing for dinner, Hannah made a point *not* to change clothes, and she was rewarded with a look, followed by a frown. Addie and Reilly wore their new "Irish" dresses which looked a lot like their American dresses.

J.D. took them to Davy Byrnes, one of Dublin's most famous pubs. It was mid-week, but the place had the energy of a Saturday night. They marveled at the pre-World War II decor, and the group took a table in high spirits. Drink orders were taken, and menus were handed around. Maggie pointed out Davy's was famous for its Irish stew and seafood.

"Did you know," Maggie said, "the Irish writer, James Joyce, was a regular here? He referenced it in his book, *Ulysses.* Let's walk over and get a good look at the murals of Joycean Dublin by Liam Proud. There are also murals of the 1940s by Cecil Ffrench Salkeld."

"Oh, Margaret," J.D. said, laying aside his menu. "Are you going to give us another Irish history lesson?"

The blood drained from Maggie's face and pooled in her

ears. She resisted the urge to clasp her hands over them. Hannah put her hand on Maggie's knee and squeezed. She leaned toward J.D., smiling her sweetest smile. She said, "Why J.D., I'm just a poor little hillbilly girl! I don't know nothing about such things. Please, don't interrupt Maggie's attempt to educate me." Then she laughed like she'd just told a hilarious joke, infecting Addie and Reilly who joined in.

After a dinner of Irish stew for the girls and oysters and salmon for the adults, not to mention exquisite wine, the group wandered down the street. Since his outburst criticizing Maggie, J.D. had said little, unless speaking directly to the girls who had chatted all evening about St. Patrick's Cathedral.

Maggie breathed in Dublin at night. Lightness was spreading through her—bringing comforting warmth with it. J.D. was leaving, and Cooper was coming. Hannah put her arm around her friend's shoulders. The girls and J.D. were far enough ahead so they couldn't hear. "I'm sorry your husband's such a jerk," Hannah said. "Don't let him ruin your vacation."

Maggie smiled. "My vacation begins tomorrow."

The group strolled back to the hotel, content with their own thoughts. In the lobby, they said their goodnights. Since he was leaving early the next day, J.D. kissed Addie and told her good-bye.

When they got back to their room, J.D. busied himself packing. Maggie asked, "Do you need help?"

"No, thank you."

Maggie took her time laying out her clothes for the next day. She remarked she was going to take a shower, but J.D. made no comment. She waited for some sort of apology or at least a remark of regret for his embarrassing comment to her at dinner. When none came, she asked, "What time will you be leaving?"

"I have a car coming at six."

"Will you be returning tomorrow night?"

J.D. sat down at the desk with his back to Maggie and started taking papers out of his briefcase. He took his reading glasses out of the case and put them on before answering. "No, I have meetings all day and an eight o'clock flight Friday morning."

"So, you knew you were coming to London this week?"

"Hum?" J.D. set aside the paper he was reading and picked up another one.

"I said," Maggie raised her voice, "if you were planning to come to London this week, why didn't you tell me?"

J.D. turned his head and glanced at her. Then he returned

to his papers. "I don't know, Margaret. I suppose I thought I told you."

Maggie walked over and stood behind him. "No," she said, "you didn't."

She stood still, anger welling up inside of her, and then, the rich scent of his cologne reached her. She closed her eyes and remembered burying her face in his neck and breathing in every part of him. Her arm went up and her hand inched toward his neck. She wanted to run her fingers through his hair and taste the patch of skin below his ear. She wanted to cry out, *Here's your chance—tell me you love me. Tell me you don't want to lose me—you can't live without me. Don't leave it like this. At least, lie to me. Say you came here to see if I was with another man because you love me and can't lose me. For once, tell me it's not about you or your career. Tell me it's about me—no, tell me it's about us.*

J.D. took off his glasses and laid them on top of his papers. He turned sideways in his chair. "Did you want something?"

Maggie dropped her arm to her side. "No, I don't want anything."

He turned and started stacking his papers into neat even piles. Maggie walked toward the bathroom.

"Margaret?"

She turned around.

"I hope you enjoy the rest of your stay."

She nodded and waited. When he didn't say anything else, she turned back and opened the bathroom door.

"Oh, and Margaret," he called. She paused but didn't turn around. "Please, remind Addie to call me."

"Of course."

Maggie returned from the bath and found J.D. asleep. When she woke in the morning, he was gone.

Maggie dressed and slipped downstairs. It was a quarter past seven, and there were only a few people in the restaurant. She took a seat by the window and ordered a pot of tea. Pearl gray clouds puddled in the morning sky. The mist stretched up toward the spot in the heavens reserved for the sun.

The first sip of tea triggered an anamnesis: "Maggie, you must try to understand your mother." She was thirteen and sitting in this restaurant with her father. He wore a black tweed jacket and red vest, and she remembered he had managed to tame his thick auburn hair that was graying more each day. She also remembered his eyes, dark with understanding. Her whole life, her father had been the buffer between her and her formidable mother. He had lavished Maggie with love and affection and done everything in his power to instill her with self-confidence. When her mother was cold and standoffish, he was warm and loving. When her mother punished her, he spoiled her. When her mother told her she was bad, he made her believe she was the best little girl in the world.

Why he chose that day, Maggie never knew. Perhaps, it was because they were an ocean away from her mother, or somehow, he sensed he wouldn't be with them much longer. Whatever the reason, he began, "Your mother loves you with all her heart, but it just isn't *in her* to show it." She remembered how he stopped and leaned toward her, looking into her eyes. "I know this is going to sound like those excuses that adults always tell children, but I'm going to say it—one day when you grow up, you'll understand what I'm about to tell you."

Maggie closed her eyes and remembered how she wanted to scream at her father, *Stop! Stop talking about my mother.* But she had sat still and listened with her hands folded in her lap, just as her mother had taught her.

A giggle came from a nearby table, and Maggie looked over at a mother, father, and two little girls. One of the girls was listening to her father with an upturned face. Maggie recalled her father's words. "Your mother was brought up with no brothers or sisters by parents who didn't show their love. They were old-fashioned, even Puritan in their beliefs about child rearing. They believed they were making her strong and independent by denying her affection. You must try to understand what that was like for her. She believes she must bring you up like she was raised. She is hard on you because they were hard on her."

All her life, Maggie had struggled to understand. When her father died, she had tried to get along with her mother, striving to be the kind and caring person he wanted her to be. A few months after his death, she read and became obsessed with *The Scarlet Letter*, remembering her father had said her mother's upbringing was puritan. She read the book over and over, looking for answers, and then she read everything she could find about puritanism. Her adolescent mind thought this would give her some secret understanding into why her mother was kind to anyone but her. Why her mother demanded the best of everything from her—grades, friends, athletic accomplishments—and why Maggie could never, no matter how hard she tried, be good enough.

Maggie cradled her teacup in her hands. She leaned her face over it so she could smell the tea's sweet fragrance. She missed Papa. How she wished for the wisdom he promised she would have when she grew up. Even though she believed him—

her mother did love her—she had never been able to understand her. She wondered if her relationship with her mother would have been different if her father had lived.

Maggie's phone buzzed. She picked it up, expecting it to be from Hannah or Addie, but the call was from Cooper. She smiled. After all, she had her father to thank for her love of everything Irish.

An hour later, Hannah, Maggie, and the girls were laughing and talking their way through breakfast. The weather was less friendly than the previous day, with bouts of drizzle. They used the Hop-On Hop-Off bus again and started the day with the National Art Gallery. From there, they went to the Guinness Factory, and the Old Jameson Distillery, where they had lunch in its charming restaurant. Hannah dubbed the morning "the Irish alcohol tour."

After lunch they toured the Kilmainham Gaol. Once a prison, it was now a museum on the history of Irish nationalism. Their tour guide was an Irish lass with long red curls and a face full of freckles. She told them the moving history of this prison built in 1796 and the horrors of life there. She explained how men, women, and even children were imprisoned. Some children were sent there for petty theft, and how the youngest prisoner was a seven-year-old boy.

Next, they went to St. Stephen's Green. The beauty of the place lightened the gray day. That night they ate at the Arlington Hotel. They were entertained by a band playing traditional Irish music and dancers doing the Irish step-dance. Hannah pointed out their dancing was like mountain clogging. Reilly said, "This music sounds a lot like the music we have back home. It reminds me of Ralph Stanley's music. Granny has some of his CDs."

Maggie said, "When the Scots-Irish immigrated to America, they brought their music with them. I guess you could say it was one of the building blocks of bluegrass music."

When they left the hotel restaurant, they walked through the cobblestone streets full of people and music. Addie and Reilly were thrilled to be in the Temple Bar District.

Addie said, "Mama, will you take us to the bar where Bono goes?"

"Please, Maggie, please!" Reilly said. "We won't drink anything."

"What are they talking about?" Hannah asked.

Maggie said, "Bono, from the band U2, owns The Clarence Hotel in the same neighborhood as the Temple Bar and is said to come by for a drink when he's in Dublin."

Hannah grabbed Addie and Reilly. "Come on! What are we waiting for?"

They made their way through the crowds to Temple Bar that was already overflowing with people. Maggie and Hannah let their daughters walk inside and have a quick look around, and then they herded them back outside. Hannah said, "Don't either one of you ever tell Granny we let you set foot in a bar."

Reilly put her hands on her hips. "Mama, all we've done since we got here is go into pubs and bars."

"Well," Hannah said. "You know what I mean!"

They wandered about for a while, listening to music floating out of the bars. When they got back to the hotel, Addie begged to stay in Reilly's room. She said, "Mama, please, I won't bother Hannah. I promise. I want to stay with Reilly."

Maggie agreed. She wondered if Addie was avoiding being alone with her because she hadn't told her that her father was coming. In truth, Maggie was relieved to be alone so she could think about Cooper. Since the fortuitous day she had shown up with pizza at Hannah's college, she had gone back many times, and by the end of the semester, she and Cooper had exchanged phone numbers and had talked for hours about everything and nothing.

Maggie and Cooper were under a sweet spell of intimacy, and Maggie was ready to throw her heart out into the void and trust Cooper would catch it. Tomorrow was their last day in Dublin before heading to the west, and he was meeting them at nine o'clock for a tour of Trinity College.

A knock at the door brought Maggie back to earth. Hannah came in yawning. She said, "I thought I'd run in while the girls were taking showers." She went straight to Maggie's bed and stretched out, patting the spot next to her. Maggie laughed and stretched out, linking her hands together under her head. For a while, they lay in silence, until their breathing became syncopated.

Hannah turned on her side to face Maggie. She raised up, resting her head on her hand. "I've had the most amazing day," she said. "Thank you for bringing me here."

Maggie stretched and sat up. She turned to face Hannah, drawing her legs up and crossing them. "I knew you would adore this place, and I can't wait until tomorrow. You will be amazed at Trinity."

"Are you looking forward to seeing Cooper?" Hannah asked.

"Oh, Hannah, I haven't told you that J.D. somehow got my phone and read all of my messages. He saw the ones from

Cooper and that's why he came here. He thought he would catch me with him."

"I knew it!" Hannah slapped the bed. "I knew that's why he showed up."

Maggie said, "We had a big fight. He said he *accidently* read *one* message from Cooper and wanted to know who the man was messaging his wife. Then he told me he was going to run for governor, and he didn't want me to 'mess it up' for him."

Hannah shot straight up in the bed. "Wait! He said what?"

"Oh, it gets better. He even said I wouldn't 'turn my back' on the governor's mansion."

Hannah faced Maggie and crossed her legs. "Do you think J.D. read anything in your messages that clued him that Cooper was coming to be here with you?"

"I tried to convince him I was talking to Cooper because I wanted him to set up a tour of Trinity for you."

"Do you think he believed you?"

"I don't know if I convinced him, or if he thought his surprise announcement about running for governor would keep me with him." Maggie paused then said, "He dared to tell me I wasn't the person he married."

"Ha," Hannah said, "I hope you told him that was exactly right—you're not the person he married—you're a better person."

"I know one thing: I'm going to be a smarter person. I won't be so careless with my phone or my messages again."

Addie and Reilly burst into the room, trailing the honeyed scent of soap and talcum powder after them. Reilly had her mother's cell phone. "It's Daddy! He wants to talk to you."

Hannah sprang from the bed and took the phone. She glanced back at Maggie. "I'll take this in my room."

Addie and Reilly sat down on the bed next to Maggie. She told them that on Saturday, a car was taking them to the western part of Ireland where they could kiss the Blarney Stone, explore the Ring of Kerry, climb up to the Cliffs of Moher, explore the Aran Islands, tour some amazing castles, and a bunch of other things that would be *grand*. She said they would be staying in different towns and hotels, and they were even spending the night in a castle.

The girls were squealing so loud Maggie almost didn't hear the phone ring. Addie said, "It's Mom. She's going to tell you we need to come to bed."

Maggie laughed and picked up the phone. "They're coming," she said.

Cooper quickly made Maggie forget about J.D. Hannah and the girls took Cooper into their group, and he became their own personal tour guide, regaling them with legends and stories. He was a gifted storyteller, and the tales he wove made this land of a thousand greens sparkle with life.

Maggie and Cooper spent every moment possible together. The day they traveled to the Cliffs of Moher was a rare sunny day in Ireland. The sky sang of true-blue perfection. There were no clouds to speak of and the temperature was a perfect seventy degrees. Hannah, Addie, and Reilly boarded a ship at Doolin Harbor to sail along the base of the Cliffs, and Maggie and Cooper walked to the top. Maggie tried to push thoughts of going home to the back of her mind; instead, she concentrated on the present—with Cooper. She stamped each second with him on her memory—every story, every laugh, every experience they had together. But this day, this place, was different.

Cooper guided Maggie to the highest point of the Cliffs, Knockardakin. There, they could see Aran Islands—Inis Oírr, Inis Meáin, and Inis Mór—and to the left were views of the beautiful Galway Bay. They also had a fantastic view of the South Cliffs.

Neither spoke. There were no words. Maggie closed her eyes against the dazzling blues and greens and concentrated on the love for Cooper growing inside of her. It swelled with each Atlantic surge. The scent of brine, warm and fertile, whispered its secrets, and she placed a hand over her heart. It beat in tune with the pounding surf. This was love—a sweet ache that made her dizzy with longing. She never wanted the moment to end.

Something blotted out the sun, and Maggie opened her eyes to find a silhouette of Cooper's six-foot-two body in front of her. The wind pushed his hair forward covering his high forehead, and she saw gray threaded among the auburn strands. He bent at the waist and came closer, and the breeze lifted his scent, musky and sweet like new grass crushed between her fingers. The leafy green of his eyes invited her to taste his lips. He grasped her elbow and pulled her hand away from her heart, placing it on his. She whispered, "Cooper," and leaned in to accept his kiss. She wrapped her arms around his neck and let him pull her against him. He kissed her, arousing a passion she thought she would never feel again.

A group of people approached where they stood, and Maggie stepped out of Cooper's embrace. Hand-in-hand they picked their way down the path, leaving a map of stolen kisses along the way. Maggie turned her face up to receive each kiss, letting the salt-tinged breeze caress her face. She couldn't stop smiling.

Back in the car, Cooper drove them to Doolin to Gus O'Connor's Pub. Once there, they secured a corner booth, and Cooper went to the bar and returned with a pint of Guinness for him and a glass of wine for Maggie. They sipped their drinks and smiled at each other like star-struck teenagers. Cooper reached across the table and took Maggie's hand. He twined his long slender fingers with hers and she shivered, imagining those hands caressing her body. When a waiter appeared and asked if she wanted another glass of wine, Maggie was surprised to see her glass was empty.

"Would you like another?" Cooper asked.

"No, thank you."

When the waiter disappeared, Cooper said, "You made me a happy man today. I shall never forget it."

"Something happened up there. On the Cliffs."

"Aye, I felt it."

Maggie studied Cooper's face. "I can be true, here. I can say whatever I want. I can do whatever I want. I can feel what I want. Oh, Cooper..." Her voice broke, and tears gathered in her eyes.

Cooper stood and held out his hand. "Come with me."

Back outside the world throbbed with sun. Cooper looked at his wristwatch. "Hannah's boat won't be back for another half-hour. Fancy a walk along the harbor?"

Maggie nodded.

They drove out to Doolin Harbor and parked. Cooper took Maggie's hand and led the way to a path that took them down to the water. They walked for a while in silence, the rocks crunching beneath their feet. Afternoon was gathering, yet the sun sang high and warm in the sky. The breeze picked up, and Maggie turned her face toward it. She drank in great draughts of bittersweet marine scents. Strands of hair escaped from her ponytail and she tucked them behind her ears. Maggie wished she and Cooper could walk until they found forever.

"There's a place on that outcrop of limestone," Cooper pointed up the beach. "It would be a nice place to sit."

They climbed to the spot, and then stood side by side, lost in the effulgence of sea and sky. Maggie said, "I feel so alive standing here—like I'm a part of this." She swept her hand up toward the sky. "I feel like this is where I am supposed to be."

Cooper took her hands and turned her to face him. "I couldn't say this in a pub. I wanted to say what is on my heart with the bloom of my home around us." He paused and smiled down at her. "*Tá grá agam duit.* I love you, Maggie."

"*Tá grá agam duit*, Cooper. I love you too."

Cooper grabbed Maggie around the waist and swung her around. She squealed and wrapped her arms around his neck. He covered her face in kisses before putting her feet on the ground. He plopped down, crossed his legs, and held his hand out to Maggie. She sat down between his legs with her back cradled against his chest. They sat in silence, content with the words that had already passed between them. Maggie wanted to stay wrapped in the safety of Cooper's arms in the wilds of Ireland, but she knew that, in another week, she'd be back in Coal Valley, and her life would resume as if this day had never happened.

Cooper placed soft kisses on her neck. He slipped Maggie's hairband off her ponytail, letting the long strands free in the wind. He coiled her hair around his hand and whispered in her ear. "I have something for you."

Cooper stood and pulled Maggie to her feet. She smiled up at him, sure this was a prelude to another kiss. She tilted her head back and said, "Oh, do you now?"

Cooper laughed. "I do, indeed." He lifted her right hand to his lips and kissed it. Then he brought it back down and slipped a ring on her finger.

A soft *ohhh* escaped from Maggie. On the ring finger of her right hand sparkled an emerald and diamond Claddagh ring. "Oh, Cooper," Maggie said. "It's beautiful."

Maggie held her hand up so the jewels winked in the afternoon sunlight. At the ring's center was a magnificent heart-shaped emerald with a diamond studded crown on top. Diamond studded hands cupped the emerald heart and diamonds circled the entire band. "But..."

"Now, no buts! There's no reason in the world why a lass wouldn't return home from Ireland sporting a Claddagh ring. Now, is there?"

Maggie shook her head. She looked down at the ring and then up at Cooper. He took her hand and brought the ring up to his lips. "This ring is my promise to you," Cooper said. "I promise I will wait for you as long as it takes."

Tears coursed down Maggie's cheeks. This time when she lifted her face to his, Cooper placed his hands one on each side of her face and brushed away her tears before gently kissing her. Then, they held each other surrounded by the sun and sea, and hope blossomed inside of her like a flower.

The time to meet Hannah and the girls at the Doolin Pier

was approaching, so Cooper and Maggie made their way back to the harbor. Cooper asked, "Do you know the meaning of the Claddagh?"

"The heart represents love, the crown represents loyalty, and the hands represent friendship," Maggie said.

"Indeed, it does. But there is a bit more to know." Cooper stopped and lifted her hand. He twisted the ring around on her finger. "The way a Claddagh ring is worn on the hand is usually intended to convey the wearer's romantic availability, or lack thereof. Traditionally, if the ring is on the right hand with the heart facing outward and away from the body, this indicates that the person wearing the ring is not in any serious relationship, or 'their heart is open.'"

Cooper pointed to her ring. "When the Claddagh is worn on the right hand with the heart facing inward toward the body, like yours is, this indicates you are in a relationship, or that 'someone has captured your heart.'"

Maggie smiled up at him and held up her hand. "Then this is the way I will wear it, forever."

Chapter 23

The forest is a healer's greatest pleasure. Coltsfoot, witch hazel, mugwort, bee balm, and foxglove—even the names sound magical. I take great joy in touching growing things, digging my fingers into the soil and helping them grow. At harvest, I admire their lacy skeletons, knowing I hold their magic in my hands. It's the forest plants, their seeds, flora and fauna I use in my healing remedies. My mother and grandmother knew the old ways of making medicine and they taught it to me.
~ from Granny Zee's Book of Dreams

"**L**OOK AT MY GIRLS!" Granny Zee held out her arms and Reilly and Addie ran to her. She laughed and turned to hug Hannah and Maggie. "It's so good to have y'all back."

As the afternoon faded into evening, Hannah, Maggie, and the girls drank sweet iced tea and ate sugar cookies while regaling Granny with stories and pictures of Ireland. They had brought along souvenirs from each place they visited, and Granny examined and exclaimed over each one. "We went to county Cork where our people come from," Reilly said.

Granny said, "I'm proud you did."

"I'm going back some day and look up our family," Reilly said.

"That you will," Granny said. "That you will."

Hannah stood. "This has been such fun, but I have to go home and get things ready for my internship, which starts in the morning at Coal Valley Hospital. Granny, are you sure about the girls staying with you tonight?"

"If it's too much, they can come home with me," Maggie said.

Granny put her arm around Hannah's waist. "I'm so proud of my girl I could bust. Me and these girls are going apple picking tomorrow, and then we're going to make crabapple jelly."

"That sounds like fun," Maggie said. "I volunteer to be the taste-tester."

"Come on," Granny said to Hannah. "I've got something to show you outside before you leave."

Granny started toward the door with Hannah in tow.

Granny said, "Maggie, we'll be just a few minutes."

Once outside, Granny steered Hannah around the house to a bench under a bank of honeysuckle. From there, they could see if anyone came out the back door.

"Now," Granny said, "what's amiss?"

Hannah told Granny Zee about the dream she'd had onboard the plane to Ireland. Granny listened, her blue eyes shining with interest.

When her recounting was finished, Hannah said, "What do you think it means?"

"I think," Granny said, "it means that you aren't sure if Travis told you the truth." She paused. "Or, you don't want it to be true."

For a long moment, Hannah looked down at her hands. She knew Granny was right. "Yes," she said, letting a big puff of air escape with the word.

"What are you going to do now?"

"Do? I don't know what to do. All I know is that Travis is a different person since the day he told me."

"How?"

"Last year, he complained constantly about school and me not being home and generally made my life a living hell. Now, he cleans house, does laundry, and—"

Granny stared into her eyes. "And what?"

"And acts like the person I always wanted him to be." Hannah sprang to her feet and with her back to Granny Zee said, "Sometimes, I wish I could fall in love with *this* Travis. It's like I don't know who the real Travis is, anymore."

Granny Zee took Hannah's hand. "Sweet girl, don't you know that Travis is afraid he's losing you?"

⁂

Granny Zee opened her eyes. A feeling passed through her not unlike the quickening she had once felt in her womb. She sat up, switching on the bedside lamp—5:02 AM. Cece stood at the foot of her bed, clutching Patty Cake to her breast. *Lost.*

Granny hurried to the girls' room, but she found them sleeping peacefully with arms and legs crisscrossed over the quilts. She went back to her room and dressed before scribbling a note— *Girls, I'm gathering in the woods. Be back soon. Love, Granny.* She placed it on the kitchen table and then donned her red sweater, got her canvas bag, and picked up her walking stick as she went out into the mist.

Lost. The word purled in front of her. Long curling fog fingers. She trailed it up the mountain to the scarlet oak that towered over her stone bench. The air was thick and electric with unseen specters, their melancholy scent superseding the forest's gentle green smell. Granny sat down, closed her eyes, and said, "Spirits of the forest—tell me who is lost," before surrendering herself to them.

When she opened them, the genesis of a new day, hot and clear was before her. The forest was full of the trills and calls of birds. Granny stood and picked up her walking stick. With heavy heart, she made her way out of the forest.

Back in her kitchen, Granny found the house quiet and the note on the table undisturbed. She put the kettle on the stove and gathered her journal and pen. When the water boiled, she poured it into a mug with a bag of ginseng tea. She sat down at the table and stared into the cup, watching the water turn aurous.

She opened the journal she called her book of dreams and wrote: *Cece woke me with this message—Lost. I went into the forest to seek help from the spirits. They say unless the young one who was born behind the veil can find what is lost, a great sadness, like a terrible trial I once faced, is coming. The spirits caution that no one will believe her, so I must be the one to tell them or death will surely come.*

After breakfast, Granny Zee led the girls to the crabapple tree. Addie said, "Those sure are little apples. Do you think they've grown enough?"

Granny chuckled. "A crabapple's supposed to be small." She snagged a low bough and pulled off two, handing one to each girl. "Did you know that all apples come from this little apple?"

Addie and Reilly shook their heads.

"This is a wild apple, and people used it to develop all the different kinds of apples we have today."

"But why do they call it crab?" Addie asked.

"My Granny said it came from the Scots. It was called scrabapple. You can trace it back four or five hundred years." Granny chuckled. "Me and my sisters used to take a knife and saltshaker out to the crabapple tree in my Granny Zee's yard and eat until we got full or a bellyache." She chuckled again. "I remember one time I got in trouble for leaving Mama's saltshaker outside, and it got rained on."

"What did you need salt for?" Reilly asked.

"We thought they tasted better with salt. Crabapples is right tart. When we get back to the house, you can try one."

By noon, a huge pot of apples simmered on the stove, and the girls had polished off a plate of grilled cheese and tomato sandwiches. Granny sat down with a bowl of sliced crab apples, sprinkled salt on a piece, and popped it into her mouth. She watched while the girls imitated her, amid shrieks of, "Ooo sour!"

Granny Zee laughed. "That's what makes 'em good."

When the apples were cooked soft, Granny showed the girls how to strain them through layers of cheesecloth she had stretched over an empty pot. When that was done, she put the pot of strained juice back on the stove and simmered it for ten minutes, and then she added sugar and cinnamon. She stirred while Reilly and Addie made labels for the row of sterilized jars lined up on the counter.

The scent of apples and cinnamon, as sweet as an orchard after a spring rain, filled the room, but Granny Zee couldn't forget the message from the spirits.

Ten jars of crabapple jelly cooled on the counter, and Addie and Reilly sat at the table drawing pictures. Granny switched the TV from her favorite home shopping network to the noon news and went back to the kitchen to wash up the apple pots. Addie suddenly dropped her marker and ran to the television.

Reilly said, "Granny, something's wrong with Addie."

Addie stared wide-eyed at the television where a news report showed rescue vehicles and swarms of people. In the corner of the report was a photograph of a smiling little boy with brown hair and blue eyes. The newscaster said, "Amanda and Derek Shortt were camping in the Breaks Park when they woke this morning around six to discover their son, Andrew, was not in their tent. The family was camping at the park to celebrate Andrew's fourth birthday. A search has been going on for seven hours with no luck."

Addie sprang to her feet. "We have to go. We have to go now!"

"Go *where*?" Reilly said.

Addie wheeled around and dropped to her knees in front of Granny. "You understand Granny Zee. You know!" She took Granny's hands in hers. "I have to find him."

Granny nodded. "Let me think a minute."

Reilly grabbed Addie's arm. "What's going on?"

Addie said, "I can find him! I can find Andrew."

She sat down next to Granny. "Please, Granny Zee. We have to go to the park."

Granny nodded slowly, looking off into the distance like she could hear a voice the girls could not. She stood. "I have to make two phone calls," she said. "While I do that, go put on your sneakers. We'll be walking."

When the girls came back wearing socks and sneakers, they found Granny in the kitchen, putting on her walking shoes. She straightened up and looked at first Reilly, then Addie. Your mothers are coming."

Addie's eyes filled with tears. "Why did you call my mother? She won't let me go!"

Granny took her hand. "It's going to be alright. Believe me."

Reilly said, "Let's check the TV to see if there are any updates."

"I don't have to check," Addie said, "he's still lost."

At the foot of the mountain, Granny Zee parked her car, and everyone piled into Maggie's waiting SUV. Hannah, still in her hospital scrubs, drove with Granny in the passenger seat. Maggie sat in the back between Addie and Reilly. Hannah said, "What's the plan?"

Granny asked, "Do you remember Anna Mullins?"

"Cousin Anna?" Hannah said.

Granny nodded. "Her oldest boy, Eli, is the sheriff."

Hannah grinned. "I see where this is going."

The closer they got to the park the worse the traffic. TV trucks from the local news were already there, and a variety of police and rescue vehicles. A helicopter circled overhead. Maggie said, "We'll never get close to that place."

"We have to," Addie said. "What I see isn't clear. I have to get closer."

Granny said, "Leave it to me."

Traffic slowed to a crawl. Ahead was a roadblock where a police officer was turning cars away from the park. Addie gripped her mother's hand, and Maggie put her arm around her. For the first time since Maggie had grasped the extent of her daughter's gift, she panicked. What would happen if Addie found this lost child? Everyone will know about her gift. She'd tried so hard to keep it hidden! Now, the press will hound her—everyone who has a missing loved one will come to her for help!

Maggie leaned forward and grabbed Hannah's shoulder. "Stop! You have to turn the car around!"

"Wait! Why?" Hannah turned.

"We can't take Addie into the middle of this!"

"Mom!"

"No!"

Granny turned around and put her hand on Maggie's arm. "Don't fret. I know just what to do. I will leave Addie out of it. I promise."

Maggie said, "I don't understand why Addie has to go? Why

can't you find the child without Addie?"

Granny fixed her eyes on Maggie's face. "Because I can only find the dead."

Maggie gasped. Granny Zee said, "Now, you know."

"Granny, I'm sorry—I don't know what to say—I'm—so sorry."

Granny Zee leaned forward and hid her face in her hands. She sobbed, and Hannah put her hand on Granny's shoulder.

Maggie said, "Please forgive me. I didn't mean to upset you." She scooted forward in the backseat, so she could pat Granny's other shoulder.

After a few moments, Granny Zee sat up and accepted tissues. She mopped her face and blew her nose before turning around and looking at Maggie, Hannah, and the girls. She said, "I'm sorry for that, but sometimes I can't bear the burden God gave me. The only lost ones I can find are the dead. They are the only ones I can hear. Let's hope I can't hear this wee boy."

Hannah said, "Granny, are you okay?" Granny nodded. "Because" she continued, "the cars are moving, and that policeman is going to stop us. It would be a good time to think about what you are going to say."

Granny Zee spoke to the police officer, who got on his radio, and in two minutes they were waved into the park to a waiting officer. They followed him through the park until he stopped, motioning them to pull over. He explained they would have to go the rest of the way on foot. He eyed Granny, who got out of the car and donned a wide-brimmed straw hat. He opened his mouth like he was going to say something—thought better of it—and pursed his lips. Granny wielded her walking stick and looked him squarely in the eyes. "You lead the way."

They were in the section of the park called the Sandy Causeway, an area heavily forested. Granny, who had Maggie and Hannah on either side of her, followed the officer with Addie and Reilly bringing up the rear. They hadn't gone far when they heard voices, and then the path turned downhill toward a clearing, crawling with police, park rangers, and various rescue individuals. They could see the faded khaki and green tent that no doubt belonged to the missing boy's family. Next to the remains of a campfire lay a child's over-size bat and balls. Across from it was the sheriff's command center, which consisted of a huge map of the park hanging on an easel, a table covered with equipment, some folding chairs, and a first aid station, all under a blue awning.

The sun jeweled the colors of the landscape. The sky, its deep beryl reminiscent of the sea and storms, rose above emerald mountains, and clumps of wildflowers glowed like citrine and amethyst. It was cooler and less humid in the park, but dangerous to a child who had been wandering without water for over nine hours.

Granny inhaled. Ozone, a scent like electrical sparks, was in the air. Storms were building. There was no time to lose.

By the time they made it to the bottom of the path, the sheriff had appeared and came striding toward them. "Granny Zee," he said, "thank you for coming. Let's get you out of the sun, and I'll bring you up to date."

Granny and the sheriff sat down, and Granny motioned for Addie to sit next to her. The others stood close by. It didn't take the sheriff long to tell Granny their search had found no sign of the boy. When three men in park ranger uniforms came out of the woods, he excused himself and went to confer with them. All three were disheveled and sweating, and it was obvious they had been searching.

"He's hiding," Addie said.

Granny said, "Tell me everything you see."

"He's under a huge piece of rock. It's cool in there."

A woman came running toward the sheriff yelling, "Did you find him? Did you see him?" A man wearing a Cookie Monster t-shirt and cut-offs followed her calling, "Amanda, honey, please..." The woman stumbled and fell. The sheriff reached her first. He helped her up and they formed a tight circle. They spoke briefly before moving to the map.

The woman turned, saw Granny Zee, and came toward her. Granny grasped Addie's hand and looked up at Hannah and Maggie. She said, "Let me do the talking," and stood, extending her hand to the child's mother.

"Are you the one?" the woman asked, grabbing Granny's hand. "Are you the seer?" The woman turned her sunburned face to Granny. Her short brown hair was plastered to her forehead, and her blue eyes were red rimmed like she hadn't slept in days. She was thin, and her oversized t-shirt had rusty sweat stains around the neck and under the arms. It looked stretched like someone had pulled on it, thinning the material until it was ready to tear. Like her husband, she wore cut-offs and tennis shoes.

Her husband and the sheriff came up behind her. The sheriff said, "This is Zelda Davis. She's come to see if she can help."

The woman started to cry. "I'm Amanda and this is my husband, Derek. We're... Andrew..."

"Call me Granny Zee." Granny helped Amanda to a chair and motioned for her husband to sit next to her, and then she pulled her chair around so she was facing them. Addie sat on the ground next to Granny's chair.

Granny held Amanda's hand and said, "I'm what some people call a granny woman or a mountain healer, and I'm going to try and help these people find your boy. Sometimes, I can see things that are lost."

The sheriff said, "I've known Granny Zee all my life and I've seen her gift with my own eyes."

"What do you need from us?" Derek Shortt said, his voice betraying his disapproval.

"Tell me a little about Andrew. Is this his first camping trip?"

While they talked, Maggie watched Addie. She kept her eyes on the ground, but her chest moved up and down like she'd been running.

Granny said, "I'm wondering if Andrew could be hiding?"

Derek Shortt snapped, "That's ridiculous! Why would he do that?"

Granny looked him in the eye. "Because he's afraid he's in trouble. Because you told him not to leave the tent and he disobeyed you."

"You did, Derek. We both did," Amanda Shortt said. "We told him over and over not to leave the tent unless one of us went with him. We also warned him about snakes, and bears, and..." She started to cry.

A commotion behind them made the sheriff turn just as a man with a huge camera and a woman with a microphone strode toward them. The woman thrust a microphone in Amanda Shortt's face while the cameraman swung his camera across the group, filming everyone sitting with her. A strangled *agg* sound escaped Maggie, and Hannah jumped up and planted herself in front of Addie and Reilly, trying to block them from view. The sheriff pushed himself between the news people and the parents and shouted, "Leave, now!"

The newswoman shouted, "Do you suspect foul play?"

Amanda Shortt screamed, and Derek jumped up and swung at the videographer, his fist connecting with his jaw. The videographer staggered backward, almost dropping his camera. Officers swarmed in, grabbing the news people and the Shortts. In the confusion, Granny, Hannah, Maggie and the girls slipped away from the fray, and went to the far end of the tent.

Maggie said, "I've got to get Addie out of here. If J.D. finds out we're here, he... oh God, he..."

"I can find him," Addie said. She grabbed her mother's hand. "Please, Mama, I know I can. If I don't he will die."

Granny said, "Look up at the sky. Clouds a-gathering. We don't have much time. Addie, can you lead me? We'll make it look like I'm the one leading but leaning on you for support. You just keep me going in the right direction and let me do the talking."

"He's asleep," Addie said. "He crawled into a space that's dug out next to a big rock that sticks out like a shelf. The rangers have walked by him, but he's afraid to show himself."

The sheriff came over and Granny said, "I'm ready to take a walk. I need my helper here to hold on to." She smiled and took Addie's arm.

The sheriff nodded. "I'm coming with you," he said.

"Bring water," Granny said. "For the boy."

Granny led the way, setting a brisk pace, with one hand on her walking stick and the other on Addie's arm. The sheriff and two park rangers accompanied them. They'd been walking about twenty minutes when one of the rangers said, "Begging your pardon, ma'am, but we've searched this part of the park."

Granny paused and looked at the man. "Yes, young man, you have, but *I* have not." She turned and headed straight ahead until Addie tugged her arm to the left. She paused and looked at the sheriff. "This way, Eli," she said, turning toward a rhododendron thicket. The park ranger who hadn't yet spoken said, "There's a trail up here on the right that leads to the hanging rocks."

Addie steered Granny onto the path which plunged into a patch of Virginia pine trees. It was shady and cool under the pines, the ground spongy with dried needles. The heady smell of resin was like a cooling balm after the hike through the forest. They continued another quarter of an hour before Addie paused, so Granny stopped and acted like she was getting her bearings. The sheriff touched her arm and asked, "Are you alright, Granny Zee? Do you need to rest?"

Addie pressed down on Granny's arm, and her anticipation passed through Granny like a volt of electricity. She looked up at the sheriff and smiled. "Eli," she said, "we're getting close."

The trail began to climb and a gust of hot wind whipped down the path, teasing Granny's curls out from under her hat. Gray velvet clouds were gathering, smothering the light from the sky and robbing the landscape of its color. Addie dug her fingers into Granny's arm and paused. They were getting close to an outcrop of rock that looked like the place Addie had described. The huge rock protruded from the side of the mountain, and it was impossible to tell there was a hole underneath it unless a person got down on the ground—or happened to be the height of a four-year-old. Granny said, "He's back up in under that rock. He's asleep."

The park ranger said, "Excuse me, ma'am, that's awful steep for a little boy to climb that far."

Granny Zee glared at him. "It appears you don't have any young'uns."

The park ranger shook his head. "No, ma'am."

The sheriff smiled at Granny.

Granny Zee said, "Young'uns like to climb. Remember that. Now, let Addie go get him. He crawled under there and hid because he's afraid. She won't scare him."

Addie stuffed a bottle of water in the waistband of her pants. She made her way up the ridge, stooping to crawl when it was too steep to stay upright. At the protruding rock she lay flat in front of the opening and spoke too softly for the others to hear. Time passed and the ranger asked, "Is he in there?"

The sheriff nodded. "Give her some time."

Addie put her hands under the rock and they heard her say, "Come on out, and I'll take you to your mama."

Two grubby hands protruded from the spot followed by a filthy but smiling face. Addie pulled him out from under the rock and Andrew Shortt wrapped his arms around her neck.

When the sheriff and park ranger came out of the woods carrying Andrew, Granny and Addie were not with them. The second ranger had led them to an access road where a golf cart waited to take them to the place where Maggie, Hannah, and Reilly waited in the car. By the time the first drops of rain fell, Andrew, sunburned and slightly dehydrated, was back with his parents, and Granny and the girls were on their way back to Rock House Mountain.

"Addie, I'm so proud of you," Maggie said. "You saved that little boy's life."

"Granny helped," Addie said.

"You guys are really cool," Reilly said, making everyone laugh. Hannah glanced in the rearview mirror and met Maggie's eyes. She smiled and nodded.

By the time they got back to Granny's house, night had come to the mountain and the rain had stopped. Maggie and Hannah brought a platter of sandwiches and a pitcher of sweet iced tea to the den, so they could watch the news while they ate.

It was the lead story, and Addie and Reilly cheered when the reporter showed the parents hugging their son who smiled, enjoying the attention. The reporter interviewed the sheriff who told how he and a park ranger had found Andrew Shortt curled up in a small recess under a rock in the part of the park called hanging rock. "The little fellow was asleep when we found him," he said.

The report swung back to the studio where a woman sitting at the news desk asked, "Sheriff Mullins, can you tell us about the elderly woman who aided you in the search?" A video flashed on the screen of Granny, holding the hand of a teary-eyed Amanda Shortt. The camera lingered on Amanda's face before swinging to Addie who sat next to Granny's knee, her eyes transfixed on Amanda Shortt's face.

Maggie gasped.

"Oh, shit!" Hannah said.

The newscast swung back to Sheriff Mullins and the reporter, who was holding a microphone in his face. He said, "I'm sorry, you're mistaken. The rescue was a concerted effort between my department and the park service."

The woman interrupted him. "My sources say the woman's name is Zelda Davis and she's known for her psychic abilities. Did you call her in on this case?" Another picture of Granny flashed on the screen. This time she had her hand on Addie's arm and the two were staring at each other. "And who was the young girl with her? Does she share Ms. Davis's abilities?"

"No! Oh God!" Maggie jumped to her feet. The phone rang.

"Daddy," Addie said and burst into tears.

On television, the sheriff walked away without answering. When the phone stopped ringing, Granny held up her hand like a teacher calling the class to attention. "Here's what happened," she said. "Maggie, the girls, and I went to the park early this morning to go walking. We didn't know anything about the boy beforehand. We came off our trail right when the sheriff and the rangers were beginning their search. We just happened to be nearby, and since I know the sheriff, I offered comfort to the poor family. If anything is said about Hannah being there, we called her, and she joined us later. That is all."

Granny sat back and the strain of the day suddenly showed on her face. She looked drawn and her skin was tinged gray.

Hannah asked, "Granny Zee, are you alright?"

Granny sighed and nodded. She said, "I was remembering another lost child I searched for. Long, long ago. She wasn't as lucky as little Andrew."

1931

Chapter 24

IT WAS A GOOD soaking rain. The kind that makes tomatoes ripen, corn tassel, and the garden bear row after row of squash, cucumber, carrots, and cabbage. Zelda stood at the end of a row of corn, hoe in her hand. After last summer's drought, she was thankful for every drop.

Times were hard, and Zelda knew they would be worse before they got better. She rubbed the small of her back and rested her hand on the new bulge in her belly. After all those times she thought a baby would come, he had waited until now when work was scarce, and a lot of mountain families were near to starving. But if there was one thing Zelda had learned from Granny Zee and her mama about babies, it was that they came in their own good time. If Zelda was lucky, her first son would wait till after the harvest, so at least she could get the food put up for winter.

Zelda and Hanson had hunkered down to weather the hard times. Granny Zee had foretold of ten hard years when the rain would be scarce, the land would hold back its growth, and the people would leave the mountains in search of work. Three of those years had passed, and in that time, Hanson's work for King Coal had dried up. They weren't building any more houses and other than a few odd jobs, Hanson had no steady work. In fact, King Coal had laid off most of its men and the mines were idle with stockpiles of coal.

A breeze filled the trees and Zelda stood still, letting it cool the sweat on her bare neck. The air held a sweetness, a promise that it would hold her fast, keep her whole, if only she trusted and held strong. And Zelda believed. Her people were one with this mountain.

Zelda saw Hanson before he saw her. He was carrying a fine piece of chestnut wood into the shed. She smiled and rubbed her belly. She knew he was making the baby's cradle. Then a cloud came over her as she remembered last night's dream.

The kitchen garden was hoed and weeded, so Zelda hurried to the house to get breakfast on the table. Afterwards, she was taking a bag of lavender to Granny Zee for soap making, and she'd promised Mama to go with her to check on Birdie Wilson who was near her time. Mama was worried Birdie would have a hard delivery.

But Zelda never got to Mama's that day. A horse and rider came over the ridge, and Zelda watched as Sheriff Mullins came into view. Hanson came out of the shed and went to meet him. Then they both turned and looked in Zelda's direction.

"I don't like it," Hanson said. "What if you hurt yourself?"

"I won't," Zelda said. She put her hand on Hanson's arm. "A little girl's gone missing. What if she was ours? I have to go. See if I can help."

Hanson nodded. He swept her into his arms and she buried her face in his chest. She inhaled his scent—the sweetness of freshly sawed wood tinged with sweat. "Promise me," Hanson said, "you will be careful? Don't do anything that will mark the baby."

Zelda stepped back and looked into her husband's eyes. "I promise," she said.

The days of Granny Zee going with Zelda were over. Granny Zee was eighty-five and her traveling days were over.

Zelda mounted her horse and she and Sheriff Mullins rode off to town where a car waited to take them to Pineville. Five days ago, a six-year-old girl had disappeared sometime between nine that night and seven the next morning. According to Pineville's sheriff, nobody had seen or heard a thing of her since.

"Tell me what you know about the girl," Zelda said.

"It's Judge and Alice Hall's little girl. George is the judge in Pineville. The girl's name is Lucy. She's six years old—long red hair, brown eyes, and freckles on her nose."

"Is there a chance she ran away?" Zelda asked.

Sheriff Mullins shook his head. "There's always a chance, but they don't think so. Right now, it looks like she disappeared into thin air."

"Is her doll missing?"

Sheriff Mullins frowned at Zelda. "I don't know."

"If she went of her own free will, she would've taken her doll. Little girls take their dolls unless—unless they can't."

From the moment she stepped into Lucy's bedroom, Zelda knew Lucy was dead. The room was down the hall from her parent's, facing the back of the house. It was painted white and had one big window with pink gingham curtains—a window big enough for a good-sized person to climb through.

The bed had been left like it was found, a hollow on the pillow where the child's head had laid, the matching pink coverlet flung back from where the child had laid. A little red rocking chair set in one corner, a row of stuffed animals and dolls in front of it. An alphabet book lay discarded next to it, face down on the floor, its spine raised in the air like it had been dropped. Zelda could see Lucy reading the book to her dolls and animals, and tears stung her eyes.

A child's rain slicker hung on a peg on the wall, tiny boots lay on their side on the floor. A white bureau stood along the wall across from the bed. Blue and red blocks tumbled across it, like they'd been stacked and then knocked over. Lucy's essence was everywhere. Her little girl scent filled the room— like the air fresh from a sudden rain.

The pain of it brought Zelda to her knees, but she used her pregnancy as an excuse, rather than give the mother any hint about her child. The mother sat on the edge of Lucy's bed, clutching Lucy's doll and crying silent tears. The doll—the child's best friend. Lucy would not have left it behind.

Zelda went to Lucy's mother and took her into her arms. She held her and listened to her beg Zelda to find her baby and bring her home. While Zelda held her, her own child stirred in her womb.

Zelda left the mother and went to Sheriff Mullins. She said, "Six rocks."

Sheriff Mullins ushered her outside where deputies milled around, searching the grounds. Zelda said, "He killed her here. He didn't mean too. He was trying to keep her quiet and he pressed too hard. He took the body to a place near water. She's buried in a rocky place near a stand of poplar trees. He wants her to be found. He marked the place with six rocks."

Pineville's sheriff, James Thomas, came striding toward them. Tall and broad-shouldered, his dark hair was threaded with gray, and his eyes, large and dark, could bore into a man's soul. He had agreed to Zelda joining the search only because the judge wanted it, and the judge was doing it because of his wife, but he had made it clear to Mullins he didn't like it. He tipped his hat and stared at Zelda, and then turned his stare on Sheriff Mullins.

Zelda repeated what she had told Sheriff Mullins who asked, "Does that sound like any place around here?"

Sheriff Thomas nodded. "Let's go."

It was about a half-mile down to the creek where they found the shallow grave near a copse of poplar trees. Six loose rocks lay on top.

Sheriff Mullins stood with Zelda until they took the body

away. He asked, "What did you mean 'he wanted her to be found'?"

Zelda frowned. "It was hate. The worst kind—a hate that has grown into this." She looked up at him and said, "I need to go home."

Zelda saw Hanson and Granny Zee on the porch, watching the road. It was late and the mountains had settled into the night. If not for this crime, she and Hanson would have spent the evening together on the porch, watching the night steal all the blue from the sky until the lines of the horizon blurred. Hanson would have talked of the garden, how the cow had tried to kick over the milk bucket that morning, his plans for the baby's cradle. Zelda would have recounted her and Granny Zee's soap making, the smell of lavender still hanging thick in the air. The evenings were their special times, when they talked and made plans until their words were no more than whispers. Instead, there was nothing about this horrible day that Zelda wished to tell anyone. When she had left her mountain this morning, she had gone from her sanctuary to a place invaded by evil—the worst kind—hate unleashed on a child.

A month later, Sheriff Mullins rode up the mountain again. He came with the news they had found the man who killed little Lucy. Ten years before, Judge Hall had sent the man to prison for robbery and the minute he got out, he had come after the judge. Sheriff Mullins said the man never intended to kill the judge; instead, he wanted him to suffer, so he planned to go after his wife until he saw they had a child.

Sheriff Mullins also brought Zelda one hundred dollars—the amount of reward the Hall's had offered. Zelda never forgot it was that money that got them through the hard times.

As her belly grew, Zelda saw Lucy in her dreams. When the harvest started, Lucy's spirit walked beside her. With her new mother's heart, she grieved for a child she had never known. She went to the faerie fort near the scarlet oak and begged the spirits for peace. Not since she first knew her gift for what it was, had Zelda fought so hard against it.

Granny Zee and Mama stayed close as Zelda's time grew near. Granny Zee had gotten so frail she spent most of her time now at Emmaline's house. She still doctored, but she no longer roamed the mountain on horseback. People came to her. As Zelda's pregnancy progressed, Granny Zee spent more time helping Zelda make remedies from the mountain plants. Zelda cherished those days with her grandmother. As the baby in her womb grew strong, Granny Zee faded. Zelda prayed the new baby would be a tonic for Granny.

October acted like a gate. It swung open on harvest and closed with Samhain and the coming of winter. It was a beautiful fall. The mountains dazzled with bright golds, reds from scarlet to ginger, and browns as rich as thick chocolate syrup. Zelda savored the frosty mornings and chilly days. After the punishing heat of summer, she relished the smell of wood smoke and the sparkle of morning sun on hoar frost.

By mid-October, Zelda was ready. Like a nesting bird, she had the house cleaned, and everything the baby would need was neatly stacked in the bureau. The canning was done, and the pantry was filled to bursting with canned vegetables and jars of preserves, pickles, relish, and crocks of sauerkraut. The root cellar was filled with apples, sweet and Irish potatoes, turnips, and strands of onions hanging like long ropes. That year, there would be much to be thankful for when they celebrated Samhain.

Two days before the baby's birth, Zelda sat in the new rocking chair Hanson had built, hemming a blue quilt she'd made for the baby's cradle. Hanson had brought it in that morning and set it up in their room. The cradle's beauty had taken Zelda's breath away, and she had gone into the room dozens of times to run her hand over and over the polished wood.

Zelda finished the last stitch, bit the thread off, and tucked the needle in her sewing basket. She rubbed her belly and stretched.

"Do you want me to help you to bed?" Hanson asked, looking up from the new seed catalog.

Zelda smiled. "No, I'm fine. Before I go to bed, I'm going to put this blanket in the baby's beautiful cradle, so I can admire it some more."

Hanson smiled. "I'm right proud of it." He rested his hand on Zelda's belly, and she covered it with her own.

Zelda hesitated at the door to her bedroom. The sweetness of lilacs hung in the air. She stepped into the room, and Cece's spirit washed over her. She went to the cradle and Patty Cake lay there. "Cece?" she whispered. "I'm happy you're back."

Zelda woke before dawn with a backache. The baby's coming had started. She eased from the bed, careful not to wake Hanson. There was no reason to tell him yet. Better to let him sleep. She wrapped a shawl around her shoulders and went to the kitchen to stir the fire in the stove until it roared to life. It was October twentieth and cold was digging deeper into the weather with each passing day.

The kettle was ready to boil when a soft knock sounded at the door. Zelda smiled. Granny Zee slipped in carrying her doctor bag. "I'm here to welcome my new great-grandson along-side the first hard frost. Your mama will be here directly. Now you set down and let me make the tea. I brought just the thing."

Hanson made twenty trips in and out of the house that day, and each time, he found Zelda either sitting in the rocking chair or slowly walking about the room, with her mother and Granny on either side of her. But it wasn't until twilight that Zelda's labor began to progress, and she moved to the bedroom. By then, Zelda's father had come for news. He had left Emerson Junior to take care of the chores. Normally, Emerson was his grandfather's shadow, but he was twelve now and a quiet boy, and he said he would come after it was all over. His mother, Isabelle, had stopped pretending she was going to raise him. Instead, she wrote long sunny letters filled with promises of visits she never intended to fulfill. She and her husband, William, were currently traveling in Europe. Isabelle claimed William's father had sent him there on business prospects since things were bad at home.

Zelda had attended many births with her mother and grandmother—births like hers where babies were welcomed and already loved beyond measure and births where babies were just another misery for a mother who could not care for the children she already had. None of those births prepared her for her own. The pain was all consuming, stretching and punch-ing and pushing her body from the inside until she thought she would give anything—anything—including her soul, to make it stop. But right at that moment when she thought the baby would never come, in a sudden rush, it was over. Her son was born and his cry, loud and strong, rang throughout the house, letting all know he had arrived.

The sun was coming up over Rock House Mountain, filling the horizon with a sky blue enough to drown in. The light caught the frost on trees and ground, setting off sparks of light into the grey mist, shrouding the hills. Louis James Davis slept in the cradle built by his father and swaddled in the blue quilt made by his mother. His little round face and thatch of reddish hair was as familiar to his mother as that of an old friend, for she had seen it in her heart. Zelda pulled the covers up to her chin and closed her eyes. She could rest, knowing her family was gathered around her hearth, celebrating her son's birth.

The last thing she heard before falling asleep was Cece singing a lullaby to her son.

2000

Chapter 25

My life has been spent in the sea of green mountains of Appalachia. When the winds roar through the trees it is like the sound of the ocean waves. When I climb the mountainside, it is like trudging through the sand. Whether it is a sea of water or trees, nature is a bountiful, beautiful experience.
~ from Granny Zee's Book of Dreams

HANNAH HAD COMPLETED THE classroom part of her physical therapy degree and was beginning the final year of supervised internships in hospitals and rehabilitation facilities. The problem was she would be interning in Colorado in the fall and California in the spring, and Travis was livid.

The demands of Hannah's schedule had left her with a mere week to call her own, but thankfully, it coincided with Granny's ninetieth birthday. Since Hannah's schedule made it impossible to plan a party, Maggie volunteered. After all, Granny was her and Addie's chosen grandmother. Maggie's first idea was to have a surprise party, but Hannah pointed out, "Do you really think she won't know?"

As Granny's birthday approached, excitement grew.

Early on Monday morning, Maggie was going over her list of things to do before the party when the phone rang. She was expecting Hannah, so she didn't look at the caller ID.

"Margaret," Judith Hudson's voice sounded like a fork scraping a plate. "I didn't know if you were awake yet, but I thought I'd take a chance."

"Mother, how are you?"

"Perfect, dear. How's my lovely granddaughter?"

"In fact, she's just come into the kitchen. I'll let her tell you herself."

Maggie handed the phone to Addie, whose mess of uncombed chestnut curls was so lovely it made Maggie smile. Addie's shock of silver hair curled over her forehead, and Maggie remembered when she had asked Addie if she wanted to get it colored to match her hair, and Addie had laughed and said, "Then I'd look like everyone else."

Maggie got a cup of coffee while Addie and her grandmother talked. She had just sat down when she heard Addie say, "Oh, Grandmother, you'll be here for our party!"

Maggie froze, coffee at her lips.

Addie said, "It's a birthday party for Granny Zee. I can't wait for you to meet her."

Maggie's stomach lurched. She went to the sink and dumped her coffee down the drain. When she turned around, Addie was balancing the phone on her shoulder while pouring cereal into a bowl. She said, "Bye, Grandmother. I can't wait to see you." Addie handed the phone to Maggie and left the kitchen.

Tomorrow.

Maggie heard the television come on in the family room. She said, "Mother?"

"Margaret, I told Addie my surprise. I'm coming to visit for a few days."

"I heard."

Maggie's mother talked on like her daughter hadn't spoken through gritted teeth.

This was the typical Judith Hudson maneuver—tell Addie first, that way if Margaret said, "You can't come," then she would have to explain to her daughter *why*. But Maggie tried, anyway. "Mother, I have a party planned for Friday night."

"I love parties. And I can help you! I'm stopping by on my way to meet friends at a new spa in Asheville, North Carolina. I'm flying out early in the morning. I'll rent a car and be there by late afternoon. Is J.D. coming home for the party?"

"No, Mother, it's not that kind of party. It's a birthday party for Hannah's grandmother. You remember Hannah?"

"Of course and that's a lovely gesture on your part, even though I should think her family would do the honors."

Maggie winced. "Everything is planned and—"

Her mother interrupted, "Don't worry about a thing. I'll be there tomorrow evening. A garden party?"

Maggie knew when she was defeated. "Yes."

"Tell Addie, and her friend who wants to be the horse veterinarian, I'll see them tomorrow. Good-bye, Margaret."

Not Granny's party! Tears stung Maggie's eyes and she leaned against the kitchen counter. She had to call the florist, and talk with the gardener, and what was it her mother said? Something about a horse veterinarian. Maggie knew Reilly wanted to be a veterinarian, but how did her mother know?

The phone was ringing when Maggie walked into the kitchen. She dropped two bags of groceries and grabbed it.

"Hey there! How's the party coming? I talked to Granny

Zee this morning and she's so excited."

"Hi Hannah."

"I called to tell you I'll be home tomorrow night. It will probably be about nine. Wait! Have you ever noticed how in the winter people say, 'It's so late? It's nine o'clock.' But in the summer, they say, 'It's not late. It's just nine o'clock.'"

Maggie laughed. "I never really thought about it."

Hannah chuckled. "I called to see if you need me to bring anything from here. I'm leaving early in the morning, but I can get it today."

"No, I can't think of a thing."

After a pause, Hannah said, "Okay, Maggie, what's wrong? You've got that sound in your voice."

Maggie didn't even bother to deny it. She was so upset about her mother's phone call she wanted to jump up and down and scream before sitting down to cry. She said, "Hannah, you know I want Granny's party to be perfect."

"And I'm sure it will be."

"I would never let anyone do anything to wreck Granny's party."

"Are you going to tell me or make me guess?"

"It's my mother. She's coming tomorrow."

"Here? I mean there?"

"I'm so sorry. I had no idea—she called this morning out of the blue—and told Addie she was making a surprise visit, so of course, Addie told her about the party, and—"

Hannah interrupted, "This is not a big deal. Everything will be fine. Don't worry."

Maggie gave a half-hearted chuckle. "You sound like a car salesman."

Hannah said, "I do not. Now, let's think about this. My Granny, my brother, my uncles, and who knows how many of my cousins and Granny's church friends, are going to be at your house for—three hours—four at the most. Your mother won't even have time to meet all of them. But Maggie, some of my cousins are borderline *The Beverly Hillbillies*."

Maggie laughed.

"No, Maggie, I'm serious. I've been meaning to tell you about my Stump Town cousins."

"Stump Town?"

"Yeah, that's the name of their holler."

Judith Hudson meets The Beverly Hillbillies sounded like a reality TV show. Maggie said, "Tell you what; I won't worry about your cousins if you don't worry about my mother."

"You'll see," Hannah said. "It will be fine."

The day of Granny's party dawned a perfect Pollyanna day. Maggie stood in the window and watched her mother pull together the perfect party that *she* had planned! With clipboard in hand, Judith checked and rechecked everything. First, she ordered more flowers. When the tent arrived and was set up, she demanded the workers add more lights. She supervised the caterer, the decorations, and the placing of every last chair.

The party was scheduled to begin at six o'clock, so Hannah and Granny arrived at five. They were seated in the sunroom sipping sweet tea when Maggie's mother breezed in fresh from her shower. She wore pale pink palazzo pants with a matching long flowing tunic. Around her neck was a long, flowered silk scarf. Her hair was swept up and diamond earrings flashed in her earlobes. Hannah and Granny stared, and Maggie looked down at her simple sundress. She smoothed back the wisps of hair that had escaped her ponytail.

Hannah sprang from her seat and came forward with her hand extended. "It's so nice to see you again."

Judith Hudson took Hannah's hand. "Lovely to see you, dear. Now, where's the guest of honor?" She smiled down at Granny Zee who wore a bright blue silk dress with a beautiful blue and white cameo brooch at the throat. The dress made Granny's blue eyes sparkle. Judith said, "It couldn't be this young lady. I thought this was a ninetieth birthday party?"

Granny Zee smiled and offered her hand. "I'm Zelda Davis, but everybody calls me Granny Zee."

"Judith Hudson." Judith took Granny's hand. "I've been looking forward to meeting you. I hope our little party will make this a special day for you."

Granny said, "Honey, when you get to be my age, every day you wake up raring to go is a special day."

Judith laughed, and Maggie and Hannah looked at each other. Hannah smiled and gave Maggie a surreptitious thumbs-up. Addie and Reilly skipped into the room and hugged Granny, singing out happy birthdays.

Maggie excused herself, saying she wanted to check a few things, and Hannah followed her. In the kitchen, they collapsed against the counter. Maggie said, "Did you hear her say 'our little party' like she did the whole thing?"

Hannah looked out the window at the workers scurrying around the pool making last minute preparations. "This is so wonderful," Hannah said. "*You* did all of this for my grandmother, and I'll never forget it."

"I was happy, no, *proud* to do it. You know how much you both mean to me." Maggie took Hannah's hand. "Anyway, nothing can go wrong, now."

By seven o'clock the tables were filled with guests, their plates piled high. Reilly and Addie and kids their age crowded around the pool. Hannah sat at the head table with Granny, who was flanked by her sons Louis and Gary. Maggie noticed Hannah repeatedly scanned the crowd, no doubt looking for Travis. Maggie didn't ask why Travis hadn't made an appearance.

Dinner had begun when the Stump Town cousins showed up. Maggie never knew exactly how many there were. For one thing, most of the men had beards and numerous tattoos, and for another, they were all dressed in faded jean cut-offs and Harley Davidson t-shirts. They depleted the beer supply in record time, and two of them jumped into the pool with their clothes on. But Granny was thrilled to see them. In fact, Granny had the time of her life.

At seven-thirty, Hannah rolled a cart into the tent with an enormous cake ablaze with 90 candles. The crowd clapped and sang Happy Birthday, and to the delight of everyone, Granny Zee managed to blow out all the candles. Maggie took a piece of cake and sat down at a table with Granny Zee, Hannah, and Judith. Maggie watched her mother smile and talk to Granny and her family like she was actually enjoying herself. She glanced at Hannah, who suddenly had a look of absolute horror on her face. Maggie followed her gaze to Travis, coming toward them, so drunk he weaved from side to side.

Hannah tried to hurry and reach Travis, but the tables were so close together that she couldn't get to him. He was pushing his way through the crowd, sloshing beer on people and practically shouting, "Where's my wife?"

Maggie froze. Hannah had reached Travis, who immediately wrapped one arm around her neck in what looked like a headlock. He swigged from a bottle of beer while he pushed Hannah back and forth, making her dance like a marionette. She tried to talk to him and move him out of the tent, but he wouldn't budge. When Judith Hudson got up and started toward them, Maggie stood, but Granny Zee, who was taking all of this in, waved her back to her seat.

Judith marched up to Travis. It had gotten quiet in the tent, so Maggie heard her say, "Why, Hannah! Who is this handsome man? And where have you been hiding him?" She looked up at Travis, who had stopped pushing Hannah back and forth. She said, "I don't suppose you'd walk with a lady over to the bar to get a drink?" Travis took his arm off Hannah's shoulder and wrapped it around Judith. She led him out of the tent and across to the bar where the bartenders were closing up. They delayed him until two of the Stump Town cousins came to take him home. Maggie watched her mother walk back in the tent and whisk Hannah back to the table like nothing had happened.

Hannah sat down across from Maggie. "I'm so sorry about Travis."

"Don't apologize. No harm done."

"Your mother was amazing."

After Travis's stunt, the party started to break up. Maggie glanced at her watch and saw that it was after nine o'clock. Granny Zee decided she wanted to go out by the pool, so she could tell everyone good-bye, so Hannah took her arm and they left the table.

Maggie looked around at the tent. Her mother's idea of putting in more lights was brilliant. The top of the tent looked like a sea of stars. The tables were covered with white table-cloths and decorated with baskets of sunflowers and battery-operated candles. Scattered around the tent area were old-fashioned streetlights that her mother had draped with ferns in hanging baskets. A huge banner read, *Happy Birthday Granny Zee,* and Maggie made a mental note to save it for Granny.

Maggie joined Granny and Hannah. A large man with a shaved head was talking to Judith. He sported a snake tattoo that coiled around his arm, its head resting on his hand. He was flexing his arm, making the snake move, while drinking from a huge bottle of beer. Maggie knew the bar had closed a while ago, so she asked one of the staff where the man got the beer. He raised an eyebrow and pointed to the man with the snake tattoo. He said that, when he told him they were out, he had gone to his pickup truck and come back with a huge cooler. Maggie stared. They brought their own beer? She edged closer, so she could hear what he was saying. It didn't take long to figure out he was *hitting* on her mother.

"Judy," he said, "a man like me knows how to treat a woman like you. I can take care of a woman, if you know what I mean." He laughed and took a long drink of beer.

Maggie watched her mother struggle to keep her composure. "I know exactly what you mean," she said. "Now, excuse me."

Judith took a step away from him and he grabbed her arm. "Aw, don't be like that."

With a look that would melt ice, Judith looked down at his hand and then up at his face. He dropped his hand, and Judith walked away. He called out, "Judy, honey, don't be like that!"

Judith winced, but she kept walking. People were turning around to see what was going on. Some of them actually pointed at her mother. Maggie was embarrassed for her, but she had to hand it to her mother, she walked away with her head held high.

What happened next was one of those moments that define an event—becomes the one thing everybody remembers whether they saw it or not. Judith's would-be suitor shouted loud enough for everyone to hear, "Woo hoo, Judy, you sure got a fine-looking swing on your back porch!" Then he raised his beer high like he was making a toast and took a long drink.

A titter went up and down through the crowd like an ocean wave. Maggie's hand flew to her mouth. She wanted to rush to her mother, but it quickly became apparent Judith didn't need any help. She wheeled around on her heel and stalked back to the man who was smiling like he'd won first prize. As she walked, her outfit caught an evening breeze and ballooned out around her, creating the illusion she was floating on a pink cloud. When she reached him, he opened his arms like he was expecting an embrace. She slapped him.

The Stump Town cousins loaded up their cooler and left, and the rest of the party broke up. Granny didn't seem the least bit upset. She walked around, dispensing hugs and good-byes, and then she asked if Maggie would take her inside so she could apologize to her mother for her great-nephew's behavior. Maggie asked Hannah if she'd rather take Granny inside, but she gave Maggie a strange look and walked away.

They found Judith sitting in the sunroom with a glass of red wine. Maggie couldn't believe it when Granny Zee accepted a glass. She sat down and watched them sip wine and laugh about the evening. She discovered her mother's "suitor" was Earl Campbell, the great-grandson of Granny Zee's late sister, Isabelle. Maggie watched while Granny and her mother talked over the evening like old friends. Before she left to see to the cleanup, she hugged Granny Zee and wished her happy birthday. Granny's eyes were as bright as a child on Christmas morning. She said, "I thank you for the best party I ever had."

It was almost midnight when Maggie came inside and found Addie in the sunroom. She asked, "Did everyone get settled for the night?"

Addie said, "Hannah took Granny Zee home, and Reilly went with her mom, and grandmother went to bed." She stood and kissed her mother. "Great party, Mom! I'm going to bed."

"Addie, did you see Hannah before they left?"

"Yeah, I told them good night. Why?"

"It's probably nothing, but Hannah left without saying good-bye."

Addie dropped her eyes.

"What is it?" Maggie took her finger and put it under Addie's chin. She gently pushed until her face lifted.

Addie said, "I don't know why, but Hannah was upset. And. And it—"

"And was it something to do with your grandmother?"

Addie's dark eyes went wide, and then she lowered her lashes. "I don't know, Mom. All I know is—it's you. She's angry with you."

Two months after Granny's ninetieth birthday party, Maggie drove the familiar road to Rock House Mountain. Hannah was in Denver, Colorado for an internship at a rehabilitation facility, and Maggie had spoken to her exactly twice since the night of the party. Both of those calls had been initiated by Maggie, and both had left her wondering what in the world had happened.

It had to be something that occurred the night of the party. There was no other explanation. Maggie had spent many sleepless nights dissecting that evening, yet she couldn't come up with an answer, so she was going where she always went when she needed answers—to see Granny Zee.

Maggie pulled in and drove around to the back of the house. She spied Granny Zee sitting outside with piles of branches spread around her. The afternoon heat had caused her to shed her big red sweater, which lay on a bench by the backdoor.

The most delightful scent greeted Maggie as she approached. She called out, "Oh, Granny Zee, what is that wonderful smell?"

Granny stood and held out her arms for Maggie's hug. An empty chair was next to hers like somehow Granny expected her. She picked up one of the branches and inhaled its heady sweetness.

"That's wild mugwort," Granny Zee said. "My grandmother called it sweet myrrh. I cut it this morning, and I'm going to dry it and make up a big wreath for the holidays. It makes the house smell like the sweet outdoors. When I was a child, Mama made us girls nibble on a leaf to ward off consumption and being attacked by wild animals. And, she told us that if a traveler put a leaf in his shoe, he won't tire. My granny always made me and my sisters a sleep pillow with mugwort."

"What's that?"

"It's a small pillow made from gauzy material like cheese-cloth and filled with dried mugwort. We put it next to our bed. It was supposed to give us vivid dreams."

"Well, it smells heavenly," Maggie said.

Granny Zee stood and picked up a couple of branches. "I'll take this in and leave the rest out here in the sun. Come on." She waved Maggie toward the door. "Tea's ready. Cece knew you were coming."

Maggie smiled. Of course, she did.

Inside Granny Zee's kitchen, drinking peppermint tea, Maggie wasted no time telling Granny why she'd come. She began, "How's Hannah?"

"She's wore out, but she's enjoying her work. I guess if you have to ask me, that means you two ain't talked."

Maggie shook her head. "Granny, I don't know what to do. She won't tell me what's wrong, but she's upset with me about something."

Granny Zee nodded.

"What is it? Please, tell me. I want to fix it."

Granny Zee creased her forehead in a half-frown. "I won't tell you because I think Hannah should tell you herself. But I will say this, Hannah is a proud person, and that's a good thing until it stands between her and a friend."

"But what do I do?" Maggie asked.

Granny took a sip of tea and then studied her cup. "Right now, would be a good time of year for a little trip." She sat back and smiled. "I'd like to get on an airplane and fly off somewhere for a few days. Wouldn't you?"

Three days later, Maggie was in Denver. She found Hannah's apartment and was standing by the front door when Hannah got home from the hospital. When Hannah saw Maggie, she started to cry and ran to her. The friends cried—talked—then cried and talked at the same time. It didn't take long for Maggie to learn that her mother had picked the night of Granny Zee's party to tell Hannah her money had financed Hannah's scholarship. Maggie apologized profusely for hiding it, and Hannah apologized for letting her stubborn pride make her act so ungrateful.

As relieved as Maggie was to find out why Hannah had been so angry with her, she was doubly furious with her mother. She had known that somehow this would lead back to her mother. Judith Hudson had struck when she caught Hannah at her most vulnerable. She had let Hannah thank her for getting Travis away from the party and then Judith had said, "Margaret is always rescuing people like you. Look how she is paying for your college."

Now, Maggie sat in a restaurant fifteen hundred miles from home, trying to undo the damage her mother had done. Hannah put her hand on Maggie's arm. She said, "I must have looked like the biggest fool in the world. Because I stupidly said, 'Maggie's not paying for my college, I have a scholarship.'" She shook her head. "I will never forget that churlish smile on her face when she said, 'You don't know, do you?'"

Maggie was so furious she wanted to throttle her mother with her bare hands. She looked at Hannah. The dark circles under her eyes stood out like bruised half-moons. Hannah leaned forward. "Your mother said, 'My dear, where did you think your scholarship came from?' And she made this phony-sounding laugh. Then, she leaned so close to me we were face-to-face and said, 'Margaret named the foundation for Augusta and Alexander, her paternal grandparents.'"

Maggie nodded.

The waiter appeared and asked if they would like dessert. Maggie said, "My friend would like a slice of double chocolate fudge cake, and I will have a chocolate mousse."

When dessert was served, Maggie said, "What my mother said is true. Your scholarship was paid for by the Augusta Alexander Scholars, set up by my father. The foundation is his legacy. He gave his life to the study of medicine, and he was a caring, generous man who wanted to see young people succeed. What my mother *didn't* tell you was that since I took over the scholarship funds, I have given away over five million dollars."

Hannah gasped. She whispered, "Five *million* dollars?"

Maggie nodded. "You see—yes, my foundation paid for your scholarship—but no, it was *not* charity. I didn't do it because I felt sorry for you. I did it because I believed in you, and I wanted to help you succeed. That is exactly the reason the recipients were given scholarships. I may have given you the money, but *you* did all the work."

2001

Chapter 26

Even a seer cannot know everything the future holds. The hardest thing I have ever faced was the loss of my child. All my remedies, all my healing abilities, all my love, could not save her. I saw her body, bleeding in the forest, and I couldn't reach her. A seer does not only see the future—what has not happened yet. She may also see what has happened in the past.
~ from Granny Zee's Book of Dreams

ALMOST—MAGGIE HATED THAT word. The denotation was bad enough. Almost meant: just about, all but, and very nearly. But the connotation got to the heart of what this word truly meant: the worst kind of disappointment—worse than a fiasco, disaster, and flat-out failure. Worse, it pointed the finger of responsibility—if someone hadn't done A, or had done B, then the outcome would have been C. And of course, C was the desired outcome and who wanted to hear, "He almost won!" The worst thing about "almost" was that it can haunt forever.

Maggie's biggest "almost" was taking Addie to D.C. for her father's speech. Addie had two weeks of school left before summer vacation, so it was a bad time for a trip, even a weekend one. She "almost" refused J.D., but in the end, it was Addie who said she would go because, "Daddy needs me."

If only Addie had known what J.D. was about to do, then things would have been different—best case scenario—she could have stopped it. Worst case scenario—she could have not been in the middle of it. But Maggie had learned that her daughter's abilities didn't work that way. Granny Zee had taught Addie there was no understanding why *an dara sealladh* knew of the coming of some things and not others. Granny said Addie's gift was strong, but she had not yet learned how to use it as Granny had learned how to use her gift. Granny Zee sought the spirits and the wee folk, but she had learned to be prepared when the spirits did not cooperate or revealed things to come that she did not want to know.

The gala was on Saturday night, and J.D. was making the official announcement—he was running for governor. It would be a big political bash, and Judith Hudson would be there with bells on. Maggie was still furious with her for telling Hannah about her scholarship. She would not, however, say one word about it because that would add to her mother's satisfaction.

In one year, Addie would graduate from high school, and whether J.D. was governor or not, Maggie was leaving him. Cooper would be returning to Ireland in August. He had been "on loan," as he called it, to Pineville's new physical therapy college, and now he was returning to University College Dublin. Maggie ached to go with him. It was Ireland where she intended to spend the rest of her life, far from J.D. and her mother.

Maggie held up her hand, and the diamonds and emeralds in her Claddagh ring caught the light. She smiled. The ring finger on her left hand was bare. She had always hated her four-carat ostentatious wedding ring. She seldom wore it, especially now. Her excuse was that she was afraid she would lose it. Maggie smiled again. She had gotten good at lying. She touched her Celtic knot necklace; like her ring, she never took it off. Cooper had given it to her for Christmas. It was easy to tell J.D. that Hannah had given it to her. Of all the things that had gotten easier, one that was getting harder—finding a way to tell Addie she was going to divorce her father and marry another man.

Already, Maggie had plans for the future. She and Cooper would marry at the Cliffs of Moher where they'd declared their love for each other, with Cooper's grandmother's diamond and emerald wedding band. Cooper had an apartment near the college where they could live until they could look for a house.

Addie was growing into an amazing young woman—smart, kind, and caring. Maggie knew she had been over-protective. Even though Addie had been cancer free for ten years—she couldn't forget the sick toddler, clinging to her neck, crying in pain. She had fiercely protected her daughter's privacy. Addie didn't want people in Coal Valley to know she had suffered through childhood leukemia. The only exceptions were Hannah, Granny Zee, and Reilly. In addition, Maggie had protected Addie's amazing gift of finding lost things and people from prying eyes.

Granny Zee had overseen this part of Addie's growth into adulthood, and as the years went by, Addie became secretive about her gift. There were times Maggie suspected she knew what was going to happen, like her father getting elected to Congress. Did Addie know Maggie was in love with Cooper? Did she know she was going to leave her father and marry him?

Spring swept across Coal Valley and overnight color returned to the landscape. The birds and creatures of the forest welcomed it like a long-lost friend. Grass sprang from the earth lush and green, and the scent of tilled earth filled the air. Like a toddler raising her arms to be picked up, the trees stretched their limbs toward a crystal sky no longer shrouded in gray. Maggie declared spring was her favorite season in Coal Valley, a proclamation she made with each season.

Maggie and Addie had invited Reilly to go with them to D.C., but she stayed behind with Granny Zee who had suffered a bout with bronchitis and still had a cough. Maggie and Addie flew out on Friday evening and planned to return on a noon flight on Sunday. On Saturday, Maggie avoided talking to J.D. alone, so they wouldn't argue.

At five o'clock, a limo whisked them downtown. As was the norm in Washington, many people used this evening as a chance to further their position or, in this case, align themselves with J.D. Whitefield. Maggie plastered a smile on her face that only faltered once, when her mother breezed in smiling and chatting to everyone like she was the one running for governor. Maggie had discovered years ago that in a crowd, her mother was on her best behavior.

Maggie kept her eyes on Addie, who smiled and shook endless hands. She admired her beautiful daughter, who had grown so tall and willowy. She wore her long hair in loose curls, and her minimal makeup was artfully done. She had chosen a pale-yellow sleeveless sheath that flattered her tan slender arms. Maggie wore a simple black dress and pearls. She recently had cut her long hair to shoulder-length layers, giving it bounce and shine. Maggie knew J.D. didn't like it by the measured look she'd got when he first saw it.

Maggie and Addie were seated at the table of honor with her mother. They were right in front of the podium where a string of politicians made short speeches that would lead up to the speech announcing the next governor of Virginia. Then J.D. would speak and make his announcement; and then it would go on and on.

During J.D.'s speech, he was wowing the crowd with his promises of how he was going to change what was wrong, and make better what was right. Maggie and Addie clapped and smiled at the appropriate times. Then he said the two words that made Maggie know the meaning of hatred. It rose in her throat, thick and putrid. She wanted to open her mouth and spit until the taste was gone.

J.D. said, "I want to talk about something near and dear to my heart—healthcare. When I become governor of Virginia, I will fight for healthcare for every person, especially every child.

I know better than some what it means to be able to get the best possible care for a sick child. My own daughter is a *cancer survivor*, and she would not be here today if she had not received proper healthcare when she needed it."

The entire crowd turned and looked at Addie. They clapped and cheered while J.D. beamed down on her.

Addie's face turned the color of cold ashes. Maggie reached under the table and clasped her daughter's trembling hands. She tried to comfort her with her touch—the way she had done when she was a toddler battling cancer. In those days, Maggie had placed her cheek on Addie's forehead, laid her hand on her back, and kissed her tiny hands, anything to place her skin next to her daughter's. Inside of her, anger erupted like a phoenix, leaving behind a new creature determined to break free. There was no excuse. J.D. knew how sensitive Addie was about her cancer, and yet, he'd just betrayed her in front of hundreds of people for his own personal gain.

At the end of his speech, J.D. walked off the stage, kissed the top of Addie's head, and sat down next to Maggie. Dessert was served, and people began milling around. Maggie played the part of the dutiful wife, while shielding Addie as much as possible from prying eyes and questions. Her mother sat on the other side of Addie, and when the first *well-meaning* woman came up to talk to Addie, Maggie gave her mother a severe look, and Judith moved in to shield her granddaughter.

As soon as she could, Maggie whispered in Addie's ear, and they started for the door. J.D. was talking to a group of people a good distance away, but he saw them and came striding over. Maggie stepped in front of Addie. She said, "We're leaving. Addie doesn't feel well."

"Margaret, you can't leave." J.D.'s smile was warm, but his voice would have frosted glass.

"Oh?" Maggie opened her purse and pulled out a gold lipstick holder. She watched J.D.'s eyes widen when he saw it. Then he looked away.

Maggie said, "I believe I need to touch up my lipstick." In one swift movement, she removed the tube and twisted the bottom until lipstick the color of dried blood appeared. "Why, that's not my lipstick!" Carefully, Maggie capped it and placed it back in the gold case. She turned it back and forth, examining it like a rare jewel, holding it up in front of J.D.'s face.

J.D. grabbed it out of Maggie's hand. He hissed, "Where did you get this?"

"Why, your daughter found it. I've kept it all these years, carrying it around, waiting for the right moment to use it."

A group of men approached J.D. Maggie said, "Excuse us." She turned, took Addie's hand, and rushed her daughter out the door without a backward glance.

Addie cried all the way back to the townhouse. Her misery filled the car, hot and thick. Maggie worried they were going to be sucked under it, drowning with no hope of rescue. Over and over Addie said, "How could Daddy do that to me?"

Back at the townhouse, Addie gathered her things while Maggie called the airline. When J.D. got home, they were already on a flight back to Tri-Cities.

Addie had to endure the last week of school with her face plastered all over the news, not to mention the looks and whispers of the students. Before they even got home, the television news did a story about J.D.'s bid for governor, with a clip of his speech telling the world his daughter was a cancer survivor. When Addie got to school on Monday, a reporter and cameraman jumped out of a car and ran toward her, shoving a microphone in her face. Reilly jumped in front of her friend and confronted the reporters so Addie could get away.

Not only had J.D. betrayed his daughter's trust, but he'd also broken her heart. The minute school closed, Maggie took the girls to stay with Hannah, who was completing her rotation at a hospital in Santa Barbara.

While Hannah worked, Maggie and the girls went sightseeing. In the evenings, they met Hannah for dinner and then went back to the hotel to go swimming before bed. When Hannah managed to get a weekend off, they went to Disneyland. They returned late, sunburned but happy to gather around the hotel pool. Addie and Reilly swam under the stars, while Maggie and Hannah stretched out in lounge chairs with a glass of wine.

After a while, Addie and Reilly bundled themselves into towels and sat down between their mothers. "Mom," Addie said, "Reilly and I want to talk to you both about something important."

Maggie sat up and looked at Hannah who had an *I don't know what this is about* expression on her face. "Okay," she said, "go ahead."

Addie looked at Reilly who nodded and smiled in encouragement. Addie blurted out, "We want to do a student exchange program next year. We've already got all of the information and have contacted the family and everything, and they're willing to take both of us, and—"

"Wait!" Hannah held up her hand. She sat up and swung her feet to the ground. "Slow down—you didn't even say where you want to go."

"Oh," Addie said. She and Reilly laughed.

Reilly said, "Ireland. We want to do a student exchange program to Dublin."

Maggie's heart leapt into her throat. She looked at Hannah who stared wide-eyed at the girls.

Addie said, "I'm not going back to school in Coal Valley. I refuse to let everyone stare at me and say, 'poor pitiful little girl,' and after what he did to me, I refuse to help my father. Besides, he's going to win, anyway."

Maggie and Hannah exchanged a look.

Addie's chest heaved, and Reilly put her arm around her shoulder. "We loved Ireland," Reilly said. "We really want to do this."

"Please, Mama, please don't send me back to school in Coal Valley." Tears trickled down Addie's face.

"Addie, honey, don't cry. We'll talk this over and check into it. I promise."

Addie shook her head and wiped her face. Reilly said, "We only have until next Friday to decide."

A *swoosh* sound escaped from Maggie. "Why didn't you tell me before now?"

"I don't know," Addie said. "I was afraid you wouldn't let me. It's something I've wanted to do for a long time. And then, Daddy..."

Hannah said, "Well, if you want to know what I think, I think it's a *grand* idea, and I think Maggie needs to go with you."

Addie and Reilly jumped up and hugged Hannah. Then they hugged Maggie who said, "Let me see the information."

"I'll get my laptop," Addie said.

Chapter 27

I believe that when we are asleep, we get access to the past and the future. When I wake, I feel like I have traveled through time. Whether I want to remember what happens on those travels, or whether or not it serves me to, remains a mystery.
~ from Granny Zee's Book of Dreams

WHEN THEY RETURNED FROM California, J.D. was in Coal Valley. At first, Addie refused to speak to him, but she finally agreed to hear him out. Maggie left the room but stayed in the kitchen where she could hear their conversation.

J.D. began like he was facing a courtroom instead of his hurt and distraught daughter. He tried to persuade Addie that he didn't know his speech would upset her. In fact, he said she should be proud her cancer story could inspire others. He went on about how much he cared about healthcare, especially for children.

When that didn't work, he talked about the voters and how important it was to make them understand that he was first a husband and father. "I need the voters to sympathize with me," he said. "That will help me get elected, and if I get elected, think of all the good I can do for the state."

He beamed at Addie, who sat stone-faced. When he'd finished his argument, she stood and faced him. "Daddy, you didn't say the one thing that matters to me." She turned away.

"Wait, Addie, what did you want me to say?"

With her back to him she said, "You didn't say, 'I'm sorry'." She ran upstairs to her room and stayed there until Hannah and Reilly came to pick her up.

The next morning, J.D. went to play golf. He was in full campaign mode, and Maggie knew he would make the best of his last day in Coal Valley before returning to D.C. When he came in that evening with the scent of summer still warm on his skin, Maggie faltered. Just for a moment. There was no good time or way to end a marriage. No matter the reason—no matter how justified it was—it was like cutting a hunk out of your heart.

J.D. poured a drink and sat down with his laptop. Maggie said, "I want to talk to you about Addie and—and about us."

He glanced at her and then looked back at his computer. "I tried to talk to her, Margaret. She's being unreasonable."

Maggie swallowed hard. She wouldn't let him upset her, not this time. "Be that as it may," she said, "Addie is going to finish high school as an exchange student in Dublin, Ireland."

J.D. didn't look up. He said, "That's impossible. I need her here for the campaign. After the November election, she can go there for the second semester, if she wants."

"It's already settled, and..." She paused. "I'm going with her."

J.D. closed his laptop and faced Maggie. "Alright, Margaret, you have my attention. Now, what's this about?"

"This is about your daughter *and your marriage*. Addie is going to Ireland for her senior year because you told the world about her cancer, even though you knew she didn't want people to know, and I'm going with her. I'm not coming back. I want a divorce."

J.D. shot to his feet. For a moment, Maggie was afraid he would strike her. Her instinct was to step back, but she held her ground.

He shouted, "You want a divorce, now? After all these years, you choose the year I run for governor to ask for a divorce. What do you expect me to say?"

Margaret went over to the sofa and sat down. She said, "Just think of all the sympathy you'll get from the voters. Imagine all the women who will throw themselves at you."

J.D. laughed, and a chill ran down Maggie's spine. He put his hands on his hips. "So, you're having an affair with this Irishman, which by the way, I knew all along, and you think I'm going to let you run off to Ireland with *my* daughter and ruin my chances of becoming governor." He walked to the kitchen. Maggie could hear the clink of ice, and he came back with a fresh drink.

Maggie sat with her hands in her lap. She waited for him to turn around and face her. "J.D., I'm not having an affair." She paused and tilted up her chin. "But I *am* in love with someone else."

He hesitated before taking a swig of bourbon, but Maggie waited.

He said, "Careful, Margaret, you forget who you're dealing with."

Maggie left the room and came back with a plain manila envelope. She handed it to him. "No, J.D., *you* have no idea who you're dealing with. I'm not the naïve little wife who sits on her hands and waits for her husband to tell her what to think. I stopped being that person years ago, but you were too busy to notice. My attorney will contact you."

Maggie went upstairs to the guest room and locked the door. She called Hannah. When Hannah answered, she said, "I did it."

"Are you alright?"

"Yes, I left him with the envelope of pictures the detective gave me. I'm upstairs in the guest room."

"What did he say?"

"He was his usual arrogant self until I gave him the envelope. I didn't wait for him to look at the contents."

"Maggie," Hannah said, "what was in the envelope?"

Maggie sighed. "Let's just say her name is Heather."

"I'm so sorry, Maggie."

"I'm not. It just made it easier."

Hannah said, "Travis, I need to talk to you."

He picked up the remote and turned the volume up on the baseball game. When he put the remote on the table, Hannah grabbed it and turned off the TV.

Travis ran his fingers through his hair. "What now?"

He sat in the same recliner that had occupied the same space since they'd moved into this house. He wore the same faded jean cut-offs and worn-out sports t-shirts, and he needed a haircut. And he was the most handsome man she'd ever seen. She waited for him to look at her, but he kept his eyes on the blank TV screen.

"I want to talk to you about Reilly," Hannah said.

"What's wrong with her."

"Nothing." Hannah went over and sat down on the couch. "She's fine. She's perfect. She is going to be a foreign exchange student next year."

"A what?"

"She's going to spend her senior year of high school in Dublin, Ireland. She and Addie Whitefield are going together."

Travis stared straight ahead. He didn't move. He didn't say a word. Maggie crossed her arms over her chest and waited.

Finally, she said, "Don't you have anything to say? Anything to ask?"

Travis dropped his head in his hands and started to cry.

Hannah had seen Travis cry once—the day his twins were born and his son died. He hadn't cried about the accident, or losing his scholarship—he had remained stoic, almost matter

Elswick

of fact about it all. To see tears after all these years shocked the rising anger right out of her, and she dropped to her knees in front of him. He mumbled something. Hannah asked, "Travis, what did you say?" When he didn't answer, she pleaded, "Travis, I couldn't hear you. What did you say?"

He dropped his hands and looked at her. Tears streaked his cheeks, and pain darkened his blue eyes—her daughter's eyes—the blue of the sky conflated with the gray of dawn. Only now, they darkened with pain. Where did that pain come from? Had it been there all along?

Travis lifted his head and looked Hannah in the eye. "I said, 'Are you leaving me?' Is that what this is?"

Hannah put her hand on his knee. "This is about Reilly."

"But, you're graduating next month," Travis said. "Are you going with her?"

Until that moment, Hannah hadn't known the answer. Many nights she'd woke, tingling with the knowledge that she was fulfilling the first part of her dream—independence. She almost had her degree in hand. Now, all she had to do was fulfill the second half—leave Travis and the mountains behind. But not yet. Even though Reilly would be in Ireland, she couldn't leave Granny Zee.

Hannah stood. "No, Travis, I'm not leaving. I'm staying here to study for my state boards."

She took a step toward the kitchen and heard Travis mumble something. She wheeled around. "What?" When he didn't say anything, she stamped her foot. "Dammit, Travis, if you have something to say, then say it!"

"I said, 'I told you I wasn't driving.'" Travis stood and looked at Hannah. "But you don't believe me. You want to think the worst of me."

Hannah stared at Travis's back as he walked away. He came back a moment later and handed her an envelope, folded so the only thing evident about it was that it had been read many times. Then he went out the door, and Hannah heard his truck start and drive away.

The phone rang, and Hannah realized she was staring at the door Travis had just exited. When she answered it, Maggie said, "Hannah, have you spoken to Granny Zee today?"

"No, why?"

"Addie just came to me and said we need to check on Granny."

"Why? What's wrong?"

"She said she doesn't know what—but something's wrong."

254

"I'm hanging up. I'll call you right back."

Hannah counted ten rings before she pushed the off button. She called Maggie who answered on the first ring. "Granny didn't answer. I'm leaving right now."

"We're right behind you."

All the way up the mountain, Hannah prayed. She tried to focus on Granny Zee and keep what had happened with Travis at bay. She remembered begging Granny to stay indoors out of the heat—that was two, no three days ago. Hannah knew people Granny's age had trouble regulating their body temperature and could be overheated before they realized it. She also knew how Granny Zee was about being outdoors with her plants.

Hannah was out of the car the second it stopped. She entered the kitchen calling, "Granny? It's Hannah! Granny!"

The reply was silence. Hannah ran to the living room, and then to Granny Zee's bedroom, but the bed was neat and tidy. She wheeled around and headed for the kitchen, planning to search outside. She called again, "Granny? Granny Zee? Where are you?" She had the door open when, suddenly, she turned on her heel—the doll room.

Hannah ran back through the house and was met with the dusky scent of lilac at the door to the doll room. She grabbed the doorknob and twisted but nothing happened. She pounded on the door, calling, "Granny Zee! Granny!"

Hannah stopped and leaned against the door, her chest heaving. She took a deep breath and tried to think of what Granny would do. Hannah made her voice high-pitched like she was talking to a child. "Cece, dear, please open the door. Please, Cece, please, open the door. Granny—Zelda wants you to." Hannah tried the door again, but it was still locked.

She heard Maggie and the girls at the door, so she ran back to the kitchen just as they tumbled inside. Maggie asked, "Did you find her?"

"I think she's..."

"She's in the doll room," Addie said. She strode across the room and disappeared through the door. Hannah, Reilly, and Maggie followed. At the doll room door, they watched while Addie leaned against the door and pressed her hands on either side of it, palms spread. Then she pressed her forehead against the door.

No one moved as Addie pressed her body against the door. She didn't speak, and for a long moment nothing happened. Just as Hannah was about to call for Granny again, the doorknob slowly turned and the door opened—just an inch. Addie stepped back, and Hannah pushed open the door.

The sweetness of lilacs rushed from the room. Granny Zee lay on the bed, dolls arranged all around her, Patty Cake in the crook of her arm.

Hannah whispered, "Granny?"

Granny's eyes fluttered open. Hannah rushed to the bed and picked up her hand. "Granny Zee, can you hear me?"

Granny spoke, her voice as thin as tissue paper. "Yes, I thought I'd rest a spell." She tried to sit up, but Hannah gently pressed her back against the pillow. "It's okay, just lie still."

Hannah took Granny's pulse, pulled down her bottom eyelids, and peered inside. She suspected Granny was dehydrated. "Have you been outside today?" Hannah asked.

Granny nodded. "This morning, I watered my flowers and vegetables."

"Have you eaten today?" Hannah asked.

Granny frowned. "I was going to fix some toast and tea after I finished my watering, but I guess I decided to rest first. What time is it?" She looked around.

Hannah stood. "It's almost five o'clock. I'm going to call your doctor. I'll be right back." She nodded to Maggie, who stepped forward and sat down next to Granny.

"I didn't mean to cause a ruckus," Granny said.

"Of course you didn't."

"How did I get in the doll room?"

"Don't you remember?"

"The last thing I remember was stepping into the kitchen."

"Cece brought you here," Addie said.

Granny Zee's eyes met Addie's. Just then, Hannah came back with orders from Granny's doctor to meet him in the emergency room. Maggie suggested Granny Zee would be more comfortable in her car, so they helped her get settled. Hannah said, "Maggie, I'll be right behind you. I have to do something first."

Hannah slipped back in the kitchen door and took off running. At the doll room, she was met with a blast of cold air. She yelled, "Is that all you've got?" and hurled herself inside the room. The door slammed behind her. She grabbed Patty Cake off the bed and swung her around in a circle over her head. She said, "Cece, if you ever try to stop me from coming in this room, I will break Patty Cake into a million pieces! Do you hear me?"

A swoosh of cold air sent the dolls on the top shelf flying at Hannah's head. She jumped back out of their way. "Ha! Is that the best you can do? You don't scare me!" Hannah held Patty Cake by the feet and hung her upside down. She lifted her into the air. "Do you see this? I will drop her and smash her to pieces if you ever try to keep Zelda away from me." She waved the doll in the air.

The lamp on the bedside table lifted into the air until it hovered just under the ceiling then dropped to the floor with the force of an explosion. Shards of glass flew at Hannah. She ducked and covered her face.

She unfolded herself and held Patty Cake out in front of her. This time she spoke to Cece like a mother admonishing a daughter. "Cece, I'm going to put Patty Cake back in her bed, but you have to promise to never lock me out again. If you do, I'll take Zelda away from here and she will never come back." She put Patty Cake down and backed up until she got to the door. She reached behind her and her hand closed around the doorknob. She opened the door and eased out of the room, never taking her eyes off Patty Cake.

Hannah was on the way down the mountain when she started to shake. She gripped the steering wheel and tried to concentrate, but the tremors bloomed from deep inside. A butterfly flew past, and she recalled a day long ago. She had been driving home after dropping Reilly off at school, when she noticed a moth clinging to her windshield wipers. She had watched, knowing it would fly away at any moment, but it hung on mile after mile. By the time she got home, she was convinced it was dead and had somehow gotten stuck, but when she got out of the car it took flight, whizzing past her face.

Hannah knew that, just like that moth, she had to hang on. She couldn't think of Travis right now. She had to concentrate on Granny. She would take care of Granny first. She punched the button and turned on the radio. Nelly Furtado's voice swelled *I'm Like A Bird*.

"Oh, God," Hannah said. She started to cry. She pulled off the road and sang through her tears. She wiped the tears from her face and saw there was blood on her hand. She pulled down the visor and looked in the mirror, finding a cut under her right eye. She found a tissue and dabbed at the cut. That damned Cece.

Back on the road, the last verse of the song cut through to her heart. Travis didn't know Hannah, and she didn't know him.

Chapter 28

Like my grandmother, I was born behind the veil. At birth, my body was covered with the birth sack, and Granny said she had to tear it to get me out. Granny saved my caul and sewed it into a small purse. It has been with me my whole life, and I believe it has protected me from many things. When I die, I want it placed in my coffin to help me on my way to the afterlife.
~ from Granny Zee's Book of Dreams

HANNAH WAS RELIEVED WHEN Granny's doctor wanted her to spend a night in the hospital and take fluids to "be on the safe side." She was even more relieved when, only an hour after the fluids started, Granny asked her to find the QVC channel on television, a sure sign she felt better. Maggie and the girls left for home, and since Hannah was staying with Granny, she made Reilly promise to tell her father what had happened.

By the time everything was settled it was late, so Hannah stretched out in the recliner next to Granny. She listened to her breathe and watched the drip, drip of the IV. She closed her eyes and prayed, *Dear Lord, thank you for sparing Granny today. Help her get her strength back.* Hannah stopped. She almost asked God to keep Granny safe from Cece, but how do you pray about a ghost? She opened her eyes and found Granny Zee watching her.

"You're supposed to be asleep," Hannah said. She sat up and took Granny's hand.

Granny smiled. "I will, directly."

"Can I get you something?"

"No, no, I'm fine."

Hannah stared into Granny Zee's blue eyes and saw her own reflected there. "You gave us a scare today. Do you remember what happened?"

Granny nodded. "I went to water my plants, and I guess I stayed out too long. I remember thinking it was so hot a body couldn't stand it for long. I remember putting the hose up and going into the kitchen. Then I woke up and you were there."

"You woke up in the doll room."

Granny Zee frowned.

"Do you remember going into the doll room?"

"No." Granny Zee paused. She looked at Hannah who smiled and patted her hand.

"It doesn't matter now," Hannah said. "I'm just happy you're okay."

"I'm sure glad you came to check on me."

"It was Addie. She told Maggie something was wrong, and Maggie called me. When I couldn't get you on the phone, we rushed to your house."

Hannah chose her words carefully. "Granny, when we got to your house, the door to the doll room was locked. It was like Cece didn't want us to get to you." She paused to see Granny's reaction.

Granny Zee looked at Hannah with serious eyes. "Don't fret about Cece. She'd never do anything to harm me. I suspect she thought it was my time."

Hannah nodded and decided to let it go. She'd figure out later how to explain the shattered lamp. She patted Granny Zee's hand. "Why don't you get some sleep?"

"I want to talk to you first."

Hannah nodded.

"There's something besides your old Granny troubling you."

Hannah sighed. "It's Travis." She paused, hoping Granny would let it go at that, but Granny said, "And?"

"Wait a minute." Hannah put her hand in her pocket. She had forgotten about the envelope she'd stuffed there. "He gave me this."

Hannah unfolded the envelope and pulled out a letter. As she read aloud, the shaking inside of her started again. Granny Zee gripped her hand. "Put this bed rail down and come here to your Granny."

Hannah moved the rail and scooted in next to Granny. She put her head on Granny's shoulder and let the tears escape. When she quieted, she said, "Granny?"

"Yes."

"Travis asked me today if I was going to leave him. He said he knew I didn't believe him when he said he wasn't driving the night of the accident." Hannah sat up and looked down at Granny. "He gave me this letter right before Maggie called about you, and I forgot I had put it in my pocket."

Granny Zee took Hannah's hand. "Well, it's clear in that letter that Roby was thanking Travis for taking the blame. Does that change anything?"

Hannah looked down at the roadmap of blue veins on

Granny's hand. She said, "It's no secret I didn't want to marry Travis, even though I went off to college with every intention of marrying the football star when he turned pro. It wasn't until I got pregnant that I realized I wasn't really in love with *him*. I was in love with the grand future I thought I'd have."

Hannah picked up Granny Zee's hand and kissed it. "But, even if we didn't have a grand future, we have a beautiful daughter."

Granny asked, "Is that all?"

Hannah sighed and scooted off the bed, settling back in the recliner. "Granny, I made Travis love me."

Granny perked up. "Did you, now?"

Hannah faced Granny. "When I was sixteen, I used Great Granny Zee's book of spells to make a love charm."

Granny made a *humm* sound.

"I know I wasn't supposed to. I'm sorry. I was some crazy teenager who thought I was in love."

"What did you do exactly?"

"I made a talisman like the book said, and then I went into the forest on the night of the Feast of Samhain and asked the spirits to do my bidding."

"And you think it worked?"

"Of course. When I started wearing the talisman, Travis fell in love with me."

Granny reached for Hannah's hand. "My dear granddaughter, you couldn't have made that spell work. You're not a caulbearer. The only person who can cast those spells is a caulbearer."

Hannah stared at Granny with wide eyes. Then she started gulping air like she was drowning. Granny asked, "Are you alright? I believe you're the one who needs to get in this bed."

"Oh, Granny! All these years I thought—I thought."

"No, dear. Travis fell in love with you of his own free will. Whether or not that changes things is up to you." She yawned. "I believe I can sleep now. Good night, dear girl. I love you."

❦

The doctor discharged Granny with strict orders to stay out of the heat. Hannah decided it would be best to stay with Granny for a few days, so she took her home, made sure she was comfortable, and then went home to pack a bag. It was also a good way to avoid Travis as long as possible. If she hurried, she could grab her things and be gone before he got home.

At home, Hannah slipped in the kitchen door and stopped

short. The floor gleamed and the room smelled like fresh lemons. She walked to the center of the room and surveyed the kitchen. It was so clean it fairly sparkled. She went through the house gaping at each dusted and vacuumed room. Even the bathrooms were spotless.

Hannah hurried downstairs to the laundry room where she found stacks of clean clothes folded on top of the washer and dryer, including her clean uniforms.

She ran back upstairs and grabbed an old Mickey Mouse duffel bag Reilly had discarded for more mature luggage. Ten minutes later, she was back in the car with her computer, some books, and clothes. She started the car before she realized she hadn't even left Travis a note.

Hannah found a pen and tore a sheet of paper from her notebook. She wiped sweat off her forehead with the tail of her shirt, trying to think of something to write. In the scant time it had taken her to put her things in the car, sweat poured from her pores. Ripples of heat rose up from the pavement and shimmered before her eyes. The air conditioner was on high, but it hadn't begun to cool the car. Hannah bent forward so the air blew in her face.

After a moment, she sat back and wrote: *Granny got out of the hospital, and I'm staying with her until I make sure she's okay. I'm worried about her. She's so frail. Reilly will stay with Maggie or me and Granny.* She signed it and opened the door. She had one leg outside the car when she stopped and picked up her pen. Under her name she scribbled. *The house looks amazing.* She left the note and Roby's letter on the kitchen counter.

By the time Hannah got to Granny's, Maggie and the girls were there, fixing dinner. Granny was propped up on the couch with so many pillows around her, she looked like she might disappear into them at any moment. Walter was on one of the pillows next to her, his purr on high volume, his green eyes adoring Granny.

Hannah laughed. "It looks like you guys have everything under control." She went to Granny and kissed her soft cheek.

Granny smiled. "A body could get used to this."

Reilly said, "Hey, Mom, come in the kitchen and see what Maggie's making for dinner."

Maggie was busy turning chicken breasts in Granny's enormous iron skillet. Hannah lifted the lid on the pots and discovered fragrant brown rice in one and potatoes cooking in another. "Mmmm, this smells delicious," Hannah said.

"Thank you; want to help me with the salad?"

Hannah poured herself a glass of iced tea and added a sprig of Granny's fresh mint. She took a long drink then started chopping vegetables.

Maggie said, "What did the doctor say?"

Hannah glanced in the other room and saw Reilly and Addie sitting on the floor next to Granny Zee, working a puzzle.

Maggie said, "They can't hear us."

Hannah sighed. "He said she was in better health than he was, and she should be one hundred percent in a few days."

Maggie smiled. "And how are you?"

Hannah looked up and met her friend's steady gaze. "I'm tired. I didn't get much sleep." She went back to slicing cucumbers.

"Is that all?"

"No," Hannah sighed, "it's not. Besides Granny scaring me to death, Travis and I had a—not a fight—I don't know what to call it."

"Today?"

"No, we were in the middle of it yesterday when you called." She put down her knife and rubbed her forehead. "I'm not even sure what day it is. Yesterday seems like a week ago."

Maggie went to her friend and put her hand on her back. "I'm sorry about all of this. Look, we'll have dinner and the girls and I will clean up and clear out so you and Granny can get some rest."

Hannah nodded. She said, "Maggie, will you do me a favor?"

"Sure."

"I need you to help me clean up the doll room before Granny sees it."

Maggie's eyes went wide. "What happened?" Surprise made her raise her voice, and Hannah saw Addie look up from the puzzle.

Hannah gave Maggie a "be quieter" signal. She went to the cabinets and started looking for a bowl. Maggie followed her. "What happened?" This time she whispered.

"I had a fight with Cece."

"What!"

"Sshh!"

"Sorry," she whispered. "How do you fight with a ghost?"

"Believe me, you can. Go look in the doll room."

Maggie disappeared. When she came back, she was carrying the trash can from the bathroom. She dumped the glass from the broken lamp into the kitchen trash and got the broom and dustpan from the closet. She glanced over at Granny and the girls, but they were absorbed in the puzzle, so she hurried back to the doll room to finish cleaning up the broken glass. When she came back, Hannah had finished the salad and drained the potatoes.

Hannah said, "Wait! You mash the potatoes and I'll take out the trash." When she came back inside, the girls were helping Granny to the table. Maggie was putting bowls of food around the platter of golden fried chicken. Hannah said, "I'm going to wash my hands and I'll be right back. Don't wait for me. Eat!"

Hannah stopped in front of the doll room. She eased the door open and took one step inside the room. With the exception of the missing lamp, the room looked like nothing had been disturbed.

Back in the kitchen, Hannah sat down and filled her plate. The girls had begged Granny to tell a story, so when she finished eating, she sat back and began her tale. Hannah tried to enjoy her food while Granny talked, but her mind kept wandering to Travis. "I wasn't driving," echoed in her head alongside, "Travis fell in love with you of his own free will."

Reilly said, "Mom, Granny's going to tell the chicken story! Hey, Mom!"

Hannah started. "I'm sorry, honey. What?"

"Granny's telling the chicken story."

"Oh, that's one of my favorites," Hannah said. She glanced over at Maggie who raised her eyebrows and gave her a "what's wrong?" look.

"Well," Granny began, her eyes sparkling, "when I was a girl, Sundays after church, my Mama and Daddy either had visitors in or went visiting. That's what people did on Sundays. They already had on their Sunday best clothes, so I guess they thought it was a good time to go see people. Anyway, one summer Sunday, Mama and Daddy took off in the wagon to go visiting, and I was left with my sisters Isabelle and Eleanor."

Granny paused to take a sip of sweet tea. "At the time of this story, I was about five years old which would've made Isabelle ten and Eleanor nine. They always bossed me around. If I didn't do what they told me, they wouldn't let me play with them, so when they said we would play church, I was ready to play."

Addie interrupted. "You played church?"

Granny chuckled. "Oh, yes, indeed. We played church lots of times—Isabelle was the preacher, Eleanor was the song leader, and I set in the congregation with our dolls. At the back of the house was a big rock, that was the pulpit, and Isabelle would climb up on it to preach. Then Eleanor would lead us in songs like "Jesus Loves Me" and "Amazing Grace," only this Sunday, they added a baptizing."

"A what?" Maggie and Addie asked in unison.

"A baptizing." Granny explained, "When somebody joined the church, the preacher took them down to the river for a baptizing. Churches in those days didn't have a baptismal inside the church, so the preacher would take them down to the river where they could be dunked under the water, as was the custom. After church that morning there was a baptizing, and our family had gone down to the river with the rest of the congregation to watch the preacher baptize some new church members. That's where Isabelle and Eleanor got the idea for us to do a baptizing."

"Did they baptize you?" Addie asked.

"No, they had a better idea. Mama's washtub was setting in the backyard right near where we was playing. There'd been rain for two days, so it was filled to the top with rainwater. Isabelle told me and Eleanor to go catch some chickens. She was going to baptize them."

"Chickens!" The girls squealed with laughter. Maggie and Hannah joined in.

"Oh, yes," Granny said. "Me and Eleanor caught two chickens a-piece and brought them to Isabelle. Isabelle took one by the legs and held it over the water. Just like the preacher, she said, 'I baptize thee in the name of the father, the son, and the holy ghost.' Then she dunked that chicken under the water. She done it to all the chickens. When Mama and Daddy got home, they found four dead chickens and a washtub with feathers floating on the water."

"Oh, those poor chickens!" Addie said, between peals of laughter.

"Isabelle never baptized no more chickens and that's a fact." Granny laughed.

After supper, Addie and Reilly cleared the table, and then went back to finish their puzzle with Granny Zee while Maggie and Hannah did the dishes. Hannah described her fight with Cece, and was telling Maggie about Travis's letter from Roby, when the girls came bouncing into the kitchen.

Reilly said, "We finished our puzzle and Granny Zee's watching QVC. She says she's ready for bed."

Maggie and Hannah got Granny settled and Reilly and Addie told her goodnight. Hannah walked them out to the car.

The darkness had not tamed the day's heat. It hung in the night like a hot wet blanket. Hannah said goodnight to Maggie and Addie and reminded Reilly to behave. She promised to call tomorrow and give them a report on Granny.

Reilly hugged her. "Night, Mom."

Hannah watched the lights from Maggie's car disappear down the mountain. She sat down in the grass and listened to the crickets calling for rain. In the sky, a few clouds chased the moon. Alone in the night, a tear splashed onto her nose. That damned Travis Lively. Hannah had thought she had him all figured out.

She wiped the tears from her cheek and lay down in the grass, brushing her hands back and forth over the ground like she did when she was making snow angels. She closed her eyes and pretended her fingers were touching icy cold snow, but the sensation of cold eluded her. Instead, the grass was so dry it felt like the plastic grass she used to put in Reilly's Easter basket.

I wasn't driving, I wasn't driving—whirled around in the moon. *You can't cast a spell, you're not a caulbearer*—danced with the stars. Hannah lay still and stared up at the heavens. She tried to get mad. She wanted to get angry and shout, "I don't care if you were driving or not! It doesn't matter now. I don't love you. I never loved you."

Tears filled her eyes and ran down into her ears. "But it does matter," she said. She and Travis had been together almost seventeen years, and now is when she'd discovered he wasn't the person she thought he was? She would swear on a stack of Bibles that Travis would have never taken the blame for anybody, and if for some unknown reason he did, he would have made sure she knew about it because that would make him a "big man" in her eyes. To Travis, being a "big man" was more important than anything, especially her.

Who was this man she'd spent her adult life with? Hannah bolted upright like her body had been wired for electricity and someone had flipped on all her switches. Suddenly, it was all so clear. The university would *not* have expelled Travis if he hadn't been driving drunk. The accident may have ended his football career, but he could've stayed in school and so could she. She would've gotten her degree and, today, she would be living a completely different life. When Travis changed the course of his life, he changed hers too. But had he loved her all along, really loved her?

The day of the accident, Hannah lost control of her life. Travis made it clear he was finished with college, and he assumed she would follow suit. When she told him she was going back, he first tried to talk her out of it, but when that failed, he pretended he was okay about it. Then, she got pregnant.

Hannah had made it so easy for him. She had started

drinking too much, and of course, Travis encouraged it. He knew she usually never drank more than one beer, but suddenly, he was pushing liquor on her. She knew the exact night she got pregnant—a football buddy had given Travis a bottle of Scotch. He kept filling her glass until she got drunk, and then they had unprotected sex. She had laid that at Travis's feet, too. She rubbed her forehead. Was that how it had happened? Was it Travis who kept filling her glass or was it her?

The rest of her life tumbled out before her—she got pregnant, married Travis, and dropped out of school. It had all happened so fast—one minute she was a college student, and the next she was a young mother dealing with the simultaneous birth and death of a child.

Hannah stood and stretched her arms out in front of her. She looked down at her hands. The moon cast a muted glow over them. Healing hands, Granny called them. Hannah placed her hands over her heart, one on top of the other. She said, "Granny Zee, I hope you're right."

Chapter 29

The Celts believed nature was inspirited—its trees, plants, water, land, caves, animals, and even its people. This I was taught by my forebears, and I saw its evidence my whole life. I also learned not all spirits are good, and stories of the mountain witch and her black magic were told around the fire at night. Those tales are why the mountain people nailed a horseshoe over the door. Metal weakens a witch's power.
~ from Granny Zee's Book of Dreams

COAL VALLEY GLOWED THAT autumn. The forest smoldered with light and flamed with color, and Hannah took refuge on Granny's Rock House Mountain. For the second time, Travis asked Hannah if she was leaving him, and Hannah let the perfect opportunity to say "yes," go by. Instead, she said Granny Zee wasn't well, and she needed a quiet place to study for state boards. The minute she said it, the absurdity of it made her wince. There is no place quieter than a house where the husband and wife merely occupy the same space—where they don't live together but parallel to one another. The truth was Hannah needed to be at the place where she had been happiest as a child. Her world was spinning so fast she was hanging on for dear life.

Hannah was alone. Addie and Reilly had been in Dublin for three weeks, and even though she could talk to them using technology, it failed miserably to stop her ache. It was some comfort that Maggie and Cooper were close to them, but still, she had never been so alone. By the holidays, her state boards would be over, and she would be waiting for the results. She already had job offers, and often received information about fellowships and PhD programs in the mail. Everything she had ever wanted was suddenly within her grasp—and she was terrified.

Mornings, Hannah packed study materials and a thermos of hot chocolate and trekked up the mountain to the spot where she could look down on Granny Zee's house. There, while the mountains around her settled in for their winter sleep, she sipped hot chocolate and studied.

She made sure to go back for lunch because it was a challenge to get Granny to eat. Each day when she returned, she found Granny Zee in front of the fire, reading from a stack of old journals. The doctor said he couldn't find anything wrong that wasn't old age, but Granny Zee was waning right before Hannah's eyes.

Hannah placed a bowl of chicken and rice soup on a tray in front of Granny Zee, who reluctantly laid her book aside. Granny took a few sips and put the spoon down. She reached for the book and Hannah intervened. "Why don't I read to you while you eat?"

Granny smiled and picked up her spoon.

1936

January 3—Snows without stopping. After a cold dry December, snow hit with a fierce fist the day after Christmas. Hanson fights his way to the barn to feed and water the animals. Thank God for the cow's fresh milk for Louis and Henry. Hanson says Henry eats like he's got a hollow leg and will soon be bigger than his older brother. Emma Rose is a month old today and starting to sleep longer at night between feedings. The extra sleep has been a blessing because the boys are balls of energy. Hanson has taken them in hand which helps. He carved them wooden trucks for Christmas, painting them red and even fashioning wheels so they roll, which the boys love. Those cars and the spinning tops Hanson made (for Santa Claus to bring) have kept them occupied while they're cooped up indoors.

January 4—Still it snows. A mist like a silver veil floats above the snow-covered ground. I marvel at the beauty of it. Today I feel more like myself. Three babies in five years has taken a toll on me. Mama's bone broth has built up my blood and her milk thistle tea has helped build up my milk. I feel like Emma nurses nonstop.

January 6—Absolute silence woke me before dawn, and I crept out of bed to the front room window. There is no quiet like a world covered by snow. For the first time in days, stars spark silver in a midnight blue sky. Drifts hide the porch, steps, and beyond. By the moon's nightglow, I see only snowscapes decorated with diamonds and pearls. In the midst of all that beauty, sadness as deep as that snow shrouds me. After Emma was born, Granny started closing in on herself like a bedsheet dried in the sun, folded end-over-end, corner to corner until it's a small square holding the fresh air and sunshine inside. New Year's Day when I sat on her bed with Emma in my arms, she raised her hand and placed it on the baby's head in blessing. I knew then Granny's time on this earth was almost over.

January 7—(I write sitting by Granny Zee's bed.) This morning Emerson appeared at my door! He'd fashioned snowshoes and walked down the mountain on top of the snow to tell us that Granny is bad. It won't be long now. He brought snowshoes for me. Hanson helped pack what I need for the baby. The boys begged to go with me, but I explained they must stay and take care of their daddy. Henry said it wasn't fair that Emma got to go. But Louis pulled him aside and explained she had to go with me because I had a special bottle under my arm that I fed her with, just like I'd fed him when he was a baby. Hanson's eyes twinkled but I shook my head to convey we mustn't laugh. After that, Henry stopped complaining. He already looks up to Louis who takes his job as big brother seriously.

I followed Emerson up the mountain. Emerson's grown into a tall slender man, almost 18—the son Daddy never had. I haven't seen his mother much since she and her husband moved to Abingdon and had two children. I don't even know if Emerson's seen his half-brother and sister. I wonder sometimes how Isabelle and I grew up to be such different people to have been cut from the same cloth.

I believe Granny Zee knows I'm here. When I took her hand she opened her eyes and tried to smile. Her body has smoothed into this round gray stone, like death is wearing away all the sharp edges life made. Even the knotted bones on her hands have flattened, leaving them smooth cool planes. The room smells like camphor and onions, and I feel soaked in death. I am not new to death, but I have always had Granny Zee to guide me. Now, I am drowning under its weight.

January 8—At 3 this morning, Granny died the way she lived her life, at peace. I pray her spirit will continue to guide me after her death.

At daylight, I helped Mama wash her with lavender soap and braid her hair. We each clipped an iron-gray strand to keep. We laid her out on the bed in a white muslin dress she had packed away years ago with instructions it was her burial dress. I thought Daddy and Hanson would have to build a coffin, but Mama said Granny had insisted they build it before cold weather set in, and she ordered them not to tell me. Daddy said there was no chance of burial, even though the grave was already dug (another thing I didn't know) until the weather warmed enough to melt some of the snow. They would seal her in her coffin and tie it to the rafters in the barn to keep it from wild animals until the thaw.

Emerson went down to tell Hanson, and came back with him pulling the boys on a makeshift sled. We lit candles around Granny's bed and said our good-byes. I read Granny Zee's favorite poem from her favorite Irish poet, William Butler Yeats: "The Lake Isle Of Innisfree."

I will arise and go now, and go to Innisfree,
And a small cabin build there, of clay and wattles made;
Nine bean-rows will I have there, a hive for the honey-bee,
And live alone in the bee-loud glade.

And I shall have some peace there, for peace comes dropping slow,
Dropping from the veils of the morning to where the cricket sings;
There midnight's all a glimmer, and noon a purple glow,
And evening full of the linnet's wings.

I will arise and go now, for always night and day

I hear lake water lapping with low sounds by the shore;
While I stand on the roadway, or on the pavements grey,
I hear it in the deep heart's core.

Few people knew that my granny was a great reader and often
sent away for books she shared with all of us.

Hannah looked up at Granny Zee who smiled with tears in her eyes. She said, "Thank you child, you can stop now."

Hannah handed the book to Granny and stood to gather the dishes. Granny's bowl was empty and the two buttered cornbread muffins she had placed on a plate were gone. Hannah grinned and took the dishes to the kitchen.

On a blustery December morning, Hannah returned to Pineville to take her state board exam. It was night when she drove back up the mountain to find Granny Zee had made a supper of pinto beans, fried potatoes, mustard greens, and cornbread. They'd agreed not to get a tree until Maggie and the girls returned, but after supper, Hannah hung a lighted wreath over the hearth and decorated the mantle with Christmas lights, pine boughs, and candles. When she was finished, she turned off the lamps and they sat together by the fire. The fire soon warmed the evergreens, and the scent of Christmas filled the room.

Granny Zee said, "I know it's been hard for you since Reilly went to Ireland. Have you thought about what you're going to do next?"

Hannah shook her head.

Granny took Hannah's hand. "Reilly's grown into a beautiful young woman, and I understand she's found her healing gift is with animals." Hannah squeezed Granny Zee's hand, while silent tears slipped down her cheeks.

Granny said, "You know, Reilly's not really coming home. She'll visit, yes, but then she'll be off to college. It's time to get on with your life. You have worked hard and prepared for it. It's time to make the next step. The New Year is soon upon us. That's always a good time to start fresh. Granny Zee rose and kissed Hannah's wet cheek. "Good night, dear. Sleep well."

◦⸻⸻◦

From the time Maggie and the girls got home on December tenth to the time they returned to Ireland in mid-January, things moved faster and faster like a run-away train. Reilly and Addie bounced between houses, spreading Christmas cheer along the way. At Granny's they baked cookies, made fudge, wrapped gifts, and watched Christmas movies.

J.D. and Maggie agreed they would have what Maggie called "Christmas truce" for Addie's sake. As the new governor-elect, J.D. breezed into town with an entourage. He spent a week in Coal Valley, attending dinners and parties in his honor, but he also spent time with his daughter, who had finally started to forgive him. They went hiking in the winter woods, cooked dinner together, and even managed to play golf. He agreed Addie could spend Christmas Eve with Maggie at Granny's and open gifts with him Christmas morning.

Christmas Eve at Granny Zee's house was the Christmas by which Hannah would measure all future Christmases. To Hannah's surprise, Travis came to dinner. He wore a new brown tweed jacket with leather patches on the sleeves over a tan pullover. His dark brown pants were new, as were his leather boots. With his blonde hair tamed, he looked like he'd stepped off the pages of *GQ*.

Maggie and Addie brought an enormous baked ham, pans of yeast rolls, and an old-style plum pudding they lit on fire after dinner in the true Irish and English tradition. Hannah and Granny had roasted a turkey and made dressing, mashed potatoes, corn pudding, and green beans.

During supper, they laughed and told stories. Granny Zee told of the Christmas her sisters had tried to bake bread, and when it didn't rise, they put it in the hog's slop bucket where her daddy had already put corn. Next, they burned a cake and added it to the bucket, not knowing the yeast in the bread and cake would ferment with the corn and wet slop. When daddy fed it to the hog, it fell asleep and when it woke up, it couldn't walk without staggering. "Lordy," Granny said, "I thought the poor hog was sick until Daddy figured out it was drunk!"

After dessert, Travis and Reilly got ready to go to his parents to exchange gifts. When Granny gave Travis a bear hug, he laughed and lifted her up, swinging her around in a circle.

Two days after Christmas, Hannah got the official notification that she had passed the state board exam. Reilly and Addie helped Granny bake a cake and decorate it with the medical symbol for physical therapy, and Maggie bought champagne.

They ate and danced, and then Addie got out the karaoke machine she got for Christmas. They sang and acted silly while Granny laughed and clapped her hands.

Around ten o'clock, Granny told Reilly and Addie to look outside. Big fat snowflakes swirled around in the outside lights. The girls grabbed their coats, and Maggie and Hannah watched them twirl and spin in the snow like they were doing an ancient dance to the goddess of winter.

Hannah recognized the blush of new love on Maggie's skin. It radiated from her, generating warmth of its own. Hannah wanted to feel like that. For almost twelve years, she had hoped and prayed for a way to leave Travis and this town behind. Now that it was so close she could taste it, she wasn't sure she wanted to go.

A week before Maggie and the girls were scheduled to return to Ireland, Hannah and Reilly went into town for lunch. They made small talk until their food arrived, and when the waiter was gone, Reilly blurted out, "Are you and Daddy getting a divorce?"

Hannah managed to remain calm. She asked, "Did Daddy say that?"

Reilly's face flushed. "No, I mean, I can tell things are bad and you stay at Granny's."

This was not the place Hannah would have chosen, but she wasn't going to put it off. "Reilly," she said, "I'm not going to lie to you. I *am* going to ask your father for a divorce." She paused, searching her daughter's pale face. She only had one chance to get this right. Reilly was her life, and she had to make her understand. "Baby, I was so young when I married and had you that I never got to do the things I wanted. That's why I worked so hard to finish college. All my life, I wanted to be a physical therapist. That was my dream when I was your age, just like yours is to be a veterinarian." She clasped Reilly's hand. "That doesn't mean I didn't want you—you have been the best thing that ever happened to me. You know that don't you?" Reilly nodded. "But now," Hannah said, "I want a life different from the one your father wants."

"Are you sure about that?"

This threw Hannah and for a moment she faltered, but she drew herself up. "Yes," she said. "When was the last time Dad went anywhere with me? He won't leave his recliner."

Reilly blurted, "Do you love somebody else?"

"No!" Hannah got up and went around to Reilly's side of the booth and scooted in next to her. "Baby, listen, there's nobody else. Please, believe me. I just want to have my own life, and whatever that turns out to be, you will always be the most important thing in it. I want you to have a million adventures like Ireland. Go, baby, go and don't look back."

Reilly lay her head against her mom's shoulder. "Mom, I love you, and I want you to be happy. But I'm sad about you and Daddy."

Hannah said, "I love you too, and I am so proud of you. And believe it or not, I'm sad about Daddy, too."

2002

Chapter 30

Deaths come in threes. This I learned as a wee child and saw it happen time and again as I grew old. And not just death, but disasters as well. Perhaps it is somehow connected to the holy trinity—father, son, and Holy Ghost.
~ from Granny Zee's Book of Dreams

ON A COLD SATURDAY morning in late February, Maggie took Reilly and Addie for brunch at the Café Kylemore in Dublin. Reilly chattered about the upcoming St. Patrick's Day, but Addie had little to say. "Addie," Maggie asked, "are you feeling alright?"

"I'm fine."

"You're so quiet."

"I was just thinking about a dream I had about Granny."

Maggie's stomach churned. "Want to tell us about it?"

"In the dream," Addie said, "Granny Zee was a little girl. She had the most beautiful long blonde hair, and she wore a blue dress with big pockets. She was walking around this old, abandoned house. The walls had fallen down, and I could see an old fireplace. I'm sure this place was on Granny's mountain because I saw the row of lilac bushes she has near her house. The little girl would walk a ways and stop, and then walk again, but she never went inside the house."

"How do you know it was Granny Zee, if it was a little girl?" Reilly asked.

Addie frowned. "I just know."

A few nights later, Addie had the same dream. She sensed how much young Zelda wanted to go into that house; it pulled her, too—a promise of comfort and something akin to peace.

A week later, Addie dreamed of Granny again. This time, the house was tilted to one side like it was going to topple over. Like the other dreams, young Zelda walked around the tilted house three times, before stopping.

The other dreams had ended here but this time, little Zelda called, "Cece it's time to go. Come and take my hand. We will go together." A little girl appeared in the doorway of the old house. She wore a brown dress with a white pinafore over it, and a big bow was in her long red hair. She cradled a doll and when Zelda called to her, she looked down at the doll and then back to Zelda. Zelda said, "It's alright. You can bring Patty Cake. Here, take my hand. It's time for us to go." The little girl came to Zelda and hand-in-hand they walked away into the woods.

Addie woke and grabbed the bedside clock. It was one in the morning. She slipped on her robe and tiptoed from the room so she wouldn't wake Reilly. She went to the kitchen and called her mother.

Maggie answered on the third ring.

"Mom, it's me. I'm sorry to wake you."

"Honey, what's wrong?"

"I don't know, but I dreamed about Granny Zee again. Only this time's different—Cece was in the dream, and Granny talked to her."

"What did she say?"

Addie hesitated.

"Addie, what did she say?"

"She said, 'Cece it's time to go. Take my hand and we'll go together.' I think we should call Hannah and check on her."

"I will. You go back to bed and try to get some sleep. I love you."

"I love you too. Call me if anything—"

"I will."

Maggie paced the room. She had to call for her own peace of mind, let alone, Addie's. She kept passing by the clock and at 1:30 PM, knowing it was 6:30 AM in Coal Valley, she made the call.

When the phone finally rang, it sounded muffled like it was wrapped in cotton. Maggie heard the *click, click, click* that meant someone answered and then Hannah's hello, faint and weak.

"Hannah, its Maggie."

"Maggie? Oh, God, Maggie!" The end of her name rose until it sounded like a wail in Maggie's ear.

"I woke up and Granny Zee was standing next to my bed, smiling. She kissed my forehead and then she was—just gone. I ran into her room and—oh, Maggie." Hannah's voice stretched into one long jagged sob. "She was—she looked asleep—but she was gone."

"Oh, honey, is someone with you? Did you call for help?"

"Yes, the ambulance is coming. But she's gone." Harsh sobs tore through Hannah.

"You need to call someone to be with you. Call Travis."

"I did. He's coming. I hear the ambulance. I have to go."

"Hang on Hannah. We're on the next flight out."

Twenty-four hours after they got the news, Maggie and the girls drove up the mountain to Granny Zee's house. Her sons, Louis and Henry, were there. Hannah and her uncles were making the arrangements and notifying family. Granny wanted a simple service in the little mountain church she loved, and they did just as she wished.

At the funeral, the little church overflowed with people who Granny Zee had doctored through the years. They filled the church with bunches of wildflowers, herbs, even wild strawberries and paw paws, instead of bought flowers. They told stories of how Granny had helped them or a loved one with her remedies.

Granny Zee was laid to rest next to her husband, in the old cemetery on Rock House Mountain. Her final resting place was in the midst of the trees and plants on the mountain she loved.

The day after the funeral, the four women sat in front of the fireplace in Granny Zee's house, sharing their memories. They laughed and cried for the woman who had been a true healer, using her gifts to heal them in body and in spirit.

Maggie and Hannah sat there long after the fire died. Hannah said, "I went into the doll room today and Patty Cake is gone."

"Gone?"

"Yes, and Cece's gone too. I can tell."

"Addie said she dreamed that Granny took Cece's hand and they left together."

"Isn't that just like my Granny Zee? Healing a lost spirit with her death."

Maggie would not leave her friend. Since Reilly and Addie had to go back to school, Maggie made arrangements for them to fly back without her. Cooper would meet them at the airport and take them to their host family. This would give her a chance to pack up things at the house. She hadn't been back since her attorney had proceeded with the divorce.

The day Hannah and Maggie went to Granny Zee's attorney for the reading of her will was a perfect example of what Granny called a "false-spring." The sun was high and white in the sky, and the temperature rose to the seventies. Anything that was frozen, thawed, and freshets poured from the mountains.

Granny Zee's will directed her money be divided between her sons and Hannah. The house and property went to Hannah. Her personal effects were to be distributed according to a list she had given the attorney. Maggie was surprised to find her name on that list. To Maggie, Granny Zee left her Christmas tea set and her blue cameo brooch. To Hannah and Reilly, she left her personal journals. She asked that Hannah and Reilly read them together.

That night, Hannah and Maggie sat in Granny's kitchen, trying to sort out her estate. It was the size of Granny Zee's estate that flabbergasted the family. Hannah couldn't stop staring at the will and cardboard boxes full of ledgers that rested on the table. She said, "How could my Granny have saved over a million dollars? All those years she insisted she could pay for me to go back to college, I never believed her."

Maggie shook her head. "What I want to know is how she learned where to sell her herbs? According to what I see, she made the bulk of the money selling ginseng to China."

Over the course of two weeks, Maggie and Hannah went through all of Granny's records and an amazing story took shape. In 1940, Granny Zee started selling ginseng to a Mr. Amos Watts, who apparently took it to a market in Ohio where it was shipped to China. Granny had meticulously recorded every transaction—date, name of herb, weight, amount, and purchaser. As time went on, she began dealing with a Mr. Yang Wei who apparently was her liaison with companies in China that wanted her herbs. Over the years, her business grew until, by the 1950s, she was recording thousands of dollars each year. Her biggest profits were in the late 1960s and 1970s, when the demand for ginseng and her herbs grew, driving up their value. The last transaction Granny had recorded was in 1988 in the amount of $10,000 dollars for ginseng and witch hazel.

By spring, Hannah had carried out all of Granny's wishes save one: she hadn't read the letter Granny left her. The morning she chose was sun-filled and laced with birdsong. Hannah packed some of Granny's journals, the letter, and a thermos of hot chocolate. As she walked up the mountain path, memories of Granny Zee mingled in her mind like music. When she got to the level place where she had studied for the state exam while looking down on Granny's house, she poured a cup of hot chocolate and opened the letter.

February 1, 2002

Dear Hannah,
Good-bye my dearest granddaughter. I pray these words will give you comfort. You are a beautiful person inside and out, and for so long,

you have sacrificed your happiness for the happiness of others. You are like your mother on that accord, so I rejoice that you have finally done something for yourself and gotten your college degree. I wish your mother was here. She would be as proud of you as I am.

You are a loving friend, mother, and granddaughter, kind and caring. I have never tried to tell you what to do, and I won't begin now, but I want my last words to you to be about what's on your heart and on mine. I must confess that I lied when I said you could not cast a love spell on Travis. You are marked with the Celtic symbols for female power, and even though you have denied that power all your life, it has been there inside of you. If you followed what was set down in my grandmother's hand, then you did indeed cast that spell. There is a way to break it, and therefore know if his love for you is true. You can do this if and only if you still have the amulet you made when you cast the spell. You must take it to the place where you called the spirits. Do this at dawn. Hold it up and say these words, "I release you from this spell. You are no longer under my power." Then place the amulet on a bed of dried leaves and twigs and burn it. The fire will break the spell.

What happens after that, I cannot know, but Hannah, I've watched you struggle for years with what to do about your marriage. You've been like a caged bird beating its wings against the bars. But my dear, I don't want you to break free from that cage, only to realize you've forgotten how to fly.

There is a whole world outside these mountains. Use the money I left you to take advantage of it. I left you my house because I know you love it as much as I do, not because I expect you to live there. Go off and have your adventures. Go on to school if you want to or travel the world, but know that this house and this mountain will always be waiting for you. And know that as long as you hold me in your heart, I will be with you wherever you go.

And my dearest girl, do not despair. Open your heart and you will find the love you long for. It waits for you.
And remember, there is power inside you.
Too-ra-loo-ra-loo-ral, hush now, don't you cry!
Love,
Granny

The next day, Hannah went to see Travis and she wasn't surprised to find him in the den, watching television. She walked up behind him and said, "It looks like your mother and sister are still cleaning house for you."

Travis sat up and switched off the television. "What?"

"I *said*, it looks like your mother and sister are still cleaning house, like they did all those times you told me *you* were the one cleaning it."

Travis grinned. "Figured that out, did you?"

Hannah nodded. She sat down on the couch, and an awkward silence rushed in and surrounded them.

Travis finally spoke. "Are you coming home?"

Hannah looked down and didn't answer.

Travis said. "What about Reilly?"

"She's looking at colleges."

"She'll make a fine veterinarian. She's smart like her Mama."

Hannah breathed in but when she exhaled, it caught in her throat. She swallowed hard. "Reilly. We may have done a lot of things wrong, but with her, we got it right."

Travis's face softened. "I thought things between me and you could get better now that you have your degree. I thought you would help me make a living." Hannah remembered Travis didn't know about Granny's money. "Hell, we could have enough money to go off and do stuff together."

"Like what?"

"We could get a camper and a boat and go to the lake."

Hannah tried to wish away his hopeful look, the blond hair slipping over his forehead, eyes as blue as a July sky. "Travis," she said, "I can't swim."

"What the hell does that have to do with it?"

"It proves that after all these years, you know nothing about me. Why would I want to spend the rest of my life with a man who doesn't even know me? Who doesn't *talk* to me! Who let me believe he threw his life away driving drunk!"

"What did you care? You've been sitting pretty with your rich friend all these years. You didn't need me."

Hannah walked to the door, but before she stepped outside, she turned. Her eyes swept around her kitchen—its familiar countertop where three-year-old Reilly had sat and watched her make grilled cheese sandwiches; the sign hanging over the sink that said, Kiss the Cook—and into the family room where Travis still sat.

Hannah said, "There's one thing I will never understand. How could you let the world think you were driving drunk to save a friend when you won't even walk across the room for me?"

She stood still, just a moment longer, hoping he would come to her, beg her not to leave. But he sat as silent as a stone. That morning she had burned the love charm just as Granny had told her.

J.D. was in Washington but would be coming to Coal Valley at the end of the week, so Maggie had the house all to herself. She had already put ten boxes of things she wanted to ship to Ireland in the car. She had packed the photo albums and Addie's baby things she wanted to keep—the outfit she wore when they brought her home from the hospital, her baby book, and odds and ends of her growing up that she didn't want to leave behind. She packed a few clothing items and the rest of her jewelry, and then she thought of the Christmas ornaments that Addie had made when she was a little girl, so she went to the garage and got out the Christmas decorations.

It was while Maggie was going through the ornaments that her thoughts turned to how she had been a slave to J.D.'s obsessiveness—the cleaning, the order, and the endless list of rules, of which the Christmas tree was one. It could not be put up before December twentieth and it had to be taken down before New Year's Day. No matter how hard Addie begged, he would not allow the tree to be put up sooner or kept up longer, and it had to be put in the formal living room in front of the window.

Maggie dragged the box containing the ten-foot tree into the family room. She went to work and soon had it put together, and then she dragged it into the center of the room. She put the ornaments *she* wanted on it, where *she* wanted to put them, and then she plugged in the lights—in the daytime. And she left the empty boxes strewn around the room.

The blood pumping through her veins, Maggie went

through the mental list of do's and don'ts she had been made to follow all these years and soon, she had a plan.

She started in the kitchen, opening the dishwasher and all the cabinet doors and leaving them open. She took the juice and condiments out of the refrigerator and opened each one, leaving them on the counter. She made coffee and left it in the pot. She fixed a grilled cheese sandwich and left it and the dishes in the sink.

Next, she went to J.D.'s bathroom and took the cap off the toothpaste. She smeared it all over the sink. Then she proceeded to take the cap off of every bottle in the room. She used the toilet and didn't flush it, and then she hopped in the tub and used J.D.'s special razor to shave her legs. She left the tub ringed with hair and shaving cream, and then she threw all of the towels on the floor. She walked out of the room, leaving the lights on. She walked through the house switching on all the lights—every lamp, every overhead light, and every closet light—because J.D.'s biggest obsession was shutting off the light when you left a room.

She went to the bedroom and opened his closet. She tore the suits off the hangers and dumped them on the floor. She walked through them like she was wading in water, kicking pants and jackets through the air. She opened the closet that held his shirts and ties and did the same. Then she dumped his socks on the bed and mismatched them. She threw all of his perfectly folded underclothes and pajamas around the room.

When she finished, she called the housekeeper and told her she would not be needed to clean until J.D. called her, but he would be happy to continue paying her, and she did the same with the gardener. Before she left, she grabbed a tube of red lipstick and ran back to J.D.'s bathroom. On the mirror she wrote: MY NAME IS MAGGIE.

It was dusk when she left, the house ablaze with light. Maggie smiled all the way back up the mountain to Granny Zee's house where she found Hannah on the patio with a bottle of wine and two glasses. The friends sipped wine and watched the stars come out until the entire night was tacked with stars.

Maggie giggled.

Hannah glanced at her. "You haven't had *that* much wine."

"No, I was thinking about something funny. Something I did today."

Hannah sat up straight. "Okay, now you have my attention."

Maggie recounted her escapades and by the time she finished, they were laughing so hard tears poured down their cheeks.

"Oh Maggie," Hannah cackled. "I haven't laughed like this since the day I met you."

Maggie held her stomach and hooted. Her words tumbled out between peals of laughter. "I know. I haven't either. Did you ever think we would still be laughing together after all these years?"

Hannah wiped her face and took a deep breath. "No, but I'm so happy we are."

Chapter 31

The fog is a part of me. I have walked many times with fog's cool touch on my skin. I took the path through the forest with a legion of fog ghosts swirling around me. I have wrapped my shoulders in fog's clammy cape and seen the fog purl on my breath. But I have always stepped out of the fog and back onto the earth. Some people live their whole lives stumbling around in the fog.
~ from Granny Zee's Book of Dreams

H ANNAH AND MAGGIE FLEW to Ireland for the girls' graduation. They found them bursting with plans for the future. Addie had planned all along to go to college in Dublin, but Hannah was surprised when Reilly announced she was staying, too.

The night before graduation, Cooper took them out to celebrate at Dublin's Pearl Brasserie restaurant. They had a table in a lovely alcove. During dinner, Cooper asked Hannah if she would be interested in hearing about opportunities in postgraduate study in physiotherapy at Trinity College. Hannah heard Granny Zee's voice say, "There's a whole world outside these mountains," so she said, "Yes, please, set up a meeting."

Summer in Ireland stretched forth—a boundless purity of colors. Hannah floated in a void of endless blue skies and green fields. Even when clouds veiled the sky, her body rose with the mists. Delectable scents of sea and salt floated on the ever-present breeze. Hannah learned a new repertoire of plants and flowers—broom, dog rose, gorse, guelder rose, hawthorn, meadow thistle, and ragged robin. As she explored, she carried on a one-sided conversation with Granny, describing every sight, every scent, and every sound of bird and insect. And she grieved for the woman who had been her constant in life.

By mid-September, Addie and Reilly were settled into university life, and Maggie and Hannah were hard at work readying the house that would be Cooper and Maggie's new home in Kilmainham, a Dublin suburb. It was a large two-story stone structure with five bedrooms and a sweeping mahogany staircase, and each bedroom had the original cast iron fireplace. It also had a garden, and a small guest house that Hannah would be occupying. Hannah already loved to go into the garden to sit and think. Granny Zee's spirit was close to her there.

As the Festival of Samhain neared, better known as Halloween, Hannah grew restless. The friends were working in the kitchen at Maggie and Cooper's new house when Hannah blurted out, "Maggie, I'm homesick."

Maggie put down the stack of napkins she was folding. "Come sit down. I'll fix us a cup of tea."

When Maggie brought the mugs to the table, she realized Hannah was trying to hide her tears. She sat down and took her hand. "Sweetie, what's wrong?"

"I miss Granny Zee. And her house. And..."

Maggie whispered, "And Travis?"

Hannah nodded.

"Have you decided about the divorce?"

Hannah wiped her eyes with the back of her hand. She nodded, and then she told her best friend about Granny Zee's letter and how she burned the amulet, breaking the spell.

Maggie drank her tea, but never took her eyes off Hannah's face.

"You know," Hannah said. "I hoped I was wrong. I wanted him to truly love me."

Hannah started to cry and Maggie put her arms around her. When Hannah pulled away, she rubbed away the tears and said, "All I wanted was for him to get out of his chair and walk across the room to me. To stop me from leaving. To say, 'You're wrong. I've always loved you.' But he sat there like a stone."

On November tenth, Maggie and Cooper stood where they had declared their love for each other, and said their wedding vows at the Cliffs of Moher. Hannah was maid of honor and Cooper's friend, Dr. Sean McClure, was best man. Addie and Reilly were their audience. Maggie was a vision in vintage beige lace. Her only jewelry was Granny's blue cameo brooch.

A reception was held at the Cliffs of Moher Hotel, and Hannah learned that the Irish did indeed know how to throw a party. Cooper's family and friends were there, as was the family who Addie and Reilly had lived with during their foreign exchange program. Thanks to Hannah urging Maggie to invite her mother, Judith Hudson was there. Ever gracious, she wished the happy couple well.

Cooper and Maggie took a trip to Greece, and Hannah officially moved into the guest house. A week after the wedding, she sat in the kitchen with a cup of Granny's ginseng tea, looking through the mail. The minute she saw the handwriting she knew the letter was from Travis. She put her hand over the envelope and it grew warm under her palm. There was no sadness here. She tore it open and found two pages filled with chatty bits of news. At the end, Travis wrote, *I miss you and Reilly. I wish you would come home?* She closed her eyes and Granny's familiar scent—the fragrance of the earth in spring—filled the room. "Granny Zee," she said, "what should I do?"

A sudden gust of wind pushed open the door. Hannah rose and walked out into the sunshine. Sitting on a branch of the garden's laurel tree was a *dreoilín*, Irish for wren. It cocked its head and studied her. She stood still and watched, her heart racing. Granny had called this tiny bird the King of all Birds.

The little wren burst into song and Hannah's eyes misted with tears. She heard Granny Zee's voice say, "Open your heart." When the bird flew away, one of its feathers drifted through the air. Hannah reached up and caught it. She whispered, "Thank you, Granny. I love you."

December came to Dublin with blue enameled skies. On an unusually warm morning, Hannah took her morning tea to the garden. She was admiring the work she was doing to tame the unruly plants when she heard her name.

There was no mistaking that voice.

Again he said, "Hannah?"

She whirled around. "Travis?"

He grinned his lopsided grin, and her heart melted. "What are you doing here?"

"I thought I'd come see what this football they have over here is all about."

Hannah smiled and her heart raced.

"And if it makes any difference, I came to tell you I love you, and I don't want a divorce. What I want is another chance. I've had a lot of time to think, and my life is nothing without you. I know you've changed. I know your world is bigger than mine. But I'd like to see that world—be a part of it—with you." His eyes searched her face.

In three quick steps, Maggie was in his arms. She said, "O spirits of land and sky above/Hear my plea/Grant me this love/I promise to love him all of my life/O spirits of the night make me his wife."

Appendix

Granny's Teas

To make your own teabags you will need coffee filters, scissors, a sewing machine, and thread. For the tags, you will need embroidery thread, construction paper, glue, a stapler and staples, a marker, or a pen. (You may hand-sew the teabags, but you must make small close stitches.)

Holding two filters together, cut the edges off. Then take the center and cut it into a rectangle. Using a sewing machine, stitch three sides together leaving the "top" (one of the smaller ends) open. Fill with your tea leaves and chosen spice. Stitch the opening closed. At the "top" fold the corners toward the center until they touch, placing the end of a 3- to 4-inch piece of embroidery floss under the flaps. Staple the corners making sure to catch the floss with the staple. If you like, you can now stitch across your fold with the sewing machine. Use construction paper to make a tag so you can identify the kind of tea. Staple or glue it to the other end of the embroidery floss. Granny used paper hearts!

AS WITH ALL OF GRANNY'S TEAS, YOU SHOULD EXPERIMENT WITH THE AMOUNTS TO TASTE. (If you prefer loose tea, add the ingredients to boiling water and pour through a strainer before drinking.)

GRANNY'S TIP FOR THE PERFECT TEA: Never heat the water in the microwave. Granny used a copper kettle. She believed the water had to come to a full boil to get the best flavor out of the tea. Steep tea for 2 to 3 minutes.

Mint Tea

1 teaspoon of tea leaves (Granny often used a blend of Indian and Sri Lankan teas.)

    1 teaspoon of dried ginseng leaves

    Fresh or dried peppermint leaves

Calming Tea

    2 to 3 teaspoons of dried Roman (or English) chamomile (*Chamaemelum nobile*)

    1 teaspoon of dried passionflower

Ginger Tea
  1 teaspoon grated dried ginger root
  2 teaspoons of English tea leaves

Ginseng Tea
  2 teaspoons of fresh grated ginseng root
  or
  1 teaspoon of ground dried ginseng root

  Chicory Tea (for those who favor the bitter flavor)
  ½ cup dried and coarsely chopped chicory root
  Boil for ten minutes and strain

Granny's Cough Syrup
  1 tablespoon of dried coltsfoot flowers
  1 tablespoon dried mullein flowers
  1 teaspoon dried violets
  1 tablespoon of dried red clover
  Steep ingredients in 1 cup of boiling water for ten minutes. Strain to remove the herbs. Add honey and molasses. Stir well. Keep in a tightly capped glass container.

Granny's Witch Hazel Liniment
  Fill a glass quart jar full of witch hazel leaves, twigs, and the bark peeled off the branches on the full of the moon.
  Cover with rubbing alcohol, filling to the top of the jar.
  Set in a cool, dark place from full moon to next full moon.
  You can pour the liquid through a strainer into a small bottle or use the liniment straight from the jar.

St. John's Wort Salve
  1 cup olive oil
  Fill oil with fresh St. John's Wort leaves and let them set for a month. Oil will be bright red.
  Strain it into a double boiler that has 2 tablespoons of melted beeswax until you get the consistency you like. Pour it into a container that you can cap and that is flat enough to reach your hand in to scoop it out.

Eye Wash
  2 cups water
  A large bunch of red clover, leaves, and flowers
  Put the water in a pot on the stove and bring it to a boil. While the water boils, wash the red clover thoroughly. Place clover in boiling water. Turn down the heat and simmer the

clover until it 'cooks down' for about 20 minutes. Let cool. Strain the water by pouring it through a cheesecloth. Put in a bottle with a tight cap. Use an eyedropper to wash out your eyes with the water. The boiled plants can be applied to the eyes and skin rashes as a soothing compress. Granny used it when her children had 'pink eye' or conjunctivitis.

Foot Bath
Fill a large pot with water.
Add 2 big fistfuls of dried mugwort.
Put on the stove and bring to a boil.
Simmer 5 minutes. Remove from heat and let cool.
Pour the water through a strainer or piece of cheesecloth into a bucket or another large pot.
For cold feet and headaches, add this water to hot water until you have enough to soak your feet in it.
For swollen tired feet, add this mixture to enough cold water to cover your feet. Soak.

Lavender Oil
You will need:
Large Stockpot
Clean brick
Measuring Cup
Stainless steel bowl filled with ice
Cut the blooms only when they have burst into bloom and are bright and vivid. Cut the stalks in the cool of the morning because heat makes the blooms release their oil. Place the clean brick in the bottom of the stockpot and set the measuring cup bowl on top of the brick. Place freshly cut lavender around the brick and fill the stockpot with water up to the brick. Close the stock pot with a lid turned upside down. A domed lid is best because it allows the steam to drip into the bowl. Place the bowl of ice on top of the lid. Heat the stock pot on medium heat until steam distillation happens. This takes 20 to 30 minutes. Cool completely.
What you collect is a lavender hydrosol that contains oil from the plants.

Gingerbread Biscuits
2 to 3 cups self-rising flour
½ cup brown sugar
1 stick of real butter (soft)
2 tablespoons of ground ginger
1 tablespoon of cinnamon

½ teaspoon nutmeg
¼ cup molasses
¼ cup buttermilk
1 large egg

Sift 2 cups of flour with ginger, nutmeg, and cinnamon. Set aside.

Cream together sugar, butter, molasses, egg, and buttermilk.

Gradually add flour with spices until the dough is the consistency of biscuit dough. You may have to do this by hand.

Add extra reserve flour as needed to thicken dough.

Pinch dough and roll it into palm-size balls.

Place on a greased cookie sheet with space between balls so biscuits can spread.

Bake 350 for 10 minutes or until brown around the edges.

Blue Violet Jelly

Violet Infusion: Fill a quart jar with blue-violet blossoms.

Cover with boiling water and cap tightly.

Let sit for 24 hours. Pour water through a strainer into a large pot.

Jelly: Into the pot of violet water add the juice of 1 lemon and 1 pkg. powdered pectin. Bring to a boil.

Stir in 4 cups of sugar and bring the water to a rolling boil. Let boil for 1 minute.

Pour into sterilized jelly jars and seal.

Persimmon Cookies

2 ripe persimmons pureed (no seeds) - can use frozen
2 cups self-rising flour
½ teaspoon cinnamon
½ teaspoon nutmeg
½ teaspoon cloves
1 cup white sugar
½ cup real butter (soft)
1 egg

Sift together flour and spices.

Blend butter, sugar, and egg until fluffy.

Add pureed persimmons.

Gradually add flour mixture.

Drop by spoonful onto greased cookie sheet.

Bake 350 for about 12 minutes.

*You may add raisins and/or nuts if desired

Persimmon Bread
>   1 cup persimmon pureed (no seeds) - can use frozen
>   2 large eggs
>   1 cup white sugar
>   2 cups self-rising flour
>   1 stick real butter (soft)
>   Chopped pecans
>
>   Mix together eggs, sugar, butter until creamy.
>   Add persimmons, mix well.
>   Gradually add flour, adding pecans last.
>   Pour into a loaf pan and bake at 325 for about an hour.

Wild Strawberry Preserves
>   Cap 1 quart of strawberries and sprinkle with enough sugar to coat completely.
>   Let the sugared strawberries set overnight.
>   The next morning, pour the liquid off the berries into a pot and bring to a boil.
>   Pour this liquid back over the strawberries and let set again overnight.
>   On the 2nd day, pour off the liquid and again boil it, then pour it back over the berries.
>   On the 3rd day, pour off the liquid and bring to a boil. Add the rest of the berries and cook on low heat until they thicken.
>   Pour and seal in jars while hot.

Shortbread
>   1 cup real butter (soft)
>   1 cup white sugar
>   2 cups all-purpose flour
>
>   Cream butter and sugar together until fluffy.
>   Gradually add flour.
>   Pat mixture into a greased baking pan.
>   Bake at 300 for about 35 minutes.
>   Cool and cut into bars.
>   *Serve with Granny's Wild Strawberry Preserves

Walnut Butter
>   ½ cup of finely chopped black walnuts
>   ½ cup real butter (soft)
>   ¼ teaspoon brown sugar
>
>   Cream ingredients together.

Homemade Vegetable Soup

The beauty of Granny's vegetable soup is its versatility. The meat and tomatoes are the base.

Choose the vegetables you prefer, or pluck from the garden what's in season. The soup can be canned to have on cold winter days.

Brown chunks of beef or venison (1 to 2 lbs.) in 2 tablespoons of oil in a Dutch oven.

Simmer the beef or venison for about 1 hour in 4 cups of water (or until tender).

Add:

2 cups of vine-ripened tomatoes crushed
2 to 3 large potatoes peeled and diced
1 cup diced summer squash
1 cup diced carrots
1 teaspoon salt
½ teaspoon pepper
Water as needed
Simmer until vegetables are tender.

Biscuits and Gravy

Biscuits:
1 cup buttermilk
4 tablespoons of oil
Approximately 2 cups of self-rising flour

Pour buttermilk and oil into a large mixing bowl.

Add flour, stirring until the mixture gets too thick to stir.

Then cover your hands with flour and pinch the dough into a ball and pat with your hands until a soft biscuit forms, adding more flour if needed.

Place biscuits side by side in a greased cake pan.

Bake at 450 until brown on top.

Gravy:

In iron skillet pour bacon or sausage grease. If there's not enough grease to cover the bottom of the skillet, add some cooking oil or lard.

When grease is hot, add 4 to 5 heaping tablespoons of flour. The mixture should have the consistency of syrup. Stir until golden brown.

Add 2 cups milk slowly, stirring constantly.

Thin mixture with cold water as needed.

*If you want super-rich gravy, substitute canned cream for milk.

<u>Crab Apple Jelly</u>
Crab apples (enough to make 8 cups when washed and quartered)
3 cups sugar
Water
Cinnamon if desired

Place apples in a large saucepan and add water until apples are covered.

Bring water to a boil, then reduce heat and simmer until the apples are tender and change color (about 10 to 15 minutes).

Strain the juice by pouring it through a cheesecloth.

Discard the apple pulp and put the juice back into the saucepan. You should have about 4 cups of juice.

Bring the juice to a boil and simmer for 10 minutes.

Slowly stir in 3 cups of white sugar and continue boiling on low. You may add 2 to 3 teaspoons of cinnamon if desired. Using a thermometer, boil until the temperature reaches 220 degrees.

Remove from heat and pour into your jars.

Seal them in a hot water bath.

<u>Granny's Sugar Cookies</u>
1 cup real butter (soft)
2 cups granulated sugar
2 eggs, well beaten
2 tablespoons milk
1 teaspoon vanilla extract
3 cups plain flour
2 teaspoons baking powder
½ teaspoon salt
Granulated sugar

Cream butter and beat in sugar. Add eggs, milk, vanilla, and blend together.

Add baking powder and salt to flour. Stir. Place in sifter and gradually add to butter mixture, blending completely.

Wrap in wax paper and refrigerate overnight.

Now that you have the dough, place it on lightly floured wax paper. You can roll it out with a floured rolling pin and use cookie cutters, or roll it out into balls, flatten, and cut out with the top of a glass that's been greased and dipped in granulated sugar.

Decorate with icing, or colored granulated sugar.

**Granny Zee always saved some dough for Reilly and Addie. She would roll it out and place their hands on the dough, carefully cutting around their slightly spread fingers to make cookies in the shape of their hands!

Colcannon
6 large russet potatoes
2 teaspoons salt
1 lb. butter
Small head of cabbage
1 cup milk or cream
½ cup chopped scallions if desired

Peel and wash potatoes then cut them into large chunks and place them in a large pot.

Cover with cold water so that the water is at least an inch over the potatoes and add 2 teaspoons of salt.

Cook potatoes until tender.

Core cabbage and wash, pulling the leaves apart. Place leaves in a pot.

Fill teapot until full and bring to a boil. Pour boiling water over the cabbage and put the lid on the pot.

Let cabbage set in boiling water for 4 to 5 minutes or until the cabbage darkens in color and becomes tender. Drain the cabbage and add 1 lb. of butter. Place on the back of the stove so the cabbage will stay warm, and the butter will melt.

Drain the potatoes until all the water is removed. It's best to use a colander. When dry, place potatoes back in the pot and add milk or cream. Mash by hand.

Cut the cabbage into bite-size pieces and add it and the melted butter to the potatoes. Mix.

Add chopped green onions if desired.

Granny Zee's Cornbread
1 ¼ cup yellow or white cornmeal
¾ cup plain flour
1 teaspoon baking powder
½ teaspoon salt
2 heaping tablespoons of sugar
1 large egg
¼ cup Crisco or lard (melted)
1 cup milk

Heat oven to 400 degrees.
Place iron skillet with 2 tablespoons of Crisco or lard into

the oven to heat.

Mix dry ingredients together. Add milk, egg, and Crisco. Mix by hand. The mixture will be somewhat lumpy.

Pour into a heated skillet.

Bake 20 to 25 minutes or until golden brown.

About the Author

Rebecca D. Elswick lives in the mountains of southwest Virginia where she was born and raised, the daughter and granddaughter of coal miners. Her award-winning debut novel, *Mama's Shoes* was published as the result of winning *Writer's Digest* Pitch2Win Contest in 2011. Her short stories and essays can be found in anthologies and journals such as *Still: The Journal* and *Appalachian Magazine*. She is currently a consultant for Buchanan County Schools and the Appalachian Writing Project. She has an MFA from West Virginia Wesleyan College.